STAR HUNT

ALYSA MISFELDT

Published by Author Alysa Misfeldt in Eden Prairie, Minnesota

ISBN: 979-8-9994858-0-9 (paperback)
ISBN: 979-8-9994858-3-0 (eBook)

Library of Congress Control Number: 2025914983

First edition September 2025

Edited by James Misfeldt
Cover Art & Map Design by Alysa Misfeldt

DEDICATION

To my sleepless baby girl,
for bringing light and magic to my nights.

And to my husband,
for loving me endlessly when the skies were dark.

LARENDI
FOR STARLIGHT, FOR EVERYONE
Havetta
Oron Mountains
The Northern Grasslands
Pakre
Brakken
Enver
Middle Forests
Tuul
Ilken
Reault
Devier Straight
Zaglian Islands
The Highlands
Vrenn
Mellin
Bay of Balst
The Southern Grasslands
Keana Islands
Carlan
Seldan
The Lowlands
To Other Lands

Content Warning

This book includes content that might not be suitable for all readers including profane language, graphic displays of death and violence, and sexual acts described on the page. Please consider these items when choosing to continue reading this story.

The time for change is now, fellow dreamers.

Too long have we let an empty sky rule our nights. The moon is magnificent, but just as the sun cannot sustain our days without the clouds, she cannot guide us without the stars. Let us gather what has fallen. Let us rebuild what makes us dream. Let the light of the stars watch over us once again from their rightful place above. Let our souls rest cloaked in beauty instead of fading into darkness.

For Starlight, For Everyone!

-King Armund to the Larendi people on the night of the first Starcast

CHAPTER 1 | TALLA

My worn boots slipped in the mud as Jetto helped me drag Callum's body to the bushes. Usually, Riggs didn't leave any survivors amongst those who got within swinging or stabbing distance. But tonight, Callum passed out in sheer anticipation of Riggs' first hit. Riggs had stared at the coward for a few seconds in disbelief before he leaned down to rifle through his jacket—I'm not sure anyone had ever just passed out in front of him like that. I know that I at least hadn't seen anything like it in the past five years of thieving together.

But we shouldn't have been too surprised. Callum was a piss poor thief. The bard was *only* interested in the star because of the notice that was posted of the King's increased reward. To think that he would lift something off a sick and helpless kid *just* for the promise of whatever King Armund had decided to part with... it made me wish he had never crossed the Brakkish gates. If he wanted to play thief, he should have at least been able to *attempt* to take a hit to defend the star. I mean, Callum had to have known that someone from Brakken would come to deliver justice for stealing what was ours. I guess he was lucky it was us, if and only if we all agreed to take a break from killing folks—for now. So, naked in the bushes he went.

As Jetto and I heaved the lump of a man into the brush, I saw Riggs unwrap the glowing package that we had been after. From Riggs' hands, the star cast a magical glow onto his weathered face. Even from this far away, I could make out a wide smile that crept across his lips. *Good*, he should be happy. That's his second star, after all.

"Oy, thanks for the help there, Riggs," Jetto cried out, wiping sweat off his brow with the collar of his new embroidered wool coat, courtesy of passed-out Callum.

Even with the cool breeze that weaved in and out of the trees of the Middle Forest, dragging Callum through the mud worked my muscles enough to cause heat to flare under my cloak.

"Coulda used you to heave the bastard out of the way instead of ol' Bossa here. She may be strong, but Callum wasn't missin' no meals." Jetto snapped a wink at me before I could let out a hiss of playful annoyance as we made our way back to our third band member.

Riggs looked up from the star that was resting in his open hand and glanced over to the bush where I could now barely make out the tips of Callum's feet.

"Oh, looks like you two managed alright." Riggs' voice was deep and raspy, and his dark eyes were locked on his new star. "Besides, *she's* the one with the physical boosts. It's about time she flexed those star-powered muscles of hers and got her hands a little dirty. She's a thief after all, not some *princess*."

He gave a crooked smile to me, one that highlighted his

uneven teeth before switching his gaze to the pendant that was poking out from under my hooded cloak. I instinctively grabbed at it, tucking it quickly under my shirt where it belonged.

Riggs was right—I wasn't the designated fighter in our group, even though we all knew I could do more than hold my own despite my smaller stature. I'd proven that time and time again in our downtime, when we would each go one v. one to determine who was to stay up for the first watch while the others slept. Neither Jetto nor Riggs could ever land a hand on me. It was something that I prided myself on... and it was also something that I *knew* ate Riggs up inside. The fact that it bothered him so much encouraged me to flash a taunting smile back at him despite his insubordinate tone.

"Come off it, Riggs. We probably wouldn't even still have our stars if it wasn't for ol' Bossa. She leads, and we follow. We all agreed, and now you've got a second star." Jetto reached out and gave Riggs a pat on the shoulder before he turned to give me a warm but sly smile.

I returned the gesture with a nod. Jetto was always helping me keep Riggs' attitude in check, even though I didn't really need him to do it—not with what was hanging around my neck.

Riggs kept his eyes on me for a few more seconds before he returned Jetto's motion with a pat of his own. His hand then slipped into his cloak pocket before he pulled out a piece of onyx nightcloth to wrap around his star. The glow faded as he tucked the orb into the black fabric before it was stuffed into one of his front pants pockets—surely just a temporary home for the treasure.

"*Well*, now I know why the girl died so quickly after Callum got ahold of this." Riggs rolled up his sleeve to show us the large cut on his arm that he had gotten a few days back in a bar brawl.

This morning, the wound was still quite red with blood crusting towards the edges, his skin stretching to close the gap. But now, the skin was smooth, with only a shallow pinkish groove indicating that a cut had ever existed in the first place. Jetto shook his head in disbelief before he spit in the direction of where we left Callum's body.

"Bastard. Maybe we shoulda killed him. A healing star *that* strong could have kept Mara's girl alive for another year. Maybe longer." A mixture of anger and grief flooded my chest.

Mara's daughter had been only seven when she passed a little over a week ago. I can still hear the echo of Mara's cries when it's quiet enough, despite being miles away from Brakken.

"May she rest soundly in darkness," I called softly, moving my fingers across my chest in a circle. It was the shape of the full moon—the *true* light of the night.

Both Riggs and Jetto copied the gesture of prayer for the girl. Her life was now added to a long list of mine of those that were taken in the name of the King. *Oh,* if I ever got my hands on him... they would definitely get dirty in that fight. We were all silent for a few moments until Riggs cleared his throat.

"Well, *Bossa,* where to next?"

The way he used Jetto's nickname for me with such contempt made me roll my eyes. But before I could say one of the several snarky comebacks that all highlighted the fact that the only reason he had his stars is because I *let* him have them, my stomach grumbled. I let out a deep and calming breath through my nose, trapping my instinct to snap back behind my teeth.

We had been tracking Callum for three days now with barely any rest. Tensions were high, and stomachs were empty. I knew better than to pick a fight within my band over something as petty as tone, especially without any food in me.

I put my hand on my chest, resting my palm over the pendant that was hidden under my shirt and closed my eyes. Breathing in deeply and slowly, I waited. The night wind blew the strands of hair that had escaped from my braid across my face and made the tree branches sway above us. Warmth bloomed from the pendant under my touch as raindrops began to fall. I opened my eyes and threw my hood up as I took a few steps past Riggs and Jetto.

"West. Follow me."

CHAPTER 2 | TALLA

It took everything in me not to smack Riggs across the face, or throw one of my daggers at his puffed-out chest, as we headed West in pursuit of the stolen stars. The cold rain whipping at our faces seemed to barely affect him or his ability to ramble on. The warm pendant on my chest was helping keep the shivers at bay for me, and had Jetto not lifted that coat from Callum, he might have turned into a big, bald icicle. The longer that he carried his new healing star, the more intolerable Riggs became. As his old wounds began to heal, Riggs recounted fight after fight to Jetto as they trailed behind me.

Riggs now had two stars in his possession, which is two more than basically anyone these days. Within my band, we now had four. Up until ten years ago, that wouldn't have been so uncommon... I think that the legendary Sento brothers used to carry six stars between the two of them. Brakken, being the furthest of the northwestern cities from Mellin, used to be a haven for starpowered crews. But over the years, as stars began to disappear, so did the bands of thieves. Nowadays, starpower in the hands of the people was rare—so rare that the three of us had to be extra careful to whom we let slip the information that we used starmagic. We probably were the last starlight enhanced crew left, and I had no intention of anyone changing that.

Most everyone from Brakken was safe and could be trusted. But, as Callum, and now these thieves from Enver that we were tracking down, proved, the King's supporters could pop up anywhere, even within the gray stones of Brakken. It wasn't always this way... things were much more fair before the selfish bastard Armund became King.

With two stars, an accuracy star and now a healing star, Riggs was feeling chuffed. He was our fighter, his accuracy star helping him throw punches or daggers on target every time. Jetto was our master lifter, and despite his big and brawny frame, with his stealth star he could lift coin or spoils off of anyone without them even batting an eye—well, anyone but me.

I was our seeker and leader, and even when we weren't in pursuit of stars, the two men followed my direction. We each had our role, and this unconventional trio of Riggs, Jetto, and I only worked because of the *particular* star that I had, encased in silver and always hidden beneath my clothes.

I tried blocking Riggs' raspy voice out of my head, putting all of my focus into feeling for the next closest stars to make sure that I didn't lead us off track. But between the cold pressing down through my damp clothes, the consuming rumbling of my empty stomach, and constantly hearing some variation of *'if I had this baby, I would have knocked him sooner,'* my focus was absolute shit.

After about an hour of trudging in the rain along the main road that skirted the edge of the Middle Forest, small lights started to flicker ahead. As we got closer, my eyes made out the words *Red Ruby Inn* painted in black on a swinging wooden sign hung above the doorway.

It was a roadside inn... one of the bigger ones in the area. This one fared well given its placement at the crossroads of two main travel paths. And though I had never passed the establishment at night before, one quick glance at the man pressing himself into the breasts of a thick and topless woman outside the door told me *just* what kind of place it might be. Not simply a place for the weary and wandering to rest, but the kind that favored those who enjoyed straying from their moral ways. Honestly, I would have been thrilled to see an overturned cart if it got me somewhere dry, but the idea of a warm drink along with some entertainment was better. *Much better.*

I turned around to ask Riggs and Jetto what they thought about stopping for the night, but before I could even get a word out, Jetto was slinging up mud as he ran past me. Riggs wasn't too far behind him as he followed Jetto into the inn, pushing past the 'couple' and straight through the wooden door.

Relief flooded over me. *Great*—decision made then. We had plenty of coin to blow after lifting a couple sacks full off Callum anyway. And besides, with Jetto's stealth star and an inn full of tired travelers focused on their drinks and the bosoms of the women that served them, we were bound to leave with even more than we were entering with. My thieving heart thudded in excitement at the prospect as I pulled my hood down and followed the rest of my band inside.

The inn was dim, lit with dripping wax candles in glass jars positioned on each of the tables and on the sides of the wooden columns that separated the room. The air was filled with the scent of roasted meat and mead with a light fruity note that came and went as people shifted through the space. My stomach was twisting, begging me to eat something. So before finding whatever corner of the tavern that Jetto and Riggs had snuck away to, I headed straight to the counter.

The floor was slick with mud, and I made sure that my hastened steps were purposeful. I wouldn't want to slip and accidentally reveal my pendant. The small crack in the silver was enough to let some of the starlight slip through, and I couldn't risk it catching anyone's eye. Not when we weren't in Brakken anymore, and not when the King's supporters could be watching.

The bartender manning the counter was old, probably as old as the bar itself, with deep set wrinkles and white hair that was cut short by his ears. Despite his eyes being an icy shade of blue, the glimmer in them was warm and inviting. Through the chaos of laughter and ladies parading the room in nothing but slitted ruffled skirts, he somehow must have seen me coming. I was barely a foot from the bar when he set down a large ceramic cup full of a dark and steaming brew on the counter before the empty stool that I was approaching.

"Did ya leave any rain outside for the plants there, gal?"

He looked me up and down, focusing on the puddle that was now pooling at my feet.

I turned around and noticed that even though the floors were already muddy and slick, the water trail left by my cloak was quite noticeable. *Oops.*

"You're dripping water all over me bar's floor. Gimme your cloak and drink this before you catch a cold and get the whole crowd sick."

I hesitated for a moment, placing my hand on my chest as if casually adjusting my cloak button, though it was really over my pendant. I took a quick breath, waiting. The old man kept looking at me, a confused expression growing on his face the longer I waited to reply. No rush of cold came over me. He could be trusted... at least for now.

"Did ya hear me gal?" He spoke a little louder this time.

I nodded, moving my hand and peeling off my sopping black cloak and handing it to him around the edge of the bar. He tossed it up on a hook next to a few others behind him while I put both my hands on the cup and sipped, scooting on to an open stool. *Thank the Moon.* Mulled Berry wine. My favorite. The drink warmed me from the inside out, bringing feeling I didn't even realize I lost back to the tips of my fingers.

"Dinner too, I reckon?" He asked, pouring a mug of mead for a stout traveler sitting on the stool to the left of me who was finishing his last sip of his current drink.

I raised my eyebrow in surprise and approval. This man didn't miss a beat, despite being ancient.

"It's beef stew, hearty and fresh from my own cows and made by my dear, Pearl. Ten coins a bowl unless you rent a room. Then we throw in a bowl for free."

I took another sip of the wine. *Ok*, it was more of a gulp. I didn't care that it burned my tongue a little going down because the notes of berry and cinnamon were just too damn delicious.

"A room would be great. One with a bath is even better. I have the coin," I responded, reaching to grab the small leather pouch that was tied to my belt.

But Ed shook his head, holding a hand out in the air to stop me.

"No need, gal. Your tab has been covered over, and then some. Your buddy warned me you were coming." The bartender gestured over to the back corner of the inn where Jetto was sitting on a chair, with a large mug pressed to his face.

After he finished downing it, he slammed it on the table. His eyes caught mine, and he raised the empty mug to me. I raised my cup back, grateful for his foresight.

I scanned the room for Riggs, quickly finding him tucked in a dark corner, his hand twirling a strand of the curled blonde hair of a woman sitting on his lap. She had her long, pale fingers tracing circles on his chest. He pulled her in closer to him with his other hand and started kissing her neck. After a few passes, his eyes opened to catch me watching him. He gave me a flash of his crooked smile before setting his focus back on the broad. My body cringed before my nose caught a whiff of the stew that the bartender had just sat down in front of me. I didn't even hesitate before devouring it.

Just as I was finishing my last spoonful, a key with a red ribbon tied on it was placed in front of me.

"Room eight is yours. I put your friends next door to's ya but yours is the one with the bigger tub. I'll have one of the ladies bring your cloak up there now to hang by the fire. Should be lit whenever you make it up there." The bartender whisked away my empty bowl.

"Quite the service, Sir." I replied, bowing my head in subtle thanks.

"Ed. Call me Ed. And it's just how we run things at the Red Ruby. We will take care of all your needs. The good and *the gray*." Ed winked at me, sliding another fresh cup of wine in place of my empty one before tending to the other patrons along the bar.

I was going to have to tell Jetto not to lift any coin from him or his staff as a more formal thank you for the good service.

I slid off my stool with my mug and made my way over to an open seat at Jetto's table, his bald head a beacon in the dim taproom. He was now engaged in a game of Flare with a big-headed fellow that had no idea that he was betting against someone with a stealth star. His brow seemed permanently furrowed as he kept losing hand after hand to Jetto. The man kept reaching into his pockets for more coin to ante up, but each time he seemed disappointed by how few he had left, like he expected to have had more.

I couldn't help but chuckle. Jetto was *quite* good at Flare, but even better at pickpocketing. Despite all of the bad that had come from the King taking back stars from folks, it did make my trio's ability to thieve a little easier. No one suspects you have an advantage these days, since almost all the stars are accounted for. Well, at least so says the King. But, I can feel there are more stars out there than the four we carry and the eight we are after. A small hoard of stars were stolen from the good people of Brakken, *my people*, and those were the ones that I was tracking. But when I focused hard enough, I could feel faint, additional pulls to the South and East.

As I watched Jetto flip his next row of tiles, my nose was filled with an overwhelming fruity scent. A soft hand landed on my shoulder. With a tilt of my head, my stare landed on a voluptuous woman with straight black hair tied up in a red ribbon smiling down at me. Her breasts were at my eye level, and they were only covered by sheer triangles held in place by strings that wrapped from her neck to her stomach. She was probably a few years younger than I was given that her face was essentially wrinkle free, but her cheekbones were well defined. Old enough to no longer look like the teenager she recently was, but so glowy and beautiful that she could tempt anyone. Even me.

"Your friend said that you might need some help relaxing tonight, shall I help you up to your room?" She batted her long eyelashes as she toyed with my messy braid, ignoring how the strands were caked in mud.

I looked past her to see Riggs, now entertaining an additional blonde woman, give me an eyebrow raise. Even with one of the girls sitting in his lap, he was watching *me* through his matted-down black hair.

Whether sending this girl over was a taunt or a gift, I couldn't know—I wasn't close enough to read his intentions very well. From working together the past five years, Riggs knew that I wasn't the whoring type, even though he was. Well, at least when I'm sober I wasn't. And with a few more mugs of wine... *Moon, save me*. I would be *far* from sober. I couldn't help but think that the smirk on his face made it clear that he knew that fact about me, too.

The girl patiently waited, leaning her exposed navel into me, her skin warm against my damp shirt. Jetto paused his game to give her a couple looks up and down before nodding in approval. I took a big sip from my wine, the aroma of my spiced drink and her clean and fruity skin mingled in harmony. And as delectable as the scent was, it only reminded me how *undelectable* I was. I thought about how there was a bath waiting for me upstairs, a bath that, in all honesty, I really wanted just to myself.

"I actually think my friend, Jetto, here could use the company. He's having a remarkable night of Flare, I'm sure he could use someone to help keep his lucky streak going."

The woman curtsied at me, understanding her dismissal, and glided past me to slide onto Jetto's lap as another opponent, a tall and lanky fellow, was replacing the big-headed man. Jetto joyfully wrapped his arm around her midsection as he shuffled his tiles in preparation for the new game, and I stood to head up the worn wooden staircase behind the bar before I could change my mind.

Room eight wasn't really that small, but the tub connected to the fireplace left little room to navigate the space not occupied by the bed. Just as Ed had said, my cloak was hanging on a hook, dripping water as it dried against a well-lit fire. Next to the wooden tub was a metal tray, topped with a bar of red soap, a mug, a bottle of wine, and a small piece of folded paper.

To keep you company.

- Ed.

I chuckled. Had I not been able to sense when stars were close, I would have guessed Ed had a premonition star with his ability to anticipate what his guests needed. I guess some people just have natural talents then. Good for them.

I peeled off my clothes into a pile, tossing my leather belt that hid two daggers in small sheaths on top, so that I was standing by the edge of the tub in nothing but my pendant. There was a mirror mounted on the back wall, and though the room was dim save for the firelight, I took a moment to examine my reflection.

My chestnut brown hair had grown longer than I usually kept it, now brushing the top of my navel, even in a braid. My frame was strong, but too slender from being on the go so much recently. A handful of scars were scattered across my toffee brown skin. They were mostly small, nicks from sleuthing in thorny bushes or scrapes from falling on stone during city raids. Those had all healed quickly from starmagic, though since my superstar wasn't purely a healing star like the one we had just collected from Callum, it didn't make my wounds disappear completely.

I didn't mind the smaller scars that left silvery blue lines across my skin. But my largest one... I touched my fingers to the jagged and raised scar that ran down my cleavage and under my left breast. Not even the strongest healing magic could fully repair the wound. I suppose I didn't really mind that one either, though. It reminded me of why I kept thieving. Why we were hunting for stars.

I popped the cork out of the bottle left for me and poured myself some wine as I let the warm water hug my clammy skin. The red soap smelled just like all of the girls downstairs, fruity and sweet. *Whore's soap*, but it was better than nothing.

I lathered the bar up and down my body slowly, enjoying the pressure the bar put on my tired muscles. I let my mind wander, wondering if I made a mistake letting Jetto take the black-haired woman. What it would be like if she was the one rubbing whores soap up and down my back. Her touch had been gentle on my shoulder, but would she touch me harder if I asked?

Before I let the vision form too clearly, I noticed that I could no longer hear the pitter patter of the rain on the roof. Instead, small collections of stars were beginning to shine in the night sky. I closed my eyes. What a damn shame, all of those stars, lost in the darkness.

Anyone who could look at that starry sky and think that it made sense was an idiot. A brainwashed, subservient idiot. I grabbed my pendant underwater, holding it tightly between my quickly pruning fingers. At least Armund will never get ahold of this one. No, this one will stay down here. Right where it belongs.

CHAPTER 3 | KIERAN

My thumbs combed over the stack of daily briefings that had been left outside my door while I was out as I watched the sun rise slowly through the large window in my chamber. I had only just returned from the Mile Dark maybe an hour or two ago, and the smell of cherries and glint of gemstone glitter was still fresh on my skin. Four new prisoners were admitted to the dungeons, charges ranging from unpaid gambling debts to attempted arson. I was reading the arrest account from the man who had tried to burn down a shop on the northern side of the city when an unexpected knock broke my focus. I quickly slapped on my belted sword and held one hand on the hilt as I made my way to the door, ready to draw it if necessary as my free hand turned the handle.

Across the threshold was Gray, the King's footman. My hold loosened on my weapon as he bowed as soon as I was in view. I returned the gesture with a subtle nod.

"Sir, K-Kieran, I apologize for the early hour," he stuttered.

I could tell that Gray was trying not to stare at me and the way that I presented myself at the door. My shirt was wrinkled, dark curls messy and unfurled, and glitter sparkled on my neck and hands. He knew *exactly* where I had been, and that I had only just returned. It didn't bother me though. It wasn't a secret that I enjoyed spending my limited free time out in the southern side of the city.

"The King has r-requested you be present in his greeting chambers b-before breakfast."

Stars, I had planned on trying to get some sleep before my training after being out all night. It was odd to receive a summons so early in the morning from the King, especially during the week before Starcast. Among many things, His Grace was notorious for sleeping in. It's thought that he stays up all night just marveling at his creation in the sky only to climb into bed at dawn. But I knew that while the King liked staring at the night sky as much as I did, he probably just was up late reading.

I sighed, running a hand through my messy hair as I looked down at Gray. His mousy brown hair was pulled back into a tight ponytail, keeping the strands away from his pale face. As I shifted my weight to lean against the door frame, the footman winced.

"Thank you, Gray," I responded. I worked a soft smile onto my face to help put Gray at ease, "I will be there shortly."

With a sigh of relief, he bowed again before turning on his heels down the hall.

About half an hour later, with the traces of my night at the Mile Dark no longer visible, I made my way up several flights of stone steps before I turned into the stained-glass hallway that led to the King's tower. The two guards clad in black armor that stood outside the large wooden door parted as I approached, their heads bowed in reverence. I didn't know their names, but I nodded to them both respectfully as I crossed the entryway into the King's chambers.

The King had over one hundred guards, stationed in several posts around the castle and the city of Mellin, Larendi's capital city. Some of the guards resided in the barracks on the east side of Mellin. The few men who had families to care for were allowed to reside in apartments just off the main square to the castle's South.

I honestly didn't know where the rest of the guards lived. All I knew was that I was the *only* guard who had the privilege of having their own personal chambers in the castle. I was the Guard the King not only trusted with running his Prisons, but with collecting his stars. Both positions were an incredible honor to be given by the Star King, an honor that I have had the pleasure of holding for the last nine years.

The fireplace in the greeting room of the King's chambers was lit, the flames casting an orange-yellow haze on the hundreds of old books that filled the shelves on the wall in the King's private collection. There were several thousands more books located in the royal libraries on the main floor, but these particular volumes were hand-picked by His Grace himself to be close at hand during his reign. From what I could gather, many of the books contained the various histories of Larendi, of the great families and the great wars.

But His Grace had been adamant about switching several of the shelves of books to contain specific volumes when he was crowned twenty years ago. He was most interested in the histories of the night and the histories of the stars, which was fitting as he was Larendi's Star King, the one who figured out how to finally return the fallen stars to the sky. Though I never read more than the volumes he so generously gifted me, I often imagined what magic and stories were tucked into the pages in his room.

When I saw that the King was sitting in the leather armchair next to the fire, I quickly dropped to my knee.

"Your Grace." My head was bowed, but I kept my gaze a little higher than the floor so that I could still see his feet.

I heard him set down the book that he was reading onto the side table. Had I not been watching his leather dressing shoes take slow steps my way, I wouldn't have known that he was on the move. The King was remarkably light-footed, which of all of his skills was probably the *least* terrifying.

"Good morning, Kieran. At ease." His voice was steady and low.

I returned myself to standing, my right hand resting on the gold hilt of my sword, my thumb passing lightly over one of the embedded onyx stones. The King stood before me, his eyes level with mine. Rarely did anyone match my height, but the King was a tall man with a dark weathered face, his wrinkles deep set in his forehead and around his dark brown eyes. His smokey hair was braided tight against his scalp, the ends tapered with small crystals that many believed were compressed stars. Of course, I *knew* that they weren't. His Grace so graciously gave up all of his own stars first to make the first Starcast ten years ago.

The King looked me up and down, examining my appearance as I stood there, still and waiting. After a few moments, he nodded with approval at me before he spoke.

"Thank you for your quick summons, especially given the hour. But something has been plaguing my sleep." He headed towards the window, looking out beyond Mellin's city walls and towards the horizon.

"Of course, Your Grace."

The King remained by the window, the back of his navy robe facing me.

"The collection of the fallen stars is almost complete. At least of those that are still retrievable. After years of our hard work sourcing them, we are down to just the final few that are left scattered across Larendi." The King turned, his shoulders now square with mine from across the room. "As you know, I have been organizing the stars into their historic groupings, and based on my research, I am left with just three constellations to complete, the Arch, the Cradle, and the Arrow."

I nodded, recognizing the groupings he mentioned. His Grace had so generously gifted me a book on the constellations after my fifth year of service in his Guard. When I wasn't patrolling the prison, training, or blowing off steam at the Mile Dark, I truly enjoyed studying it. There was something so satisfying about seeing my hard work, *our* hard work, depicted in drawings on the page during the day, and then finding it sparkling in the sky at night.

I glanced at the small door that was to the left of his fireplace. It was a barrier that I myself had never seen past; the wooden door always pulled tightly shut. But despite never having set foot inside, I knew that the door led to the room where the King performed the Starcasts. Beyond that door resided the stars that had been returned or that I had collected before they were sent back up to the sky.

"We have waited long enough to return the entirety of the stars back to the sky for all of our people to enjoy. So…"

The King hesitated a moment, as if to build suspense for whatever he was about to say next. I willed my body to stay calm, using my training to keep my heart rate slow and steady despite the anticipation building in my chest.

"I have decided that the final Starcast will be on the winter solstice. The night will be its longest, and we have been graced by the Stars themselves that the moon will be new, giving us no competition for nighttime light…."

The only manifestation of my surprise that I allowed to show on my body was the light raise of my eyebrows. The *final* Starcast? The winter solstice was only two months away. Which meant the King was only planning for three more Starcasts… ever.

After ten years, the magical phenomenon of watching the blue orbs soar skyward would finally come to an end. Of course, I knew that it would happen eventually. But it would be hard to imagine life without the monthly displays. Not only because of their beauty, which was unmatched by anything else that I had ever seen, but particularly because of the frivolity that led up to them.

The citizens of Mellin were always generous to members of the King's guard. But the week before Starcast, people were *especially* thankful. Within the yellow stones of the capital, if I took just one step beyond the castle walls, my arms would become flooded with pies and drinks and flowers woven into necklaces.

When I was a younger man, fresh off the streets of Vrenn and new to my role both in the King's Guard and as King Armund's chosen starhunter, I used to turn down the gifts of the people. I was just *so* honored to have the attention and favor of the King, that accepting anything else felt like too much. The position was a gift in and of itself. And on top of it, being gifted my own chambers in the castle was more than I could have ever imagined at only eighteen.

So, at the time, the idea of accepting any other kindnesses felt like stealing. But after years of grueling training and constant negotiations on *top* of managing volatile and dangerous prisoners, it got easier for me to accept them. Mostly because I had decided the gifts, especially from the ladies at the Mile Dark, did help make my time more... fun.

It also became easier to accept the gratitude of Larendians as I arrested more rebels. Most of the prisoners rotting in the Royal prisons that committed crimes in Mellin were from way beyond the city walls. Usually they were folk from Enver, Brakken, and sometimes even Parre; all cities north of the Middle Forests and known for harsh, cold, and heartless demeanors. Too often, when rebels unfortunately crossed my path, they made my job harder than it needed to be, whether that job was collecting stars or managing the prisons.

I can understand how at first, when King Armund started collecting the stars, it might have been difficult to adjust to a world without unregulated access to the stars. A thousand years is a long time, and entire cities were built around dealing in starmagic. But as the sky began to fill, beauty filled the void in the night sky. The patterns of starlight inspired Larendians of all ages to embrace an era *other* than darkness. Soon, the distribution of starpower became more equitable, and with the generous help from His Grace in exchange for stars, cities became newer, more sustainable, and safer versions of themselves.

So, over the years as the remaining rebels began to fight harder and became more reckless, I made an effort to make the most of what the loyal and kind supporters offered me.

The King looked at me, his face waiting, so I quickly regained focus on our conversation and pulled together what I imagined his greater plans were to form a response.

"Your goal then is to release a constellation on each of the remaining Starcasts, and you are worried because the next Starcast is only a few days away."

A knowing smile spread across his dark lips as he gave one joyous clap of his hands.

"Yes, yes! Always quick to understand, my boy. You are exactly right."

Pride filled my chest from the praise.

"How many individual stars are left then?"

I don't think anyone in Larendi knew how many stars it took to fill the sky. I tried to keep track of how many stars I personally had helped gather over the past nine years, but after one particular day when hundreds of citizens from the eastern coast came returning sacks full that they had mined from the sea, I lost count. Even my constellation book wasn't clear on the original starcount. The pages alluded to some flexibility within the groupings' makeups, but the book didn't go into any more detail. Maybe the answer was in that book the King was always reading, he at least had to have some sort of idea of the true starcount if he was ready to stop his beloved Starcasts.

"Based on my research, there are only fifteen stars that are left recoverable. Those fifteen happen to perfectly complete the three constellations! It's serendipitous, really. I couldn't have planned it better if I had tried." His Grace glanced upwards, as if he could see the stars through his ceiling and smiled. "To think. In two months, the night sky will be essentially whole again after over one thousand years."

The weight of his statement tugged at my heart, squeezing it enough to threaten mist to form in my eyes. I quickly blinked the sensation away.

"What an incredible legacy, Your Grace." I bowed my head.

The King took a few silent steps towards me, his navy cloak billowing behind him. His smile faded.

"It is not legacy that I'm after, Kieran. Only justice. And once the stars are all back in the sky, they will finally be where they were meant to be. They shouldn't have fallen all of those years ago. It wasn't meant for everyone to have access to the power they possess. And soon, all will be right again."

I nodded, holding my breath a bit as the King stared directly into my eyes.

"Now," the King continued, reaching into his pocket. He pulled out a velvet pouch before he handed it to me. I opened it to reveal the shining gold cuff that I'd grown accustomed to wearing on starhunts. It was simple in its design, the only differentiation between it and any other metal cuff being the raised circle with the faintest blue glow at its midpoint.

I rolled up my sleeve and slipped it onto my right forearm, fastening the clasps at the ends. The metal, so thin and lightweight, was barely noticeable on my arm. But the warmth that spread through my body and the unexplainable pulling sensation made me catch my breath. It always took me a little to adjust to wearing starpower.

"Which way does it pull you, Kieran?"

I focused on the humming power on my wrist. The King always liked to confirm the star's powers hadn't faded or altered before sending me off.

"Northwest, Your Grace."

"Yes. Very good. Now, when you come across their holders, offer the usual for their return. Gray will have the bags loaded on your horse by the time you get down to the stables. But, do note that if these people haven't returned the stars by now, they likely aren't interested in the gifts of the Kingdom."

The King headed back towards his chair by the fireplace and picked up his old book, flipping through the pages to return to where I assume he left off. "It is critical that these stars make their way back, Keiran. Do I make myself clear?"

I nodded in understanding.

"And what should I do if they refuse, Your Grace?"

My question hung in the air between us, the fire crackling softly in the silence. I shifted in my boots in anticipation of his response. I could count on one hand the times that folks had refused to trade with me, their stars for gold and spoils of the Kingdom. But the King was right. These remaining stars *must* be held by nonbelievers if they have held onto them this long.

The King didn't look up from his book as he responded.

"I trust your *particular* training will be of use. It is most important that power doesn't lie with individuals lost in the wind. They pose too great a threat to our Kingdom. For the sake of the people of Larendi, refusal is no longer an option. I trust you'll *handle* them with tact, especially if they prove particularly dangerous."

I nodded, my hand tightening around my sword. It had been a while since anyone had given me a fight that had caused me to break a sweat. In truth, most people weren't dumb enough to go toe to toe with me. But still, every day I trained against the King's personal guards, all equipped with different levels of starpower loaned from the King's collection before he cast them back to the sky. The training kept me fast and strong and ready—ready for what, I didn't know. Some threat that the King envisioned might be out there lurking. Waiting for the right moment to dismantle everything he had worked for and the beauty he had created.

The King flipped another page in his book.

"I expect you to return before Starcast, Kieran. Without those stars, I will have to release an incomplete constellation.

And the people of Mellin, the people of Larendi, deserve it all. Don't you agree?"

I took a step forward, toward the King in his chair, and returned to one knee.

"I have been serving you for nine years, Your Grace. I have yet to fail you, and I don't intend on starting now."

He held out his hand, leaning his fingers down to expose his gold star-stamped ring. I kissed it and then uttered the words that constantly ran through my mind, the final phrase of the King's Guard oath that would be the legacy of King Armund's reign.

"For Starlight, for Everyone."

CHAPTER 4 | TALLA

Blaring rays of sunlight burned my tired eyes as I opened them the next morning after the dull pounding in my head woke me. The bottle of wine that Ed had left me the night before now laid empty on the tray. My toes glided quickly against the cold floor after I emerged from the warm cocoon of the sheets and scampered towards the clothes that I left hanging on the hooks of the fireplace mantel. They smelled faintly of cherries and smoke, but the dirt and sweat from a few days on the road were well washed out. I didn't remember washing my clothes, but good for drunk me for doing a decent job.

After fastening my dagger belt, I closed my eyes and focused on the warmth of my star pendant. The pain behind my eyes retreated enough that the sun was no longer such an aggressive source of light. I headed downstairs, my nose following the smell of toast and chicory brew.

The taproom of the inn had a noticeably different vibe this morning—cleaner and brighter. The sunlight through the glass windows brought a warmth that bounced off of the honey oak tones of the walls and floor. The floors had been mopped free of its coating of mud and booze. Most notably, the tables were no longer overflowing with travelers either with their faces tucked into uncovered bosoms or engaged in some sort of gambling game.

Ed, also, wasn't behind the bar. Instead, a short and plump woman with tight black curls was refilling the mugs of the sleepy eyed patrons. One of those being served was Jetto, his bald head now covered by a green knit cap that I'm sure belonged to someone else not too long ago. A quick and fruitless scan of the room for black hair told me that Riggs hadn't come downstairs yet.

I slid onto the open barstool next to Jetto who was just being served breakfast. The plate before him had a healthy serving of eggs, sausage, and bread that I had no doubt the woman serving it to him had baked herself. The woman's teeth were bright against the darkness of her skin as she flashed me a smile before I settled into my seat.

"Ah, finally up then, darling." She poured me a steaming mug and placed it in front of me. "My name is Pearl, dear. Ed mentioned to keep an eye out for you. Said to make sure the young gal with toffee brown skin and eyes like an evergreen got a healthy heaping of breakfast. Said you'd need it after all the wine."

Her voice was a little *too* chipper for my taste, but I gave a polite smile back to her before taking a sip of my drink. I knew that my eyes were unique. They were a dark shade of green that was rare across Larendi, especially with my darker skin and hair. But, even so, I did *truly* hate it when people identified me by them. Probably because I hated how it reminded me of who gave them to me... and how I lost her.

"How'd you fair against the tall fellow last night?" I turned to Jetto, trying to distract myself from the painful memory.

"Chap was a better Flare player than the dud before him. But I still managed to come out on top." He took another bite of his breakfast, crumbs falling across his reddish beard as he chewed. "Riggs shouldn't be too long now, he was wakin' up as I was leavin'. Turns out neither of the blondes that he was with were enticin' enough to bring back last night. It wasn't ten minutes after you turned away that black-haired beauty that he was over at my table, braggin' about how good of a shot he was. He and her stayed down here 'til dawn I think. Not sure they ever made it up to the room. Course even if they did, I wouldn't have noticed. That bed was so comfortable, the King's Guard could have barged through the door and it wouldn't have woken me."

My heart sank a little. Riggs... with *her*? I thought back to her face, youthful but strong. Dark hair tied back with a bright red ribbon. She wasn't really his type. I had never seen Riggs go for anyone, *whore* or not, without light hair. It was easy to remember because the girls he messed around with were always the opposite of him.

With his dark hair and broad shoulders, Riggs never had a problem finding someone to toy with, paid or unpaid. If it wasn't for his crooked smile and slightly hooked nose, not to mention his overly pompous personality, he might actually be sort of handsome. Well, handsome as far as thieves go. But to think, it could have been *me* this morning she was waking up with....

I gave myself a little shake back to reality as I forked a crisp piece of sausage into my mouth. Jealousy between band members *never* ended well.

"But, that's Riggs for ya," Jetto continued on, finally dusting the crumbs that had collected in his beard, "Never stays happy with what he's got. Always wantin' somethin' else."

I snorted. Jetto couldn't have been more spot on. Riggs was insatiable, but it was that never-ending drive that helped keep our band going. His constant need to find and chase and take kept us busy, even when we weren't hunting down stolen stars. He might be an insufferable asshole a lot of the time, but he helped keep me awake in a world that seemed to desperately want us to sleep.

"Makes for a good thief, though." I added, which made Jetto chuckle.

"Aye. Indeed, Bossa. And a *good* thief he is. Speakin' of thievin', how far d'we have to go today?" Jetto turned toward me, his blue eyes glancing down at the pendant he knew was hidden under my shirt, mindlessly twisting the bronze ring he wore on his right pointer finger.

"Not far," I replied quickly.

I could feel that the hoard of stars we were after were close by, having barely moved since we arrived at the Red Ruby last night. It was why I was content with taking the morning so slowly. We would take those stars back before the night was over, no problem.

"Home by the end of the week, then?" He continued.

His eyes narrowed a bit, the deeper question looming. I nodded, and Jetto gave a content smile. Being back in Brakken by the new moon was imperative, for *all* of us. It was the only place any of my band wanted to be during the night of Starcasts.

That was another one of the few details that made us, this trio of, Jetto, Riggs, and me, work. We all had something to mourn on the nights the sky should be black, but wasn't. And we all wanted to mourn with our people, in true Brakkish fashion. Riggs might not have been Brakkish by birth, but with his disdain for the bastard King, we adopted him all the same.

It wasn't until after Jetto and I had both finished our breakfasts and downed a couple mugs of chicory brew that Riggs finally joined us. Despite Pearl's best efforts to serve him a full plate of breakfast, he insisted on just taking a sausage to go. Pearl's dark eyes dimmed as he refused her a final time. And though I'm sure that she took his resistance personally, I knew that it had just been because he was eager to get moving towards our next target.

Jetto settled up our tab with her as Riggs and I both slid into our cloaks. As we stood there waiting for Jetto, my eyes curiously scanned Riggs. *Where* had he hidden his new star on him? I was unable to see any outline on his tunic or pants, but I could feel that both of the stars that he held were on his person. A cloak was a dangerous place to store stars because it was too easily pickpocketed. Night cloth helped hide their blueish glow, but stars, which were typically the size of crabapple, could even be spotted wrapped if someone was looking hard enough. *Especially* if you were showcasing any signs of starmagic.

My eyeline drifted to his hands before he submerged them into the dark fabric of his cloak. Some stars, like my superstar, Jetto's stealth star, and Rigg's accuracy star, had been compressed into special casings and worked into wearable jewelry. Jetto wore his star in a ring and Riggs wore his in a leather cuff around his wrist. But the one we had lifted from Callum had been raw.

Casing stars was not cheap, especially if you wanted them to be hidden in plain sight. It was easier to conceal the stars if they were cased, but with everyone in Brakken these days scraping by for meals, there was essentially no extra funds to pay for metals or leather or the services of someone skilled in star compression. I often found myself wondering how my mother could even have afforded casing the star I wore around my neck. Maybe she had gotten a deal on it. After all, it's not like it was a perfect casing job. On the backside, a hairline crack spread across the silver, letting the tiniest bit of starlight through to shine in the dark unless it was pressed against my skin.

As for Riggs' new star, between necking the blondes and doing who knows what with the black-haired gal from last night, he couldn't have had time to case it last night. So where was it?

Riggs noticed me staring at him and flashed a signature crooked smile at me.

"Like what you see, *Bossa*? Here I thought you only got randy when the wine was flowing."

I rolled my eyes at him, and he let out a raspy laugh.

"Sorry you didn't like my gift last night. But I must admit that I'm not truly *that* sorry. She was just... delightful." Riggs smirked and licked his lips.

"I was happy to bathe and have a night's sleep without hearing your loud ass snoring," I bit back.

"Ah, Dayla didn't mention anything about me snoring. Not that we slept all that much anyways...." His dark eyes locked on mine as one of his eyebrows raised.

He was clearly baiting me, which he liked to do more than I liked. He waited patiently in the silence between us for my reaction. When I didn't give one, he continued.

"Perhaps my new friend here made the snoring disappear." His voice was low and hushed as he leaned in towards me. "I've never held healing magic so closely before, it's marvelous. Tell me, *Bossa*. How are you not always beaming from ear to ear, clicking your heels wearing your star? No aches or pains in addition to your other skills... you must feel like you could rule the world."

He glanced down at my chest, looking at where he knew my star lay close to my body. I instinctively took a guarding step back.

"You know it doesn't exactly work like that."

I trusted Riggs and Jetto enough to let them know my superstar gave me access to all of the starmagics: healing, accuracy, premonition, stealth, elemental manipulation, and seeking. But they didn't exactly know how much of each magic I had access to. And that's because *I* didn't even truly know.

My ability to access starmagic ebbed and flowed, and it's not like there was a book on the science of activating superstars. It was more of a learned art, one that I had pieced together from the various stories and tricks that I had heard over the years. Even though I had been wearing mine for almost ten years, I knew I didn't have all of the magics down perfectly. Thankfully, I didn't need to be perfect to be better than everyone else.

"So you say," he replied at an uncomfortably slow pace.

"I'm glad you had a good time last night," I lied, switching the conversation away from my particular star. "We needed the rest after that grueling hunt for Callum. Sneaky coward. Today should be much simpler."

"Ah, but where is the fun in simple, Talla? I want to try out these instant healing powers in a real fight before we bring her back home to Brakken. I still have the itch for some slogging after Callum turned out to be as tough as a baby bunny, even after staying up *all* night." His beady eyes flared as he again lifted his brows.

Moon, save me. I hated how he knew that even though I hadn't wanted to sleep with the girl, Dayla I guess her name was, that it bothered me that he had gotten to. He probably could read the slight twinge of jealousy plain as day on my face—Jetto has always told me that I'm not very good at disguising my true emotions. I couldn't see my own reactions in real time to be sure, but I had a feeling he was right.

"Well, I'm happy to go head-to-head with you, if you'd like. After all, you said I need to get my hands dirty more often." I pulled my hand up, flipping it back and forth, checking for dirt under my nails. "Mmm, freshly bathed. Should we fix that?"

Riggs' smirk quickly fell, and then I flashed a saccharine smile. He could taunt me all he wanted, but he knew that he couldn't take me, even with his added star. He had embarrassed himself every time that he tried to prove otherwise.

A jingling sound pulled my attention away from Riggs as Jetto finally joined us, sliding a small velvet bag of coins to each of us. No doubt these were the spoils he collected in his games the night before. A solo thief would have kept it all to himself, but that was the benefit of having a band. Jetto, Riggs, and I had an understanding. Jetto slyly lifts the coin. Riggs, more or less, keeps us safe. I lead us to stars. And all of us together bring goods and stolen starpower back to the people of Brakken where we then revel in their gratitude.

My mother had always told me that people worked stronger together if you were lucky enough to find the right ones to trust. Fortunately, my luck manifested in the form of my superstar. My access to premonition magic helped me determine who to keep by my side, or else there's no way in hell I would have entered into a band with a balding gambler and a cocky capital city reject both at least fifteen years my senior.

"Are we's ready?" The sound of Jetto's light and diffusive voice cooled the heat of my temper that had flared while waiting with Riggs.

"Ready." I replied as my hands worked their way deep into my cloak pockets.

Jetto adjusted his knit hat to cover both his ears better as we stepped out into the chilly autumn air. Still west, my star was telling me. I nodded my head in the direction that I could feel the seeking magic pulling me in before stepping out towards the thick tree line of the Middle Forests with Riggs and Jetto in tow.

CHAPTER 5 | KIERAN

The royal stables were tucked around the east tower of the castle, and while they had been constructed mostly of the same sand-colored stone that made up the city walls and the castle itself, the upper level of the barn was built from strong and sturdy wood. The top of the stable walls joined together at the top to form a remarkable arched roof that was home to probably half of Mellin's bird population. As I passed through the human-sized doorway on the barn's side, I could see Gray busy with attaching various velvet and canvas bags to a chestnut mare. The horse's coat and mane were sleek and polished, and her orange-brown hues contrasted beautifully with the navy blue saddle pad that extended from her back across her hindquarters. Gray's pace quickened when he noticed that I had entered, his fingers fumbling with the buckle on the last bag as I closed the distance.

"My a-apologies, Sir K-Kieran. I didn't think you would be down so soon." As soon as he finished the clasp, he went to bow, but I reached my arm out to his shoulder to stop him.

"Gray, you have nothing to fear from me. I have told you this before."

Gray shifted his attention up, his blue eyes hollow in his pale face as he met my gaze. I wanted him to trust me, to know that despite my reputation, I wouldn't *dare* lay a hand on him. The King had appointed Gray as his footman at the beginning of his reign. It spoke volumes about Gray's character and loyalty that the King had never decided to replace him over the past two decades. I wouldn't threaten such a relationship so important to His Grace, especially after everything the King had done for me.

Gray's glance slipped from me to the onyx studded gold sword on my hip a few times as he leaned into my extended arm. It wasn't the first time that I had noticed his eyes linger on the weapon over the years. As I watched his gaze flutter between what I read as fear and longing, an idea quickly formed in my head. Footmen weren't allowed to carry swords, naturally, but to my knowledge, there was nothing against them training with them.

"You know, after Solstice I am likely going to have more time on my hands. I'll still have my rounds at the prisons to do, but I'd be happy to teach you how to use a blade if you are interested."

Gray's face lit up as he took a step back, returning his body to his full height. A small spark of hope shot through me.

"That is..." I continued, reaching out to take the reins of the horse from him. He happily slid the leather straps into my hand before taking another step back, giving me room to mount the mare, "as long as you promise not to use my own tricks against me."

I shot him a wink, but he must have missed the joke in my tone, because he frantically started to shake his head. All happiness and excitement had drained from his face.

"I have seen you t-train, Sir Kieran. I may be a mere footman but I am not a fool."

My lips settled into a flat line as I nodded. I wanted to tell him that there was nothing '*mere*' about serving the King so closely, but the magical sensation humming along the skin of my arm stopped me. The pull on my wrist reminded me to get going in pursuit of the stars as I had been ordered. So instead of saying anything else, I glumly shared a soft grin before I lifted my boot into the extended stirrup and pulled my way up onto the horse.

Once I was settled in the saddle, I pulled at the bottom hem of my tunic, readjusting the fabric before bending my torso down to greet the familiar horse with a hearty run pat on her neck. Of all of the castle's horses, she was the one I preferred to take on starhunts. She was brave and fast, but still gentle on the ground. She had never failed me on my numerous journeys across Larendi, no matter the terrain. The only flaw that the mare had was that while she was most often quite sweet, she could also be quite stubborn. Over the years, I had learned how to better communicate with her in her more trying moments, and since they never seemed to really impact the outcome of our journey, I never let them stop me from choosing her as my steed. I wasn't sure if she had a formal name—I didn't get to spend much time in the stables between my training and overseeing the prisons. But, to me she was Boli.

She snorted in response to my gesture, beginning to take small and antsy steps beneath me as I tightened the reins. Gray opened the larger stable doors for us, which let the morning sunshine flood the concrete aisle. The sudden shift in light caused several of the other royal mounts to stir in their stalls.

Boli tugged at the reins that I held in one hand as I pulled my mask that I had tucked underneath my tunic up over my face. It was a simple piece of fabric, but one that was necessary to shield my mouth and nose from the impending wind. Gray seemed to quiver on the threshold of the barn as he looked at my covered face, but I didn't have time for another attempt at calming him because the second I released the tension that I held at the horse's mouth, the chestnut mare and I were off.

I steered Boli out beyond the sandstone city walls, letting the star on my wrist pull me towards the closest hoard. She happily charged forward, her hooves thunderously pounding down on Mellin's main entrance road before turning right to head along a northern path.

The magic of the Seeker star tucked under my sleeve constantly hummed along my skin, the pull growing in strength as the distance between me and other stars lessened. While this star could lead me towards any of the six types of stars, it couldn't tell me what kind of star it was. The only way to know what kind of power that a star held was to hold it and activate it. Depending on the type of star, the difficulty of accessing the magic varied.

When the King started collecting the fallen stars, the Seekers were the first that were returned. Not surprising—after all, what good was it to be able to find nearby stars if you knew that everyone around you already had one? Especially when their stars equipped them with more tangible abilities like enhanced accuracy and stealth.

But as more stars were collected and returned, suddenly having a seeker star was like having a map to hidden treasure. Three years ago, the King had had me trade almost a cartful of coins in exchange for the last known Seeker star. That hunt took me south, down into the wet and grassy lowlands. The towns in that part of Larendi are smaller, the largest being only a quarter of the size of Mellin, and poorer as well.

The swamps offer little as far as resources go, so for the man who had found the Seeker star lost in one of the shallow pools, the ten chests of gold instantly made him local royalty. He probably would have taken less, but His Grace was adamant about paying the man fairly in exchange for such an orb.

The King had also provided me with extra coins to exchange for its immediate compression, but no one in the lowlands was skilled in the art of encasing a star. The trade had become almost taboo as people all over Larendi began to fall in love with the star-filled sky, and those who once knew how to compress the magic stopped teaching others how to do so. Luckily, I knew of a skilled metalworker with ample practice on star pieces in Vrenn just east of the city wall. Though, getting Lor to agree to the job wasn't easy, even with the ample payment. My sister's attitude towards the King, his magnificent dream, and my role in it was the *exact* reason why I made my visits to Vrenn short and infrequent.

But in the end, the uncomfortable venture back to my home city was more than worth it. There was no other way to track the location of stars without the power of the Seeker star that flared on my wrist. Without this magic, I can't imagine how the King would have ever been able to find all of the stars to complete the night sky.

By the time the sun started to set, Boli had swiftly carried me over the rough hilly terrain of the Highlands that separated Mellin from the Middle Forests. My eyes were watery from the whipping winds, and had it not been for my mask, my skin would have surely been burned from the cold. I pulled Boli back to a trot as we crossed over a ridge that faded down to flatter and softer ground. The cooler weather meant we could travel faster and longer than our starhunts in the warmer seasons, but I knew Boli could use a rest.

The road we followed approached a creek, an offshoot of the River Linvel, roaring from last night's heavy rainfall. I pulled her to the side, and dismounted, my boots squishing in the wet grass as my feet hit the earth. After tying up her reins in a knot on her neck so she could freely graze and drink, I approached the creek to get a drink myself. The bank was slick with mud, but after pulling down my mask, with cupped hands I scooped a few cold mouthfuls of water to my face. It tasted like metal and algae, but it was refreshing all the same.

I was reaching down for a fourth handful, when an unexpected shadow moved under the wooden bridge a couple dozen yards to my right. My instincts flared, and I dropped the water that I had been drinking, opting to grab at my sword on my back. There were few beasts in the Highlands, the rocky and exposed terrain wasn't suitable for them like the mountains and forests were. But with winter approaching, I wouldn't put it past a mountain cat or a ground bear to venture this far south.

The figure came into view again, and by the shaking silhouette, it appeared to be a man, trying to traverse the underside of the bridge without slipping on the wet rocks that lined the water.

"Boli, stay put." I said over my shoulder, pulling my mask back up over my face.

She snorted in reply between the large mouthfuls of clover that she managed to find between the grasses. My attention never shifted from the man. He was so focused on not falling into the creek that he didn't even see me approach, taking my own careful steps down the bank. My hand rested on my sword—he didn't appear to be a threat, but not every danger in this world was dressed like one. In fact, this one wasn't dressed at all.

After a few moments of watching how the man moved with such a lack of skill or stealth, I decided to call out to him.

"Lovely day for a stroll," I shouted.

My voice caught him by surprise, and the startle sent him tumbling backwards onto his bare ass. I suppressed a smirk under my mask, but quickly closed the distance between us to go and help him up. "Bit chilly, though, isn't it?" I went to reach my arm out, but the movement caused him to cry out.

"Please no!" He threw his hands up to shield his face, "don't hurt me. They already took it... I have nothing to offer you."

I took my other hand off my sword and crouched down to be near eye level with him. His hefty frame was shivering as the cooler winds had picked back up. I surveyed the round, naked man that sat bare on the ground. He had small cuts that covered his skin, and his messy blonde hair was filled with twigs and leaves.

My wrist sensed no stars on this man, not that I could imagine where he could even be hiding them. According to his comment, my guess was that he had been robbed. I didn't realize the people beyond Mellin had grown so uncivilized to strip a man of everything, including his clothes, when robbing someone.

I whistled to Boli, who came trotting over without hesitation. When he realized that I wasn't going to strike him, the naked man opened his eyes. His scared blue gaze darted back and forth between me and Boli. Between the glances, I could see something new registering on his face replacing his fear—shame.

"You're... you're a member of the King's Guard," he muttered softly between the chatter of his teeth.

He tried to cover himself, pulling at the long grass and gathering it at his waist. He must have seen Boli's saddle pad, embroidered with the sigil of King Armund, because nothing on me could have given it away. I always travel in plain black clothes.

"Yes, I am," I replied.

His eyes were wide in shock and admiration.

"What are you doing out here?" he asked, still shaking.

I stood up and turned around to rifle through one of my saddle bags, pulling out the extra blanket that Gray had packed for me before setting it on the ground. With a quick draw of my hand, I unsheathed my sword. The naked man flinched as I stabbed my blade through it, right into the soft earth.

I flicked my wrist a few times, using the sharp edges of my blade to make tears in the fabric before I sheathed my weapon. With a few tugs at the hole I had created, there was a large enough gap in the fibers to slide over his head. Before crouching before the man again. I pulled my mask down, revealing my full face to display my sincerity.

"Besides my Royal duties, I'm apparently saving you from freezing to death. Lower your head."

He obeyed, and I slipped the hole right over his head so the blanket was resting draped in a circle around his shoulders. I grabbed at his arm and pulled him up to stand. The blanket just grazed the top of his knees, his round belly taking up most of the fabric's real estate. It wasn't much for clothing, but it should keep him from dying. Probably.

"Of course. So foolish of me to ask questions when the Stars have graced me with such luck. Your kindness is unmatched, Sir. I am honored to receive such kindness from a member of His Grace's court."

Pride swelled in my chest as the man wiped away tears as he continued on.

"I... they. They attacked me. I was planning on bringing it to the King. And they took it from me. And took my clothes. They left me in the bushes." The man's words became muffled as his hands shot over his face to hide his tears.

My brow raised.

"What were you planning on bringing to the King, Mister..."

"Callum." He choked out his name at my pause before continuing, "A star. I had a star for King Armund. I was touring in Brakken as a bard. Nasty town, full of selfish thieves and stingy tippers. But the bars were always full, so it evened out. Been there for a few months before realizing the people there were hoarding their stars from everyone else. People talk, and they think bards don't listen while they are singing. But they do. I had heard of the grace of the King. The gifts in exchange for returning a star. I figured I'd stayed long enough in Brakken. I wanted to settle back within the castle walls. It's where I'm from, you know. *Stars*, I shouldn't have ever left home. Mama said not to, you know. Said there were dark and dangerous people with unchecked power, more dangerous than any wild beasts, beyond the woods. I thought that was just a tale her mom told her, and her mom before that. But those three... Mama was right. Those thieves are using the stars! They are using them to steal and fight and bring darkness to this world. It's unnatural. The stars need to be up there, where they belong!" Callum gestured to the cloudy sky above before wiping his face.

Huh. I could always feel a weak pull while wearing the star cuff to the northwest, way beyond the River Linvel. I figured that I would have to make my way out to that disheveled town sooner or later. Since most of the Brakkish people seemed to be unreasonably rebellious against the King, I wasn't surprised to hear that there were now bands of star thieves lurking beyond the gray stone gates.

I kept my face neutral as the man rambled on about his love and appreciation for the work of the King. All the while I was pondering what he had recounted regarding his attack. If what Callum was saying was true, and these star thieves were using starmagic to help them rob and steal from the good people of Larendi, then they would of course need to be stopped as soon as possible.

This was one of the rare moments that I *almost* wished that I didn't complete my starhunts alone. It would be impossible to bring several thieves back with me to serve an appropriate sentence in the prisons. Boli was strong, but she could only carry one other rider over such a great distance. But even that would be risky. The far simpler solution would just be to *handle* them. His Grace had given me permission, after all.

My attention shifted back to Callum, who was now recounting every member in his family's history and their acts of allegiance towards the crown.

"Can you describe them to me?" My words interrupted him mid-sentence, his mouth left open as he processed my question.

"The thieves who robbed you," I continued, my tone calm and curious. "If they're that dangerous, I should be on the lookout for them... the King's Guard should be made aware of such a threat to King Armund's vision."

"There's three of them," his eyes brightened as he started to stand a little taller. "A big dark-haired fellow, kinda like yourself. But with a crooked nose. Riggs, they call him. Real troublemaker. I've seen him fight in the bars I was playing in. He's deadly. And then there's a big, tall bald man. I forget his name, but he's always playing cards or betting with tiles at the bars. He's a sneaky one. And then there's a girl... she seems to lead them. Gosh I forget her name, too...." Shame started creeping back onto his face, but I tried to nod to reassure him that his information was still helpful. It was, after all.

"What type of star did they steal, do you know? Or what kind of starmagic did they wield?"

It ultimately didn't matter what the answers were to those questions, but they would help me anticipate any potential attacks from them. Callum shook his head, looking utterly dejected.

"That's alright. That's plenty for me to recognize them should I be so unlucky to cross paths with them."

I reached into my pocket and handed him a gold coin. He held it gingerly in his hands.

"It's not the same reward as the King gives for stars, but consider it a thank you on behalf of the King's Guard for the tip on the thieves."

"Thank you. Thank you, Guard." Callum bowed his head.

"And keep the blanket. It's made of fine wool from Reaultan sheep. That coin will do you no good if you freeze to death." I gave him a wink before grabbing at Boli's reins.

As I mounted, the man saluted me before shouting, *'For Starlight, for Everyone!'* so loudly and proudly that I squinted my eyes, but I still gave him a polite smile in return.

As I was pulling my mask back up to cover my nose and nudging Boli onward, away from the man named Callum who was naked no more, he shouted again.

"Guard! I remember!" I turned my head in his direction, waiting for him to continue. "Talla. That's the girl's name. Talla. And she has these *unique* green eyes. Everyone knows her by them. But don't let them fool you! Her and the others, they are dangerous folk even if they don't all look it!"

I nodded again in thanks before pushing my heels into Boli's sides and sending her off towards the pull of the stars. As she picked up her pace, her strides now at a canter down the road, Callum's words played back in my head.

'They are dangerous folk, even if they don't all look it!'

I laughed a bit to myself. Dangerous for him, sure. But I was doubtful that these thieves could show me any sort of fight that I hadn't seen while I had training against starmagic for almost a decade. Talla, Riggs, and the bald thief were surely no different than the thieves that I had locked away in the Royal Prisons. Selfish, self-righteous criminals.

CHAPTER 6 | TALLA

The assholes that we were hunting, the ones who had come through Brakken to steal our stars, sure seemed comfortable in these woods. Either that, or they were already dead. By the direction of the pull on my wrist, I could tell that they were stalled deep in the Middle Forests.

Traveling through these woods at night was dangerous this time of year as the ground bears were preparing for their long Winter sleep. Even during the other seasons, many Larendians avoided the Middle Forests all together, save to use the edge travel road. That road, however, took at least five days to travel end to end, and these particular thieves were likely trying to find a shortcut through to the Highlands near the castle. But they hadn't moved the entire day. Their questionable choices at least made tracking them even quicker work than I had anticipated.

After we had realized that Brakken's few remaining elemental stars were missing, it didn't take long to figure out that the thieves we would be after were from Enver. That fact didn't surprise me—while folk from Enver aren't big fans of

Armund either, they did have a reputation for being selfish and foolish.

Realistically, I do suppose the fact that Armund, in his desperation, had increased his offerings for the return of the stars was *theoretically* tempting. We all probably should have seen it coming, in hindsight.

The Enver thieves made their heist during a cloudy night when Brakken was covered in a nowadays rare, but comfortable, layer of darkness. With so many stars lighting up the sky most nights, we tend to celebrate when their light is obstructed. So, when the hooded figures came slinking through the fields, everyone in town was either asleep or too drunk to notice.

It was mid-afternoon when the cool winds first carried the thieves' voices to us through the tall evergreens. I thought that I could hear at least three different voices, both male and female, so I held my hand up, signaling to Riggs and Jetto to freeze. Both men did so with no hesitation. Turning my head slightly to my right, I gave a silent nod to Jetto. He silently ran ahead, dodging the trees swiftly until he was out of sight.

Riggs and I stood quietly in the clearing, wind roaring and whipping around us. Three thieves we could take easily. In fact, anything under six would be manageable. The three of us once bested a cohort of nine thieves, but that fight had left me so sore that I didn't leave my bath for a week. Superstar or not, it's pretty fucking hard to dodge three daggers at once.

With about a day's worth of walking needed to get us back to Brakken after a week on the road, an easier fight would probably be best. I looked up to the sky, noting how the sun hung low, fighting to peek out behind thick gray clouds. Colder days and nights were coming.

I didn't hear Jetto return until he spoke, his breath a little labored from running through the woods.

"There's four of 'em, Bossa. Drunk off their asses it seems."

I smiled. Even *easier* than anticipated then. I faced Riggs to see delight dancing in his eyes. He was clearly thirsty for a fight, and I had to admit that I was a little, too. Callum had gone down too easy. Several days of tracking that fast bastard only for him to collapse out of fear? Talk about anticlimactic. But if there's one group of people who do indeed like to fight, it's drunk thieves.

"Well, shall we go have some fun?" I said as I turned to face both of my crew.

"After last night, I was starting to think you had lost your taste for fun, dear Talla." Riggs responded.

I rolled my eyes at him.

"Only joking. Lead the way, *Bossa.*"

With a huff, I started to walk towards their voices, the pull of the star around my chest guiding my feet towards our target.

◊

The thieves were sitting around a bright orange fire with two rabbits roasting on a spit above the flames. Two men were seated on a downed log to the left of it, taking sips from mugs in between hearty laughs. It was obvious that the two were twins. Both of them shared the same square jawline and the same shade of dirty blonde hair tied into buns on their neck.

Next to them, there was a girl with her back to us. By the way she twirled a loose strand of her raven-colored hair, she clearly was admiring one, maybe even both, of the twins. The rest of her hair laid in a braid down her back, the plait laced with a shiny gold ribbon tied in a bow at the end.

The final thief was also female, and she stood opposite the fire, facing us. A long bow was strapped around her cloaked shoulders, and she wore navy trousers tucked into some *nice* fur-lined boots. Had her long face been looking up instead of being buried in her drink, she might have seen us approaching through the trees.

But she didn't, and my crew and I were able to approach the thieves without alerting any of them of our presence. The pull at my chest increased with every step we took, the sensation becoming overwhelming as my foot hit a hard object buried underneath the pine needles. I scanned the perimeter of the area, noting the very faint blue glow under small pine piles scattered in a circle encasing them.

"Excuse me, fellow travelers?" I shouted as we approached so that they could hear me over the swaying branches.

But my voice came out louder than I intended. I looked up, and sure enough the branches above us weren't swaying anymore. It also was notably warmer in this part of the woods than the others. I couldn't help but be a little impressed, or at least surprised, at their abilities to activate elemental stars this way. Enver was located further south than Brakken, opposite the River Linvel on extremely fertile ground—the town didn't share the same difficulties as Brakken did.

One of the twins responded to me, standing up as he spoke.

"No need to shout girl. We can hear ya just fine!" He swayed a bit, clearly unsteady from how much he had to drink. His shoulders were broad and covered in a thick fur shawl, while the rest of him was clad in a dark leather. I scanned him from head to toe. No visible weapons.

"What can we do yas for, milady? Are you lot in need of directions? Not often do we find stray travelers in these parts of the woods." He took a swig from the mug he was holding.

Unarmed. No fear or worry in his posture. He was such a fool.

Jetto piped in from a few steps behind me, already fully in character.

"My kin and I are on our way back to Reault from some time in Enver. Merely seeking shelter from the wintering winds and noticed the smoke from your fire." He tugged at his coat trying to pull it close around him. He took a few steps forward, adding a convincing limp. "Can we bother you for a few minutes around your fire? My knees don't tolerate the cold as much as they used to."

Riggs rushed to his side, pretending to help him hobble along. I suppressed a smile as I watched them play their parts so well.

The standing twin gave a nod to his brother who stood to join him. He was dressed similarly, but I quickly noted the dagger that he wore around his waist. The two surveyed us for a few moments before the second twin walked over to the other side of Jetto than Riggs, offering his hand to lean on.

"Oh, thank you for your kindness!" I added, batting my eyelashes and giving the second twin a soft and sweet smile.

He stared at my face for a few moments with his brow lifted and mouth open like he was searching for the words on the tip of his tongue. His search must have failed him, because the expression faded. He smiled back at me, and I could feel the black-haired girl shooting daggers at me with her eyes, though she didn't move from her spot on the log. I made sure she saw me pretend to blush, *just* for fun.

"Indeed, many thanks." Jetto added. The three men hobbled towards the fire.

"Admittedly I feel warmer already! The magic of fire never ceases to amaze me."

"Indeed." The long-faced woman responded through a chuckle, brew still coating her lips.

I watched as the group shared knowing looks to each other, but I pretended like I didn't notice. They had absolutely *no idea* that we knew how they were able to reduce the winds. They also didn't know that between us, we had more than enough starpower to take the lot of them down without breaking a sweat.

The long-faced woman shuffled her foot to move some needles to try to cover the star closest to her, but ended up just better exposing the backside. I counted eight small piles of leaves around the group—all of the stolen stars accounted for.

These glances of mine, though, were *not* unnoticed. Her brown eyes locked on to mine, but I played it off, giving the woman a soft, doe-eyed smile. The long-faced woman nodded to me, albeit a little suspiciously, before the second twin stood and spoke, much louder than his brother had.

"Our cart broke down along the road over there." He gestured through the trees, and we all looked.

I could barely see the lopsided pile of wood and chains, but it was there.

"We sent word with our horses for supplies to mend it last night. Until help finds us, we are just enjoying the woods!" He walked a few paces before sitting back down on the log, slinging an arm around the black-haired girl as she giggled into his shoulder.

Riggs rolled his eyes before setting them on me. The words '*I'm done playing this game*' were written all over his face. I gave him a nod—I was getting tired of the charade as well. He returned the motion with a crooked smile before taking a few steps backwards.

"Well, it's a good thing you have all of these little *stars* to help keep you warm while you wait!" Riggs plucked one out of the ground, holding it in the middle of his flattened palm for everyone to see.

The entire mood of the group shifted from jovial to tense. I could see the gears turning in the long-faced woman's head. I saw how she thought about reaching for her bow before she stopped as the louder twin waved her off.

"Careful there," he was speaking to us like we were children who had gotten ahold of something they shouldn't have. "Those aren't just toys. It takes practice to be able to work them, and we need them to—" he was interrupted by a gust of cold wind to the face.

Riggs had deactivated the star, causing a break in the circle that was keeping the warmth in. The twin's face dropped.

"You lot know how to wield elemental stars then?" The dark-haired girl's voice shuttered with such apprehension, it made me giddy.

I walked over to a spot where another star was hidden, and picked it up, the power buzzing through my body as soft blue light peeked through my fingers.

"Well, seeing how they were *our* people's to begin with, it would be embarrassing if we didn't know how to use them." I deactivated it, causing another burst of cold air to move through their camp.

One twin turned his head towards me, shock and disgust settled on his brow. He took his arm off of the girl's shoulder and made a few sloppy steps my way. Once in front of me, he leaned his face down to look into mine, his breath hot and stale like the air inside the Brakken pubs in the middle of summer.

"Finders. Keepers." He shook a finger at my face, punctuating each word with a point before reaching to grab the star in my hand.

His face grew angry as I pulled it back, just out of his reach. When he went to give me a shove, I effortlessly sidestepped him, dodging his hands. The swing into the air caused him to topple forward a few steps before he could regain his balance. I let out a huff of disapproval before reaching under my cloak and fisting a dagger in my right hand. As I pulled the blade into the daylight, I twisted it enough to glint the small amount of sunshine that was now managing to peek through the clouds back up at his face.

"Not all girls with braids care for your hands on them, you know. Some of us have *taste*." I shot a quick look at the girl with the raven braid to see her face flare with red embarrassment or rage... I couldn't tell which.

"You're playing a dangerous game, girl," he spat through gritted teeth.

He went to reach for his own dagger... only to find it missing. Panic flooded his face as he looked around for it quickly. Jetto stepped up beside me, holding it in his hand. The twin stuttered in disbelief.

"Looking for this? Won't do you any good. Not against this gal." He clapped me on the shoulder.

"Doubtful." The other twin was now by his brother's side.

He managed to find a small axe that was now held tightly by his chest. *That's fine*. He didn't need to believe Jetto. He would be eating his words soon enough.

"Should we test it?" I replied in a light and airy tone.

I flicked my dagger again so the sun gleamed in both their faces. The joyous sound of drunk and angry growls filled my ears.

"No amount of starpower is going to revive Brakken to its good ol' days. And stars aren't worth dying over. So why don't you just *leave* before this gets ugly."

I let the wind howl around us for a few seconds while I contemplated my response. We *could* show mercy. But, then again...

"Can't do that I'm afraid." I shot Riggs a wink, letting him know it was time.

Riggs started rolling up his sleeves as he walked over and gave an antagonizing push to the louder twin to start the brawl.

Both twins descended on Riggs, and it was a mess of fists and leaves and grunts. The older woman dropped her mug and finally reached for the bow that she had slung around her shoulder, but her hands only found air. Frantic, she turned around, only to see Jetto aiming down a cocked arrow that was inches from her forehead. She was less foolish than her companions and quickly put her hands up in surrender.

Thinking that I was distracted, the dark-haired girl launched herself at me. Within a few seconds I had my dagger pressed against her throat, my arms wrapped around her from behind. Even though she was about my size, my grip was unbreakable on her. She couldn't move, and with no weapon of her own, her only option was to scream for the help of one of the twins.

And scream she did. But her loud calls fell on deaf ears as the two men were too busy stumbling around trying to lay a successful blow on Riggs to respond to her. The twin with the axe finally managed to nick Riggs' arm with a faked out sideways swing. Riggs grasped at his wound as blood started to seep through his tunic. His pause of attacks left room for the other twin to finally land a punch on his jaw. The impact of the hit sent Riggs slamming to the ground.

I tried not to hold my breath as I watched him lay there, spitting blood as he tried to push himself up with his good arm. I hardly ever saw Riggs get hit by someone other than me, and I almost never saw him lose blood. The twins laughed as they towered over his downed body, kicking out his supporting arm, causing him to fall again.

I knew then that not all four of these thieves would live until nightfall, not with how they were playing with Riggs. The twins continued their drunken laughter, thinking that they had bested him.

They didn't know that somewhere, though I'm still not sure exactly where, Riggs held a very powerful healing star. Or, that if you push Riggs too far, he won't hold back.

In a flash, Riggs had popped himself back up, and using the arm that had been sliced into, he reached out and grabbed the axe bearer's hair and yanked. With the help of his accuracy magic, Riggs was able to pull against the man's spine perfectly for it to snap. The crack of the twin's neck breaking was loud enough to echo over the howling winds. With a thud, one of the twin's bodies hit the forest floor, eyes wide open but completely lifeless.

Riggs grabbed the axe and swung it at the other brother, who had been standing watching the events in shock. The blade sliced his throat. After a few seconds of strained and desperate gurgling, he too fell to his knees before his body fell alongside his brother's, never to stir again.

Two perfectly executed deaths in less than thirty seconds. It was a little dramatic for my taste, but it's not my fault the dumb bastards picked a fight with the wrong man.

The girl in my arms wailed as she clawed at my hand that was holding the dagger, trying to pull the sharp tip of my blade away from her skin. I pressed it tighter into her smooth neck, drawing a thin line of blood. Her hair tickled my chilled nose as I leaned in to whisper in her ear.

"He was right, you know, these stars aren't worth dying for. It's your choice. But in case you're thinking of calling my bluff," I nudged her gaze back up from the body into Rigg's grinning face. "I can kick that man's ass with my eyes closed."

The girl stopped fidgeting, and I moved my arm away from her neck and pushed her forward. Jetto nodded to the older woman, the arrow still cocked. The two ladies quickly looked at each other before simultaneously running in the opposite direction of their cart they had abandoned.

"Hopefully that'll scratch the itch, Riggs," I said to him as I watched the girls disappear into the Middle Forests.

I headed towards Jetto, who had already started digging up some of the stars and putting them in a nightcloth pouch.

"It helped, that's for sure." Riggs replied, wiping the blood from the axe off on the twin's fur shrug.

When the blade was clean, he secured the handle through a loop on his belt before he tossed me the elemental star he had picked up earlier. Even one star could create a small pull at my chest, the feeling of its power subtly washing over me as it zoomed closer. It's how I knew only a few moments later, away from the pile of stars in front of me and away from my star-powered comrades, a new star was coming towards us, and quickly.

The moment I recognized the feeling, I turned my head from side to side, trying to spot it or its wielder. Jetto and Riggs, too, started looking, noting my frantic movements.

"There." It was Jetto who spotted the figure in black first.

He was on a gleaming orange-brown horse that was clad with a navy-blue pad. Even though I couldn't see the symbol embroidered on it, I knew who those colors represented.

"The *fucking* King's guard? What are they doing out here." Annoyed, I continued to help Jetto pull up the stars.

"Looks like a lone rider, Bossa" Jetto added, "Do you think he's after..."

"He won't get them." I cut Jetto off and looked at Riggs.

There was no way that Royal Asshole would be taking the stars from us. I wouldn't allow it.

"Still got an itch? Jetto and I can finish up here. We will meet you when we are done. I wouldn't mind having a horse to help us make the trip back to Brakken anyways."

Riggs looked at me for a few seconds, clearly debating saying something that he probably shouldn't. I rolled my eyes and took a step towards the guard, as if I was just going to take care of him myself. You'd think Riggs would be a little less insubordinate now that he had two stars of his own and a winning fight under his belt for this trip.

"I got it, *Bossa,*" he replied with the familiar mocking tone before taking off in a run towards the black figure in the distance.

It was bad luck to come across any members of the

King's Guard, especially with two dead bodies and a handful of stars at your feet. At least it was a solo rider. A small hiccup in today's plan, but the fight should be over quickly. Riggs would take care of him, I had no doubt about that. And we would be heading back to Brakken by nightfall *happily* knowing that the King had one less man alive in this world to do his bidding.

CHAPTER 7 | KIERAN

I saw a man with dark hair and blood splattered clothes approaching with long and quick strides through gaps in the trees. He was coming right for me, so before he could get too close, I made sure to secure Boli behind a tight grouping of trees. *Thank the Stars*, she didn't give me any of her usual protest about being left behind for a bit. I had traveled across almost all of Larendi during my time in the King's Guard, and I still hadn't come across a place *less* predictable than the Middle Forests. There were always some sort of beasts roaming these woods. Today it looked like it was one of the two-legged and rebellious variety.

I took a quick backwards glance at Boli before walking on foot to meet the man, guilt squeezing at my chest. By the way her brown eyes widened, and her tail swished back and forth, she seemed to be aware of *exactly* where we were and the dangers associated with these woods. But, she diligently stayed put. Leaving a horse unguarded in these trees was a risk, but less of one than dealing with whatever weapons this man was wielding.

The blood on the man was bright, and by the patterns in which it stained his clothes, it wasn't just his own. In the few seconds before we were upon each other, I quickly searched for signs of others in tow who might cause me grief. I could barely make out two others. Their forms were only shadows moving amongst the trees, one larger and one more slender, both bent over shuffling something from the ground into a jet-black bag. My wrist pulled hard in their direction—they were likely the trio of star thieves that Callum had warned me about.

Riggs... that's what Callum had said the hooked-nosed man's name was right? Well, if these people were the very same thieves that had stripped that poor man of his star and his clothes... they sure did seem like a confident bunch—but criminals always were. His comrades foolishly paid no attention to him as he headed my way.

As he stormed closer to me, it dawned on me why that was. Power skidded across my skin, the pull from the Seeker on my wrist becoming stronger with each step. This man had starmagic. While it was impossible for me to know which kind he had equipped himself with, it was *very* clear that he wielded more than one power.

Selfish bastard. Carrying at least two stars himself when the night sky needed them back. The odds of a peaceful negotiation like I was accustomed to was low with someone like him—if he and his comrades were in the business of stealing stars and using their magic, they didn't have one shred of respect for the King, let alone his guard. But, even though my efforts might be pointless, I still had to try. After all, a thief is a thief. And starthief or not, *all* thieves like coin.

I didn't waste any time sharing my first offer—a sack of gold and silver coins—once we were face-to-face in between the tall trees.

Riggs let out a cold laugh before *'No'* slipped from his lips as he cocked his arm and swung at my face. After I had side-stepped him, I decided to double it. Two bags of coin would be enough to set a man like Riggs up for the next three seasons, even if he did share it with his comrades.

That offer got me the swing of his axe. After dodging his second blow, I couldn't hold back the smirk that formed on my face as I surveyed him—his nostrils flared, skin scrunched around his hooked nose as he lifted his top lip, baring his teeth. He looked completely and entirely pissed off, which I found completely and entirely amusing. Clearly, he wasn't used to anyone evading his attacks. Too bad for him, I was more than used to beating down star-powered brutes.

Unphased as I was, his drawn blade *did* mean that I needed to at least unsheathe my sword. I grabbed onto the gold and onyx hilt that had been poking up over my shoulder, swinging it up and across my body. Riggs was quick and had a fighter's instincts, and he managed to time another swing of his axe in my direction so that I was only just able to block it at the last second. Sparks flew in all directions as the two blades met, my sword blocking each of his blows.

The constant clanging of metal didn't give me much room to negotiate with him, but it did give me time to study him. He didn't move with calculated steps, instead choosing quick and aggressive ones. The way that the blood stained the inside of his sleeve cuff meant that he wiped it from his nose or mouth. But despite being oily and unpleasantly tainted by greed, Riggs' face didn't have an actual mark on it. It was a safe bet that he had a healing star, then.

In the short breaks between his attacks, I listened closely against the wind. I could hear his feet shuffle along the needles and leaves. He wasn't wielding stealth magic. So, his other star, or stars, had to be elemental or accuracy. Those were the only other starmagics left in the world on the ground, according to His Grace.

The remaining types of stars, Illusion and Seeking, had all been recovered. It didn't *really* matter what kind of stars Riggs had though—I had fought against every combination of known starmagic there was left. I had seen it all. But I still needed a plan if I wanted to stop this parrying and attempt to recover his stars. In the opposite direction of where I had left Boli, I noticed a crooked cart with a few long chains lying along the path.

Frustrated by his lack of success with his axe, Riggs threw it to the ground, letting out a deafening howl that, had I been anyone else, I might have found terrifying. No wonder Callum was so shaken up. I took a small step backwards towards the cart. I was hoping he'd follow me on instinct, too distracted by rage to see the trap that I was luring him into. It worked, and in the lull of the hits, I decided to again use my voice.

"Wise to put your blade down, sir. I think we both know that you weren't going to be able to land a hit on me." I looked him right in the eyes as I took another small step before continuing on. "Surely thieving must be exhausting. A simple trade, the stars for enough coin and jewels, courtesy of King Armund, to keep you and your comrades over there well-funded for the seasons to come."

He took another step closer to me, cracking his knuckles in both his hands.

"What's *exhausting* is having to continuously track down the stars that were stolen from their rightful owners. And yet you call *us* thieves." He spat at the ground toward my feet.

I cocked my head a bit.

"Well, no one person can own the stars. They belong to the sky. King Armund is just working to help return them all, and from the looks of it, you and your friends are working to keep them for yourselves." I braved another step, which he instinctually matched as he chuckled at me, his dark eyes wide.

"But why shouldn't we? Last I checked, the sky has plenty. What's the King need with our pesky few?"

"Your few stars will help complete the night sky, bringing beauty back to the night sky for thousands!"

He rolled his eyes.

"Spare me the brainwashed bullshit, Guard. I've heard my fair share." He took another step towards me, clearly itching to close the gap between us and lay a blow on me.

I was close to the cart now, to the chains that lay on the ground behind my feet.

"Strange. You're so willing to run your mouth, but hesitant to use your sword. Not much of a King's Guard if you aren't willing to shed a little blood," Riggs twisted his face into a demonizing sneer, "no wonder the King sent you off as his errand boy."

I didn't even flinch at his poor attempt to shame me, which quickly hardened his face.

"Oh, I'm willing to shed blood. But why when we are having *such* a good time conversing?" I slammed my sword into the ground so that it stood tall in the earth. With one arm, I leaned on the hilt, slouching into the blade so that it carried my weight. "Tell me more about these exhausting efforts of yours. Is it just stars that you steal, or are there other goods that your trio gets their thrills from? With no seeker stars left in public, you'd have to rob every man, woman, and child you came across. Surely you must have found something else to take to keep your purses full. It's no wonder you're so tired! A man of your age can't possibly keep up that level of nefarious activity for long."

He growled again, clenching his fists tightly beside him. I unstuck my blade and raised it, taking the final step back that I needed. My shoulder was to the cart now. I wiggled my back foot under the chain that sat in a heap, hooking it precisely over the top of my boot. The trap was fully set; all I needed was for him to lunge. Considering how I could almost see the steam pouring out of his ears, I knew it wouldn't be long.

I couldn't help but let out a sly grin.

"Tell me this then. Do you really prefer the darkness to the stars in the sky? Is it because in the dark, you finally get a relief from having to see your reflection in the mirror?" I raised my eyebrows as I gave him a disapproving look up and down, "I've never understood the dissent for the King's vision before, but now that I've been staring at your mug for so long, perhaps I get it."

"What we like or do is none of your fucking business. We thieves *thrive* in darkness. And when I'm done with you, your sorry ass will be swimming in it. Forever."

"Agree to disagree on that." I flashed him a taunting grin and reached for my sword like I was finally going to make an opposing strike.

Instead, I reached to the side and grabbed the chain from my foot as I kicked it up. He had launched himself at my waist, an attempt to take me to the ground where my height wasn't such an advantage. Theoretically a smart move, but it was the exact one I was hoping he would make.

In a second I had the chain locking him to the ground, wrapped so tightly around his arms and chest that he couldn't move. He bellowed with fury, fighting against the metal links, but it was to no avail. The chains were made of strong, thick iron, and I had fastened them to the cart four times over. He wasn't going *anywhere*, and with how hard the wind was blowing, the odds of the sound of his yells making it to his comrades' ears were non-existent.

"You fucking royal piece of *trash*. You fucking brainwashed *coward*. Fight me like a man, Guard! I will end you."

I lowered my body so I was inches from his seething face, a smile wide across my teeth.

"You could try, but you would fail."

The cuff on my wrist was pulling tightly against my skin, both towards him and towards his crew.

"Now be a good chap and stay put. I do hope that your partners are in a better mood to negotiate. While I don't like to capture folks and bring them back to Mellin to *persuade* them to hand over their stars, I have the orders to do so. Think about that while I'm gone. Are a couple of stars worth rotting in a cell for?"

He spat at my face, but I dodged it, grabbing his neck tightly with my hand before his spit hit the ground

"Careful," I warned, my voice low and unwavering. I was squeezing tight enough to make his beady eyes pop. "My orders include *disposing* of complications as well."

After he took a few strangled and desperate gasps, I let him go, his breath heavy trying to compensate for the lost air.

"But, I'd rather not." I pulled on his chains, double checking that they would hold while I was off looking for his comrades. He wiggled and fussed hard against them, but they didn't budge. "I'm going to get those stars one way or another. Dead or alive. It's your choice, Riggs."

His jaw fell open at my drop of his name, and I gave him a quick eyebrow raise before turning on my heels, leaving him in a bundle of fury and awe.

I had walked about a hundred yards through the thick forest, hearing and seeing nothing. The afternoon light was quickly fading, and though the wind was still blowing strongly, the tight forest shielded me from the worst of it. If Riggs was yelling or calling for help, I couldn't hear him in the slightest.

Cruel, maybe, to leave him tied up there while I tried to negotiate with his peers. But it was more merciful than killing him on the spot. The likelihood of him coming around to my offer was low, I knew that. But, at least if he was going to take his last breath by my hand, he would have had a chance to do the right thing.

The faintest whizzing sound was my only warning of the blade careening towards my head. I turned my head slightly just in time for the tip to shave off the end of one of my longer curls before sticking into the tree next to me. I looked up, surprise filling me as I saw a girl, hooded in a black cloak with a long braid pouring down the front of her.

I heard her swear under her breath, clearly she wasn't used to missing her mark either. *Damn*, her aim had been impressive. Surely, she was working with accuracy magic... anyone else it would have killed.

I didn't even have time to take a breath before I unsheathed my sword, instinctively swinging high to the right. It caught on the knife of a tall and bald thief, the sound of clanging metal echoing between the trees. The force of my block knocked him back a step, which handed me the advantage.

With one swing of my non-sword arm, my elbow hit his bearded jaw squarely, knocking his large body straight to the ground. A hard hit, for sure, but not a fatal one. With no sound echoing from the fall, it was likely that he was using stealth magic. These thieves really were well equipped—how had they managed to find all of these stars considering how few there were left unrecovered? I hadn't been exaggerating when taunting Riggs. Without any seeking magic, it would be *exhausting* trying to scour the land for them.

As the bald thief lay unconscious by my feet, I scanned my surroundings. That was two of them down, one left. *Where did that girl go?*

A loud thump drew my attention, and in the middle of a clearing up ahead, I could now see that a black bag sat squarely in the open. Surely a trap, but I grinned, knowing that it meant the girl, *Talla*, must be waiting nearby.

I slowly made my way towards it, sheathing my sword and acting like I had completely forgotten that a knife throwing thief was lurking somewhere in the trees. With every step, my eyes carefully hunted the branches, looking for any sign of movement. I strained my ears, parsing through the wind whispering through the treetops for any hint of her whereabouts. Surely the trio hadn't been able to secure two stealth stars. She had to make *some* sort of sound as she moved through these woods.

Despite my efforts, the only sound that reached my ears was my own footsteps. My chest twisted in frustration. *Stars, help me.* Where did she go? Why couldn't I track her?

I willed my heating temper to cool, commanding my ears and eyes to remain calm. Open. Focused. I didn't know if she had any more daggers, but her aim was too good to take the chance of bending down to grab the bag that was now a few feet away from me. I took a deep breath. And another.

My ears had already grown accustomed to the sound of the harsh winds, so against the lack of other noises, my breaths started to sound like gusts of their own. That is, until a twig snapped behind me. On instinct, I launched my body backwards, slamming into the nearest tree, praying to the Stars that I hadn't miscalculated her attack.

The warm and soft body I now had pressed tightly against the front of me told me that I hadn't been wrong. I had her caught against a tree with my forearm pressed tight across her chest. My legs straddled hers so that my hips locked hers between me and the trunk. I had at least a head on her, and from this position, this thief wasn't going *anywhere*.

"You know, you're faster than you look," I said to her leaning in so that my nose was mere inches from hers.

My eyes flared for a moment, her scent catching me by surprise. Under the smell of campfire, I could detect a faint fruity aroma, one that I had come to know and love from my nights at the Mile Dark. *Intriguing*.

It was generally frowned upon in Mellin for ladies to partake in the dance houses... unless they were performing, of course. Perhaps ladies out beyond the castle walls played by different rules. Or, perhaps this thief just didn't give a damn. Considering that she lived her life as a ringleader of thieves, and that she showed no ounce of hesitation with throwing a dagger at my head, I assumed it was the latter.

She squirmed for a bit, trying to break my hold, but I pressed against her tighter. She let out a faint squeak, my arm so tight that I could feel the ridges of the chain of the necklace she was wearing under her shirt. With the level of warmth radiating from my wrist, I knew that she was wearing an encased star. Her chest wasn't heaving, but her heart was beating quickly.

"Now that your comrades are taken care of, I'll try one more time. Care to make a trade? Stars for coin? You can name your price." I unsheathed my sword with my free hand and dug it into the ground behind me. A small and temporary, albeit risky, gesture of peace. "I'm sure that I can meet it. Otherwise I have jewels? Tuulish leather? Lowland glassware even? Surely these stars can't be worth passing up an opportunity to bring such goods and riches to your family?" I let the questions hang in-between us, trying not to breathe too deeply... her scent was too distracting.

After a few breaths, she turned her head upwards and our eyes locked. I couldn't help but study them. Round and... *yes* they were actually dark *green* like Callum had said. They were magnificent, like the deepest emerald of fresh evergreen branches.

She didn't answer my offer, so I selfishly continued to stare. I have seen the faces of a thousand criminals, looked them in the eyes as I locked them behind bars and then for years afterwards. Thieves always have the glint of greed dancing in their pupils.

But not this thief. Staring into her eyes, there was something else. Something else lit the spark that flickered across the pools of green. For a second, I let my mind drift, wondering what had happened to such a young woman to lead her to a life such as this.

That second cost me.

Before I knew it, a sharp blade cut through my pants leg, the tip poking right into the sensitive skin of my groin. Had I not been wearing my thicker winter riding pants, she would have sliced right into my manhood.

Bitch.

The shock caused me to loosen my hold just enough for her to slip down through my arms and between my legs. She was running towards the bag of stars behind us, her steps unbelievably silent. When I turned around to face her, she was standing hovering over the bag, her long braid peeking out from under her cloak and cascading down like a chestnut waterfall. I pulled her dagger out of my pants, the end lightly covered with my blood.

She gave me a saccharine smile.

"Fuck the King." Her voice was devious.

Without thinking, I pulled my sword from the dirt and launched it. My aim hit true. Just as she was pulling the bag upwards, the blade sliced cleanly through the nightcloth. Stars cascaded around her feet, their soft lights sprinkling the forest floor. She managed to scoop up a few of the stars in the half of the shredded bag she held before taking off through the woods. I went to launch her dagger at her, but she was already out of range.

I instead pocketed the small knife. The cut on my groin stung with each step that I took toward the stars. Luckily, it was a shallow wound that would heal quickly, but still. It wasn't one I wasn't looking forward to having for the ride back to the castle.

I gathered up the glowing orbs that she had left on the ground. *Four.* Which meant eleven stars still remained at large for me to hunt down before Solstice. I had a sinking feeling that many of those stars lied with the trio of thieves I had just encountered. Looking out into the woods in the direction her silent footsteps followed, I wished I had more time to chase after them. To take them back from these thieves and be done with my starhunt duties once and for all. But the next Starcast was just a few days away, and the King did insist on my return.

My jaw ticked the entire walk back towards where I had left Boli, safely behind a stand of trees, sniffing through the fallen tree needles on the ground.

I was getting those stars back, one way or another. If these thieves weren't going to cooperate... my stomach dropped a bit as I worked it though in my head. I'd have no choice but to put an end to them. It was my duty to my people, and to my King, to recover the fallen stars. I wouldn't let them down.

CHAPTER 8 | TALLA

I couldn't stop thinking about that royal fucking prick of a guard the entire journey back to Brakken. How was it that one stupid guard was able to take out both Riggs and Jetto? I knew that he had a star on him—that much was clear from the intense pull and warmth that I felt on my chest as he held me against that tree. But what was the magic that he wielded? He managed to miraculously dodge the dagger I threw from the tree... but that was most definitely a rare stroke of luck—it had to be. There wasn't any magic that I knew of that helped you evade a blade.

At least I was able to do some intimate damage to him. A pretty boy like him, with his smooth curls and close shaven face... he would miss the part of his manhood that I was able to slice. I smiled to myself as I strode down the road, Jetto and Riggs at my side, the memory of the Guard's face flushed with surprise, then pain, as my blade dug into him filling my thoughts. He deserved *that,* and more. That brainwashed bastard not only cost me one of my daggers *and* half of the stars, but tying Riggs up and leaving him out in the cold like that....

I shot Riggs a quick glance as we continued walking down the road, looking to see if his expression had changed since the last time I checked. His eyes were wide and fixed, seemingly focused on the path ahead... or on something else entirely.

I shook my head as I replayed the events that had occurred after I escaped with the stars two days ago. My first move after escaping the Guard had been to find Riggs, because with Jetto lying on the floor of the Middle Forests unconscious, we didn't have time to spare. Together, Riggs and I could heal Jetto faster than I could on my own anyways.

I had run towards the pull of Riggs' stars, ultimately finding him wrapped in iron chains and foaming at the mouth. His face strained as he pulled against the metal. I couldn't even fathom what in the Moon had happened between Riggs and the Guard to land him in that position, and I knew it would do me no good to ask. With a few intentional blows of some nearby rocks, I was able to crack some of the links that were binding him. As soon as there was some slack in the chains, Riggs tore himself free.

The Guard's actions did something to Riggs. I *thought* I had seen Riggs at his angriest after working together for the greater part of five years. But when he stood, and the metal chains lay still in piles around his feet...

I'll never forget the way his eyes, which were already such a dark shade of brown that they were almost black, became as dark as the old night sky during a new moon. No ounce of light and completely full of rage.

It took me three attempts to snap him out of his angry haze before he agreed to help me heal Jetto. The two of us quickly made our way through the trees to the spot that Jetto had fallen. Riggs didn't even blink as he reached his hand down next to mine on Jetto's head. Though he was physically with us, using the healing magic from his star to bring Jetto back to consciousness, he mentally was somewhere else.

I knew Riggs. He would want—*no. Need* revenge on the Guard. And that revenge would be bloody.

Riggs wasn't fond of anyone slipping past his attacks and getting a hand on him. What he did enjoy, as he had displayed earlier that evening with the twins, was making his kills a show. I had to admit, envisioning what Riggs might do to the Guard the next time they met was *exciting*. Because, there would absolutely be a next time the two of them met.

Riggs claims that he would never set foot in his birth city again, but if making a trip back to Mellin meant a chance to rip that Guard into pieces... well I think that he might make an exception. We might have our differences, Riggs and I, but we both do enjoy a spectacular hunt for revenge.

Time dragged as the three of us completed the walk from the Middle Forests to Brakken in utter silence. With it being so close to the new moon, there was no moonlight to illuminate our journey as night creeped across the sky.

Thankfully, the darkness doesn't bother us—in fact, it does quite the opposite. And since there's only one road connecting the Forests to Brakken, I could have found my way home blindfolded. Still, it was on trips like these, when morale was low and the air around us turned colder by the minute, that I *really* wished that Brakken still had horses.

On horseback, this journey might take only a few hours. Several times I had considered stealing one, but even with the amount of coin that we brought in, Brakken just wasn't favorable to animals anymore. With a limited food supply, anything *not* human that made its way past the stone gates would quickly find itself in someone's supper pot. And if they happened to avoid the slaughter, Brakken's extreme weather would take them soon enough.

It was fully night by the time that we reached Brakken's entry gates, the small torches on either side of the gray stone arch lit like orange beacons in the black. The hastening sound of footsteps drew my attention away from the comforting sight of home. I looked around to see that Riggs had picked up his pace, quickly striding out ahead of Jetto and me into town without even a glance of farewell. I raised an eyebrow toward Jetto, looking for a response. He clearly was still a little groggy from taking that hilt to the head, and he only nodded goodbye in my direction before he, too, headed home.

A sinking feeling bloomed in my stomach. This wasn't how we three normally separated after a trip. I tried to shove the uncomfortable uncertainty of the exchange aside, focusing on the familiar silhouettes of Brakken's weathered stone buildings. We would reconvene in the morning as we always did. At least we were home now, and at least we had managed to save some of the stars and bring them back here.

My feet mindlessly followed the packed gravel streets of Brakken. We had activated the four elemental stars during our trip home, their magic shielding us from the dropping temperatures. Even so, the skin around my eyes ached and the tips of my toes longed for the hot bath that I knew was waiting for me once I arrived at my house.

I forced my frozen feet to push faster as I turned down the main mercantile street of my city. Small candles, lit on the sills of the windows tucked in the gray stone walls, flooded the interiors of the shops with a soft yellow glow. There weren't many shops left nowadays in Brakken—a small bakery. A woven goods store. A tool and weapon shop.

I could remember when there used to be merchant carts posted along the roads all year long. Traders and craftsmen alike lined this very street, selling fresh pastries, smoked meats, and in-season produce all gathered and grown by Brakkens themselves. Flowers of a thousand colors exploded among the neutral gray rock that the entirety of the city was constructed of, and birds swooped overhead as they gathered materials to build their nests safely in the blooms. But now...

I studied the shadows cast from the trailing dried flower husks as I passed them—yet another set of annuals that lived shorter than the year before.

While the market street had been essentially empty, just one street over the walkways and building fronts were packed with cloaked and hooded figures. All the wooden doors of Brakken's well-loved bars were swung open, their inner circuses aired out into the street. The symphony of boisterous laughter and breaking glasses filled my ears as the passing breezes laced my breaths with the smell of wine and smoke. Over the last decade, as our temperate weather disappeared and more extreme patterns settled in, the already robust bar scene in Brakken exploded. Fresh fruit became scarce in these parts year-round, so the best way to preserve any extra from our shortening growing season was to ferment it and bottle it. Brakken is a pain in the ass to get to for the rest of Larendi, but with our reputation for revelry, we still find ourselves visited by travelers who hope to survive a night out in the city of drunk and stubborn rebels.

With the effects of the alcohol blocking the chill, a few patrons leaned against the outside of the corner bar, Scuro. Seemingly immune to the cold winds, their bare hands passed a pipe back and forth as gray and blue smoke billowed from their noses. I could see that one of them was Asha, a girl with silver hair as long as mine and large eyes that matched. She was a thief as well, and while we weren't exactly friends, we did try to look out for one another should anyone try to give one of us trouble.

As she exhaled after a particularly long drag, she nodded to me before passing her piece to her comrade. I returned the gesture just as I turned down the sleepy residential road that culminated at my house. I pulled my hood tightly around my ears as the change in direction put me face-on against the wind. If only I wasn't so consumed with exhaustion from being on my feet for days... perhaps I could have spared some time to stop for a smoke.

The echoes of the town faded as I headed down the hill towards the house that I had lived in all my life. The small standalone cottage backed up to an old orchard, with the rolling hills still sporting the small, weathered trees. All of it—the house and the orchard—had been my mother's before she died. When she did, it all went to me.

I'm not sure why, but my father never lived here with us. I don't even think he ever lived in Brakken. I often forgot that I even had a father. My mother had never mentioned him, and I never thought to ask her.

I walked through my weathered wooden door to cross the threshold into my house, breathing a sigh of relief as I did. Though outside the front door my mother was gone, inside, she was everywhere. Her favorite mugs with a cross-hatched glaze were sitting on the shelf, her hand knit blanket was draped around the couch, and the glass jars of herbal salve and scrubs she used to make lined the bathroom window. The only things I had allowed myself to change in the house were the plain gray walls.

A few years after she was taken from me, I painted three large canvases with some paints and brushes that I lifted off this asshole merchant. One was of a dog, white and shaggy, sitting patiently with a bone at her feet. Another of the sea, or at least how I imagined the sea to be from piecing together mother's stories. And one of the very house I was now standing in, small yet sturdy gray stone, cloaked in the darkness of the true night sky.

I dusted off the fresh cobweb that had formed above the final painting during my week away as I walked past it on my way to the bathroom to draw myself a hot bath. As I settled into the warm water, I let out a long exhale and closed my eyes.

My star rested in-between my breasts as I settled deeper in the water, my chin barely above the surface. There were slight pulls to the north and east that I knew were Riggs and Jetto, settling into their own homes. Beyond that, the most predominant pull that I could feel was faint, meaning the stars were far away. I knew that could only be the stars that the Royal Prick had taken back to the castle.

Soon, I wouldn't be able to feel their pull at all—once the King shoots the stars beyond the clouds, I can barely feel them. The first few months of Starcasts, I tried to Seek them. I thought that if I could at least track their powers as they went skyward, it would help lessen the sadness I felt knowing they were gone. But the sensation of their pull fading away left a cold emptiness in my veins. I quickly learned it's easier just to avoid activating any of my superstar's powers on Starcast nights. That way, there was no chance of feeling the part of this world, part of me, that was now lost.

I played some with the bubbles that were floating on the surface of my bath, mulling over the events of the past week. After tomorrow, we would have to decide what our next move would be. We wouldn't go after the guard, despite how much I'm sure Riggs might want to now. The stars would already be lost by the time we got there, and with the season sitting on the edge of winter, it would be near impossible to make the trip to Mellin without proper supplies.

I weighed our usual options, flipping my star pendant back and forth between my fingers under the water. We had just done a swing-through raid of the two closest towns that were more protected from the harsh sun and winds that

Brakken got... we could do that again, but it's best to keep at least a month between visits for best spoils, giving the patrons plenty of time to restock.

I thought back to the convincing performance by Jetto and Riggs with the thieves from Enver—another option could be to station ourselves on one of the roads posing as lost and helpless travelers. But true winter was coming quickly, and the idea of setting such a trap and waiting in the cold made my bones begin to ache again.

My fingers worked at my braided hair, loosening the plats and letting my long curls flow around me as I sunk all the way under the water. I had nothing as far as a plan, and frankly was too tired from the day's events to try and brainstorm anymore. Hopefully, one of the guys at breakfast would have a lead on something or else we might just be sitting in Brakken for a bit, waiting for the next opportunity to strike.

◊

The next morning, I laced up my boots and buttoned my long dark cloak around a thick wool shirt and headed to meet the crew at our normal spot. We liked to convene in a small pub, off the main drag of Brakken, that only had enough seats for the three of us and *maybe* one party more. Because it was so small, we were always comfortable planning our next moves or divvying up spoils from our trip prior. It didn't hurt that the owner happened to be Jetto's cousin, York.

Cousins by blood, but they looked and acted like brothers. He made sure we got the service and privacy we needed. Not to mention, he served the best breakfast pies this side of the River—with Jetto helping him out, York was able to afford decent and filling ingredients. They were always a welcome meal after being on the road, and while I wanted York's business to do well, I secretly prayed that the Moon kept our spot off of the Brakkish radar. If I ever tried to get a breakfast pie and York had already run out....

York was behind the bar wiping down glasses when I strode in.

"Mooorning, Talla." He didn't even look up when he greeted me, his hands busy at work on his glassware.

I walked up to him, pulling aside a worn leather stool to take a seat.

"How do you always know it's me, York? I barely made a sound."

"Ah. It's because you *don't* make a sound that I know it's you. I can tell who enters this place just by the sounds of their footsteps. You, lady, are the only person I know that is so light footed. Well, besides Jetto, but the day he walks in here and keeps his mouth shut is a day the moon doesn't rise. So if I hear the door open, but nothing after, I know it's you." He shifted his gaze to me and flashed me a smile.

He looked so much like Jetto when he smiled, except for the fact that York's hair hadn't all fallen out, and he kept his red beard longer with three tiny braids. I returned him a small smile.

"Fair enough. Is Jetto here yet?"

"Yes, he's upstairs with the girls."

Right on queue, I could hear the shuffling sounds of tiny footsteps followed by a familiar *'Oy!'* overhead. York had two small daughters that lived in the apartment upstairs with him. Though Jetto lived across town, he came by every morning he was home to watch them while York opened up and his wife slept.

"Did you hear the news from while you lot were away?" York's face was somber as he grabbed a plate from a stack and placed a hot slice of breakfast pie on it before handing it to me.

I knew the tone of his voice could only mean one thing. Death.

"Who?" I replied.

I hoped it had been someone old, someone who had lived a long life. York looked me square in the face.

"Mara. They say it was from grief."

My heart sank. It was Mara's girl who died when Callum stole her healing star.

"When?" My voice was short as I took a bite from my pie.

"Yesterday morning. We burned her last night." York replied.

My face started to heat. We had been just *hours* too late. Had that stupid King's guard not interrupted us, we would have made it back in time to save her. We could have given her back the healing star to mend her heart. Or I could have at least taken the sting off with my superstar.

But, we didn't make it back in time. And now she, like her little girl, is just another name added on to the long list of lives that were taken by King Armund's 'dream'. *Fuck* that.

York traced a circle in prayer in his chest, and I followed just as Jetto was making his way down the pub side stairs.

"So, I guess York told ya, Bossa?" He took a few steps to meet me at the bar and sat down on the stool next to me as York prepared him a plate of pie as well.

"He did."

"Damn shame. She deserved better. Guess Riggs gets to keep it after all."

York had turned away, his ability to sense when to give us privacy one of the many reasons why we liked to meet here. Yes, that did mean Riggs could keep his mysteriously hidden healing star—that was the agreement we had all come to.

When we hunted down stars, anytime we reclaimed ones that were stolen from our people, we always returned them. On the rare chance we found stars not from Brakken, I agreed to let Jetto and Riggs keep them. It only felt fair since I held a superstar and the series of starmagics that went with it. And, since there were so few stars left in the world that were ownerless, I wasn't worried about either of them getting too powerful.

I nodded, then switched the conversation to plan our future moves. We brainstormed ideas for over an hour waiting for Riggs to join us, but he didn't show. Around mid-morning, Jetto clapped me on the shoulder as he stood up to leave, crumbs of breakfast pie all tucked in his beard.

"He's probably just bankin' some extra rest before tonight. I know I plan on drinkin' double since the outlook is for a clear sky."

Tonight. I had been so busy trying to come up with our next move that I had almost forgotten that tonight was the dreaded Starcast.

"I'll swing by his place on my way out tonight. Don't worry, Bossa. You know how Riggs can get."

But as I walked out of York's, the annoying and uncomfortable sinking feeling from the night before returned. We knew Riggs had a temper. *Moon, save me*—everyone in Brakken knew that if anything so much as dented his ego, it would be completely normal for him to brood and sulk for days. But no matter what happened, he had never missed a meeting with Jetto and me before. He might enjoy pushing my buttons, but he valued thieving with Jetto and me.

I placed my hand on my chest, hovering over my hidden star pendant. I hoped that I would get some sort of inkling from my star, but it was cool to the touch. I never quite understood how the premonition magic worked in my superstar.

I used it most to read people's intentions, but it wasn't fool proof. I couldn't get clear ideas of what they were planning on doing, or any visions of what was about to happen. I mostly just got a feeling... it was hard to describe. And I had never come across anyone else with a premonition star to compare notes with.

Regardless... I was certain that Riggs wouldn't miss the anti-Starcast celebrations. Drinking and debauchery were the only things that made any of us feel any better when more stars were lost to the skies. I waved goodbye to York as I silently headed out of the door. Until then, it was my job to return the four elemental stars that we were able to bring home back to the ground. I would dig them deep into the soil myself this time so that no future thieves could find them.

Moon, save us, hopefully just the four stars could give us some chance of a fruitful growing season next year. Despite how much we might act like it, Brakkish folk can only survive the harsh winters on bread, wine, and the occasional breakfast pie for so long.

CHAPTER 9 | KIERAN

The fading daylit skies had fallen from orange to violet when Boli and I made our way up the smooth stone street that approached the city walls. I hadn't wanted to spend any more nights than necessary away from Mellin the week before Starcast. With the northern winds at our backs instead of our faces, Boli was able to cover the ground between the Middle Forests and Mellin in record time.

The roar of Larendi's capital city was deafening in comparison to the sounds of the wind and Boli's thundering strides that I had been listening to for hours as we entered through the city gate. The combination of suppertime dishes clanking, rambunctious children laughing and shouting, and the thuds and dings of drums and bells was enough to make me close my eyes once we were safely behind the tan stone border.

The cacophony worsened as a few of the citizens recognized me. Even with my mask covering half of my face, the people knew that the Guard clad in back with golden eyes was the King's personal starhunter. Their shrieks and cheers layered with the other sounds of the city, bouncing overwhelmingly between my ears. Several passersby reached their hands out to me with flowers or baskets of goods. I lowered my mask and offered a practiced smile in return, but kept the tired mare moving. While I normally would have stopped, delighting in the kindnesses of the people, the combination of both the stinging pain from the cut on my groin and the skeletal ache from riding in the cold was already enough to keep my heels digging into Boli, pushing her as darkness descended over the city.

Despite my best efforts, by the time Boli and I crossed into the castle yard we were both adorned with freshly assembled necklaces of flowers dyed navy and gold. Now, instead of the many sounds of the city, Boli's labored breaths and the sound of her hooves clacking on the road blended together as a calming closing track to our evening. I let out a deep breath, trying to release as much of the painful sensations as I could. For a moment, I felt some relief. But, no sooner than the first bit of air filled back into my lungs did the uncomfortable sensations resurface.

Gray was standing by the large entryway of the stable. He smiled at me as we trotted through the arched door, his cheeks and nose rosy. It was nowhere near as chilly in Mellin as it had been out beyond the walls, but once the warmth of the sunlight disappeared, even the castle could feel uncomfortably cool in the evenings.

I watched Gray carefully take the reins from me before I swung my leg over the saddle to dismount. I winced with the motion. The cut on my groin, though minor in the grand scheme of things, was still a bit raw and burning from the ride home. I hadn't bothered with a healing tonic, though in hindsight I probably should have.

"You are hurt, Sir Kieran?" Gray's eyes grew wide with concern as he stood there holding Boli, watching me gather the pouch that I had housed the stars in from one of the saddle bags. There was no stutter in his voice this time.

My answer flew out of my mouth before I could stop it, the pain from the ride and the frustration from the day hindering my ability to check my tone.

"It'll heal." I barked at him, my voice echoing a bit in the lofted barn.

I was immediately filled with regret as I saw the fear settling back on his face in place of his smile.

I let out another deep breath, this time forcing the effects of the pain to have a lesser hold on me than before. It wasn't Gray's fault that I hadn't acquired all of the stars or that the green-eyed thief was able to make a mark on me before she ran off with them. It wasn't his fault that despite not being able to shake the fact that something was different about her, I couldn't figure out what exactly it was. I swallowed the guilt that was creeping up in my throat as I looked at him.

"I'm sorry, Gray. I'm fine, truly. Nothing a tonic won't heal." I gave him a soft smile, to which he only nodded in return.

"His Grace is waiting for you in his chambers. He is expecting you right away, as always."

I gave Boli a soft pet on her neck before Gray pulled at her reins to move her to her stall. My body ached from the long ride in the cold, each step sending tremors from my frozen feet up through my legs. As I walked into the castle, the familiar buzzing on my wrist vanished as it always did.

His Grace had found a method in one of his books to negate Starmagic in the public areas within the castle, including the main entryway, his throne room, and the first-floor staircases. It was a fortuitous protection mechanism—I can recall a few times that dissenters and rebels had traveled to the castle in hopes of collecting a reward in exchange for their stars, only to try to use the opportunity to harm the King. He was even able to extend the protection into the prisons below, which meant if any criminal managed to smuggle starpower when they were brought in, they wouldn't be able to use it to break themselves out.

The buzz of power returned as I crossed onto the second floor, sending waves of warmth skidding across my skin. I followed the most direct path to the King's chambers, up the six flights of stairs, down the corridor and through the large oak doors that led to his stained glass hallway. I clutched the pouch of elemental stars tightly under my arm, their magic humming lightly.

Elemental stars were interesting, and far less predictable than the other startypes. Activate them correctly and they could block the effects of the elements, change or predict the weather, and even help plants grow. But knowing how to access the right power within each elemental star took more practice.

And, of all the star types, the elemental stars also were the weakest. You needed more than one to really make a difference against the active forces of nature, so you had to almost always be working more than one star at a time. It had been tempting to try to activate the ones in the pouch for the ride home, just to block the chill of the Northern winds for myself and for Boli. But I was given strict orders when I accepted my role nine years ago to *never* utilize starmagic for myself. Except, of course, when wearing the Seeker cuff that was on my wrist.

The guards at the King's chamber door parted for me to enter as I approached. Just like our last encounter, once I was inside, I was met with the image of the King's face being shielded by a large leather book. When he heard my footsteps against his marbled floor, he looked up, and I paused in my tracks to bow.

"You're limping, my dear boy."

I swallowed. *Shit*, was I? The return of feeling in my toes and legs had been enough of a distraction from the small, annoying twinge in my groin that I had almost forgotten what that thief did to me. Maybe the cut had been worse than I thought.

Heat threatened to flood my face in embarrassment, but with a deep breath I was able to chase it away. The King didn't appreciate such emotion amongst his Guards. I'd be damned if I added that to the list of reasons why the King might be disappointed in me tonight.

His Grace stood up, his crystaled braids clinking slightly against each other as he pushed them away from his dark face. With no other sounds, he made his way towards me and held out his expectant hands. I first unlatched the cuff on my arm that housed the Seeker star and handed it over, followed by the bag of elemental stars that I had collected from the thieves.

As the King held the bag, his expression turned dark and cold. Even though I knew that reaction was coming, my stomach still dropped. He could tell without me muttering a word that something had not gone to plan, that I had not collected all of the stars that I was after. I said nothing, choking down another swallow as his eyes drilled into mine.

"Care to explain?"

I didn't really—I had never not fully delivered before. But when the King asks you a question, especially one regarding the beloved Stars... well avoiding answering isn't an option.

"Your Grace. The stars were being held by a band of star-powered thieves. They were not open to negotiations, as you expected."

The King did not move. He did not say anything. He just stared at me with a look so icy, I swear the room around us grew colder.

I continued on, subtly wiping away the little bit of sweat that was beading on my palms against my pants.

"I was able to deal with two of them easily, Your Grace. But the third thief...." My cheeks heated despite my skin stinging with cold.

The true and full embarrassment of what had occurred in the woods crashed over me for the first time. *How* in the Stars was I supposed to explain exactly how a young, female thief was able to prevent me, the best trained member of the King's Guard, from bringing back all of the stars?

A vision of her dark green eyes flashed in my mind, the smell of campfire and petals filling my nose as if she was standing in front of me again, our faces inches apart against the tree in the woods. My chest tightened and sent a different kind of heat through my stomach, and I cursed the fact that despite standing before a displeased King, my body was betraying me with arousal.

"Out with it." His words were sharp enough to slice through metal, and any sense of titillation was wiped clean from my body.

I could have tried to bend the truth, to say that she had in fact been as large as me, wielding weapons sharper and stronger than my own. I looked down at the sword on my hip. It was an impressive piece that felt more like a limb than a blade, but it wasn't the deadliest of weapons out there. Of course, in combination with my training, that might not exactly be true. But there was no honor in lying to the King... or trying to even stretch the truth. He could always sense deception, anyways, it was one of his many admirable skills.

"The third... well she eluded me. She stabbed me, it's why I'm limping. By the time I could react, she had run off with the stars to revive the others. I wanted to follow them, Your Grace, but I had tracked them to the Middle Forests, and with my mare in hiding behind a group of trees, for her safety I didn't want to risk being there into the night. Without the horse, I would not have been able to make it back before Starcast."

The King blinked before he turned his back on me to head towards the small door on the other end of the room. I didn't dare move a muscle in my body, but with my eyes I glanced at my surroundings. The book lined walls were less organized than normal, several books were stacked on the shelves with their decorative spines facing in rather than out. The stack of books by the King's chair near the fireplace was at least twice as high as it had been before. Clearly, he had been busy reading in the hours that I was away.

The King returned, his hands empty after apparently depositing the stars and the cuff in the back room. "Did I not provide you with enough goods to make the trade convincing?"

I nodded, "You did, Your Grace."

"And did I not provide you with years of top-notch training against those working with activated stars?"

I had to wipe the sweat again from my palms on my pants. "You did, Your Grace."

"And did I not explain to you why it is imperative to get the stars back at all costs?"

"You did, Your Grace." I hung my head, closing my eyes as I replied.

"Look. At. Me." His words left no room for disobedience.

My eyes nervously watched the King's jaw tick.

"You've never disappointed me before, Kieran."

I forced my body to remain still, despite wanting to lean over and vomit. But instead of the contents of my stomach, words started tumbling out of my mouth as I stared into the King's dark and disapproving eyes.

"I'm sorry, Your Grace. It is never my intention to let you down. But the last thief..." I knew better than to ramble, but I was at the mercy of my lack of understanding regarding Talla the thief's abilities. The stream of thoughts and questions that had filled my mind filled the tense air that stood between me and the King. "She only wore one star, but she... she was so sneaky. And her aim was impeccable. Not to mention how fast she was able to get to her comrades and revive them. I'm not sure how to explain it. It was like her one star had more than one magic. Or that she could activate more than—"

"ENOUGH!" His voice bellowed through the room, shaking the wine glasses on the table to my left and knocking the stack of books by the fireplace over so they spilled over the rug.

I quickly snapped my mouth shut, slamming closed the gate and forcing my words to catch behind my teeth. My heart pounded nervously against the inside of my ribs. When the King raised his voice like that, it *never* ended well for the person on the receiving end.

He silently crossed the rug, effortlessly stepping over the scattered books without even giving them a glance and sat down in his chair. He reached and picked up a small leather book, furiously flipping through the pages until he landed on one. He scanned the page a few times up and down, his dark eyes moving furiously over the lines.

"Starcast. Ten o'clock. The training hall. Leave your sword in your chambers," he muttered, never lifting his eyes off the page.

Well shit. Any time the King scheduled me to train at night, I knew that I was likely going to end up back in bed hours later covered in blood and bruises. The daily sessions kept my skills sharp, but the nightly sessions were to have me learn new ones.

I nodded.

"Yes, Your Grace."

"Now go."

With that dismissal, I bowed again and walked out of his chamber door. I didn't realize I was holding my breath until I had made it all the way down three flights of stairs to the hallway that lead to my own chambers.

CHAPTER 10 | Kieran

Over the next few days, I channeled all the disappointment, annoyance, and shame from the failed starhunt into each swing of my blade during my morning training sessions. I vowed to leave every ounce of feeling on the training hall floor to be able to greet the new day with a clean slate. Working through my reps against the King's starpowered guards reminded me that *I* was Kieran Amdiffyn: the first, and only, chosen Royal starhunter.

With each clang of my sword against theirs, it was hard to ignore the simple fact that my natural skills and instincts were unmatched, even against magic. It didn't matter that I had been distracted by Talla or that she had found and took advantage of a brief moment when my concentration lapsed. *I* was the best swordsman... *Stars,* probably the best fighter, in Larendi. And there's no way that blade against blade or hand against hand, a simple thief would be a match for me. Her outwitting me had been a fluke. Nothing more.

It took nearly an hour and a half of grueling sparring in the mornings before I was satisfied enough with my abilities to pick up with the rest of my duties and patrol the Royal Prisons. As Prison Captain, when I wasn't out on official starhunting business, it was my responsibility to ensure that all of criminals that had been arrested and held for their crimes against the Kingdom were accounted for and managed.

On the night of Starcast, I made my way down the darkened stone staircase that laid behind a thick wooden door on the castle's first floor. Rows of iron barred cells framed both sides of a narrow candle lit walkway, the air still and damp from the moisture seeping through the natural walls.

There had only been one new arrest since I had left the day before last, an older woman who tried to pull a blade out during the King's visiting hours. When I walked past her cell, she spit at my feet.

"Fuck you, Guard. And fuck the King."

Her hands gripped the bars of her cell as she pulled her face tightly against them. This woman's gray brows were furrowed on her deeply wrinkled tan face. I watched her for a moment, the words *Fuck the King*' ringing in my ear. I was unable to stop myself from wondering if this was what the future held for the green-eyed thief. How old was Talla anyways? She couldn't have been older than me, but much younger and it would be hard to imagine how she was hanging out with the two older men, the bald one and Riggs.

I turned to the older woman, smiling, knowing that at least this blade happy rebel was properly accounted for.

"Welcome home, Ma'am." I tipped my head down towards her as she lunged to grab at me.

Her fingertips caught only air though as I had kept walking. I laughed against her wails of rage, before I turned down a darker hallway.

This was where we kept the convicted murderers, the ones who would die in these cells with no chance of retribution. Many of the prisoners were sleeping, their bodies confused whether it was day or night given the complete lack of sunlight that reached this deep into the prison. One murderer, however, had his face pressed tightly against his bars, repeating the same phrase over and over.

"I was framed. It wasn't me. I was framed. It wasn't me."

I shook my head in disgust as I walked past him, remembering the multiple eyewitness accounts that saw him stab an entire family of four, one by one, through the heart in broad daylight. It's amazing how some people can commit such gruesome acts and then act like it never happened. I wasn't sure how you could ever forget the feeling of taking a life with your own hands.

When I was done with ensuring all cells were secure, all prisoners were still alive, and nothing out of the ordinary was occurring, I finally made my way back above ground.

The last rays of the fading sun illuminated the horizon before I made my way down to the training hall that jetted out from the second floor of the castle.

The hall was made of two parts. The first was a large stone room, the ceiling supported by arched wooden beams that ran down the length of the walls and connected to the floor with interlocking wooden platforms situated at various heights. For training purposes, each landing provided their own set of advantages and disadvantages for combat. The tallest one has easily the best view of the entire room, but if you were to fall as you reached for the adjacent beam, you were likely to break a few bones. Alternatively, the shortest platform provided the most options for escaping attacks, but you would rarely see enemies coming if attacked from above, due to the beams obstructing the view. For two weeks when I first started in the King's Guard, the King had me battle the same guards over and over again until I won three matches from each platform.

The back wall of the hall could open up with tall glass doors that stretched from the floor and the ceiling leading to the second section—an outdoor arena. This was my favorite place to train. No platforms, no beams. No walls even save for the surrounding hedges, twenty-feet tall.

The thick wall of green encased its entrants in an oval of soft compacted dirt underneath the changing skies. There were no hiding places in the outdoor arena. No way for your opponent to get an unexpected drop on you. In the outdoor training hall, giving everything that you had to a fight was all that you had to work with.

That was especially true tonight. With no sword on my belt, as instructed by the King, tonight's battle would take all of the strength and skills I had. Luckily, the dagger wound on my groin had mostly healed, my limp fully gone. I walked through the dark indoor section of the hall, my boots clomping against the floor. The back doors were open, and I could see a small torch was lit in the middle of the clearing. When I finally reached it, I looked around, flaring my senses to examine any possible clues for tonight's training.

All I could hear was the wind blowing through the hedges, carrying faint echoes of the Starcast celebrations that I was missing on the other side of the castle wall. The sky had darkened completely now, with small, faint pinpricks starting to make their appearance. They would gradually get brighter as the night aged, and when the King sent up more stars to join them, they would all flash together for a few moments.

One second I was admiring the sky, and the next I had a foot make silent contact with the back of my knee. It buckled, but I saved myself before my joint crashed into the ground. There was no sound to indicate that I was no longer alone. *Stealth Magic.*

The star-powered guard I was to fight was nearby, and my lesson had started. Sure enough, I turned around to see a hooded figure walking casually away from me, as if he had not just made an attempt to ground me. His cloaked back would have made a perfect target if I'd had any weapons on me.

I scrambled, getting my feet back under me. The torch flame flickered across the ground that separated me and the guard, who had now stopped moving. He just stood there, silently, with his back to me—baiting me. Clearly, he wanted me to make the next move then.

I considered my options. With this distance, and no stealth star of my own, there was no way to effectively sneak up on him. I could charge directly at him... but the point of these night training lessons, especially the ones without weapons, wasn't just to use brute force but to sharpen some other aspect of my skills that the King deemed lacking.

Out of the corner of my eye, I noticed two large black iron nails sticking up out of the base of the torch. It wasn't really a weapon, but it might just work assuming I could retrieve it without being noticed. I bent down, keeping my eye on the back of the guard. With barely a jiggle, the first nail pulled free.

I smiled when I saw that the end was still sharp. It was tiny, but it had enough weight to launch. Without hesitation, I flicked the nail through the air, aiming at the back of the guard's left shoulder. My smile fell when, without turning around, the cloaked guard caught the nail midair with his right hand after he carefully stepped to the side. *Accuracy magic.*

Going with the only other plan I could think of, I grabbed the second nail from by my feet and ran towards him. The guard had expected me to charge nail first, but before I closed the gap between us completely, I dropped my body to the ground, the side of my hip sliding against the dirt with the momentum from my run. I aimed my foot directly at his ankle, and the swift contact knocked his feet straight out from under him.

This guard was one of the tallest I've seen, and his long body came crashing down to the ground, his head whipping to the side and exposing his neck. It was an opening—an opportunity to end the lesson right now. I had the nail in my right hand, and one hard swing upward and the sharp iron would be through his neck.

But these lessons were never supposed to be fatal, and underneath that cloak was a Royal Guard member, just like me. One who worked hard for the honor to wear blue and gold and protect the King's dream of uniting the stars in the sky. I might not know his name or face, but that didn't make him any less deserving of being here....

I swung the nail towards his leg, instead, aiming for a flesh wound that a salve could heal within the week. But before I could make contact, the Guard had silently scrambled out of the way.

That's when it started feeling like I was breathing in ice. The air around me had started to freeze, each inhale slicing through my working lungs. As I coughed through the pain, the nail in my hand instantly burned with an unbearable cold. I dropped the metal to the ground out of reflex, knowing that this was elemental magic. And not just any elemental magic... this was the work of someone well-practiced in activating elemental stars.

My gloveless fingers were seizing from the sudden drop in temperature, and as I blew hot air on my fingers to rework them into fists, I searched for the guard's location. A shadow popped up on my right, so without hesitation, I swung.

As my fist soared only to cut through cold air, I realized that he had vanished... only to pop up again over my left shoulder. I changed my tactic, quickly dropping low and kicking my leg out to the side. Still, my efforts made no contact. When I stood up, I could no longer see any evidence that there had been anyone outside with me at all. My heart started to race. *Shit.*

This must be Illusion magic—the rarest of all the starmagics, even more rare than Seeking. I hadn't ever trained against it: there were so few illusion stars to begin with that the King either hadn't deemed it necessary *or* didn't trust any of the guards to wield the power. I only knew of it from the books that the King had lent me. I don't think even the general public knows this star ever existed.

The King had been so relieved when a mysterious white-haired sailor returned what had been Larendi's last illusion star a few years back that he walked around the castle smiling for weeks afterwards. But it made sense. I couldn't imagine the chaos that would ensue, or the crimes that could be committed, if this type of star got in the wrong hands.

Without weapons, you have to fight with your senses and instincts. But I quickly learned that my senses were rendered frustratingly useless against illusion magic. I backed up closer to the light of the flame, the small amount of warmth helping me focus. The outdoor arena around me was quiet, the trees suspiciously still. I closed my eyes, hoping to call upon fighting instincts that I had honed over the years as a guard.

Something in me screamed to open my eyes, and when I did, I was encircled by seven different guards, each holding a small black nail like the one I had thrown. I wanted to panic at being so grossly outnumbered, but the same voice that had urged me to open my eyes also told me to *breathe*, so I did.

After a few calming breaths, I stared at each of the frozen guards. One by one I surveyed them. Firelight reflected off of the sheen of the cloak, the orange and red dancing against the dark fabric with each flicker. Until, that is, I noticed that on one of the guards, the light was much dimmer. It clicked then—this wasn't seven guards at all, but one guard and six illusions.

I turned to take a step towards the figure I was assuming was the real guard when he lunged. He whipped by me with super speed. Pain immediately shot across my leg—he had cut my pants with the nail at the back of my calf, blood starting to trickle down the outer seam.

I blocked the hurt out as I tried to identify the guard amongst the newly positioned set of illusions, searching for the one which reflected light just a bit differently. But each time, at the moment that I could identify him, he rushed me, slicing a new wound through my leg. I could feel the blood running down the back of me as the shreds of skin and muscle struggled to support my weight. I likely had one more chance to take down this guard before they would crumble completely.

Once again, the guard and the illusions circled me. But this time, I didn't survey them. I couldn't afford the time it took to look for the light, I had to just act. The moment they encircled me, I lunged to the left. The six illusions faded into mist, leaving only the guard that I had thrown myself at in view.

My body went soaring through the night air, pain propelling me towards my target. I reached for anything I could grab—an arm, a leg. *Something* that could bring this guard down so that I wasn't the only one that would be fighting on the ground. The tips of my fingers clawed at fabric, and then at air before my body slammed against the dirt. I had successfully snagged part of his cloak, but not enough of it to pull it off of him.

A sly laugh filled the air and my stomach dropped. I *knew* that laugh, but it couldn't be. Not him....

As I looked up at the guard in terror, he simply unlatched the cloak from under his hidden chin, letting the fabric slide effortlessly off his body. When the cloak fell, my eyes confirmed what I already knew. It hadn't been a random King's Guard that had sliced my legs, or that I had tried to stab. Dark eyes and small crystals at the end of braids glinted back at me, both reflecting a mixture of fire and starlight set against his dark and weathered skin. I *hadn't* been fighting and dodging a guard... it had been King Armund himself.

CHAPTER 11 | KIERAN

The King's deep laughter filled the sky as I scrambled back to my feet. He took a silent step forward, shaking his head. I tried to keep my face neutral, to calm my racing heart and quickened breaths, but the knowing gaze of the King told me I was failing.

"I see two problems with you, Kieran." He discarded the bloody nail so it rolled softly off of his hand and clattered on the ground. "The first, you are too used to having the upper hand in fights. Normally, having your guards so well trained that they don't expect to lose would be a King's dream. And in fact, for years, the way your natural ability and combat instincts blossomed under my particular training methods has been more than I could have hoped for.

But your latest starhunt revealed a weakness to me, and your face just now confirmed it. Losing the upper hand catches you off guard, makes your reaction times slower. It should not have taken you so many attempts to make contact with *me* versus my many illusions."

I swallowed loudly. He was right, of course. Until yesterday, no one had even come close to laying a finger on me. My aim, my strength, my stamina, all matched, if not surpassed, the skills of anyone wielding starmagic. I *had* gotten too comfortable in my invincibility.

Talla had been... unexpected. A distraction. Her speed and accuracy, and the way her eyes alluded to the fact that she was someone... different. I tried not to let my mind wander to think about her as the King continued his evaluation of me.

"The second, and likely more serious of the two, is that you are clearly not willing to do what is necessary. From what you told me, you left those star thieves alive, and for what? What did showing mercy do for you but cost you your ability to bring back more stars?"

I held back my tongue, choking down the words that were dancing behind my teeth. Without mercy, we were savages. No different than the many criminals rotting behind bars in the prison below us.

I had never needed to turn to lethal measures to accomplish my orders before, and I liked it that way. Not to say that I hadn't *ever* killed someone, I had killed plenty before joining the King's Guard. But that was for survival, that was different. *That* was necessary.

"Well? Are you going to answer me or should I find another Guard to replace you who will take this role seriously?" The King's eyes were wide, glowing orbs in the night.

Never before had he threatened to remove me from my role. The King had poured his trust in me, using lots of time and effort to meticulously train me over the past nine years to be his chosen starhunter. So, even though the odds of him simply finding another guard to take my place, especially with so few stars now left to recover, were slim at best, I didn't like the idea sitting in the King's mind.

"Your Grace, I take the honor of being in the King's guard seriously. I have shown mercy, yes, but it—" I started.

Without warning his flat hand struck the side of my face. My skin stung from the contact, but I did not react, despite my spine tingling with fear.

"Your job is not to be *merciful*. Your *job* is to help me retrieve the lost stars so that I," he paused and cupped his hand to the cheek he had just slapped. The sting from the hit instantly vanished. "So that *we* can restore the night sky and bring the beauty of starlight for everyone."

His hand warmed my entire face, and within moments the air around us was no longer frigid. The muscles in my hands started to relax, regaining their full range of motion as the night warmed around them. The King's face had fully softened now. He reached down and picked up his cloak, draping it over his arm.

"No more mercy, Kieran. It's time to bring those stars home. Find them. At all costs."

The King stepped away, and I nodded my head. Those had been my orders before, and even though I had indeed brought back several stars, I had failed by letting some slip away.

My calves stung from the slices against them, but all in all, it wasn't the most painful lesson that I had had to learn over the years. Perhaps after cleaning up the cuts, I would even be able to make it out to the Starcast celebrations. The vision of diamond-covered ladies down at the Mile Dark, twisting and sparkling under the starlit sky put a small smirk on my face.

But the King saw that smirk, and clicked his tongue at me in response.

"Not so fast, Kieran." He motioned to the doors that opened to the interior training hall behind us.

I turned around. Lamps were now lit and they illuminated five guards standing in battle gear, blocking the exit. It was a sight that quickly drained any hope of celebrating from my body. The pain in my legs reared up the length of my limbs.

Stars, help me. The match against the King had only been the *beginning* of this lesson. I was a fool to think the king was going to let me off so easily, not for failing him this close to the end of his life's journey to complete the skies. Just as I had been a fool to spare those thieves, to let the girl run off to save them, and ultimately leave more stars than necessary unrecovered.

I forced myself to swallow back some of the burning pain, willing it to disappear—I wouldn't stand a chance against these guards if I let it consume me. Despite the way my wounds were still dripping blood, I wasn't going to get out of fighting these guards.

As if sensing my thoughts, the King placed his hand on my shoulder, and a warm, buzzing sensation flooded my body. I could feel the tears in my flesh mending, the skin slowly stitching itself together—the King was using the magic from a healing star on me. But before my wounds had healed completely, he lifted his hand, and the realization of his intentions sunk in—he had used starmagic to heal me, but only enough so that I wouldn't bleed out during my next fight.

"Remember that those willing to steal beauty and light for their own gains are *not* friends to this Kingdom. For continuing to wield starmagic, they are to be treated as enemies." The King's eyes met mine, and I nodded again.

"Good." He responded, "Solstice is quickly approaching. Find them, Kieran. And bring them home."

And with that the King silently and swiftly strode back towards the castle. The guards parted for him to pass through before reforming. Once he was out of sight, they charged forward, straight towards me to battle underneath the night sky.

◊

Battered and bruised, I laid on the floor in my chambers, gazing through the framed window. The guards had been brutal. But after about an hour, the two guards that I had not managed to knock out finally dropped their weapons and retreated back inside, dragging their fallen comrades behind them.

I had pulled my aching body up the many flights of stairs back to my chambers with the last remaining bits of strength. When I finally crossed the threshold of my room and shut the door, I collapsed. My entire body ached and throbbed, and after the climb back through the castle it would be at least a few hours before I had the strength to pull myself to the shelf that stored my healing supplies and brew a tonic.

The stars were almost at their brightest now, the dark purple and blue sky illuminated with tiny pinpricks scattered in various formations. I searched for what I considered my favorite star, the one that sat in the right tailfin position of the Siren. But with my limited view, my search was fruitless.

From this angle, I could barely even make out the King's tower. So when the magic of Starcast was occurring, I was lucky to catch part of the cluster of glowing orbs shooting from his window, soaring skyward leaving small trails of light in their wake that faded after a few seconds. I knew when they finally reached their destination by the way the entirety of the sky blinked. To my relief, the new constellation filled a space that was completely in view. I hadn't even realized it had been empty until now.

My Stars, *how* did the world not fall into despair once the stars had fallen? The poor people who lived during the most recent times of the dark skies… how had they lived without such immense beauty?

Cheers from the town below echoed to my ears. While part of me desperately wished I was celebrating tonight, a kernel of pride bloomed in my chest. No one was going to have to live without such beauty again because of the work that I was doing; the work that my body was currently bleeding and bruising for so I could do it better in the future.

I sighed. The King had been right, of course. I had grown too comfortable. I had forgotten what the true meaning behind my particular role in the King's Guard was. I was to get the stars back at all costs, with no room for mercy. No room for distractions. The everlasting beauty of the night sky, and the joy and hope that it so clearly brought our people, depended on it.

I tried to pull myself up to sitting, but the strong protest in my muscles and bones prevented me from moving even an inch. Resigned, I closed my eyes. I tried not to envy the people outside of the castle, immersed in celebration and filled with mirth, while I laid aching on my floor.

Instead, I let their voices consume me, their cheers mixing and layering into soft songs that would surely lull me to sleep. Right before my body succumbed to my exhaustion, a vision of a dark and wintery forest settled in my brain. One tree came into focus, the evergreen branches still as what must have been red firelight danced upon the limbs buried in snow.

CHAPTER 12 | TALLA

As a young girl, I used to *love* when winter settled over the gray stones of Brakken. Of course it was sad to see the harvest season go. The many orchards of Brakken's hillsides became bare, with only smaller and bruised apples left at the foot of the trees for animals to gather before they froze through completely. The merchant tents that lined the streets changed, no longer selling fresh items but opting for those that were dried or jarred. The flowers that had lined the streets all summer withered away, the combinations of delightful floral scents replaced with the smell of wood smoke and spices.

But winter meant less daylight, which meant longer nights. And Brakkens didn't just thrive under the thick and dark cover of night.... No—we reveled in it.

All winter long we gathered and celebrated with great feasts, plentiful cider and wine, and communal frivolity that filled the streets once the sun set and the moon was high. Children and elders alike danced in the firelight, embracing the cool winds against their skin and filling their lungs. The harshest of the winter winds were kept at bay as Brakken was meticulously shielded against the extremes by a dome of starmagic. It allowed Brakken to thrive as a city of the night tucked away in the northern corner of Larendi.

But all of that changed when the bulk of the elemental stars were returned to the King and then eventually to the sky. Gone was our ability to sufficiently block the extreme heat or cold. Gone was the well of magic that kept our vast hills fertile. And, so, gone was the wealth and the cheerful and vivacious nature that made Brakken home. Nowadays, yes, the Brakkish folk still probably feasted and drank more than any other town, even with our limited supply, but the only time Brakkish folks had truly good parties—you know, the kind where you could feel like you're a part of something bigger than yourself—was when we gathered to mourn the loss of stars on anti-Starcast.

The sun had just set, and the kaleidoscope of pinks and oranges and purples had nearly faded from the sky, leaving only shadowy versions of their hues behind in the clear evening. I stood against one of Brakken's signature gray stone walls, my leg kicked up behind me for support, just... watching.

I could see Jetto's nieces twirling in their black dresses, their reddish hair mimicking the flames in the torches that lined the large fabric tent that had been set up in the main square. Those lengths of billowing fabric might block the view of the stars that were starting to creep out, but it couldn't make me forget they were there.

Some of the long tables and chairs from the bars lining the square had been pulled out to host a variety of anti-Starcast activities. There were women dancing on some of them, their long bodies moving in silky black dresses, with men and women sitting around their bases in awe as they watched. Other tables were loaded with cakes and pies and other Brakkish treats, baked with provisions set aside each month for *this* party in particular, for all to refuel during the long night of distraction. The rest of the tables were being used to host Brakkens of all kinds, including a familiar bald redhead, playing rounds of Flare.

My star pendant sat tucked beneath my shirt, like always, but I didn't dare search for its powers tonight. No, not when the feeling of stars fading away and crossing into an unreachable world felt like losing a part of myself....

Besides, though Jetto's stealth star gave him amazing sleight of hand and the perfect edge during his games. I didn't need to press into my premonition magic to know that he didn't intend on robbing anyone. His games tonight were for pure amusement and distraction only. And from the way his blue eyes shined even from across the square that was darkening by the minute, and from how his laugh lines were scrunching up at the edge of his brows as his bearded mouth widened in apparent victory, his games were serving their purpose well.

Someone moved into the empty space beside me, and I didn't need to look to know that it was now occupied by the broodiest member of our crew, Riggs. Jetto had informed me that Riggs was *'just fine'* when he caught sight of me twenty minutes ago. Jetto had checked in on him, like he said that he would this morning, and chalked up his refusal to show this morning to an extended case of extreme brooding. I knew that Riggs would find his way to me eventually this evening, Moon knows that I wouldn't be bothered to seek him out. Not when he's the one that owed me an explanation for diverting from our trio's usual plan.

The smell of tobacco flooded my lungs as he must have lit his pipe.

"Another month, another anti-Starcast," he started. His voice was light, with very little rasp in it before he took a deep inhale, causing the dried leaves in front of his face to glow orange for a bit before fading back to black. "I have to say, of all the places I've lived, you Brakkens make the most out of these shitty evenings. You mourn in the best way... well. At least the most fun way." He exhaled a cloud of smoke skillfully towards the ground.

I shifted my gaze from Jetto, who was now taking on a rather small and gray woman in a round of Flare, to the dancers on the table a couple feet away. Their long silky dresses reminded me of the hair of the girl that Riggs had offered me at the Red Ruby. My core tightened.

I really fucked up handing her off that night given how long it's been since another warmed my bed. And any urge I had to find someone in Brakken to do so, to properly mourn the loss of the stars, needed to be squashed. There was no one in Brakken that I hadn't already ruled out as an option.

Riggs continued on, "I know I missed the meeting today. But I can make up for it." He held his pipe out in front of me, the smell of the leaves even stronger now.

My nose picked up on the sweet notes of the smoke—*Yarla Root*. The herb was rare and only harvested in the lowlands, usually only used by royals or truly successful merchants. My eyebrows raised at the recognition—he was burning extremely expensive tobacco this evening. Well, expensive if he would have paid for it, which knowing him, he didn't.

Acknowledging the peace offering, I took the pipe from him, bringing the mouthpiece to my lips and taking a long, deep breath. The burning in my lungs was short before the calming effect of the leaves washed over me, flooding my body with a soft warmth, before I, too, released a plume of smoke towards our feet.

"I'm listening." I replied, my voice short, handing the pipe back to Riggs, my gaze still on the dancers. He didn't seem to mind.

"There's a merchants fair in Tuul that's starting in two days—"

"Tuul?" It was hard to keep the surprised tone out of my voice as I cut him off.

Tuul was at least a three-day journey on foot, and after tracking down Callum and our run in with the Royal Prick, I couldn't imagine setting out right away on such a journey.

"Yes, Tuul. But before you say what I know you're thinking, we won't be walking, and we will get there by tomorrow evening."

That was enough to bring my attention to him, making contact with those dark, beady eyes.

"How? No one in Brakken has horses anymore."

No one could afford to keep them fed.

Riggs took his pipe and pointed across the crowd starting to build under the tent towards the firepit at the edge of the square. He was directing my eyes to see two men, both with deeply tanned skin and sharp, dark eyes and brows. One was clean shaved, the other had a mustache, but both stood awkwardly by the fire, warming their hands with unsure looks on their faces. If those eyebrows didn't give them away, their apparent lack of familiarity with Brakken and the frivolity that anti-Starcast did. They clearly weren't from here.

"Visiting merchants, on their way to Tuul but sheltering in Brakken this evening."

"I'm not helping you steal their wagon ton—"

"Lucky for us," he cut me off, handing me the pipe again which I took. I wasn't going to turn down more Yarla Root, not when the smoke tasted better than half of the meals I've had in the past ten years, York's breakfast pies excluded. "I spared the mustached one's life several years ago after he tried to shortchange me on a sale. He is offering us passage on their wagon as they head to the fair."

I exhaled the smoke I had pulled from my most recent drag, considering Rigg's words and the mustached man by the fire.

"Why didn't you kill him? Letting a guy live for days, let alone *years*, doesn't sound much like you after getting ripped off."

The Riggs I knew would have ripped that guy's hand off just to call it even. From what I could see this far away, the man still had all his tawny appendages.

"I was younger then, naive. I lacked... *confidence*." His voice dropped on the last word, and Rigg's raised his eyebrows just ever so slightly.

I knew that tone shift of his, how he talked about his days before he was able to access magic anytime that he wanted. He was starless, then, when this man had wronged him. And without the enhanced accuracy, the job of killing him had been a bit trickier, though not impossible.

It was clear that Riggs had been a good fighter before he claimed his accuracy star. He had freshly acquired it when Jetto met him five years ago, and that was when Riggs had only just found his way to Brakken. I wondered how much earlier the encounter between this merchant and Riggs had been.

I contemplated Riggs' idea as I continued to eye the dancers. Jetto and I hadn't come up with much of a plan for our next move during our meeting, and Tuul was known to attract merchants from across the continent. Perhaps it was exactly the opportunity that we needed.

My eyes shifted away from the silk-wearing ladies as I spotted Jetto heading towards us with three large mugs in his hands. As he approached, he handed one to both me and Riggs.

"Don't tell me that small frail lady beat you..." I asked, grasping the mug and letting the warm spiced notes of the drink fill my nose.

Jetto threw up his free hand, almost in surrender.

"The Moon has decided that all the strength in that little old gal would be kept in her mind. She was slicker than any player ever I've played. I'm not even embarrassed to've lost to her."

I chuckled and took a sip from the mug. The mix of the wine and the Yarla Root set pleasant stars in my vision.

Jetto turned to Riggs. "So, did'ya share your plan with her?"

Riggs nodded, and looked at me. "She hasn't agreed yet."

I looked between both members of my crew. The contrast between their features, Riggs's dark hair and eyes with Jetto's bright counterparts, started to become less apparent as the haze of the smoke and drink filtered my vision. Firelight bounced along their faces, turning everything under the tent a bit orange.

But Riggs was right. I hadn't yet agreed to the last minute trip to Tuul. I let the plan that he had proposed stir in my mind as I took a few more sips of wine. I didn't know these merchants that would be driving us, and it wasn't like any of us to go with folks we didn't trust. Surely, we could take anyone down, I wasn't worried about that. But sleeping... especially after a night of anti-Starcast level partying... we would be extra vulnerable.

As if reading my thoughts, Riggs chimed in.

"I'll stay up even if you're worried about the ride after..." he motioned to the drinks and pipe, "and it's been a while since we have been able to raid a good merchants fair. Tuul will bring the best. You know this."

I titled my head in consideration. He had a point there. Tuul was known for their leather goods, due to the ample livestock that their grassy fields could harbor.

The finest leather was tradable across the entirety of the continent. I even heard a rumor that the Kings cavalry themselves were outfitted with tack made of Tuulish leather. I glanced down at my boots, noting how cracked the leather was, giving way at the point where my toes could bend. At the very least, the trip would allow me to swipe some new boots.

"That'll work for me. I figure a couple more mugs of this, and I won't care wheres it is I sleep tonight. Maybe you can even use that healing boost of yers whilst we sleep? Prevent that dreaded post-anti-Starcast hangover?" Jetto nudged Riggs in the side with his elbows, but Riggs didn't even flinch.

His dark eyes were fixed on me. Sharp and... was that a hint of desperation I saw? My hand instinctively reached up to my chest to check his intentions, but before I could grab hold of my pendant, I stopped myself. No starmagic, not tonight. Not unless my life depended on it.

If Jetto was on board, it was two versus one anyways. When it came to our trio, of course, as the leader my vote mattered the most, but after our last trip... I figured that Riggs needed a win. I held my hand out expectantly to Riggs. He quickly put the pipe in my fingers, and I brought it to my mouth.

"At dawn then." I muttered, my lips around the mouthpiece.

The crushed Yarla Root was almost burned through completely, but with a deep inhale, I was able to ignite the last of the herb into dark orange embers.

"Let's hope I'm still standing by then." Jetto replied, lifting his mug of wine towards Riggs and me.

I nodded as I exhaled the smoke upward, lifting my own mug in cheers. Riggs smiled, and maybe it was the herb or the drink or the combination of the two, but I could have sworn that it was bigger than I had ever seen him smile before.

"At dawn. The wagon will meet us at the Brakken gates." We clinked our mugs before we downed them.

I chuckled a bit at the beads of wine that dribbled down into Jetto's beard as he wiped it with his sleeve and gave me a signature wink. Jetto moved between Riggs and I, slinging an arm around each of our shoulders as he pulled us in tightly for a makeshift hug. He nodded with his head forward, towards the festivities under the tent.

"Enough of the planning you'z two. It's time we revel in the darkness.

CHAPTER 13 | TALLA

When I cracked my eyes, the wagon was bouncing along the cobbled entry road that led to Tuul's large metal gate. I knew that we were close because the smell of manure from Tuul's well-known livestock filled my nose. Warm sun was peeking through the canvas seams of the wagon that the three of us had just spent the day in.

I had taken the tufted seat towards the front, which after a night of drinking and dancing felt like the most comfortable cloud. Jetto, like a gentleman, had slept on the wooden floor, using his jacket as a blanket and his arms as a pillow. Riggs, true to his word, kept watch at the back near the only door.

"Good morning, or should I say afternoon? Seems like you slept well enough. How are you feeling?" Riggs said to me, his greasy black hair covering half his face as he leaned over.

I sat up. No sudden rush of blood or familiar pounding surfaced. It's like I hadn't even touched a drink or a smoke the night before. I then did a mental scan of my body. My legs, my feet. There was no fatigue. I felt fine. Better than fine, actually.

"I feel great... did you...?" my voice dropped off as he shrugged.

"I had to do something to help pass the time while I kept watch. I knew Jetto was a deep sleeper, but I was surprised you didn't even flinch when I was... *working*." He flashed a teasing smile at me that made me crinkle my nose at him.

While the thought of Riggs putting his hands on me while I had slept sent a shiver up my spine, I was grateful that his healing magic made it so I was without a hangover this morning.

My superstar can heal me well enough, but activating healing magic takes concentration, and often time. Both of those things are hard to come by when you had been up twenty-four hours and you inhaled the equivalent of a jug of wine and a sachet of Yarla Root.

"Well, thanks. You must be tired...." I said, looking down at Jetto as he started to stir.

His big arms lifted over his head in a sleepy stretch, hitting my legs. One little shake from me and his eyes popped open.

"Ooo wee. Are we'z there already?" His bearded mouth opened wide as he yawned but was cut short as something crinkled his nose. "*Smells* like we're there. Thank the Moon that it doesn't smell like shit in the city! You know, I miss having the company of livestock in Brakken, but I don't miss the smell."

Jetto tilted his head up at Riggs. "Tells you what, that's the best floor sleep I've ever had. And I reckon I haven't ever felt this right after an anti-Starcast in my life."

"Anything for the team." Riggs said as he reached out a hand to help Jetto sit up.

I shook my head a bit—was this the same man that thirty-six hours ago wouldn't even talk to us because he was too busy brooding over the run in with the Royal Prick? I don't think I've ever seen Riggs this... genial.

I didn't have long to contemplate his drastic mood shift. The cart stopped, and Riggs leaned over to jump out the back. His hair swished in the air as he exited, and I could hear him as he walked around the wagon to thank our drivers. I pulled my fraying braid into a quick bun and followed him out, my eyes squinting as they adjusted to the bright afternoon light.

Tuul was covered in fresh snow, with sunlight gleaming off the ground and bouncing between the metal buildings that lined the gate. The street was packed, full of merchant tents of various colors. I could see hides, jewels, and leather goods for sale in just the first few tents alone.

Glee crept up my chest and curled a smile across my face, suddenly thrilled by our decision to make the trek here last night. We were going to make out like Kings and Queens.

We split up for the day to cover more ground. I successfully switched out my old boots for some supple brown ones that fit like a glove without the merchant noticing, then satisfied my sweet tooth with delicious chocolates from a cart that was too busy trying to tame the crowd of children before it. My cloak pockets jingled with gemstone bracelets and gold and silver rings, enough to trade for a season of goods and services back in Brakken, allowing our good people to come out on top. Even with all of our thieving efforts, the money and starpower that the three of us could bring back to Brakken wasn't enough to revive it to what it used to be. But every bit counted, and it was all that we could do.

The only problem with arriving right in the middle of a merchant fair, though, was that once we were done doing what we do best and we were ready to settle somewhere for the night, all of the rooms in both of the nicer inns were already booked. Annoyingly, there wasn't even a point in trying to lift a key off of one of the occupants. According to information that Riggs was given by one of the merchants who drove us here, the keys were changed daily. The Tuulish innkeepers swapped out keys each morning to ensure something called *'a safe and hospitable respite'* for their guests. Lame, if you ask me. And trying to work around that was honestly too much effort just for a place to sleep for a night or two.

The three of us, luckily, were able to secure lodging at an inn that was tucked away off of a side road. The street was quiet, away from the hustle and bustle of the fair, and when we had approached the building around suppertime, it was quite obvious why there was a vacancy. Unlike the rest of Tuul that was constructed of gleaming metalwork, this inn looked as if the four wooden walls were one kick away from toppling onto each other.

The rooms opened directly to the outside, which is less preferable in the colder seasons. I prayed that the wind didn't shift, bringing the faint smell of livestock across the city and directly into our rooms. The bottom floor of the inn, where usually there was a restaurant or bar, was left entirely to the open air, the space hosting a few fire pits with large pots or spits suspended over the rings.

Beyond the lodgings, I could see a few rows of dilapidated wooden houses and an old church before the tree line at the back of an old pasture swallowed the view. *Clearly*, this street was forgotten during any reconstruction and rehabilitation efforts over the last century.

"Wellum. Better than the floor of a wagon I reckon." Jetto had said.

Despite my initial disappointment, he was right. This place might be shitty, but we had slept in worse. I mean, at the very least it should shelter us from the bitter cold that was blowing in on the northerly winds that made their appearance once the sun started to set.

"I'll get started on supper," Riggs said. He motioned to the sack he had slung over his shoulder. He had secured us a couple of cuts of beef, some potatoes, and some wild onions during his raid. "I'm thinking a stew?"

My stomach gurgled. It had been unsettled from my stellar choice of following a night of drinking with heaps of chocolate. A hearty stew, warm and thick, sounded *more* than delicious.

"Do you need a hand? I can help with the potatoes," I offered, taking a step towards Riggs, reaching for my dagger.

"No, no, no" Riggs held a hand out, motioning for me to stop, his voice was quick. "Consider it part two of my apology for missing our meeting." I lifted my brow.

"… Are you sure?" I countered. I couldn't think of a single time I had ever seen Riggs cook. "Do you even know how to make stew?"

His face went white. Was he starting to sweat?

Jetto wrapped an arm around me,

"Bossa, stew ain't nothing more than throwin' the goods in a hot pot and stirrin'. The man wants to cook so let him cook." He leaned in close to me, dropping his voice low so that his next words could only be heard by me. "You don't always have to challenge him, you'z know. You might be our Bossa, but we are all a part of this crew."

I let out a sigh and nodded. Riggs and I were great at pushing each other's buttons, and Jetto was our perfect diffuser. Jetto gave me a signature wink and nudged me towards the main door of the inn. As we were walking away, I had the urge to check over my shoulder, looking back at where we had left Riggs. He was still standing there, watching us as we strode away from him.

Jetto and I checked us all in as Riggs prepared our dinner. We were handed our keys by a strikingly beautiful, androgynous individual with tawny skin and hazel eyes that had various bird feathers clamped into their dreaded hair. Their name tag had read Plume, and the entire walk up the stairs Jetto and I debated on which we thought came first, the name or the hairstyle.

My door was just down the hall from the room Jetto and Riggs would share this evening. And inside it was a small wooden bed, a small arched window, and two round connected

CHAPTER 14 | Talla

Hours later, when the moon was high in the sky, the sensation of my stomach dropping jolted my body awake. I gripped the edge of the sheets, my fingers digging into the dusty mattress clinging to it for dear life. After a few breaths, my eyes were able to focus, and I recognized the dirty walls of the shitty room that I had surprisingly managed to fall asleep in.

It must have been a dream sensation that woke me, because I was safely in bed. Not like *that* gave me much relief. Still, I could count on one hand the number of times that I had gotten a nightmare that made me feel like I was falling, and each time it had been before something gravely wrong occurred. The last time it happened, I got the scar that was on my chest, and my mother was killed by that bastard who broke into our house.

I reached for my star, making sure the pendant was still there. The weight and warmth in my hand helped soothe my racing breath, until...

Wait. Something was off in the mix of sensations that I could normally feel from my star's multiple magics. The pull from the stars that I recognized as Jetto and Riggs felt different... weaker. *Definitely* weaker than it had when I had fallen asleep.

I closed my eyes and focused harder. It shouldn't be weak, they were only in a room down the hall. *Moon, save me.* The pull should be strong enough to make my hairs stand on end. After a few more seconds of me concentrating on the seeking magic passed, I dropped my star, the pendant thumping against my chest. The pull was still getting weaker—which meant that for some reason, Jetto and Riggs were on the move... without me.

I jumped out of bed, tossing the sheets and quilt to the side. Darkness poured through my window, and by the height of the moon, it must have been around two. Where the *fuck* would they both be going at this hour, especially without me?

The room started to spin a bit, but I shook my head to clear my vision, dousing any spark of hope for more sleep that lingered in my head. Thankful that I had chosen to go to bed in my clothes last night, I slipped on my new boots in two quick motions. My blisters that had started to form last night after a day of breaking them in had vanished thanks to my star, and already the boots were starting to mold to my feet, feeling like home.

Within seconds, I was out the door, dagger strapped to my belt and cloak wrapped around my shoulders. My hand reached back to my star, hoping to nail down the direction that Riggs and Jetto were heading in as I moved along the corridor.

The inn was quiet, as most places—besides Brakken—were in the dead of night. The guests were all asleep and making little noise beyond a few stray snores.

I kept going, my steps silent on the floor, towards the stairs, the ones that scaled the side of the inn and exited directly on to the road. I was almost there when I passed the door to the room Jetto and Riggs had been staying in and…

Hang on. I paused. The door was slightly ajar. My mind tried to work quickly, but sleep must have still had a hold on me because the questions were slow to form in my head. Had they left in a hurry, the door would be wide open. If they took their time, they would have shut it. But *ajar*? Why leave it just cracked?

It wasn't until I was close enough to grab the knob that I heard a sound that turned my stomach upside down. Heart racing, I pushed it open with more strength than needed. Had I not been aided by stealth magic, the sound of the door slamming against the wall stop would have been enough to wake the adjacent rooms.

Jetto and Riggs' room was dark save for a tiny bit of moonlight flowing in through their window. The beam was just enough to illuminate the outlines of furniture. The layout of the room was similar to mine, except that this room had two small beds pushed against the walls. One of which currently had a large figure kneeling against it.

My nose crinkled at the familiar metallic scent that filled the air. *Blood.* I didn't need any more light to know that it was blood causing the dark spots that were splattered all over the bed and the floor.

Shallow, near silent gasps were escaping from the figure. They turned their head, clearly sensing someone was in the room with them. I would have drawn my dagger had I not immediately recognized the shiny bald head that was reflecting the moonbeams back at me—*Jetto.*

One second I was in the doorway, and the next, I was kneeling down next to Jetto, firmly pushing my hand into his shoulder. The fibers of his clothes were warm and wet. With my other hand I grazed him for injuries in the area, and it didn't take long to discover the fresh jagged wound on his neck. I quickly put my flattened hand over it, his pulse thumping under my palm as more blood escaped. This was bad, so *fucking* bad.

"Jetto." His name was a gasp that escaped my lips.

I willed the healing power of my star to flood my body, channeling warm magic through my palm and fingers into him. I could feel the bleeding slow under my palm, but my efforts weren't enough to stop it completely. I pulled at my magic harder, trying to focus completely on healing the wound, imagining his skin stitching back together like I did anytime I had healed my own wounds.

Seconds ticked by slowly, and with each labored breath of his, each tremor that his wounded body made, the reality before me started to become clear. There was too much blood. The pulse under my fingers was growing too weak. *Fuck.* I might not be able to save him.

It was then that it dawned on me—Jetto was alone. Where was Riggs? I glanced around, making sure that I didn't miss a second shadowed figure in the room. I saw nothing but the other bed, perfectly made and appearing unslept in. The sight made me feel uneasy, like there was some unknown puzzle in front of me but I didn't have all of the pieces to put it together.

Jetto moved his legs a bit, hitting the bedframe and causing it to screech against the worn floor. As my ears registered the sound, another realization crashed over me. Jetto hardly ever made noise with his movements because of his stealth star... but I couldn't feel the presence of any stars in the room. I used my magic to reach out to the nearest stars, and the pulling sensation was even weaker than before.

Jetto had clearly been attacked and then robbed of his star... but how? How was that possible? *Moon, save me.*

Where the fuck was Riggs and his healing star? I needed him. *We* needed him. Or, did the attacker take his star, too? If Riggs was still alive, he would most definitely hunt after his attacker, magic or not, to make him pay for what he did. Perhaps that's why he wasn't here.

I looked into Jetto's blue eyes as worry flooded my system. To my horror, they were starting to glass over. *No.*

I silently pleaded with the Moon as I shoved another wave of healing magic into him. I couldn't give up. I pushed all of the energy that wasn't being used to apply pressure to the wound into concentrating on healing.

Faster.

I needed the magic faster. He had lost too much blood. He maybe had a minute of life left. I was running out of time. It would have done me no use to scream out for help—with wounds this large, my magic was Jetto's best hope at survival.

Jetto was growing colder in my arms. Besides, I knew that there was nothing anyone here could do. Not now. Not as the darkness was so dangerously close to claiming him. But I couldn't even bring myself to say anything to him, my mind was too busy working all angles of my superstar.

Once his pulse had slowed to the pace that I had been desperately trying to avoid, I had instinctively started to divert my attention away from healing and to making the room more comfortable instead. I tapped into my elemental magic, warming the room the best I could with just my one star.

After a few seconds, I could see his suffering lifting. It would be seconds now before he was resting in darkness. My eyes burned, tears threatening to fall, but I blinked them away. My comrade, my friend. At least he wouldn't be alone when the darkness came to claim him.

My healing efforts had closed the wound on his neck almost completely. With what appeared to be immense effort, he lifted his right hand to my thigh. I glanced down at it, noticing the patch of paler skin on his ring finger, exactly where his encased stealth star ring used to sit. He hadn't needed to show me for me to know that it had been taken, but if he used what little strength that he had left to show me, he wanted me to ask about it. I inhaled deep, demanding my voice break free from its hiding place inside my chest.

"Who, Jetto? Who did this?"

I tried to stay calm. Hysterics now couldn't save him. But it was hard not to burst into emotion as Jetto coughed before muttering his reply.

"Riggs."

No… I couldn't have heard him correctly. I titled my head a bit in question, and he nodded, collapsing a little more into my arms as he did so.

I had been worried that I wouldn't be able to hold back my tears much longer. But with that one word, my eyes dried completely. It wasn't sadness that I immediately became overcome with. It was rage, pure unfiltered rage.

No. Absolutely fucking no. It was as if someone lit my blood on fire. I wanted to scream so loudly the flames could burst through my mouth and burn the entire inn down. I didn't want to believe it, but I didn't have time to try to make sense of it.

Jetto tried to grab my hand to soothe me, but he was too weak, his fingers barely moving. I dropped my hand from his throat, my skin slick with blood as I grasped his. He gave a very faint smile.

"Be careful, Talla… po" he coughed and wheezed a bit.

I swallowed. He almost never said my real name. It was always Bossa. A nickname he gave me the day he agreed to work with me. I tried to sit him up a bit more, which was futile considering our size difference. He tried to speak again.

"Po…" his voice was thick and desperate, the word coming out as a cross between a cough and a gasp.

I tried again to shift him, but a second later, Jetto's body went limp against mine, and I knew that his soul had finally been called home.

An eerie quiet settled over the room, no longer filled with his labored breaths. After a few moments, I set him down, leaning on his bed alongside him. *Dead.* Jetto was dead. And he said that Riggs... Riggs had killed him. Or rather, left him for dead.

But why? What happened after I went to bed? The two of them got along fairly well, better than Riggs and I did at least. I knew that Riggs was selfish and ruthless. It's what made him a good thief. I knew he was capable of horrible things, but I didn't think he was capable of this.

I surveyed Jetto and the room as if the answer was written somewhere, and I was just missing it. If Riggs wanted to kill someone, he could in an instant with his accuracy magic. Leaving Jetto like this, barely alive...

It all clicked.

This... all of this was on purpose. He knew I would sense the stars leaving. Knew that I would find the cracked door, find Jetto. Riggs left him alive hedging his bets that I would find him before he died. That Jetto would tell me it was Riggs who hurt him so that I would go after him.

He must have stolen Jetto's star, that greedy power hungry bastard. And now, he wanted to lure me alone to take mine. How long had he planned to do this? Was this entire trip a trap? How the *fuck* did I not see this coming? How did I not read it on him?

I reached out again with my star. Riggs was no longer moving, the pull just as far as the last time I had checked. Wherever he was, he was waiting for me. Challenge *fucking* accepted, bastard.

I stood up, gripping the footboard of Jetto's bed for stability. I was shaky, my body probably just in shock, as I drew a full circle across my chest, leaving a thin line of Jetto's blood behind as I did so.

"Rest in the darkness, my friend. I'll get that son of a bitch." I muttered, the prayer giving me some new energy, though my mind felt foggy.

I looked at Jetto, draped over the side of his bed, lifeless. I would come back for him, for his body at least, to help burn at sundown after his death, as was the custom. But there was nothing I could do until then except seek his vengeance. So with my single dagger, my cloak, and my star, I raced out of the door, following the pull to find and kill Riggs.

I ran down the stairs and across the road down a small side path, blindly following the sensation at my chest. *Where did you go you fucking traitor*? Anger propelled me through the night as I raced towards the stars, past a few rows of small wooden houses and an old stone church towards the woods that loomed on the edges of town.

How had I been *so* foolish? It had been too easy of a trip. Too rushed. He had been too desperate. It was all clear to me now. But between the drink and the smoke, and the lure of Tuul, I missed it before.

Now, not only was one of my trio members dead, I was about to murder the surviving one. From three to one in just one night. I didn't let myself think about what that would mean for me, and how I would be facing this world alone again come dawn.

Snow was starting to fall, the wind blowing it sideways right into my face. The flakes hitting my eyes kept blurring my vision, but onward I charged. My mind was spinning. I didn't take any time to mark my surroundings, my feet silently pounding against the cold, hard ground.

My new boots were warm, with excellent traction. Each step was taking me closer to what I'm sure was going to be a hell of a fight. He had taken Jetto's star, so he was now equipped with accuracy, healing, and stealth magic. That was a lethal combination... unlikely to go down easy.

But *Moon, save me,* I would rip into that bastard's skin, tearing him apart, to make him bleed like Jetto did. I had a fucking superstar, and I would make sure to remind him what that meant.

I wasn't sure how long I had been running, but I had gone far enough that the cold air burned my lungs with every breath that I took. The pull of his stars was strong as I came across a small clearing. The snow was settling on the ground around me, unprotected from the tree cover unlike the rest of the forest. Close. I was close.

I looked around, trying to catch my breath. But it was then that I was struck with the sudden and violent urge to vomit. I leaned over and heaved. The snowy ground became tinted with sick as I spewed again. I spit and wiped my mouth clean.

As I looked back up towards the trees, my vision began to spin again. Something was wrong. Weakness shuttered through my body as I collapsed to my knees. The contact with the ground, the snow soaking through my pants and icing my skin flipped a switch in my head. I thought back to Jetto, a large and sturdy man, lying helplessly in my arms. I had asked myself why Riggs would do this a thousand times while tracking him, but this was the first time my brain thought to ask how.

How had Riggs attacked him so silently? How did he manage to take Jetto's star off of his hand without any sort of clamor? Jetto wasn't as skilled as Riggs or I were with a dagger, but as big as he was... Riggs must have had some sort of advantage over him to bring him down.

As I coughed and spit on the ground, the specs of blood that I saw on the snow gave me my answer. *Poison*. That's what Jetto had been trying to say. I instantly regretted not grabbing the few daggers that were still strapped to Jetto's belt before I left him. If I had been poisoned, I was likely going to need more than just my one blade to take Riggs down.

As if on queue, laughter filled the cold night air, echoing against the surrounding tree trunks. I turned my head around to see a dark hooded figure emerge from the shadows of the forest.

"The dosage was tricky to determine, you know." He moved closer to me, and I reached for my dagger but I missed, my senses all disoriented.

Fucking hell.

This had been a trap. And I played right into it. I tried again to grab my blade and managed to graze my fingers over the handle. The effects of the poison were coming in waves. My starmagic was desperately trying to combat the effects, but it was ultimately failing.

"As you know, grayweed has compounding effects. A little bit will kill you slowly, but a lot will make it quick. I miscalculated with Jetto... the big brick. Gave him too little. But

I think I got yours just right, even considering that superstar of yours."

Grayweed. When did he get his hands on that? Despite its seemingly common name, it grew in near impossible conditions near the mountains. It also was a master camouflager, blending in effortlessly with the surrounding vegetation so that even the trained eyes of an herbalist might miss it growing at their feet.

Though it was safe to the touch, it was deadly if ingested in any way. All of this, of course, made the herb insanely valuable amongst assassins and criminals alike. Especially since the plant was both odorless and tasteless, even when cooked.

It's why neither Jetto nor I noticed that the stew Riggs had prepared last night was laced with it. No wonder he was so adamant about cooking it—he didn't want to take any chances in case either one of us recognized the deadly herb.

There were a million words I wanted to blare at him, but "I'm going to fucking kill you, you Bastard," was all I could choke out.

I reached again for my dagger, this time making full contact with my fist and swung. But my blade only cut through air. I vomited again, and Riggs laughed. A wide smile was plastered on his oily face as he bent down and looked me in the eyes.

"You wish."

He snatched my dagger from my hand, and before I could stop him, he sliced upwards, severing the chain that held my star pendant. His cut slashed the skin on my ribs, but the pain wasn't what I felt the most. Suddenly the warmth I had come to know on my chest vanished. Despite being fully clothed, I felt naked.

"No" I cried out, barely louder than a whisper.

The trees and the sky and the ground all started blending together as I tried to push myself up. I couldn't let him take it. Not just because of the power it gave him—in addition to his other stars, a superstar would make him unstoppable—but because my mother had given her life that night ten years ago for me to keep this star.

A hard thud on the side of my face let me know that I had failed, my cheek resting on the cold, frozen ground. Riggs' deep and raspy chuckle echoed in my head. Was he still one man? I swore that I could see two of him. His footsteps stopped and I willed myself to see straight, looking up at the man that I had worked alongside for years... a man I thought I knew.

"Riggs. Please." I choked.

It wasn't like me to beg. But without my star, I wasn't sure I could do anything. Had the Grayweed not finally rendered my body useless, I would have kept trying to fight anyway.

Begging was the only move I had left. But as my vision cleared for a second, I saw how his eyes were wide—excited, ready. He cracked his knuckles on both his hands, the sound sending a chill down my spine. *Oh fuck*.

This close, Riggs never missed. I muttered a soft prayer under my breath. At least I would see my mother again soon. I guess I wouldn't end up alone after all.

"Nice knowing ya, *Bossa.*" He lifted his boot, and

within an instant, the whole world went black.

CHAPTER 15 | KIERAN

I awoke the next morning still on my floor, but thankfully with significantly more strength. The sun was shining so bright through the arched window of my chamber that I had to squint until my eyes adjusted. I pulled myself up and immediately stepped to my small apothecary cabinet located on the side wall. Like second nature, I added the combination of herbs that made a fast-acting healing tonic and drank the entire portion in a single gulp. Within minutes, the lingering twinges of pain in my muscles disappeared.

I gazed at myself in the ornate mirror that was mounted next to the cabinet, making sure not to stare directly into the bright beam of sun that it reflected. Dark stubble now covered my jaw and mouth. I quite liked the look of it, but in the summer months, clean shaven skin was far more comfortable. The northern winter winds were blowing stronger every day, though, and since the hair added an extra layer of protection for my face against the chill, I decided to leave it.

My golden eyes were bright, as they were on most sunny days, and glowed in contrast to the darkness of my eyebrows. I looked down at my clothes, dirt and blood covered my tunic and pants. I had been too weak and tired to change last night, but now that I was healed I quickly ripped them off, throwing them right into the garbage bin—the shredded pants were no good anymore anyways.

I pulled out two new sets of clothes, both woven of dark dyed wool. One I put on immediately, the other I threw onto the bed to pack for my upcoming starhunt. When the clothes hit the blanket, I couldn't help but stare at them as they sat plainly on top of my unslept-in bed. This wasn't just my upcoming starhunt. Assuming all went to plan, which after last time there's *no* way I would be letting it go otherwise... this trip would be my *last* starhunt.

I glanced back at my reflection in the mirror, letting the magnitude of the trip sink in. This was *it*. This trip would be the culmination of nine years of service to the King. The scrawny, but scrappy, eighteen-year-old street rat that accepted this role couldn't have dreamed of what that decision had in store for him; what he would learn, what he would see. That boy could never imagine that he would become the skilled fighter, the beloved guard, or any bit of *the man* that was in the mirror now.

I added several healing tonics and salves, an extra pair of gloves, and the dagger that the thief Talla had used to stab me to the pile that I was planning to pack. I had to admit that the thief's blade was a clever one—sharp with a beautiful wooden handle that had just enough stick in your hand, making it perfect for throwing. If I had to guess, the metal wasn't pure steel, which was the most common makeup of weapons throughout Larendi. This dagger felt heavier than it should, meaning that there was some other metal laced within the blade.

From what I knew about metalwork, such a task was no easy feat. I could distinctly remember Lor all but quitting her job at the forge when Neet, the best metalworker in Vrenn at the time, had her practicing crafting weapons with alternative alloys. She mastered it eventually, as Lor always did with every skill she tried to learn.

But because of their complexity, knives such as this one were pricey, likely going for triple the cost of a comparable steel dagger. Given that Brakken was no longer known for their flush finances, the likelihood that Talla had swiped her daggers off of someone was high. I didn't want to condone stealing by any means, but I had to appreciate the green-eyed thief's taste.

A small rustling sound caught my attention, and I turned to see a small, folded piece of paper that had been slid under my door. I walked over to it, hearing the retreating sound of footsteps down the hall on the other side. The paper was wrapped around an envelope still sealed with the King's wax mark. My eyes scanned the scribbled cursive writing that was etched on the inside of the outer paper.

"Sir Kieran, see enclosed this letter from His Grace. 'Boli' will be packed and ready when you are. FSFE, Gray"

I quickly pulled open the door to try to greet Gray, but the hall approaching my chambers was already empty. Another wave of guilt crashed over me for how I had snapped at him yesterday. After I returned from this starhunt, I would have to make good on my offer to sword train him. It would be nice, after all, to have someone to talk to once my starhunt duties disappeared. Someone to spar with rather than against.

I broke the shiny seal on the note from King Armund and read the elaborate midnight blue lettering.

Dearest Kieran,

I trust that your wounds have healed completely by now. The Seeker cuff will be waiting on my chair by the fireplace in my chambers. I, unfortunately, do not have time to meet you in person today, but the door guards are expecting you and only you to enter. Eleven stars are left to be recovered; the cuff should lead you to them all. Your prison duties will be handled in full starting at sunrise today, so there will be no need to complete any rounds. We need the stars back before Solstice Eve, or else everything that we have worked for over the years is for nought. Remember, Kieran. At all costs.

For Starlight, for Everyone.
Your King,
D.A. Armund

I read through the message three times to make sure that my eyes were not deceiving me. I had *never* been instructed to enter the King's chambers without His Grace present, let alone to retrieve the star cuff on my own. Perhaps after last night's training, he had figured that I was worthy of the added trust; that I had learned my lesson, and now fully understood what exactly my role was.

Pride swelled a bit in my chest. After almost a decade of rigorous daily training sessions, of nights on the road, of long public hearings, and the rightful return of what must be a thousand stars... eleven to go. I wouldn't let my Star King down. I was going to bring the stars home, at all costs.

I grabbed my belongings, throwing them into a canvas sack, and headed out my door and down the hall towards the stairs. Up and up the stories I went, my feet light on the stone steps, my sword thumping against my back. By the time I reached the King's floor, the mid-morning light was pouring through the stained-glass windows that lined the hallway that led to his chambers. I walked through the multicolor beams, heading straight towards the opening between the two guards who had already parted for me. They bowed their heads as I walked past them, through the King's wooden door and across the threshold.

It was quiet in the King's chambers. Unlike every other time that I had been here, there was no fire lit in the main hearth. The chair adjacent to the fireplace, though lacking royal presence, had a familiar box perched on its green velvet cushion. *The starcuff.*

My footsteps echoed through the quiet room as I made my way over to the chair. I opened the box, the ornate gold lock clicking as I lifted the latch free. The golden cuff lay upon the navy satin lining, and the star that was compressed into the center glowed softly. I slid the metal on, welcoming the familiar rush and warmth of starmagic dancing across my skin.

As I went to set the box back on the King's chair where it had been waiting for me, I couldn't stop my eyes from wandering to the side table. There was a book, open and facing up with the corner of the cover gently touching a wine goblet that still smelled of fermented fruit. From where I was standing, I could faintly make out some of the black printed text on the page, and my eyes widened.

Some of the books held in the Kings Chambers were the only copies known on the continent. They contained our histories, our conquests, and what knowledge was left of the Great Star Drop a thousand years ago. Somewhere in the volumes stored in his chambers, the King had discovered how to return the stars back home. Somewhere in the pages I was surrounded by was the answer to the beauty of the night sky... was it in *this* book that was on the table?

Curiosity got the best of me, and I leaned in closer to the open page. Under the heading *'Known'*, there was a list of words, most of which were crossed out. *Altair. Renfred. Nazra. Arason.* Instantly I recognized them as surnames, though many were no longer common amongst Larendians. The list continued, some of the names had question marks scribbled next to them, and others had more than one pen strike through the letters. My eyes skipped to read the only name that was left uncrossed out. *Aftan.*

I took a step closer to the table to try to read the list again, but my knee bumped the table, causing the book and the goblet to fall towards the floor. With quick reflexes, I was able to catch them both before they hit the rug, saving the small drop of wine left in the cup from leaving an identifiable stain.

But with the book now open to the first page, I noticed another name written in familiar script on the inside cover, one that was printed to indicate whose book this was. *Drake Aftan*.

Realization quickly settled into my mind. Drake Aftan. *D.A.* Armund had been the name taken by the Star King when he assumed power after the great fall of King Trewan, the King before Armund. This practice was common throughout our history, usually with the King keeping his given surname as an unused middle name.

The new name would serve as the King's legacy in history, and any references to their former names were kept from the public view. As a display of trust, the King always used the shortened version of his full name, D.A., when addressing members of his Guard. Looking at the name scribbled in the King's handwriting was the first time that I had ever heard what the letters stood for. What the King chose to be called, like many things, was none of anyone's business besides his own.

I swallowed a bit of guilt at the thought, the feeling sinking down into my stomach. I was snooping... in the King's chambers. I shouldn't be touching this book, *Stars help me*. I shouldn't be lingering, unsupervised, in here *at all*. I was instructed to retrieve the star cuff and retrieve Boli from the stables, not peer through the King's personal research.

I quickly flipped the book pages to find the one that had been left facing open. Once I came across the familiar sight of the crossed-out list, I set the book back near exactly how it had been laid on the table, barely grazing the goblet. Paranoia pricked at the back of my neck, the same way it did during a fight when someone was approaching me from behind.

I turned my head from side to side quickly, looking to see if one of the door guards had somehow entered without me hearing to investigate what was taking me so long. But I saw and heard nothing, so I shook my head, causing the worry to fade. I had to get out of here—I had work to do and stars to find. With the starcuff safely secured on my wrist, I turned on my heel and headed back towards the door to make my way down to the stables.

◊

The winds were behind us, which gave me and Boli an edge as we raced onward. From cross checking the strength of the pull on my wrist with the map I carried, it seemed that the closest star was located somewhere between Mellin and Tuul, east of the Middle Forests.

We rode all morning, only breaking once for a drink of water from the larger part of the River Linvel that still ran quickly. It appeared that the land north of the river had experienced a heavy snowfall, the landscape fresh with sparkling powder that was still loose on the surface. Thankfully, my mask protected most of my face from the tiny cold flakes that were swirling up in the air.

I muttered words of encouragement to Boli, who fearlessly treaded on, despite the flurry of white that was surely impeding her vision. She managed to keep her pace despite the weather, and I couldn't help but share my gratitude for the mare. She was tenacious. A fighter. And brave. *Stars, bless her* for it.

About mid-day, my wrist heated, signaling that we were *very* close to another star. I shifted the reins into one hand, moving the other onto the hilt of my sword on my back. With some pressure on my seat, Boli slowed her gait to a controlled trot. After my last run in with the thieves, I wasn't taking any chances. I would be ready to demand the star they carried, no matter who they were or how much they protested.

My orders were clear from the King. *At all costs.* It's why instead of my saddlebags being filled with the usual treasures that I used to bargain for trades, Gray had stuffed them only with provisions. And since I doubted anyone would be desperate enough to trade a star for some bread or dried meat, my sword was my best shot at convincing whoever we were approaching to give up the star. If they were foolish enough to fight back, my sword would handle them.

I tugged lightly on Boli's reins, forcing her to slow even more. Her hooves shuffled through the snow on the frozen road as we walked in circles. There was... nothing. Nothing around us indicated that a star was nearby. There was only the sun bouncing off of fresh snowfall. If it hadn't been for my cuff sending sparks of warm energy up my arm, I would have ridden right through this area... but the stars knew better than I did, so I dismounted.

I could see nothing but endless evergreens, white blankets of snow untouched on their branches. In the distance, I could hear the sound of a few crows, their caws faint in the wind. We had followed the main road most of the way here, but as I stood next to the saddled mare in the bare and white landscape, you would never know. It was vacant, last night's storm clearly still keeping all of the travelers and merchants at bay.

I could see no other footprints, no tracks besides Boli's. But yet, we were close to a star? I turned my head back and forth, reaching out with the power of the seeker star on my wrist, double checking what I had already known. There were no other stars nearby, just the one. *But where?*

I took a few steps towards the edge of the road. The land sloped down to what looked like a shallow creek bed. My eyes scanned it. Bent reeds poked out of the fresh snow, their yellow brown stems messy and tangled. There was a spot where a larger rock protruded, the snow not yet deep enough to cover it completely, there was a....

Wait. There. My eyes thankfully caught just the faintest blue glow from a patch of snow a few feet from where I was standing. I shuffled down the hill and bent over, scooping both my hands into the snow where the glow was. Power buzzed in my hands from the raw elemental star as I stared down at it, eyes wide with surprise.

It had been centuries since true lone stars were found, save for the stars that had fallen into the sea. All of the stars had been found and claimed by at least someone. But as I tried to clear off some of the snow from the glowing orb, I noticed that it was not all that I had scooped up. Also in my hands were some pieces of silver, bent and cracked with a thin chain.

Now that made more sense. Perhaps this had been a poorly compressed star that finally exploded, and not originally an ownerless one after all. Star compression was a dying art, and if attempted by unskilled hands, this was bound to happen.

Though, it was odd that its carrier chose to discard it over carrying it raw.

Perhaps they didn't know how to activate elemental stars properly? Or perhaps they were tired of carrying just one since their magic worked better in multiples. Whatever the case was, it was one more that would soon be finding its way back home in the skies.

I reached into my tunic pocket and ripped a small piece of fabric out of the lining, wrapping the silver pieces inside it before turning to trudge up the small slope that led back to Boli. It might be a long trip, this final starhunt. There was no point in discarding a good bit of silver when it could come in handy later.

"Well, looks like the stars are on my side..." I said under my mask, looking at Boli.

Her soulful eyes blinked at me. I know horses can't talk, but I knew that Boli could understand me. It helped make these trips alone more tolerable. I rummaged through my canvas pack, placing the star and wrapped silver pieces into a nightcloth bag.

"One down, ten to go."

CHAPTER 16 | KIERAN

About an hour later, Boli and I were deep in the trees. I pulled her back to a walk as the terrain was less certain in the forest than on the road. The cuff had, to my disappointment, pulled me away from Tuul and towards what I could only guess was somewhere along the front range of the mountains. I aimed Boli towards Ilken, a town I had not yet visited myself, but by the small size of the dot on the map, I doubted that I had been missing much.

When we were first heading this way, I had really hoped to stay in Tuul. The inns there were updated, lavish, and comfortable, and likely my best chance for a good night's sleep until I recovered the missing stars. Tuul had been the first town to completely return all of the stars within its limits during the beginning of King Armund's quest to reconstruct the night sky, and for that they were thanked generously. With a sudden influx of funds, they were able to complete a rehabilitation of almost every building, swapping their flimsy wooden exteriors to those of metal and ore. The main inn even had added heated marble floors, fueled with clever redirection of geothermal energy.

I crinkled my frozen toes in my boots and sighed. With solstice fast approaching and no time for detours, I couldn't justify heading towards Tuul when Ilken was directly on the path my wrist was leading us down. I tried not to belabor my disappointment—every town, big or small, had stables and bars. Surely, there would be nights on this hunt that I might not even have access to those luxuries.

After we emerged from a dense patch of trees, I saw something that brought my attention to the ground up ahead. There was a large object resting in the shaded snow that looked like it did not belong. It was too dark to be an exposed piece of rock, especially considering the snow fall. Was it a downed ground bear? Maybe, but all of the ground bears I had heard of had brownish tan fur, and this figure was definitely black.

Boli took a few steps forward so that I could get a better view and my stomach dropped.

Shit. It was a body.

I scanned my surroundings. No signs of anyone. I dismounted, swinging my leg around the saddle and bracing for the impact of the ground on my cold feet. I walked Boli to a tight grouping of trees out of the blows of the wind and sightline of the figure. I tied her reins into a knot by her neck so she wouldn't trip on them, tucking the ball under the raised pommel.

"Stay here." I whispered, and she snorted back in my direction, puffs of breath flooding from around her nostrils before taking a defying step towards me.

I furrowed my brow. She could definitely understand me, but after a long morning ride in the cold, she seemingly didn't care.

"Stay here... please?" I whispered again, the end of my command coming out more like a question.

The chestnut mare stared at me, her big brown eyes looking at me as if to ask *what's in it for me?* I rolled my eyes and walked back over to her, reaching into the saddle bag that I knew housed some grain. I grabbed a handful and let her nibble some, her lips tickling my hand through my glove.

I scattered the rest in front of her. She snorted again, but this time, seemingly out of contentment as she immediately started nibbling at them, her nose sifting through the snow. Tenacious. A fighter. And stubborn.

I gave her a pat on the neck and reached into another bag, grabbing a vial of healing tonic and the small dagger I had packed. If the person was dead, which was the most likely situation given how cold it was out here, both items would be rendered useless. If by some blessing of the Stars they weren't... well. Either I'd help them live or give them their own way out if it was already too late.

I made my way towards the figure. The body was so still. Was it already frozen? The backside of a dark cloak was all that I could see, giving me no clues as to what shape this person was in.

I squinted my eyes, but I couldn't see the chest cavity moving up and down like it should be doing. We were a few miles from Ilken still, and even further from Tuul. What had this individual been doing out here? Had they gotten caught in the snowstorm?

I willed my feet to take shallower steps, softening the crunch of the snow beneath them. When I was close enough, I could see that the body was that of a girl, long brown hair cascading out of the cloak, her face down into a pile of crimson snow.

Yikes. She must have been attacked.

I placed my hand gently on the cloak and relief shuddered through me. The girl was breathing, but barely. A few more minutes, and she'd probably be turned to ice. Had it been an animal attack? I checked for signs of claw marks on the cloak or scattered blood from bites, but the red was localized to just around her. And, her cloak was fully intact.

"Looks like the Stars are on your side today, too, girl." I muttered, reaching for the tonic in my pocket.

The purple liquid shined in the afternoon sun as I palmed it. I wasn't sure how she got herself bloody and alone in these winter woods, but no one deserved to die like this. I wouldn't let her. I would heal her and help her get—

My mind went blank as I gently rolled the body over, careful to keep her head in line with her spine. Blood had soaked through the front of her clothes and covered the bottom half of a tan face that I recognized instantly. Something in my chest tightened, and my stomach dropped as I gazed down at Talla, the thief, her body limp on the ground.

Her face was calm, and peaceful, with no trace of the wicked smile she had flashed at me the last moment that I saw her. My wrist was cold as I held her. *Interesting.* She was now starless. I scanned her body, noting the lack of weapons and the blood seeping slowly from two stab wounds in her gut.

Minutes... She would have only minutes left in this cold.

'Fuck the King.'

That's what she had said to me before I had thrown my sword at her. I gripped the glass vial of tonic in my hand, hesitating.

The odds of her wanting me, a member of the King's Guard, to heal her was absolutely and positively zero. And the King made it clear that the likes of her were dangerous. But looking down at her soft face, her long dark eyelashes laced with trapped snowflakes... it was hard to believe this was the same thief that had stabbed me in my groin only days earlier. I grimaced at the memory, but looked at my vial.

'Your job isn't to be merciful.'

The King's words echoed in my head. *True.* But what was my alternative? Leave her here and just forget the image of her turning into ice that was now occupying the forefront of my mind? Who cared what she would want, anyways? I most definitely didn't.

My heart started to race. Every second I spent contemplating my decision, the fewer I had left to make one. It was just a tonic. Thief or no thief, she was still a girl.

I slammed the doors shut in my brain that kept the doubt and hesitation flowing. Decision made. I just hoped it wouldn't come to bite me in the ass. I unscrewed the glass top and tipped the vial into her mouth until I had poured in every last drop.

CHAPTER 17 | TALLA

My lantern bobbed in the wind as I ran barefooted down the path towards the house. Laughter escaped my mouth as I turned back to make sure she was still playing our game. Sure enough, a glowing white fluffball was gaining on me, her ears flopping in the wind.

When I reached the front stoop, I tried to turn mid-stride, but two paws landed on my feet, soft fur rubbing against my legs and stopping me in my tracks.

"You caught me! You're getting faster!" I laughed, rubbing my little hands through her fur.

Her tail wagged back and forth in delight as I pulled a dried sausage bit from the pocket of my skirt for her to catch.

"Taaaallla!" I heard my mama call from the back garden.

I set my lantern down and followed her voice through the side gate until I was standing at her side. Mama was sitting next to a fire, wrapped in a thick wool blanket and drinking from a steaming cup that smelled of cinnamon and clove. She held out a hand for me.

"There you are, honey. The clouds are clearing. Come and watch the moon with me."

Using all of my strength, I pulled myself up onto the bench that she was sitting on. My legs were too short to set on the ground like hers, so I tucked them behind me as I leaned my head on her blanket-covered arm.

The moon was full tonight, shining like a beacon in the pitch-black sky. The apple grove, the forest, everything her light touched had a gray glow to it, like a soft blanket covering the landscape. There was nowhere in the whole wide world more beautiful than Brakken, I was sure of it.

As the night grew older, the temperature started to drop. Mama opened up her arms for me to crawl under her blanket and onto her lap. Her skin was warm, and she held me just right. She smelled different than she normally did, but I breathed it in all the same. I felt safe there, hearing the thuds of her heart beating. Thuds that, despite the two of us sitting still, seemed to be getting louder. Wait. Too loud... they were too loud for the soft and gentle heart of my mama—

My eyes flipped open, my vision flooded with the light of the daytime sky. I blinked, confused by where or when I was. I turned my head slightly to see a masked face above me and dark curls bobbing with each step. My movement must have alerted him, because within an instant a pair of gold eyes fixed on me.

I would recognize that brainwashed gaze *anywhere* after the other night. I pushed against his solid chest, flailing my legs to try to flip my way out, but the little strength I had was no match for his grip. What the *actual fuck* was I doing in the arms of the royal prick of the King's Guard?

"Easy there, Talla." His voice was low and smooth like waves in my ears.

For a second, I wanted to relax back into his arms. *Moon*, I must be dead if my body thought being carried by one of Armund's men was *relaxing*. But he spoke again, and my traitorous heart had the nerve to remain calm instead of pumping the adrenaline I would need to fight him off.

"Though... you've been healing much quicker than I anticipated, even with the help of the tonic I brewed."

I closed my eyes tightly and opened them again. I didn't *feel* dead. But *shouldn't* I be dead? Between the poison and the kick to the head, Riggs had tried to kill me. He should have killed me. He would have killed anyone else.

The Guard kept on walking, his feet crunching on snow with each step. I made a subtle effort to turn my head in hopes to gain more information about where we were headed. But from my angle in the Guard's arms, all I could make out was the tops of snowy trees. Wherever it was, I *definitely* did not want to go there with him, that much was certain.

I pushed again to try to free myself from the Guard's arms, but his grip didn't budge. I cursed under my breath as I closed my eyes, silently begging the Moon to give me some answers. What day was it? Had they already burned Jetto? Where was Riggs now? Where the fuck was this Guard taking me? And....

I ran the Guard's words that he had spoken back through my head, this time not focusing on the way they sounded, but the words themselves.

"How... how do you know my name?"

The prick ignored my question.

"A shattered nose, two deep puncture wounds. Plus, you were left in the middle of the woods, completely exposed to the elements. How in the Stars did you survive the deep freeze last night?" The disbelief suggested by his words didn't make its way to his tone, his voice and steady heartbeat threatening to lull me back into my childhood vision.

I bit down hard on my lip until the metallic tang of blood tinted my saliva to keep that from happening.

"Where are we going?" I demanded in response.

With every step, we were probably getting closer to the castle, which meant getting closer to prison and closer to breathing the same sickening air as the bastard Armund. I had to escape.

If Riggs stabbed me *twice*, after a close-up kick to the face, it meant that he really wanted to make sure that I was dead. It meant he hadn't been immediately filled with regret when he realized that he had tried to murder one of his comrades. That fact shouldn't surprise me—if he hadn't felt remorse after what he did to Jetto, the member of our trio that he actually *liked*, then he wasn't going to feel it for me.

Heat flooded my skin as the memory of Jetto fading in my arms settled in my brain. *Thank the Moon* that Riggs hadn't killed me because now, I got to kill *him*. I'd make sure to carve two matching wounds in his traitorous body—one for betraying me, and a deeper one for Jetto.

And that asshole had taken my star, leaving a cold gap on my chest where the pendant had lived for so many years. I had to get it back as soon as possible. I had to get revenge for what he did to our crew. Which all meant that I had to find a way out of this Guard's grasp *now* before he took me any further from Riggs' trail.

I used all of my strength and willed my body to soar backwards. While the attempt was more successful than my last, the Guard just squeezed his arms tighter around me. His muscles flexed as they held their position. He wasn't going to let me go, and without weapons or my starmagic, I wasn't going to be able to escape on my own—I was trapped. By the way the Royal Prick looked down at me, his golden eyes shining, he clearly knew it, too. *Fuck*.

The Guard shifted his gaze back upward before speaking again, his tone now noticeably jovial.

"You know, I'd be lying if I said I wasn't a bit surprised that someone bested you. You had nearly impeccable aim in the Middle Forests. Admittedly, I'm a little jealous that I wasn't the one to do it, but perhaps the Stars will favor me and give me another opportunity soon." The bastard winked.

Moon, I hated that he wasn't afraid of me, and I hated it even more that I didn't have my star to shut him up.

"How's life with one ball, you prick?" I spat out at him. I expected him to wince, or at least drop those cocky raised brows. Instead, I found myself being lightly shamed in his arms... from his laughter.

"Barely an ounce of strength and yet you still choose to fight? You're either the bravest or the most naive criminal that I've come across."

I rolled my eyes—if I had a silver coin for every macho asshole that underestimated me, I'd probably have enough to feed half of Brakken through the winter.

"Despite your impeccable aim, *thief*," I noted how his golden gaze shot down his mask-covered nose at me, his voice sharp around the last word as if 'thief' was supposed to be some sort of insult. "The royal riding clothes are made of incredibly tight weave. Your little nick healed in a matter of days, with both my balls still very much intact."

The sunlight glinted in his eyes as they crinkled a bit on the side, making them shine even brighter gold. Oh, how I longed for anything sharp to be within my reach to make a second attempt at slicing him.

I heard a horse whinny, almost as if it was greeting the Guard, and instantly my plane of vision shifted. The sky and ground tumbled over each other until I was sitting upright on my ass in the snow. I looked around, trying to spot anything that would clue me in as to where I was.

Everything was a blinding white, the fresh snow reflecting the daytime sun in millions of tiny glimmers. I couldn't see the horizon through the dense forest, but judging by the way the trees towered over us, we were still North of the river. Maybe we weren't too far from where I had found Riggs the night before. Hope fluttered in my chest as I quickly searched for the path of steps through the snow. If I acted quickly, I could follow the Guard's path back to wherever he had found me and pick up Riggs' trail from there.

I wanted to stand up, but a prickling sensation in my nose and lungs stopped me. The breaths I was taking were freezing into tiny crystals, tearing at my insides with each inhale. It had been years since cold had affected me such—I had become so used to the warming effect that my starmagic granted me that I had almost forgotten what the deep freeze air felt like.

Was this my starless future? Was this what was in store for the other Brakkens this winter? Would the four elemental stars that I had buried in the ground be enough to keep the city alive through the deep freezes to come?

I finally pushed myself up to standing to find myself staring into two big brown eyes. The horse snorted at me, sending a plume of warm mist into the space between us as I admired her. It had been years since I had been so close to a horse, or close to any creature that I wasn't planning on slaughtering. She was tall and beautiful, with fur of a color not too different than my hair.

Her big eyes were locked on to me, the animal barely blinking as I regarded her. If I didn't know any better, I'd think she was sizing me up, determining whether or not I was some sort of threat. She stomped her foot a few times before the Guard stepped up next to me to put a calming hand on her neck.

I could feel the heat rippling off of his body as he stood at my shoulder, and I hated myself for missing how warm it had felt in his arms just moments earlier. I switched my attention to him, preparing to take one final glance before I made a run for it, when my jaw dropped.

Holy shit.

He was enormous. He was much, *much* taller than I remembered from the last time I had been face to face with him in the Middle Forests. Taller than both Riggs and Jetto who had each had at least a head over me. My eyes only met the Guard's chest, which was clad in a dark black tunic that was cut tightly to his muscled form.

Stunned by the sheer grandiosity of his physique, I just watched him and his horse for a few moments. He tenderly stroked her neck until she curled her head into him, nudging him slightly. The Guard pulled his mask down, revealing a strong jaw, with dark hair growing tightly around his mouth. I wasn't sure why I was still watching him when I should have been planning my escape, but something made me want to step closer to him.

I hadn't realized that I had been staring until he whipped his head in my direction, sending a sharp golden stare of his own in my direction. I blinked and closed my mouth, but I held his gaze.

"Well. Now that you're awake and apparently stable, my job is done." He unclipped something from his horse's saddle and tossed it to me.

It was an empty leather canteen with Armund's symbol embossed in gold. The canteen alone would trade for a week's worth of meals to the right merchant.

"You're a few miles from Tuul, and even closer to Ilken. I assume you can find your way back to wherever you're hoping to pillage next from there. Consider the canteen a parting gift to remember the kindness of the King's Guard."

I lifted my brows in astonishment.

"You're just… letting me go."

Surely, he wasn't just going to walk off. The King's Guard was known for arresting folk for even minor rebellion towards them or the King. And between yelling *'fuck the King'* and stabbing this Guard between his legs… well I had done *much* worse than that.

"Yes," he grunted.

I looked down at the canteen, then back at him, but he had turned back towards his horse. I wanted to come up with a clever response, something disparaging to both him and the King, but my mind was drawing a blank. Absolutely nothing about any of this made any sense. I watched the Guard adjust his saddle, preparing to mount.

"You're welcome for saving you," he said without turning around.

I folded my arms across my chest, relishing in the added warmth the position gave me.

"No one asked you to save me, Guard."

He turned back around to glare at me over his shoulder.

"No, but it's against my honor to leave a young woman to die in the woods. Even if she wouldn't grant me the same courtesy."

I rolled my eyes.

"Psh. Your honor? You're a subservient sheep at Armund's mercy. Serving a bastard like him doesn't make you honorable, it makes you a *disgrace*." I spat the last word out at him, but before I could blink there was the sharp tip of a dagger pressing lightly against the skin of my throat.

My eyes traveled down the silver of the blade to see a familiar wooden handle tucked in between his fingers. He was wielding *my* dagger—the one I had used to make my escape during our last encounter by stabbing his groin. The way his golden eyes were narrow under his dark furrowed brow made my breath catch in my throat, but I held my ground.

"I have been more than kind to you, *thief*. But my patience only goes so far." Gone was his joking tone from a few moments ago and gone was any ounce of levity in his eyes. "You're lucky I don't arrest you now, and bring you back to the castle."

He was acting exactly how I'd expect a power tripping asshole under Armund's spell to, and I couldn't help but laugh. While apparently saving me from freezing to death and just letting me leave unscathed had been surprising, this display of pompous anger was not.

"So why don't you, *Prick?*" I kept my voice steady, my eyes challenging his.

I was acting far more confident than I should have been, considering that he was armed. But I could feel my strength returning a little at a time. I didn't have my star, but I might be able to take him. Maybe not to the ground, but all I needed was to snag some sort of a weapon off of him. His sword, my dagger, *something* to use as I ran off to find Riggs.

The Guard and I both breathed, locked in a battle of pointed gazes. The vapor from our breaths mingled together to form a white cloud of mist around our faces, fogging my view of the forest around us.

He eventually lowered my dagger, tucking it into his tunic side pocket. "I don't have time to bring you in and complete my duties before Solstice."

I remembered then that this Guard had been out collecting stars the other day when he crossed paths with my trio. He had been willing to trade *riches* in exchange for the stars that were now buried safely in the ground in Brakken. He must still be searching for stars... would that search lead him to Brakken? Or would it lead him to....

A risky plan quickly formed in my head. Royal Prick or not, this Guard had coin, weapons, a horse, and some way of tracking down stars. I had... well. I had nothing. It was going to be incredibly difficult for me to just wander by myself through the trees, hoping that I could find my way to Tuul or Ilken before I froze or became something's dinner with only snowy tracks to guide me.

And if I made it to town, what then? All of the skills that made me a good thief—my stealth, my aim—they came from my superstar. Could I even make my way in this world without it?

I shook my head, not letting that kernel of doubt sink too deeply in my thoughts to distract me from what I needed to do to ensure I had a chance at finding Riggs and getting my revenge.

"Assuming you're after the stars, I know where you'll find them." I twirled my finger around my blood-matted braid, batting my eyelashes a few times.

The Guard paused as he was grabbing onto the saddle to climb on to his steed, his eyes both curious and concerned.

"I'm almost sure the man who did this to me has whatever stars are left. Clearly, you have some royal star tracking ability..." I paused, seeing if in the silence he would reveal what sort of tool or magic he used to track down stars.

But the guard's face didn't break in the slightest. No small eye twitch, no shifting in his seat. He maintained an annoying stature of composure atop his chestnut horse.

I continued on before I lost his attention, and he really did decide to leave me here with nothing but an empty canteen.

"You're going to need help. The man that has many of the stars is not going to just let them go easily. It'll be helpful to have someone with you who knows him... knows his moves. You might have a fancy sword and large muscles, but he has access to incredible magic right now. Take me with you and I can help you get those stars back...."

I forced the disgust that was creeping up my throat back down to my stomach as I ground out the last words, hoping to seal the attractiveness of my offer.

"To the Star King."

I hated that people actually called him that, but it was a term that supporters of Armund and his ridiculous dream used lovingly. Of course, what I actually meant as I was offering my help to the Guard was, *take me with you so I can find Riggs, steal the stars back, and then make sure you never get your hands on them.* Remembering all of the times that Jetto teased that I say a lot with my expressions, I worked hard at making sure my face kept my true intentions hidden as my offer hung in the silence.

I watched the Guard think. His golden eyes were bright against the darkness of his hair and mask. I moved my toes up and down in my boots to try to warm them up a bit and pulled my cloak around me a little tighter.

"What do you say?"

If I could just figure out how he was tracking stars, I could use it to get my star back and get my revenge with a fraction of the effort. And, with my body properly healed and equipped, stealing the rest of the stars back from this Prick would be a breeze, even if he was double my size. Sure, to get what I wanted I would have to ride alongside the King's cocky errand boy, but it was only temporary. Perhaps I would get another chance at stabbing him along the way... and this time, I'd be sure not to miss.

I fluttered my lashes again before giving him the kindest, sweetest smile that I could muster. I might have to work a little for it, but he was going to say yes.

CHAPTER 18 | KIERAN

"No." I responded to Talla's offer with absolutely no hesitation. I hooked my leg into the stirrup and pulled myself up as Boli shook her head.

Talla's doe-eyed face dropped, her striking green eyes wide with disbelief. Clearly, 'no' wasn't a word that she heard often.

"You hardly even thought about it."

I pulled my mask back over my nose and mouth, my skin grateful to no longer be exposed to the elements.

"I didn't need to," I replied curtly.

It was the truth. Even if I hadn't been explicitly told by His Grace to steer clear of people like her—people who used starmagic for their own personal gains—I had no interest in keeping the company of a thief. I had already risked enough and wasted too much time by saving her life.

I went to tug on Boli's reins when something cold exploded on my shoulder. I looked down to see my black tunic splattered with tiny white crystals. Did she actually just throw a snowball at me?

Annoyed, I turned to look back at her. She was standing with a hand on her hip, her face painted with a *'yeah, so what?'* expression.

"Are you a *child*?" I bit at her.

Maybe she was younger than I had originally pegged her to be. Clearly younger than me, but I thought she might at least be twenty by the way her frame curved in and out at her waist. Those curves were hidden under her cloak as she stood before me, but I remember how perfectly my arms fit around her as I had scooped her up from the forest floor.

She bent down and scooped up another pile of snow in her hands before she launched a second snowball in my direction. This one I dodged, causing it to explode on the thin trunk of a tree behind me.

"Leaving me here now is no better than if you would have left me over there." She pointed in the direction of my path of footprints.

I followed them with my eyes, remembering seeing the figure lying there just a bit ago. Had I known it had been her lying there, would I still have approached it? I turned back towards her.

"You're not seconds away from death now. You were then."

"Well, without any weapons to hunt or defend myself with, it'll only be a matter of time before that's the case again! Especially in this cold."

I raised a brow at her.

"You're a thief, aren't you? Surely this can't be the toughest bind you've been in. You'll figure it out. I have already wasted too much time as it is helping you."

I nudged my heels into Boli's side to move her forward, but the mare was reluctant to move. A soft and unexpected sound caught my attention before I could nudge her again.

"Please."

The word felt just like the kicks to my stomach that I had endured as a child before I learned how to fight back. It sounded so helpless, so earnest. *Too* earnest, in fact.

Her plea was such a departure from her previous tone that I found it hard to believe. Where was the defiant voice of the girl that had stabbed me only a few days prior? The thief that all but spat on the King's name so that her rebellion echoed with conviction through the trees. Who was this girl that now not only requested aid from me, a member of the King's Guard, but actually pleaded for it?

The King viewed people like her as a threat. *Well,* people who continued to use starmagic in spite of the Royal effort to return them to the sky. But she no longer was using starmagic....

I stared at her, taking the entirety of her in. Medium height. Brown hair. Brown skin. Black cloak. Blood soaked shirt and pants. Leather boots. Green eyes. *My Stars,* those eyes were even more magnificent in the daylight. Truly the shade of an evergreen bough, yet brighter now that the fading sunlight directly hit them.

Wait. Were they now lined with silver? A small tear rolled down her cheek. *Stars, help me.* I hated it when women cried. She must really be afraid to be out here alone, or else she's a *damn* good actress.

The entire time that I focused on her, the pull from the seeker cuff on my wrist didn't change. She was starless, though clearly not by her own choice. But it still meant that she currently wasn't as much of a threat to me, or to Larendi, as she had been before. She was just an average, albeit attractive, criminal. At least as average as a thief covered in blood, who mysteriously didn't die despite being left to freeze, after being stabbed twice, could be.

I took a breath, pondering my options. She had no weapons. No star. And she hadn't really fought back when she came to and realized I had saved her. I was almost sure I was going to regret the words that came out of my mouth next, but I said them anyway.

"Only to Ilken. Then you're on your own, *thief*."

She quickly smiled, and something in my chest warmed. She wiped at her eyes, and I couldn't help but question whether I had just been played or if her desperation had been real. *Stars*, maybe I didn't really want to know the answer to that.

"Deal."

Had I not met her previously… had I just encountered her today, cold and hurt in the woods, I might have thought she was a gift from the stars themselves. Her smile was bright even against the gleaming snow. Her brown cheeks were round, and their fullness caused her green eyes to bunch together at the sides. Even covered in blood, her's was maybe the most remarkable face my eyes had come across, and that was saying something. The Mile Dark, a habitual dance house of mine for its proximity to the castle and elite service for members of the King's Guard, attracted the most beautiful women from all over the Larendi.

The phantom sensation of her blade poking through to my groin reminded me that I had, in fact, met her. It reminded me that she was not just some girl that I had somehow stumbled across in a Star-fated meeting. But despite being a stubborn and dangerous thief, she was right. The air was still too cold to be out here for too long. If I left her, I might as well not have given her that tonic in the first place.

Talla walked towards Boli, who huffed a thick cloud of vapor in her face. To anyone else, that would probably be a normal horse mannerism. But, I knew Boli better than that.

"She wants to know if you know how to ride," I said, translating the horse's actions.

Talla stopped in her tracks, her face suddenly shifting from victory to confusion. She looked at Boli, then looked back at me.

"You can speak horse?"

I shrugged, smiling softly under my mask.

"We understand each other." Boli snorted again in agreement.

"Funny. I didn't think anyone working for the King could understand anything other than how to ruin people's lives."

And just like that, my smile was wiped from my face. *There* she was, the snappy and self-righteous thief I had met in the woods. I furrowed my brows, but she didn't seem to notice... or care. She continued forward with her steps. Steps, I realized, that were surprisingly silent despite crossing over the hardened snow we were standing on.

Boli stomped her front foot twice and then retreated a few steps of her own, keeping the distance between her and the thief. I couldn't help but chuckle when surprise flew across the thief's face.

"She's waiting for an answer, you know." I said, looking down at Talla. "she's not going to let you get any closer until you do. She's stubborn like that. Something I'm sure *you* can relate to."

Talla glared at me, crossing her arms and shifting her weight into her hip again.

"Don't act like you know me, Prick. Besides, you never answered my question. Why should I answer yours?"

"It's not my question. I couldn't give a shit if you know how to ride or not. But it matters to Boli. And what question of yours did I avoid?" I didn't remember her asking me anything besides where we were going. And that question had already been answered.

"How do you know my name?"

Ah. I contemplated whether or not I should share exactly how I learned her name. Keeping it from her clearly was driving her crazy, which could provide some good entertainment for the next hour as we rode to Ilken. But this whole charade was taking longer than I had intended.

The sun would be set soon, and it was too cold to be out here after it went down. If giving her an answer would speed up Boli's approval process, then I had to do it. So I opted for the truth... sort of.

"I ran into a rather scared and naked fellow before having the pleasure of making your acquaintance the other day. Said he had a run in with a band of thieves who robbed him of everything, including his star. Enter you, your comrades, and your horde of stars. It wasn't that hard to put two and two together, though it did throw me off a bit to find that you were only half as striking as he described..." I paused, "Maybe a quarter."

I'm not sure exactly why I added the last bit. She was, of course, the definition of striking. I swallowed hard as the lie sat heavy on my tongue.

I could almost see the steam pouring out of her ears. I was a little bit surprised that she found that offensive. Had she hoped that I had found her pretty or something?

"Callum is a coward who is lucky to be alive." Each word was louder than the next, followed by a very sharp "... and of course I can fucking ride."

Her voice echoed in the silence of the forest, against the icy bark of the trees. Boli must not have appreciated her tone just as much as I hadn't, because she threw up her head, her front hooves lifting off the ground a little before stomping back into the snow.

"Easy, easy," I said, switching the reins into one hand while I used the other to settle her.

Talla had retreated a few steps to move out of the horse's way. When my eyes found hers again, I glared at her. Mostly because she scared my horse, but also because she was testing my patience and my generosity. I don't know why I even kept bothering to talk to her, but for some reason I did.

"You know for someone who is so desperate for a ride, you sure know how to scare one off."

Talla's face scrunched, her rounded nose wrinkling. I was expecting some sort of snotty comeback, but after a few seconds, she conceded.

"Fine." She faced Boli head on. Her face softened as she addressed the horse, putting a palm up in the gap between them. "I'm sorry, horse. I can ride. I learned from my mother at a young age, and she had ridden all of her life."

Talla's hand hung out in the frozen air for a few breaths before Boli met her, giving her a few curious sniffs. Talla didn't budge until Boli's entire muzzle rubbed against her fingers. She cupped the horse with a sort of half embrace, stroking Boli's cheekbone with gentle familiarity.

Talla's braid was fully visible now, lying down the front of her clothes, the end hitting where I assumed her navel would be. I noticed how the parts that weren't crusted in blood and ice were the exact same shade as Boli's coat, and I wondered if perhaps these two weren't cut from the same cloth. Brave, tenacious... and sometimes a pain in the ass.

Boli stepped close enough to Talla that she could mount. I took my foot out of the stirrup, making room for her to step into the silver hold. I reached down my starless arm to aid her, but she bypassed it. Her brown fingers reached right to the pommel of the saddle, and with a swift kick up into the air, she effortlessly pulled herself to sit in front of me.

Her hood had fallen during her lift, but she made no effort to pull it back up as she settled herself into the seat. Her hair had swung behind her, and I gently moved it out of the way before readjusting my seat. Even through my mask I could make out the same campfire scent I had smelled on her the other day, though the fruity notes had completely faded.

"Just to the gates, *thief*," I muttered, regrouping the reins so there was enough slack for Boli to move despite me sitting further back.

"Playing with my hair is cute and all, Prick. But it's fucking freezing. Let's go."

I grumbled.

"The name is Kieran, by the way."

"Didn't ask, did I?"

My temper flared—*Stars*, help me. I took a deep breath in and out, calling upon my years of training to maintain my body in a state of calm. I went to send Boli forward, but before I could even move my feet, Talla gave Boli a nudge with her heels. Boli quickly launched into a canter, and the sudden movement sent Talla's body hard into my chest.

We each quickly adjusted ourselves so that there was a visible gap between her back and my front. And while I was grateful that our bodies were no longer touching, our new positions were *incredibly* uncomfortable. I reminded myself that at least it was only a few miles to Ilken. Just a few miles of discomfort, and then I'd be rid of her and back on my way.

CHAPTER 19 | TALLA

True to his word, the Prick all but pushed me off his horse the second we crossed the Ilken gate. It was simple enough to get a ride from him here—men are just *so* easily manipulated by women in distress. Though, truthfully, I felt so naked without my star, for that split second after he denied me I thought he might actually leave me in the woods. Fear was an emotion that was rare for me. Once I mostly figured out how to use the starmagic in my pendant, I didn't need to be afraid of anything. But standing in the woods, considering the possibility of wandering through Larendi weaponless and magicless, I was starting to wonder if fear would start to feel as familiar as my magic once had.

I luckily landed on my feet during the forced moving dismount. *Thank the Moon* for my new boots because I surely would have slipped if I had still been wearing my old ones. Snagging these was probably the only good thing that came from my trip to Tuul, the rest of the journey had been true and utter shit.

I watched the Guard trot away from me down the firelit main road of Ilken, his broad frame clad in all black moving effortlessly with his horse's steps. The other city dwellers that were moving about from building to building or climbing in and out of carriages made way for him, clearing a path so that he didn't have to slow or weave. I couldn't help but scoff at the sight. He had nothing on him that indicated he was anything but a normal rider, save for the beautiful onyx and gold sword that was slung over his back. And yet, somehow everyone just knew to get out of his way. It was likely due to the pompous *'I'm doing something very important that you couldn't possibly understand'* attitude that radiated off of his broad shoulders.

Kieran. That's what he had said his name was. I sorta liked Royal Prick better, though I suppose both names suited him well.

It wasn't until I noticed a third person staring at me like I might be a monster that had emerged from the woods that I remembered the state of my appearance. I looked down at myself, the firelight from the roadside torches illuminating the dried blood in my hair and on my shirt. I needed new clothes and a bath as soon as possible. A sinking feeling filled my chest—without any money or magic to help me steal it, *how* was I going to pay for them?

I had been a thief from the moment my mother was taken from me at the age of thirteen, and that was ten years ago. But my star had *always* helped me. Especially in Armund's new version of Larendi, sleight of hand was imperative for stealing without consequences. Could I even *be* stealthy without magic?

Another wave of concern flooded me. My thumb rubbed over the thick scar that lay between my breasts, palpable over my shirt now that there was no pendant to block it. If anyone had spotted me while trying to lift something and it came to a fight... how would I heal if I got hurt?

I had taken all of my abilities for granted these years, never thinking I would ever be without them. And while losing my stealth or accuracy or seeking abilities was unsettling, the idea of not being able to heal myself was *terrifying*. It's not like I had a stash of tonic vials in my pockets like Kieran had—

A light went off in my head.

My pocket! I reached deep in my cloak, my fingers frantically searching for what I hoped still remained. Relief shuddered through me as I retrieved a handful of jewels. I looked towards a building on my right that had a small wooden sign hung by two strips of iron chain from a post above the door.

I couldn't make out the name of the establishment from where I was standing, but the last word definitely said *'inn'* and that was good enough for me. I clutched the jewels tightly in my hand and closed my eyes. I wasn't sure who I was without my star, but these jewels would be enough to at least get me a bath and some dinner. And for now, that had to be enough.

The inn reminded me of the last one I had stayed in, except where there had been warmth in the wood tones of the Red Ruby, there was a coolness in this one's murky black stone. The bartender of this inn was also nowhere near as attentive as Ed had been. But despite taking several minutes to acknowledge my presence at the bar, he did accept the majority of the rings from my pocket as payment for a fresh pair of clothes, the laundering of my old ones, and a room with a small tub and meal package.

Later, when he finally got around to handing me a serving of dinner, my heart sank. On the bar top, he sat down a wooden bowl that had steam wafting up from what looked like vegetable stew. An uncomfortable sensation of prickling started at the back of my neck before skidding over my entire body, memories of the previous night consuming me. Already, this sensation was becoming all too familiar. *Fear.* I almost started trying to push into the bartender's intentions out of habit, but before I could, I stopped myself. I didn't want to know what it felt like to reach for my magic and not have it answer me.

I sighed, staring down at the stew. *Surely* this bowl of stew wasn't poisoned, and I needed to eat it before my stomach decided to eat itself. Above me, the bartender let out a big huff as I continued to stare warily at the meal. Only because he seemed inclined to take my bowl away if I continued to frown at it did I swallow any hesitation and dug in.

The entire time that I was eating, I found myself watching one particular table that was positioned against the far wall of the tavern. One at a time, I watched several people approach the very slender faced individual with tightly cut white micro bangs who was sitting there. In front of them was a Flare board and two stacks of tiles, enough for both players.

Between my bites of stew, I noted how each approaching person would sit down and show the white-haired individual their ante. For some, it was coin. For others, it was something else of value—like a metal pocket watch or a knife.

Every time, the mysterious Flare game leader showed nothing in return, and yet they began to play anyway.

The white-haired player must have been quite good based on how often they seemed to collect their challenger's treasures. From my seat at the bar, I did my best to track their movements, looking for any indication that they might be starpowered. I saw no rings or obvious necklaces, and they always kept their hands above board, which was often not the case for individuals using stealth magic. Those observations weren't definitive 'no's, but it did lead me to believe that perhaps this person truly was just good at the game.

Only once did a game end where they didn't collect a treasure from their challenger at the end. Assuming that meant they lost, I waited to see what type of payment would be exchanged. However, instead of handing over a traditional ante, they just leaned over the table and whispered something into the victor's ear.

I had *never* seen payment in the form of a whisper before. Flare was a betting game of goods and greed—what words could possibly hold the same value as gold and silver? Even in Brakken, where items of value were becoming rarer by the day, you didn't sit down to play the game if you didn't have something good to give.

The question silently rang through my ears as I watched a brawny man sit down to play next. After a few minutes of hesitation, my curiosity grew strong enough to get me out of my seat, leaving a few uneaten bits of soggy vegetables at the bottom of my bowl on the bar top.

CHAPTER 20 | TALLA

I arrived at the table after the latest opponent, a short but brawny man, left as a second apparent victor. As he passed by me with a mischievous grin on his face, the white-haired person sat back in their seat, resetting their Flare pieces at their edge of the board. Noticing my presence, they looked up with what I could only describe as an extremely annoyed expression.

"Yes?" Their voice took me by surprise—it was higher pitched than I expected considering their strong jawline.

"I've seen you play several rounds of Flare tonight. When you win, you take your opponent's ante, but when you lose, you give up nothing." It wasn't so much a question as a statement.

They didn't even shift in their seat as I spoke to them, their focus honed in on stacking their tiles up neatly on the Flare board's edge. I cleared my throat to indicate that I was waiting for some sort of response.

"... And?" They didn't meet my gaze as they lazily replied.

"Well how have you convinced people you don't need to pony up your fair share of the game?"

The question was enough to bring their eyes up. Despite the snowy hair, their eyes were dark and murky, the way a pool of water gets just before the height of the summer months, before the colorful algae begins to bloom. They raised one of their fluffy white brows before speaking again.

"*Who* says that I'm not ponying up, *girl*? There's more things to trade than just coin and goods."

My lips hardened into a straight line as I bit my tongue behind them—I did *not* like how they threw that word *'girl'* at me. I thought about telling them that, but I instead opted to push further.

"But Flare is a betting game. How are you betting with words against coin?"

They gave me a quick and aggressive look up and down, their gaze lingering nowhere before they lifted a hand to wave me off.

"It's not for the likes of you, I'm afraid."

I shifted my weight onto one hip and crossed my arms. My lips scrunched into a full scowl now.

"Try me."

They eyed me for a moment, as if considering whether or not I was worth their time. Picking up one of their Flare pieces and flipping it nimbly between their long fingers, they replied.

"Ok, Princess."

Heat pressed against my cheeks as I dug my nails into the skin of my forearm, almost hard enough to draw blood. If I didn't *like* being called *'girl'*, I *hated* being called *'princess'*.

"I have a passkey, one that can get you into the most daring event in Larendi. Entertainment and riches beyond your wildest dreams."

I relaxed my fingers as I let the information settle, and I could feel my expression shift from annoyed to intrigued.

"Are you familiar with the sea cave arenas outside of Havetta?"

My brows shot skyward as my jaw threatened to drop. I had *definitely* heard about the earthen areas that lay hidden in the rocks near Larendi's northern most coastal city. But since the man who had made me aware of them had just recently tried to kill me, I tried not to focus on the reason for my familiarity.

"Yes, I know of them," I nodded as my stomach twisted.

I couldn't stop my mind from flashing back to nights seated next to Jetto and Riggs by the campfire over the years. Particularly on evenings when Riggs had indulged in too much wine, he would share stories from his past. Many of them included the Cave Matches that used to run quarterly during King Trewan's reign and the early days of Armund's.

Riggs delighted in his memories of spectating the blood and brutality under a red-lit ceiling, in a roaring crowd of young and fight-hungry men like himself. The matches didn't sound as fun as he clearly thought they were, but Riggs so rarely talked about his years between living in Mellin and Brakken that Jetto and I would let him ramble on.

I don't even know what happened to his old crew he used to attend them with. All he told us was that they cut ties after selling out for one of the King's offers in exchange for their stars. I could almost feel my freshly healed stab wounds throb—I wondered if Riggs had tried to kill off those comrades, too.

The movement of white eyebrows as the Flare player's face lit with amusement pulled my attention back to the inn.

"Well, I'll be damned. You're more well-traveled than you look."

The tile that they had been fidgeting with traveled overtop and between their fingers, like a coin might in the hand of an illusionist. The practice seemed to be second nature for the white-haired individual because despite them never looking down at their hand, the tile never fell to the table.

"After a decade of drought, the coastal communities have recently re-formed their infamous Cave Matches. Win the round against me, win the passkey needed to enter. I'm one of many set forth to spread the news. But we are only seeking the hungriest minds and the fittest warriors for entry... and after I play twelve rounds, I move on to the next town."

"Why only twelve?" I asked, trying to count how many rounds I had already watched them play. I didn't think it was twelve, but it was probably close.

"There's a fine line between promoting and publicizing, girl. Surely you can imagine that while we want people to participate, we aren't interested in being dismantled before we regain our traction."

I could imagine it. There was no way that fights to the death for sport would be supported under Armund's new version of Larendi, which is probably why they disappeared. The asshole King claimed that by adding starlight back to the night sky, he was also removing the temptation for crime, which would transform Larendi into a safer, and more vibrant land.

What a load of shit that was. It wasn't starmagic making people commit crimes the past thousand years. But now that so few stars were left to maintain our ways of living, engaging in unsanctioned activities was the *only* way to survive.

They paused, looking me up and down once again before trying to peer around me, seemingly looking to see if anyone else was waiting to play.

"But, as I said. My game is not for the likes of *you*."

I opened my mouth to snap back at them, but I quickly shut it. I knew how I looked to others—young and feminine. It was especially true when, like now, my long chestnut hair was visible and there wasn't a knife in my hand. I had started to rely on people underestimating me. It honestly is what made being a thief... well. *Fun*.

The coin, the spoils, those were necessary to live off of. But now that I was starless... *Moon, save me*. How could I be sure that, even if I managed to get my hands on a weapon, I could even hit a barn without my starmagic? I had never tried to throw a dagger without wearing my pendant. I didn't even get my daggers until my mother was killed. They had been hers, after all.

Even if I had still been equipped with my magic, I still wouldn't have been interested in competing in the matches. But, even starless, I was still a thief. I refrained from saying something snarky in reply and risking being fully dismissed by this mysterious passkey holder and instead pressed them about the part I did care about.

"And when you say *riches...*"

"The fortune alone would be enough to make any man as rich as the King. But, that's not all." They leaned in closer to me so that their torso hovered over the Flare set up as they lowered their voice into a hush of daring and excitement. "There is also power... and the right to say that you're the best there is. Now is there anything *richer* than that?"

Well. If I had any doubts on why Riggs spoke so dreamily of these cave matches, I didn't anymore. Sounds like the exact place that would attract a murderous, power hungry, secretly star-powered thief like him. Had he known about the matches? Is *that* why he wanted my stars?

Clarity washed over me in an icy wave. That had to be it—the resurgence of the Cave Matches was the answer that I had been looking for. Those sniveling merchants that gave us a ride to Tuul with their linen clothes... they were *coastal.* They must have tipped Riggs off that the matches were back up and running.

For an ego as large and fragile as Riggs', being called the best fighter in Larendi would be too enticing. It would even be alluring enough to kill your partners and steal their stars, that's

for sure. And with my superstar on top of his other starmagic…
Riggs would win the entire thing.

"I wanna play." I pulled the chair out from the table
and sat down.

I received an incredulous look from the other end of the
table.

"You can play me for the passkey, but you won't be
allowed to enter without a male warrior to fight for you."

"You're joking," I countered, unable to hide my
disbelief.

The white-haired person threw their hands up in
surrender.

"I don't make the regulations. And if you can't accept
that measly one, you don't have a chance of getting past the
gates to the match anyways."

Fuck that. I absolutely hated how some parts of this
world still made such antiquated and backwards assumptions
about what women were able to do. A dagger does the same
amount of damage no matter what kind of hand holds it, as
long as the blade is sharp.

"And what if I showed up at the gates in search of
entering without some '*warrior*'?" I threw up my fingers in air
quotes around that last word.

"The guard posted at the entry wouldn't let you
through."

"Even with the passkey?" I pushed further in protest.

"Even so."

Of course not. Without thinking, I tried to push into
their intentions to see if they were just trying to rile me up.

Impossibly, a spark flew through my body—I felt something warm against my chest. My hand quickly scrambled, reaching up to where my pendant used to lay hidden against my breastbone.

My fingers found nothing but the opened buttons of the shirt that the bartender had just sold me. And then, as quickly as it had appeared, the warmth vanished. I wondered how long I would be feeling the phantom sensations of starmagic—how long was enough to heal the mark it so clearly left in my brain?

Even if what this person was saying was ridiculous, it didn't mean that it wasn't likely to be true. If there was anywhere that was untouched by a modern sense of equality, it would be those underground arenas... and if I wanted a shot at finding Riggs, at retrieving my star and getting revenge, I was not only going to need to find some *'warrior,'* but I was also going to need to play their game.

I reached into my pocket and grabbed the last remaining ring that was floating around in the fabric. I pulled it out with my fingers gripping into the gold band. The reddish orange stone was small, but it was cut nicely and sparkled like flames in the dark.

I had watched Jetto play enough over the years that I knew my way around a Flare board. However, since he rarely played fairly, neither did I. Without the help of my star, without my added stealth and slight of hand, was I good enough to win?

I spent a few moments looking at the ring, moving it around my palm before I closed my hand around it tightly. I *had* to be good enough. Something in me knew that Riggs was going to be at the Cave Matches. He had to be—without my star tracking abilities, it would be impossible to find him otherwise.

That annoying prickling sensation of fear started to creep back along my neck as I worked up the courage to hand my ring over. I had nothing but this damn ring. Small as it was, this ring was enough to buy me a few more meals, perhaps another few nights at this inn. Losing it would be risky... but now everything without my star felt like a risk.

The sound of nails tapping on the flare board brought me back to the moment. I opened my hand again, admiring the ring's reddish orange stone one last time in case I lost. The color reminded me of Jetto's beard, and I could almost hear him in my head, egging me on.

Come on, Bossa. You can take 'em.

I smiled, his voice fading back into the bar chatter. I leaned forward, grabbing a stack of tiles from the pile in the center of the board, leaving the ring in its place.

"There's my ante. Let's deal."

◊

As I flipped over the last tile on the board, my lips curled into a triumphant smile. I had won, which meant not only did I get to keep my last gemstone ring, but I also got the passkey to enter the Cave Matches. *Take that,* asshole.

My white-haired competitor grumbled and slid back in their chair, donning their now familiar annoyed expression.

Hopefully, they had learned something about judging someone's abilities by the way they looked.

True to their word, after a few seconds they leaned forward to share the treasure that I had earned—the passkey. I brought my face close enough to hear them over the loud bar patrons. In a hushed voice, I was given both a passkey and the description of a symbol that was carved into a rock formation above the entrance to the hidden arena.

As I leaned back, I repeated the phrase in my head. It was an odd combination of words that felt more like a poem than a passkey... and an incomplete, kind of bad one at that. The symbol was simple enough to remember—it sounded just like the four points of a star without the connecting lines. Satisfied that I had memorized my prize, and with the ring still in my possession, I thought that I should treat myself to another drink.

I pushed my chair back to stand up and return to the bar, but it stopped moving before I could get to my feet. A man with a long gray mustache stood directly behind me, impatiently tapping his foot. *Clearly*, he wanted a chance to play before this passkey holder moved on. Didn't he realize he needed to get out of my way before he could do so?

The high pitch voice of my competitor then regained my attention as I was able to push past the man.

"Find the symbol, find the gates. There will be someone there to share your passkey with, but without a warrior to fight, *you* won't be permitted to enter. Choose wisely."

"Ya. I got it," I snapped, moving out of the way to let the eager man sit down.

My eyes lingered a bit as he pulled out his ante—a shiny gold pocket watch. I imagined how if Jetto were here, he would have found a way to slip that watch on while the two were busy flipping their tiles.

The white-haired player shot me an icy warning glare, and I simply bowed my head and took my leave. I didn't have time to daydream about lifting something as simple as a watch right now... I needed to focus all of my efforts on finding something else. Something that was, unfortunately, necessary for me to get into the Cave Matches. I needed a warrior.

I surveyed the bar, sizing up anyone I could get eyes on. I had never been to Ilken before. I didn't even know of anyone from here. Perhaps I could find someone near Havetta. Or, I could come across someone along the way who was already en route to the matches.

It would be best to find someone around here, though, who didn't have the passkey themselves. After all, those words were my only bargaining power to help even make the trip to Havetta. It was probably a week and a half's journey, and that's if you were lucky enough to travel on horseback. My one gold ring definitely wasn't going to be able to take me that far.

I turned my attention back to the gray-haired man that was currently playing. Maybe he would lose, then I could offer my knowledge in exchange for travel and entry? He was meticulously pondering each of the tiles, still having not flipped a single one despite playing for several minutes. I sighed. *No.* That level of indecision might cause me to either leave him or kill him on the trek there, and then I would be back at square one.

I needed someone strong and willful, someone who had the means to help me get to Havetta, and fast. Someone who I didn't really care if they lived or died once we entered those caves. Someone who I could convince that entering the matches, despite their reputation, was a good idea.

As if the Moon herself heard me, a cool breeze rustled the free strands of my braid along the side of my face. I felt pulled to turn my head, looking for the person that caused the unpleasant temperature change. My eyes widened, taking in every warrior-like inch of the darkly clad man that was making his way to a small corner table.

He was absolutely perfect.

CHAPTER 21 | KIERAN

"How many times do I have to tell you *'no'* before you get it through your head, *thief*?" I set down my mug and stared at Talla, who was now sitting across from me.

All I had wanted when I entered the bar was a quick drink before bed. Just a sip of something to help take the edge off of a long day of storming through the cold and to forget a certain pair of green eyes. The stable hand of the place that I had boarded Boli told me that there were only two bars in Ilken. And with just my luck, I had walked into the one where *she* had decided to get a drink as well.

Talla had made no hesitation to take a seat at my table and share her proposition for the two of us to travel to Havetta together in search of some revamped version of the outlawed cave matches. I actually wasn't paying the *closest* attention to her as she was outlining her plan. I was too distracted by how much *better* she looked since I left her. It had only been about an hour, but she looked like she had been healing for weeks.

Her full cheeks were rosy, now flush with life. She wore all new clothes that were clean and bloodless. Her cloak was missing, and she wore a faded gray shirt that buttoned down the front of her. Since the piece swallowed her frame, she had rolled the sleeves up several times leaving a sizable cuff resting just below her elbow. This had exposed her forearms which were covered in a myriad of small silver blue scars. The bar was dimly lit, but I swear they almost sparkled against her toffee skin.

"… so, I know that Havetta has what we both are looking for," she continued with such conviction, bringing my attention back to her and her plan. I may not have memorized every detail, but I caught that the gist revolved around finding that ego-charged, hook-nosed thief, Riggs, that I had left chained to a cart in the Middle Forests.

I took a long sip of my drink. While the warmth and lightening sensation that it gave me was familiar, the taste was foreign. The brew here was more earthy with a heavier influence of spices than the drinks in Mellin.

The fact that she had suggested the stars would be in Havetta was the only reason I was still sharing a table with her. After I had settled Boli in at the stables, I had taken some time to examine my map. There was really only one main direction that I could sense the pull of the stars, and it was northeast. By how weak the feeling was, they likely were at least a few days ride away, maybe more.

I had decided on my own that I would follow the road that went along the front range of the mountains and eventually ended in the coastal city of Havetta. It seemed too coincidental that this thief was now begging me to go in that very direction. I had to at least pretend to hear her out—what else was I doing, anyways? It was too dangerous to travel at night, even with the help of both starlight and moonlight.

"Tell me again why you are so eager to find a man who tried to kill you?" I asked, trying not to sound more interested than I actually was.

I didn't really care why she wanted to travel across Larendi. But of all of the details that I caught, that was the bit that had made the least sense to me.

It seemed like a lot of effort to go through *just* for revenge. But, I suppose many of the criminals rotting in the prisons at that very moment had done more for less... and Talla *was* a Brakkish rebel like the worst of them.

She rolled her eyes at me, and as she let out a frustrated sigh, I wondered if a day went by that Talla didn't roll her eyes at someone.

"I told you, *Guard*," her tone indicating her level of annoyance.

Even though she knew my name, it didn't bother me that she didn't use it. *'Guard'* was better than the endearing *'Prick'* that she had been using earlier... though both names coming out of her mouth had sounded equally as condescending.

"He didn't just try to kill *me*, he *actually* killed my friend. He can't just get away with that. That's not how things work on *this* side of the river. He deserves to die."

I wanted to correct her and let her know that, actually, *many* people living north of the Linvel knew how to suppress the savage desires that she was planning to act on. Not only that, but also that it was exactly that type of rash and merciless attitude that landed many of her peers in the prisons below the castle. But before I could get a word out, she adjusted her braid to fall behind her back, exposing the bit of chest that was visible beneath the unbuttoned top of her shirt.

She leaned into a heavy sigh, like she was contemplating something else but was holding back. I set my mug down, watching her tenderly bite her bottom lip as she leaned forward to speak again.

"He also... stole something," she started, her voice as vulnerable as it had sounded when she had pleaded to me in the woods. "Something very important to me. And I want it back."

I suppressed the urge to shake my head in disapproval of her or even to point out the irony in her sentiment. This thief wasn't vulnerable, she was upset—upset that she had been robbed by someone better at her game than her. I should have guessed that was really what it had been about. *Someone* was missing their access to magic.

"So let me get this straight," I started, leaning back in my own chair and crossing my arms against my chest, making sure that my starcuffed wrist was tucked closer to my body. "You want *me* to lead you to Riggs, not only to commit a murder, but more importantly to regain your ability to wield magic on your own?"

Her eyes widened at my drop of the word *'magic'* in such a public setting. There was no point in hiding the fact that I knew she used to have a star, and now she didn't. She clearly knew that I was able to track them, though by the way she had been fishing about my methods earlier, she didn't know the details. The gentle buzzing from the cuff was a constant reminder of the power that magic lent its wearer—if she knew what was mere inches away from her, how long until she tried to take it for herself?

I continued on, focusing again on Talla rather than the magic.

"You do understand that I am a member of the King's Guard, right? With the power to arrest you not only for the crimes you have committed, but the ones you're *planning* on committing?"

She scrunched her face a bit in confusion, like she didn't see anything relevant about what I was saying. I brought my non-starcuffed arm up, rubbing the bridge of my nose with my fingers. I knew that rebels were impossible to reason with, and it seemed like Talla was no different.

"So you clearly don't care about that. What is it, then? Are you hoping that you can get another chance to slice my balls off before you run to rob and pillage the continent with ease?"

Her expression softened as she cocked her head to the side for a moment, contemplating. I instinctively grabbed at the sword on my hip under the table, ready to draw in case I had inadvertently inspired her to try and complete her attack from a few days earlier.

"While that *is* a tempting offer, no. That wasn't my plan. I don't want to take the chance of heading all the way out there just for him to have changed direction."

My grip on my sword relaxed as I gave her an eye roll of my own.

"Well *sure*. Why waste time hunting when there are crimes to commit!"

She shot me a foul and icy look that felt too familiar for how little I knew her.

"Do you have a family, Kieran? Are you close?"

I nodded affirmatively, slightly taken aback by her use of my name along with the change in subject. My acknowledgement wasn't fully a lie, I *did* have a family. It's not like I was about to go into the details of the state of my relationship with my sister with someone like *her*.

"Well, my condolences to them, because you're an *ass*. But my only family risked everything for me to have what he took from me. And whether or not you want to believe it, I have been using it to help the people in my town survive after your '*precious King*'s' dream left them to starve. And *then* Riggs stole it from me after eliminating the closest thing to family I have been able to find since I lost mine."

I willed my face to stay neutral as a tiny pang of guilt bounced in the bottom of my stomach. Misguided rebel or not, I found myself feeling a bit sorry for her, despite her having just called me an ass.

She continued on, her voice quieting down a bit.

"So. No. I don't want to waste time because I can't afford to waste time. Not on my own like this."

I couldn't look away from her as her words sank in. I knew that sentiment all too well, and the familiarity of it made me think that perhaps this thief and I understood each other more than I thought.

I shook my head—I had nothing in common with this girl, and as enticing as her emerald stare was, it was getting late. I needed to get back to my room and sleep before continuing on the hunt at dawn. If the stars *were* heading to Havetta like I suspected, it should take me about a week to get there. It would be another to return back to the castle, and that's *if* I pushed Boli to the max in cooperative weather.

I took the last sip from my mug, cherishing the potent bits of spices that had settled to the bottom. I allowed myself one last lingering glance at the girl in front of me, fully knowing that it would be the last time that I saw her, before I set my mug back on the table.

"Well, thief. That sounds like an epic quest of self-righteousness to take some unsuspecting man on. But as for me, I travel alone."

And that was that. As she looked at me with pure disbelief, I forced my attention elsewhere. I was not going to fall for her silver lined doe eyes this time. I had already helped her enough.

Stars. I saved her life, didn't I? I didn't owe her anything else. With no hesitation, I stood up and turned towards the door, walking out of the inn without looking back.

◊

I rose before the sun the next morning, which was getting easier to do now that the days were shortening rapidly. I strapped on my golden-hilted sword and canvas bag containing the recovered star and silver before heading down the stairs. I forced my feet to step lightly, treading carefully so as to not wake the other guests as I passed their rooms. When I made it to the ground floor, I pushed through a tiny wooden door and was welcomed by a light breeze. The air was much milder than the harsh and icy winds that blew yesterday, and I filled my lungs deeply with it, savoring the change.

All of the stars had faded in the sky above, signaling that dawn had almost arrived even though the moon still shined brightly. The remaining bits of moonlight illuminated the sleepy streets of Ilken as I navigated my way towards the stables. By the time the first pink light of day peeked out over the horizon, my feet were shuffling in the snow, my sword swinging through the air as I completed my reps.

When out on starhunts, I had to make time to train on my own. Though I had no starpowered guards to spar against, keeping my muscles moving was the next best thing for keeping my skills sharp. My reps became a meditative practice; first slashing my sword up, then down, then shifting my feet to the right before turning, switching my blade from one hand to another and striking upwards again. Finally, I would drop to the ground, rolling before I popped up just to repeat the exact sequence on the other side.

My body and blade moved seamlessly together until sweat finally started to break on my brow. After what must have been the thirtieth rep that morning, I sheathed my sword and took a deep and centering breath before aiming my steps at the stable door to retrieve Boli.

Ilken's rentable stables were small—just a few stalls available in a wooden barn on the edge of town. The front door creaked loudly as I slid it open on its rusting wheels. Morning light filtered in behind me, barely illuminating the narrow dirt aisle between the two rows of stalls. The stables had been empty last night save for Boli, and at the end of the barn, I could see a lone horse's head peeking over a stall's edge. Her head was twisted to the side, almost as if she was looking at something in the shadows behind her.

"Good morning, Boli. Let's get going, shall we?"

Expecting a snort or whinny in return as a greeting, I gave her a smile, but it faded quickly as I was met with silence.

No, not exactly silence. I could just make out a small, ruffling sound towards the back of the barn. My instincts flared, and with my hand on my sword I took a few careful steps. In the midst of the shadows, my eyes deciphered the dark outline of a hooded figure. The sound of metal whirring against leather as I pulled out my blade sent the birds that had been asleep in the rafters soaring through the door behind me.

My heart raced as I took a few bounding steps forward. I was prepared to take down whoever was here attempting to take Boli from me. Even as I closed the gap, the hooded figure remained still.

The closer I got, the more of them came into view. My eyes registered a pair of leather boots poking out the bottom of a long cloak. Then, a hand, held out palm up and covered with small blueish-silver scars that glowed in the darkness. Finally, a long and wild braid that was the same shade as my favorite mare.

I lowered my sword and let out a long and frustrated breath as I realized who the figure was.

"If you're here to steal Boli, your opportunity just ended."

Talla looked up at me from under her hood, green eyes blazing in the darkness. Her dark brows were raised as a small smirk found its way to her mouth. Boli's muzzle was furiously nibbling at her flattened hand, bits of what must be grain stuck to her lips.

"Relax, Guard. I'm just saying good morning to my friend here."

Boli finally decided to give me her attention, her brown eyes wide with delight as she let out a snort of approval.

I looked between the two of them, almost lost for words.

"I told you that I travel alone." It was all I could get out, my body reeling from the whiplash of feeling threatened then annoyed.

"Yes, I remember you saying that. But the more I got to thinking, I realized that wasn't entirely true." Talla rubbed her now empty hand along the side of her cloak before giving Boli an endearing pet on her cheek. "You travel with *her*. So, I figured if I could get her on board, then you would have to let me come along."

I stood watching the girl, half taken aback by her nerve, but also half impressed. I stormed past her, heading to the back wall of the barn that held Boli's tack and saddle bags.

"You're not riding with us." My voice was short as I grabbed them off of the hook and made my way into Boli's stall.

I started dressing her, fastening the leather pieces along her face and belly, making sure not to give Talla even the slightest glance as I did so.

"Well, I'd take my own horse, but it looks like this stable is fresh out," Talla said, walking up and down the barn aisle as I worked.

The only reason I knew she was moving was the change in the sound of her voice. Her steps were silent, just as they had been in the forest. She apparently was skilled at moving quietly through the shadows, which was all the more reason why I didn't want this particular rebel as a travel companion.

"Besides," she continued, her tone now *too* confident, "Boli seems to like me."

Boli snorted again with approval, and I shot the mare a quick glare. She just swished her tail from side to side, not caring in the slightest. *Figures.*

There was no point in continuing to argue with Talla about the matter as it was time for Boli and I to get going. As soon as I was done attaching my last bag to the saddle, I gathered her reins to lead her out of the stall. But when I took my steps forward, Boli didn't move. Her hooves were planted in her stall, her head pulling back against every attempt I made to bring her with me.

I gritted my teeth as I pulled harder.

"Boli. Let's. Go." Each word came out as its own sentence with each tug on the leather.

She forcefully threw her head up in protest, signaling that I could keep pulling at her, but she wasn't going *anywhere*. I closed my eyes, my hand finding its way to my temple. I reminded myself of the reasons I liked this horse—her fearlessness, her strength, her speed—and to get those things, I remembered that I also had to deal with her sporadic displays of stubbornness.

Sensing the movement, I opened my eyes and watched Talla take a few steps forward, motioning for Boli to follow.

Stars, help me. The mare moved.

Talla turned to me, her eyes looking particularly green this morning.

"So, Kieran. Do you really travel alone? Or would you like some company?"

We locked eyes. Everything in my brain was telling me to leave this girl behind. She was a thief and a rebel. She was someone who actively seeks out starmagic to use for herself instead of letting all of Larendi benefit from the starlight.

She might not seem like a threat now, standing before me with no weapons or magic... but eventually, when we found the stars, she could be. She would try to take them from me. She would fail, but did I really want to deal with her when she did? The King had made it very clear that people like her were threats to the Kingdom and to the dream of reuniting the night sky.

At all costs.

But as she stood there before me, some foreign force pulled at me, telling me to keep her close. If the stars *were* with Riggs, and he was at these cave matches, I would in fact need the passkey that she claimed she had. I doubted that anyone trying to revive the outlawed matches would give a shit that I was a member of the King's Guard who was demanding entry on behalf of the King.

Taking her with me based just on that very large *'what if'* was a risk. But she was just one thief. Even if she somehow gained back access to starmagic, it wouldn't be like last time. I wouldn't underestimate her. I would be ready for her to try to take them from me. And when that inevitably happened, I wouldn't fail at keeping all of the stars.

The sun was fully up now, and every minute standing there in the barn was a minute closer to the Solstice. I could feel the stars on the move, their pull weakening ever so slightly each time I checked in with the sensations on my wrist. Still moving East, heading closer and closer to Havetta.

I let the attractive force win, at least for now, ultimately deciding that some risks are necessary to do what is right. Besides, if Boli wasn't going to move without her, fighting would only waste more time.

"I'm not giving you a weapon. And you have to promise that you won't do *anything* to slow us down." I fidgeted with the ends of my sleeves, making sure the end buttons were fastened tightly around my wrists.

Was I really bargaining with a criminal?

Talla nodded.

"Thieves don't make promises, but how about..." she reached into her cloak pocket and pulled something out. It was a gold ring, dainty, with a small but sparkling fire-like stone. "Consider this a sign of my good faith. This is all I have left, and it should cover any necessities of mine for the trip. *And* I won't lift anything off of anyone while we travel together."

I *highly* doubted that would be true—in my experience, once a thief, always a thief. But still, I grabbed the ring she held in her hand and pocketed it. I pulled my mask up over my face and made room for Talla to mount Boli while I was still holding on to her. She quickly found her way atop the saddle, sitting near the front of the seat and leaving me room to slide behind her. With my foot in the stirrup, I pulled myself up, settling in and readjusting my reins to accommodate the two of us.

I let out a sigh, willing my brain and body to focus on the pull of the stars and not the feel of her warm body in front me. Once we were both settled, Boli headed out of the barn towards the road on her own accord. I steered her towards the Ilken gates, grateful to be on our way again. And though my sense of relief prevailed, the fact that I had somehow managed to secure the company of a starthief for my final starhunt gnawed at my insides as it settled in my mind.

CHAPTER 22 | TALLA

Thank the Moon that I'm good with animals, because I don't think there was anything that I could have said to change Kieran's mind. But Boli, *Moon, bless her*, made it impossible to leave me behind. I thought men were uniquely easy to manipulate, but it turns out that horses like treats as much as they do.

Traveling with Kieran, though necessary if I wanted to be *sure* that I was heading towards Riggs, wasn't ideal. It was very different being his extra passenger all day than it had been for the hour ride between the woods and Ilken. In order to reduce contact between our bodies, I had to sit slightly perched between him and the pommel of the saddle. I held on to Boli's mane while Kieran curved his arms awkwardly around me to control the reins.

After a few hours, I desperately wanted to lean back and rest, but if I slouched even just a little, I could feel his broad chest against my shoulders and his hips moving lightly with each thunderous stride. I would have had to lean my body fully into his motions to prevent uncomfortable friction between his tunic and my cloak, and there was no way *that* was happening. Leaning forward, I did manage to keep an eye on the light blue glow that was visible on his wrist whenever we passed through a shadow. I thought that I had noticed it last night at the bar, but I had assumed that it had just been a trick of the light. I mean, Armund wouldn't trust a simple Guard with one of his stolen stars, would he?

I found it hard to imagine that the King would let any star out of his sight once he got his selfish hands on it, save for the few he used during his performative Starcasts. But in the barn this morning there was no mistaking it. Kieran wore an encased star on his wrist, the magic surely pulled him towards the stars just as mine had for me. Maybe he wasn't just a simple King's Guard, then. Perhaps there was more to Kieran, and his ability to fight, than I had thought.

Regardless, his wrist was a clever placement for a star. By the way that he had drawn both my dagger and his sword with his right hand in our earlier confrontations, it was safe to assume it was his dominant side. Without any enhanced accuracy or stealth from starmagic to help me out, the likelihood of being able to snag that cuff was damned near impossible.

During the day, Kieran and I rode in silence. After all, what were we supposed to talk about? Neither of us wanted each other's company. I needed him to get me to Havetta so that I could use him as my *'warrior'* to gain entrance into the cave matches. There, I would find Riggs, *end* him, and take back my star. Kieran needed me around because I had cleverly woo'd his horse, his apparent weakness, into requiring my company. Our current companionship was purely strategic, so there was no need to waste words on such a fleeting arrangement.

In the silence, Boli charged down the road with impressive speed considering the fact that she was carrying two of us. We passed through woods and over hills, loud wind buffeting our faces and filling our ears as the mountains drew nearer. Though I myself had never explored the northeastern quarter of Larendi, my mother had told me stories from her own adventures. She described the eastern edge of the Orun Mountains as a special place, filled with what she called transient energy.

She said a similar strange force existed where the sea met the land, in the sandy shores that are reachable if you head south from Havetta. Of course, children don't understand what words like *transient* mean. Before she died, I had probably asked her a hundred times to try to explain it to me. The best explanation that I was able to get was that in some areas, the land changed so quickly, like from dirt to rock in the mountains or from water to sand in the beaches, that you could *feel*, and not just see, the difference in the landscape as you crossed over their barriers.

She was very into that stuff, the energies of the land and the hidden magics of the world. I think that's why she was willing to give her life for me to keep our superstar—to her, having such access to magic was the most incredible gift. Now that the space where the pendant used to lay on my chest was without it, I couldn't help but think that she was right.

To pass the time, when I wasn't plotting how I was going to get my revenge on Riggs without any starmagic, I stared in awe at my increasing view of the Orun Mountains. The range was filled with tall and snowy peaks that looked like they were piercing the daylight; the blue of the sky and the white of the snow all but faded together whenever clouds passed by. I couldn't help but wonder if there was the same sort of *transient* energy up at the tops of the mountains, where the land and the sky met, as well. Surely there had to be some feeling of magic at the summits. How could there not be some mysterious magic so close to where so many stars now lived?

We barely took breaks, and if we did it was only to refuel or relieve our bodies. During those stops Kieran tried not to meet my eyes, even as he reluctantly threw scraps of dried meat and fruit my way. I was grateful for the food, though I would never admit it—the road across the mountains was not very fruitful for scavenging or hunting. I had also given him my only means of buying provisions to secure my place in his company.

The bits of food, even dried, tasted *rich*. After my first bite, I couldn't help but curse Armund under my breath. Brakken used to have food this flavorful—used to be *known* for it. No one in Brakken cared that the King would ship us boxes of 'quality' goods if we decided to return the stars willingly—we wanted to be able to grow it on our own.

When we weren't eating, Kieran focused all of his attention either on his map or on Boli. I stayed close to the two of them on the off chance that he decided to try to give me the slip while I was crouched behind some rock or bush. As the day went on, I found myself unexpectedly entertained by the Guard and the mare's dynamic.

Often, the two appeared deep in conversation together—though since Boli can't actually talk, the actual words shared were one sided. Sometimes the exchange would even get *heated*. Kieran and Boli seemed to argue often, such as when Boli wasn't drinking water quickly enough or Kieran didn't tie her reins up the *right* way for her to graze comfortably.

But their marital-spat-like interactions weren't even the most surprising part. Despite apparently always being on the losing side of their battles, Kieran never took action against the horse beyond raising his voice. And even then, he *barely* did so. The loudest and sharpest his words ever got were during their arguments about me.

It wasn't until Kieran's fifth failed attempt to move her more than five steps away from me that he finally resigned, putting his hands up in the air in defeat. Royal Guards were simply not known for their self-control or willingness to step aside. Another Guard might have just abandoned the horse altogether in search of a more obedient steed. Was Boli a horse of particular value to the King and that's why he remained so patient with her? Or was it something else?

Only when the last light of the day was fading away did we stop riding. There was a small roadside inn that was built just a few paces off of the road. The building was simple and unassuming, and though it clearly had no bar, or likely even running water, my heart skipped at the prospect of lying down. *Moon, save me*, how my body ached. My thighs were burning from leaning forward for almost the entirety of the day, unwilling to sit back and risk the contact with Kieran. I mentioned nothing of my discomfort to Kieran, though, unwilling to share even a shred of my vulnerability.

After Boli halted just outside the small inn's door, Kieran dismounted in a huff. I watched his broad frame stretch then glide across the ground, never letting go of Boli's reins even as he walked through the door. He didn't trust me—which was fair.

But even though there was a time a few days ago that I would have delighted in stealing the Guard's horse, that desire had passed. Boli might get me to Havetta, but without Kieran, I wouldn't be able to enter the matches. Plus, he had the map, and the weapons. Without my star enhancing my abilities and leading the way, I would just be a lost fool on horseback without him.

He used his first words to me since early that morning to begrudgingly let me know that he booked us each a room. Later that evening as I laid in the tiny room upon the small, yet soft, wood framed bed, memories of Jetto, his body bloody and lifeless in my arms, haunted me. As shadows danced around my body, fear pricked the back of my neck.

Alone and afraid, I found no comfort or rest in the small bed. How had I never realized how truly vulnerable a person is while sleeping? Anyone who wanted to harm me could bust through the shaky wooden door. And there would be absolutely nothing I could do about it.

The next morning, just before dawn had broken, Kieran found me and Boli snuggled up in the pile of sawdust that laid at the bottom of her stall. I met his eyes defiantly, waiting for him to sling some sort of insult my way for choosing to sleep in a barn over the room that he had paid for. He simply raised a dark brow at me before reaching for Boli's saddle on the rack by her door.

I couldn't tell if the expression had been one of surprise or judgement, but he didn't try to book me a room the next night or any of the nights after. He even left Boli's side a few times during our breaks or when he went into the inns to secure his own lodgings. I guess he finally realized that if I was going to take his horse and bolt, I would have done it by now.

CHAPTER 23 | TALLA

The trees along the Orun Mountains were sparser than in the forests I had come across on my own travels. Thieving never led me too far from Brakken, since most of the time me and my crew—when I *had* a crew, had to travel on foot. The pointy leaves were clustered in clumps high up on branches, leaving their skinny trunks with peeling bark bare. While snow covered the peaks within the range, the thin limbs dropped any snowfall to the ground to melt in the midday sun. Large boulders jutted out from the ground, and though I appreciated the rugged feel of the landscape, it did cause a problem—ice.

The uneven and exposed rock surfaces funneled the melting snow into pools that froze in patches along the road. Navigating around them slowed our pace dramatically. I couldn't hide my smirk each time Kieran huffed in frustration behind me as he weaved the mare back and forth to prevent her from slipping. Despite my amusement, I too was annoyed—I wanted to get to Havetta as fast as possible like he did. But I couldn't help that there was something rewarding knowing that this Royal Guard wasn't getting exactly what he wanted.

While on one particularly glazed section of the road, Kieran was forced to quickly pull Boli back to nearly a walk. The sudden shift in speed was enough to make my shaky legs buckle, sending my back straight into Kieran's chest. After three days of supporting all of my weight leaning forward, I couldn't deny the relief it was to sit in the saddle properly.

Kieran shifted his own seat behind me, and though I could feel his hips moving with each step, the contact was manageable. Once the ground leveled out a bit more, reducing the icy patches and therefore allowing Boli to move faster, I didn't reclaim my perched position... even when the ache in my legs vanished.

It was after midday when the three of us passed through a natural archway formed by a bent over tree that I felt a sudden and unexplainable pulse of energy through my body. Boli and Kieran must have felt it too, because they both simultaneously reacted, their bodies tensing both behind and under me. My mother's words filled my head. *Transient energy*. Was that what we had just felt?

I noticed that just ahead the road split into two. I glanced down at Kieran's hands as they held the reins—by the way that he was pulling slightly to the side, he was planning on taking the road to the right. I wasn't sure why, but I was suddenly consumed with the desire to go to the left.

"Hold on a second." I said, using my sit bones to put pressure into the saddle, the motion signaling to Boli to slow down.

"What are you doing?" he protested.

It was odd hearing his voice directed at me instead of the horse after riding in mostly silence the last few days. His tone with Boli had much less of the *'fuck you'* vibe that he was giving me, but I ignored it to answer him.

"I think we should go left," I said as Boli then slowed to a halt.

"The main road continues right." His words were deep and commanding, which made them all the easier to ignore.

Before he had even finished his sentence, I had already swung my leg over the top of Boli's neck to dismount. With my feet planted on the ground, I breathed in the mountain air—it felt *good* to stand here.

"What *are* you doing?" Kieran's voice was a little more desperate this time as he looked down on me, his golden eyes glowing against the darkness of his features and mask.

"What's it look like I'm doing?" I took a few steps down the path, marveling at the feeling that was working its way up my legs and into my chest.

The humming was both foreign and familiar, giving me the strangest sense that I had been here before, even though I hadn't. If this *was* the transient energy that my mother had experienced, I now knew why it was difficult for her to explain it to me. Kieran cleared his throat.

"Didn't you agree that you weren't going to do anything to slow us down?"

I rolled my eyes before shouting my response over my shoulder, not letting him distract me from the path that was pulling me ahead.

"Didn't you hear me when I said that thieves don't make promises? Besides, I'm sure Boli wants to come."

The trees echoed with the sound of a hearty whinny. I turned completely around to see that Boli was, sure enough, pulling Kieran to the left to follow me. Kieran kept the tension tight against her reins for a bit before letting out an exasperated sigh.

"Stars, help me with the two of you. I swear."

I winked at Boli and gave a silent prayer of thanks to the Moon for granting me such a pull over the mare before I continued to walk.

The tree limbs lining the path squeezed at the space around me, quickly becoming almost too narrow to navigate. I heard a thud on the ground, signaling that Kieran had dismounted to lead Boli on foot. The sound of their steps soon became muffled by an increasing whizzing sound, the same that water makes when it escapes the kettle after being boiled. The air grew damper and milder around us as I followed the dirt trail towards whatever hidden energy was lurking in this part of the land.

The path ended at a bank before a large glittering pond with water tinted a soft bluish green. My eyes widened as I stepped closer, realizing that I could see straight through the clear water and down to the rocky bottom. Though the wind couldn't reach it through the dense tree cover, the surface seemed to dance. Steam wafted up from the water, and I understood that the mist must have been the cause of the whizzing.

I walked right up to the edge to stare at the mesmerizing water. I crouched down and held my hand above the surface for a moment before instinctively dipping in my fingers. It was warm, the sensation sent waves of comfort across my body. If I had thought that stepping on the path felt good, the contact with the water had felt even *better*. I needed more.

An idea popped into my head as I quickly submerged my hand under the surface. Without hesitation, I started stripping my clothes, tossing them into a pile on the bank. I guess Kieran had been watching me, because the second that I pulled my shirt over my head, I heard him swear under his breath.

I didn't care that I stood there naked in front of him— *all* I wanted was to dive into the pond, to soak in the mysterious comfort. Wading into the water, I dismantled my braid, letting my long curls hang down my back. The deeper that I went, the more I could feel my skin sing. When the water was deep enough that my toes could barely touch the smooth rocks at the bottom, I closed my eyes. I took a deep breath and sank my entire body into it.

I let the warmth consume me, slowing my heart rate into a rhythm of ultimate relaxation. The water cradled me as I floated beneath the surface. I could have been home in Brakken, lounging in my own tub surrounded by my mother's herbal salves and soaps. I could almost smell them around me as I exhaled some of my breath through my nose. After two nights of sleeping in a stall, and almost a week since I had taken a decent bath of my own, this moment floating in the warm water was nothing short of bliss.

I could have stayed under the surface forever if my lungs hadn't been screaming in protest, begging me to take a breath of air. With a push of my feet against the bottom, I popped up out of the water and inhaled. Comforting steam filled my chest.

I moved my wet hair around the front of my body to cover my breasts and turned to see Kieran sitting on the bank. His mask was pulled down to rest along his neck. His golden eyes were focused, apparently fixed on something beyond me. I turned my head to see what could be drawing his attention so intently. But when my eyes saw nothing save for the waters of the pond, I realized that his steadfast gaze had, in fact, been on me.

It should have bothered me, seeing the way he looked at me as I stood there. I glanced down, checking to see if I was still completely covered. I was—my thick chestnut hair and the rippling water perfectly cloaked my breasts and midsection. When I looked back at him, he was still looking, but in a softer way than I had ever seen him look at me before.

It was the first time that it even crossed my mind that Kieran was not just a member of the King's Guard, but also a *man*. A man with his own wants and needs and dreams, just like everyone else. He might have chosen a shit cause to devote his life to, but he was at least giving his all to it.

In the midst of the mist, I think I caught him *smiling*. Actually smiling, and not one of those half-assed smirk-smiles he would make every now and then. I hated that the sight made me want to smile back at him.

The moment was over quickly as he seemingly remembered who exactly he was looking at and turned his attention away from me and back towards the main road. My cheeks flushed from the heat of the steam as I made my way towards the water's edge.

Boli, who had been standing dutifully next to Kieran, suddenly hopped down the bank and into the shallow edge of the pond. With all four hooves submerged, she picked up her front one and pawed at the surface. The result was a large, steaming bluegreen splash that completely drenched Kieran's upper body.

"Boli!!!" He exclaimed as he jumped out of the way.

I tried to hold back my laughter as he stood there, arms out in surprise. His dark curls sent drips down the front of his face, and a glint of gold and starlight caught my eye as he wiped the excess water away. I watched him flip his head over, shaking more of the pond water off.

As Boli continued to play, he carefully reached for her with his starcuffed arm stretched out through the rising steam. His forearm muscles flexed as he grabbed ahold of her mane, effortlessly guiding her back up the bank while avoiding any further splashes. Boli snorted and shook her entire body, making sure to get as much of her discarded water onto Kieran as possible. A smile erupted on my face.

I was getting ready to call out to Kieran through my laughter, but before I could, I spotted something along the bank. I blinked a few times, wondering if the steam was distorting my vision, but each time I looked, what I thought I saw remained. I waded over to examine a small plant with viny stems that was growing just next to my pile of clothes.

Adrenaline soared through me as I distinguished the bunches of little gray-green leaves growing amidst the other vegetation. I reached out and grabbed a chunk, taking extra care not to bring it into the warm water lest the entire pond be turned into a poisonous and lethal diffuser. *Grayweed*.

I nervously looked up, wondering if Kieran had seen me pluck the rare stems. To my relief, his back was to me, fully focused on retrieving something from one of the saddle bags. I quickly shoved the bit of grayweed into one of the exposed pockets of my cloak before pulling myself out and shaking myself dry. *How in the Moon* I was able to spot it amongst the other plants, I didn't know, but I was grateful. I might not have a weapon at my disposal, but without magic, grayweed honestly might be my preferred choice anyways.

As I dressed, I expected to overhear Kieran and Boli in another one of their arguments after she doused him in pond water. But the only sound that I could hear over the gentle whizzing of the water was laughter. And not the kind that was made up of his annoying *'I think that I'm better than you'* laugh. This was a laughter that was full, joyous, and... *intoxicating*. I couldn't help but laugh along with him as I watched him bend over to rub down her legs with some fabric. Boli curled her head around him as he did so, nuzzling softly at his back.

My laughter faded as I watched the two of them share such a tender moment. I realized then why Kieran chose to bargain and argue with Boli. She was more than a beast to get him from point A to point B. More than just a commodity that could be traded for gold or jewels. Anyone who tried would see that *this* horse was different from other horses. Boli was special. She was his friend.

I had never imagined what being in the King's Guard was like before because, well. Why would I? But in that moment, when I watched a man laugh alongside his steed that he so lovingly cared for, I figured that the life of a King's Guard must be a lonely one. After all, when your life is the King's... what of you could possibly be left for anyone else.

CHAPTER 24 | KIERAN

I couldn't get the image of Talla standing in the pond out of my mind. And not just because she had been wearing nothing but her chestnut curls and the steam that was wafting up from the surface, but because of the dozens—no, *hundreds* of silver blue scars that marred her rich brown skin. The worst of them snaked up her ribs, the skin raised and smooth. A scar like that could only come from a near fatal wound.

Just *how* many times had the thief in front of me evaded someone's attempt to kill her? More importantly, how had she managed to heal such dire wounds so well? I had seen what the magic of healing stars were capable of, and this felt like more than that.

To my surprise, traveling with Talla had been... well. *Fine.* Sure, the first few days were extremely awkward, but had I not known who or what she was, I would have never guessed that the cloaked girl riding in front of me was a Brakkish thief. Talla hadn't been lying—she was a fair rider. Not too many people could stay on at high speed with her seat barely in the saddle, but she made it look easy.

She also made no attempt to arm herself or fight against me, nor did she try to run off with the starcuff or the stars in my bag. I hadn't exactly admitted to the stars' presence, but by the way her gaze kept finding its way to my wrist and my back, I knew that she could probably guess they were there. But, maybe the most surprising thing was that she hadn't tried to lift anything off of anyone else since we had left Ilken.

It probably helped that despite traveling on the main northern road, we hadn't come across many other travelers. But from my years of experience managing the prisoners below the castle, thieves rarely can contain their instincts to steal. And, Talla apparently had.

For whatever worries that previously weighed heavy in my chest about allowing Talla to accompany me, she really hadn't acted like the rebel who stabbed me in the forest at all. Perhaps Boli could sense something that I couldn't. *Stars*, I must have asked the stubborn mare a hundred times why she held such an attraction to the thief. Of course, I never got an answer. All I could discern from her snorts and whinnies was that wherever we went, Talla had to come with, and I had to be okay with that.

And honestly, I was. Mostly because with every stride that Boli took, I could feel us gaining on the stars. The buzzing power snaked up my arms and hummed in my body alongside my pulse, continuously growing stronger and pulling me to the East. The destination of my starhunt never changed—we were heading to Havetta, alright.

On the fifth day, we crossed beyond the ridge known as the Horn. Soon, our options for roadside lodging and provisions would disappear until the road turned, north of Havetta. The grasslands between the mountains and the coast were vast and mostly uninhabitable, which meant charging on as far as we could by day before setting up camp overnight.

Gray had thankfully packed me enough dried meat and fruit to care for both me and Talla under those conditions. I didn't particularly care for either meal option—the leathery feel left my tongue with a longing for the juices and flavor that had been dried away. But, they would keep me fed and strong.

By day seven of traveling together, we were finally crossing into the open grasslands. Talla and I had found such a comfortable rhythm in the saddle that if it wasn't for the constant aroma of warm campfire flooding my nose, I might have forgotten she was there in front of me.

As the sun was just setting over the horizon, the three of us found a spot to set up camp. A grassy knoll a couple hundred paces off of the road was dry and flat, save for a few large boulders that provided shelter from any winds. I used the remaining bits of daylight to tie up one side of a tarp around a boulder's edge with some rope that had been stowed in one of Boli's saddle bags while strategically maneuvering medium sized rocks to hold the other side to the ground. Luckily, the grasslands were shielded from the worst of the icy blasts thanks to the Orun Mountains that trapped the temperate sea air wafting in from our east. It would still be chilly, especially if the winds picked up speed... but with a fire it would be warm enough to find sleep.

While I had been pitching the shelter, Talla had tended to a roaring fire with such remarkable speed that I couldn't help but be impressed with her skills. She had skillfully constructed the fire in the center of a circle of rocks that absorbed the growing heat and radiated it back outwards. I suppose it shouldn't have completely surprised me. The Northwestern cities had recently experienced extremely harsh winters—the odds of that technique saving her and her crew's lives while out pillaging the neighbors were high.

Once we had finished eating some warmed dry sausages as the fire crackled loudly between us, Talla stood up to make her way to the tent that I had pitched. I, as a gentleman, had offered it for her to sleep in, just as I had the night before while I slept by the fire. She had denied my offer both times, her gaze shifting nervously to the chestnut mare.

But as if she could understand us completely, Boli had made her way to the opening, circling a few times before lowering her body down to rest by the tent. When I offered again, Talla accepted. Tonight, I swore I even heard a *'thanks'* mumbled under her breath.

I felt honored that for these nights out in the open, the sky was exceptionally clear. Sleeping out of the tent allowed me to fall asleep counting the thousands of stars that I had helped gather for the King. I watched intently as the sky shifted from a soft indigo to midnight blue, the pinpricks of starlight growing with intensity with each passing second.

The air was chilly, but the matted grasses beneath my body were soft and comfortable. With the fire still crackling next to me, I breathed in. The smell of wood and smoke warmed my body from the inside out. Though I missed my castle chambers, with my cozy sheets and large stargazing window, I found myself completely content as I stared at the stars.

By the light snores that I could hear over the fire, Boli must have fallen asleep. I glanced backwards, watching Talla stroke the mare's mane gently without waking her. My calm heart rate ticked up, and before she made her way into the tent, a sudden urge to speak filled my body.

"Do you want to sit with me?" the words were out of my mouth before I could even think, my lips moving without permission from my brain.

Talla turned on her heel, her braid whipping in the night air as she stared at me. My breath caught in my throat looking into her round eyes that now reflected glints of both fire and starlight.

"Sit with you? And do... what?"

Her questioning tone made my palms dampen. I casually wiped them on the dried grass next to me as I propped myself up onto my elbows.

I had no idea where I was going with this, but *Stars help me*, I couldn't stop myself from replying.

"I don't know. It's been a long time since I've had someone to sit with." My cheeks flushed at the kernel of vulnerability that I shared, then utterly heated when she responded with a scoff.

"No thanks." She turned back towards the tent that I had fashioned, silently crossing over the grass.

The dismissal from her shouldn't have bothered me...
but it did. I wanted to curse the Stars for whatever had
possessed me to try and engage with her, tainting my perfectly
peaceful evening with the sting of rejection. The two of us
hadn't shared more than a few phrases this entire week. Why I
had thought for even the *slightest* moment that she might want
to share an evening now was beyond me. I let out a sigh of
frustration before returning my gaze skyward, hoping to salvage
my night.

The clouds from the daytime were completely gone,
leaving an endless landscape of dark blue and purple sprinkled
with bits of light. I strained my tired eyes while searching for
any of the constellations I knew. The sound of flames roaring
and wood burning was my only company as I identified both
the Bear and the Siren. The latter, made of seven stars that
curved up towards the side, ending with two points to represent
the fins, held my *favorite* star.

It didn't have a name—or at least if it did, I didn't know
it. I had searched through the books that His Grace had given
me, but I could never find it. Even nameless, the star was special
to me. The right fin tip was just a tad brighter than the others in
Siren, and my eyes always seemed to gravitate towards it. There
was something comforting in being able to find it night after
night—a constant guidepost in the darkness, an anchor in an
unruly sea.

Seeing that star, bright and shining no matter what day
of the week it was or what had unfurled in the sunlight hours
before, relaxed me. It reminded me that while so many things
can change in this life, *some* things never do. That was the

hidden magic of the stars—even though they rested in the skies, their ethereal light and magnificent glow could still find a way to ground you.

My concentration broke as a barely audible *'sigh'* filled my ears. I couldn't hear Talla move in my direction, but I could feel her presence next to me as she lowered herself to the ground. My lips threatened to curl into a small smile, but I quickly neutralized them before turning my head to her, acknowledging her arrival.

"Only because I am not tired and there is literally nothing better to do right now." Her tone was dripping with her usual sass. I ignored it.

"That's fine." I replied, and I meant it.

We carried on for a few moments just sitting in silence, letting the warmth of the fire soak into our limbs. How it managed to continuously burn so evenly was a mystery to me. My attention was back on the tailfin of the Siren.

"Do you have a favorite star?" I asked.

I surprised myself with how light and genuine my voice was. It was like how I might speak to a friend. She answered me quickly, as if she was anxiously waiting for me to break the silence first.

"You mean besides the one that was *stolen* from me before Riggs tried to kill me?"

I shifted uncomfortably against the ground. *Right*, that. She had been so quiet this entire journey; so un-criminal that I had almost forgotten she was on a revenge trip. I swallowed before continuing my train of thought.

"I mean up there. I know you hate that they're up there, but surely you have a favorite. One that you notice time and time again."

She shook her head.

"How could you possibly pick one star out of the mess. It's chaos up there."

Her comment surprised me—never once before had I considered the kaleidoscope of starlight anything akin to chaos.

"Chaos?" I couldn't help but chuckle at her word choice, "It's the opposite of chaos."

She rolled her eyes.

"How is *that*," She motioned grandly with her arms to the vast sky above us, "the opposite of chaos? They're scattered in the sky, hanging indefinitely wherever the King told them to go. Their powers rendered useless. It's such a waste."

A wave of pity rolled over me. I couldn't help but feel sorry for Talla. She held onto such animosity for the King and for his vision of a reunited night sky. If she thought that the stars being up there was a *waste*, she didn't know the truth or the power of starlight. If only she could see that while on the ground, starmagic fueled the few... up in the sky, starlight inspired the masses.

"I promise it's not chaos." I started, but she leaned forward like she was going to push herself up. I instinctively reached out to stop her, my non starcuffed hand grabbing her arm. "Humor me?" I asked her.

I knew she didn't want to talk about the King or his mission that I had been working towards for nine years. But for some reason, I wanted to try to help her understand. If she could see that it wasn't all just for him... that there was some greater order to the stars in the sky, an order that superseded us all, maybe she wouldn't—

Her round eyes instantly laser focused on the touch of my hand. I quickly let her go, holding my hand up in the air a few inches away from her. I was convinced she was going to storm off. With one movement I had squandered this opportunity to change the mind of a rebel before it even began.

She eyed my open hand, studying it as I held it still as stone. I let out a sigh of relief as she leaned back on to the ground.

"They did choose their places," I continued, willing my heart to settle whilst nodding my head up to the sky.

I saw confusion register on her face as her brows scrunched together, as if it was the first time the idea had ever been mentioned to her. After a few minutes passed without her speaking, I dared to reach my hand out again, this time prepared for her sharp gaze. She didn't resist me as I shifted her to face further north. She didn't resist as my hand slid down to rest at the small of her back, either.

"Do you see the three bigger stars in a line there? Just above the mountain peaks?" I pointed slightly up to where I had been looking earlier, and I watched her eyes follow the sightline of my finger.

She nodded, "I guess so."

"Ok, so to the right of that, it curves up, then splits into two. That's the Siren Constellation."

"What's a constellation?"

I bit my lip a bit, trying to remember exactly how the book that was currently sitting on my bedside table in the castle defined them.

"It's a star pattern. It's like a home for the stars up in the sky. They never change, though some nights it's easier to see them than others."

She kept staring but said nothing.

"And the one at the top right of that little split? That's my favorite star."

She nodded again, acknowledging that she could see it, though remained frustratingly silent. The fire continued crackling beside us as I stared at the side of her face, trying to use any clues I could to read her current thoughts.

Her dark eyebrows were relaxed. Her lips were neutral. Her eyes were soft. Was it working? Was she starting to understand that everything that the King had done, everything that *I* had done had been a part of some greater plan?

I swallowed hard before continuing on, pointing to each constellation that I knew of. My finger navigated her gaze across the night sky. As she was trying to piece together my description of the Crane that sat high in the sky above us, I couldn't help but look back at her, to gauge whether any of what I was saying was really landing. My chest tightened at the sight of her round eyes opened wide, the dark green of her irises sprinkled with little reflections of starlight.

She leaned back against my arm that had been resting on the ground behind her as she wrapped her own arms around her tucked knees.

"And where did you learn such information about the stars? In everything I've ever heard about them, I have never heard of these constellations."

I leaned in towards her, crossing my ankles in front of me.

"The King has a whole library of books about stars."

She shot up, turning her body to face me.

"There are books about the stars?" Her words were quick and full of shock.

How did she not know that? I thought that *everyone* knew that the King's Chambers were home to a variety of histories, including those of the stars. It's how His Grace discovered how to return them back to the sky in the first place. He was the first King to focus on making sense of the stories rather than ignoring them.

"Hundreds of them." I replied, my brows raised.

"And how many have you read?"

I hesitated a bit before responding.

"Just a few."

"What, does the King not trust his personal star-fetcher to know more?"

My brows quickly fell, as I suddenly found myself on the defensive.

"He trusts me enough."

She let out an incredulous puff of air through her mouth.

"Doesn't sound like it." She shifted her body so that she was sitting with her legs crossed, now facing me directly.

"Didn't you ever think to snoop? Snag a few of the books and learn more for yourself?"

I shook my head, my cheeks hot as my fingers found some of the grass beneath my seat. I breathed in and out, working to control the rise of emotions. I pulled at the blades beneath me, hard enough to feel the tension of their roots in the ground, but not hard enough to remove them.

"I mean, the King put you through extensive training to send you out on seemingly dangerous missions to steal—"

"Recover." I couldn't help but correct her as I struggled to keep my calm.

In typical Talla fashion, she just rolled her eyes and kept talking.

"Steal…" she continued on, "stars. Imagine the valuable information that those books carry!"

"Taking those books without permission of the King *would* be stealing, and any actions made by the King's Guard without explicit permission from His Grace are not only grounds for dismissal, but also *arrest*." I don't know why I expected her to be phased by the prospect of my job, my *way of life*, being taken from me just to read a couple of books, but she wasn't. "Besides, even if I wanted to do something of the sort, I never had the chance. The volumes are greatly protected; you would have to be a fool to even try to access them without an invitation."

My mind drifted to the last time that I was in the King's chambers, right before I had embarked on this final starhunt. I wasn't being fully honest with Talla—I *had* just recently had a chance to do the very thing that she was suggesting. Of course I had wanted to learn more about the stars, but I wanted to serve my King, in the role that I had been gifted by him, with honor, more.

I thought back to my momentary lapse in judgement when I read over the page with his list of crossed out names. I *had* snooped a little, but I didn't learn anything of interest. But what if it had been a different book lying open on that table? What else was there to learn about the mysteries of the fallen stars?

I snapped my attention back to Talla.

"It's not in my orders to learn more about the stars. Only to retrieve them and bring them back to the King."

"Right. Honor. Orders." Her tone had shifted into mocking me, and I began to regret ever bringing up the subject of stars in the first place.

My hand grasped at the ground, pulling a few blades of grass free.

"You really think that the darkness is better than the starlight? That emptiness is better without the beauty that the stars add?" My question was sharp, but she was quick to reply, as if she had been waiting the entire time to share her opinion on the matter.

"Just because you can't see anything up there, doesn't mean it's empty. The darkness is full of peace. Of silence. Is *that* not beautiful?"

"No." I replied with no hesitation. "Not compared to this." I pointed up at the sky, and she just shook her head.

Her face was clear to read now, and I hated every ounce of the emotion that I could see. Pity.

"Well. I guess that's why you work for the King, and I work to undermine him."

My jaw ticked as I stared at her.

"You really don't think that the world is better off now that so few stars are left on the ground? The cities are *safer*. The streets are filled with more musicians and artists than ever before. Children aren't afraid to run around and play at night now that they can see even when the moon is hiding."

She shook her head defiantly at me.

"Brakken isn't like that."

This time, I rolled my eyes.

"Well, maybe you're all too drunk to notice. Or just too stubborn to accept that sometimes change in this world can be a *good* thing."

Her nostrils flared as her eyes narrowed into slits.

"So, you think families struggling to feed their children or people dying from curable illnesses are *good* things?"

"King Armund sends more than adequate provisions to all of the cities who have cooperated. You can't blame him for your people's inability to distribute them."

"But what if we don't want handouts from King *Ass*mund? What if we *like* being able to support ourselves?"

Stars, help me. Why couldn't she understand?

"You're impossible." I huffed.

"And you're a fool, Kieran."

The insult hit me like a rock to my chest, cracking the cool and composed lid that I kept on my emotions, the one that kept my head free and clear so that my instincts could prevail during any fight, no matter my opponent's magical enhancements.

"At least I'm working towards something *meaningful*." The words came out of my mouth quickly and loudly.

My heart rate climbed at a rapid pace. With the lid cracked, my emotions started to run rampant underneath my skin. Anger. Confusion. Grief. Fear. I didn't care that Talla had moved backwards an inch in the grass, clearly taken aback by my sudden shift in energy. I felt like I could grind the blades of grass that were tucked in my fingers into a fine powder as my fists clenched around them.

"I'm doing something that gives the *good* people of Larendi more power than the stars on the ground ever did. And I'm so damn tired of dealing with rebels like you who think they, for some reason, *deserve* the stars. Like they're your own precious magic source cosmically designed for you and your needs. The stars belong in the sky. The constellations are *proof* of that. And if that wasn't enough, seeing the amount of joy and hope and inspiration that a starry sky gives to people should be.

I guess I shouldn't be surprised that you can't see the truth of it for yourself. You are just a self-righteous thief. You could never understand what it would mean to work towards giving people something. All you do is *take*." I all but spat the last word at her as I thought about the hundreds of criminals that I had managed over the years in the Castle prisons.

Every one of them was selfish. Every one of them, no matter their crime, was always after taking something for themselves.

I breathed heavily into the silence between us as I glared at her. I watched her expression shift from surprised to lethal. The air between us felt icy, like a cool breeze had somehow plummeted the temperature in an instant. It cooled the fury and adrenaline that pumped through my veins. With a handle on my emotions, my mind cleared, leaving room for me to acknowledge any of my own instincts that were flaring. That's when I realized that maybe my outburst at Talla had been a mistake.

Without blinking, her gaze burrowed into my soul. And with each passing second, regret of my harshness bloomed in my chest. But I couldn't find any words that might amend the situation. The damage was done.

"Your mission has taken more away from me than it could ever give, you fucking *Prick*."

Talla stood up and stormed off to the tent. The fire next to us had gone out completely. I sat there for a moment, the lack of her presence stinging more than I had wanted it to. Rebel thief or not, I probably shouldn't have yelled at her. Even if I knew in my heart that she was wrong, we still had about a three-day ride to Havetta.

I looked around the grassy knoll, noting all of the rocks that were scattered through the grass. She might not have any weapons anymore, and might not have tried to do anything so far on our trip, but that didn't mean that she wouldn't find a way to bludgeon me in my sleep. My head started to ache. I took a swig of water from my canteen that was strapped to my hip before letting out a long sigh.

I wasn't going to be able to sleep tonight, not now, knowing that I might have just poked a sleeping groundbear. I glanced over to Boli. She was laying still with her head and neck tucked over her hooves. *Thank the Stars,* our argument didn't seem to disrupt her sleep. After a hard and fast day on the hilly terrain, she sure needed it. Plus, if I had to deal with another stubborn soul this evening, I might just explode.

There was no noise coming from the tent. Though I doubted Talla had fallen asleep so quickly, I was sure that she wasn't going to make another appearance. I laid out and got as comfortable as I could on the ground, placing my head on my arms raised above me. The stars were magnificent, twinkling in rounds between the constellations.

After about an hour of my mind replaying the evening over and over in my head, my eyes slowly started to close. One final thought washed over me as I was drifting off to sleep— perhaps Talla was right about one thing after all. I *was* a fool alright. I had been a fool for thinking that such a beautiful thing could be understood by such a beautiful woman.

CHAPTER 25 | Kieran

It took us three days to completely cross over the grasslands. I was expecting Talla to be silent the morning after our dispute, much like she had been during the first few days of the trip. Instead, she was chattier than ever. Not to me, of course. But she did seem to all of a sudden have lots to say to Boli. The two of them would sneak off a few paces during our riding breaks—never far enough that it felt like they were escaping. But Talla would lead her *just* out of my reach before launching into conversation.

I overheard her most of these times as she made no effort to keep quiet. Mostly, Talla told Boli about Brakken. She shared anecdotes from her childhood, like how she used to ride through her orchards that carried apples and stonefruit all year round or how she and her friends would run through the streets, weaving through the market street tents on a busy afternoon. Whenever she could, she made an effort to weave in that while it would have once been an excellent place to visit, it wasn't safe for a horse in Brakken now.

Those particular comments were always accompanied with a sharp glare in my direction, as if it was *my* fault that Brakken had time and again refused the help of King Armund over the years to transition their city and thrive beyond the era of the darkness. I didn't want her immature way of coping with our discussion to get under my skin, and it *shouldn't* have. But during one stop, after hearing her refer to His Grace as King *'Assmund'* for the third time in ten minutes, I snapped.

With my hand on the hilt of my sword, I stormed towards the two of them, insisting that if she did it again, I would make her run beside Boli for the remainder of our trip with the point of my sword pressed into her back. I wouldn't have *actually* done that, but with Boli still showing a great affinity to her, it wasn't like I had any other threat to pose.

As if finally getting a reaction out of me was all she wanted, her lips curled into a smile as she whispered back, "Fine."

Her passive-aggressive tactics immediately waned, though her chattiness didn't. She knew a lot about plants, easily identifying ones that were growing alongside the road. She was more familiar with salve and soap making than tonic brewing, so we went back and forth a bit sharing which plants were better for each purpose.

She knew a lot about wine, too. That had been less surprising than her botanical knowledge—having grown up in Brakken, she probably was given wine instead of milk as a babe. Brakken's reputation for imbibement is one thing that hadn't changed too much between King Trewan's reign and King

Armund's. When I told her that, she actually *laughed* as she agreed.

The rebound in her demeanor from the night before was a relief. I had been so concerned that I may have awakened something in her, given fresh air to the burning embers of her rebellious spirit and setting it ablaze. Maybe it was just easier now that our true feelings about each other were out in the air. Now that our roles had so plainly been identified, we didn't have to hide away from them.

When the three of us crested over a large hill, we were met with an expansive view of jagged land meeting with crashing blue gray waters. It had been at least five years since I had breathed in the mild, salty coastal air, and the sensation sent my mind back—back when there were still thousands of stars left to recover and each starhunt felt like the grandest adventure of my life. Now there were only ten stars left to hunt before I was consumed by duties that would likely rarely lead me beyond Mellin's yellow stone walls.

The cliffs were the same reddish brown as I remembered them, though the drop off appeared steeper than it was before. According to my map, Havetta was still a bit further south, as were the cave arenas. We would need to follow the dirt path that winded down the cliffs and navigate our way around the increasingly sharp turns as we made our way.

The cuff on my wrist felt warm, the magical pull from the Seeker star indicating that other sources of magic were nearby. We were in the right place, alright. After over a week of traveling across Larendi, we had found the remaining stars.

Talla, who had been fully reclined against me, her head tilted to the side in a light sleep, jolted upright when the sea was finally in sight. Cool air funneled through the newly forged spot between our bodies. It was as if the sudden burst of salt-air woke her, and I had to shake off the slight twinge of disappointment that it had as the warmth of her body on mine quickly dissipated.

"Wow." The word escaped her so softly, it was almost like she didn't mean to say it out loud.

"Have you seen the sea before?" I asked with genuine curiosity.

"In a way," she replied. She seemed almost sad.

Like it was a latent instinct being called to action, I found myself overcome with the urge to wrap my arms around her. I refrained, instead gathering the reins in one hand as I reached for my canteen. As I was drinking, I noticed that a group of men had emerged from the other side of the cliff up ahead along the road.

Half of them had hair as white as snow, while the others had longer, black hair adorned in braids and beads. Even though they were a couple hundred paces ahead and their clothes were dusty with red clay from their climb, I could still make out the splatterings of dark crimson that decorated them. *Blood*.

I handed Talla my canteen. She took it, swallowing a few hearty gulps of water before she returned it to me. She then leaned forward in the saddle as if the few inches would help her see the oncomers more clearly. Once they had pulled their last man up onto the road from the cliff side, they turned as a group, facing us from further down the road.

One white haired man seemed particularly revved up, swinging his fists through the air before launching himself at his friend. The contact took the two men to the ground. The man who had been hit screamed as if he had been mortally wounded, clutching at his chest as he writhed in the dirt before dramatically faking his death. Seconds later, the entire party erupted in laughter before helping both men up to their feet.

I moved the reins to my other hand as I reached back to make contact with my sword, not drawing it, but ready to if I needed.

"Do you think they've come from the cave matches?" Talla asked as the group turned away from us now, heading down the road in the direction of Havetta.

"Either that, or someone just told him that he was doomed to have you as a travel companion for their journey home. A little too reserved of a response, if you ask me." I tried to say it in jest, though I wasn't sure how successful my attempt was as I heard the words leave my mouth.

I held my breath as Talla turned her head, glancing over her shoulder at me.

"Ok, Kier-*ass*. If you're not careful, I'm going to give you the wrong passkey and watch you pout from outside the entry gate as I find some other warrior to get me to the stars."

I couldn't help that a chuckle escaped me as I exhaled.

"Kier-*ass*? What happened to *Prick*?"

She shrugged her shoulders.

"I don't know. Trying something new out."

I clicked my tongue.

"Well, Kier-ass is not *that* creative. I heard you use that already several times when referring to the King. Or is creativity not a skill that is valued amongst thieves?"

Still looking at me over her shoulder, she raised one of her dark eyebrows.

"After I get my star back, I'll be more than happy to show you *just* how creative I can be."

Though her words ended in a playful smile, they made my stomach drop. We had never talked about that part of the plan. I tried not to let myself think about why she was even on this trip with me, especially over the past few days. But now that we were here, outside of Havetta and closer than ever to the stars, I couldn't ignore the reality of our situation.

She wanted to get her revenge on Riggs and to regain her access to starmagic. I might look the other way when she took on Riggs, but I *wasn't* going to let her keep her star when we found it. So what would happen next?

"He's there isn't he?" Talla asked, breaking my train of thought.

I nodded back to her and sighed, letting go of the concern that was building in my chest. No matter what happened, I would handle it. I would return the stars to the King by Solstice. At all costs.

"I knew it. I can almost feel it."

I wasn't sure what she meant by that. But, before giving it too much thought, I reached for the dagger I had strapped under my tunic and pulled out the perfectly molded wooden handle of the weapon that once belonged to her. I slid my arm around in front of her, holding it out for her to take.

It was a risk giving her a weapon, but one I felt like I needed to take. If we *were* entering the caves, and the newly organized matches were anything like the old ones, she would need it. There was a good chance that we would get separated in the underground tunnels. She was a good enough fighter to find her way out of a jam, but it wouldn't feel right letting her walk in there empty-handed.

She grabbed the blade almost instantly, looking down at the dagger for a few moments before lowering it to her side.

I exhaled a breath of relief.

"Just please don't use it on me."

"No promises," she replied, laughing a little.

The sound was sweet in my ears. I rolled my eyes playfully.

"Between us? No. But I at least hope by now that we have an understanding?"

"Hmm... I suppose we do." She leaned down to pat Boli on the neck, the mare whinnied in response.

She sat back up and nestled her seat back so that she was leaning on me slightly again. *Stars. Hopefully* I hadn't just handed her the blade that would somehow be the end of me.

"Cmon," she said as she tucked her dagger into her cloak pocket, "let's go get some stars, my *warrior*."

CHAPTER 26 | TALLA

Close. Kieran confirmed it. We were close to the stars, which meant I was close to getting my revenge and also getting my magic. I didn't *exactly* have a plan for how I would do either, beyond getting through the entry gates and into the Cave Matches. I had been sending silent prayers to the Moon this entire trip to guide me—to lead me away from the annoying and pervasive prickling of fear that had followed me since Tuul and towards what I knew was mine. I had to trust that a plan would come to me.

I knew enough about the Cave Matches from Riggs to be confident in two things: the matches were *loud* and the arenas were *dark*. Loud spaces were perfect for sneaking around, even without stealth magic. And starless or not, I was from Brakken, damn it. We didn't just *thrive* in darkness, we *reveled* in it.

Kieran mentioned the idea of boarding Boli in the stables in Havetta, and I agreed with him. I didn't want her anywhere near such a hostile and dangerous environment. And if the past week was any indication, unless she was tucked safely in a stall, where I went, she would follow. Boli was incredibly sweet and loyal... I would miss her after all of this was over.

Havetta was filled with thatched roofs and clay buildings. The city itself wasn't at sea level. It had been built into the side of the sea cliffs, giving the entire town a remarkable view of the ocean. The streets were packed, filled with people of all shapes and colors wandering between the open-aired shops and markets. Tall curved trees lined the walk, and though they looked nothing like the evergreens of the forests that I knew, they still held onto their fan-like leaves even with the winter upon us.

Looking around, it was hard to believe that we were just about five weeks from the winter solstice—the weather was much milder here, the winds were more forgiving and brought in warmer, wet air from the sea rather than the frigid and dry air from the north. I searched, but there was no indication that winter would be arriving soon. Maybe winter came later on the coast. Or maybe it never came at all.

After a tip from a fellow rider that we passed on the main road, Kieran arranged for Boli to stay at Havetta's nicer stable by supplying the stablehand a sizable pouch of coin. He had paid the woman extra to compensate for his not knowing exactly when Boli's stay would end. She happily took his money and suggested that if we wanted to ensure lodging for us as well, we should make a similar deal with the inn across the street that her brother ran. I could tell that the stable hand was just trying to get Kieran to fork over more gold to support her family, but I didn't mention anything to him.

The streets of the city had been busy, so there was a real chance that there might not be a convenient room for him when we were done in the caves. I, of course, wouldn't need a place to stay—I would have my star and all of my abilities to thieve my way into the best room in town. I also didn't mention it to him because I appreciated the stable hand's hustle—the less that Kieran had to return to Armund, the better, even if the woman didn't know that Kieran was working for the King.

I leaned myself against the outer wall of the inn, my cloak catching on the breeze as I held it draped over my arms. Through the window I watched an ivory-skinned woman, probably not much older than me, helping Kieran make his arrangements. I couldn't help but stare at her flowing blonde hair and distractingly blue eyes as I watched her all but throw her body on to Kieran as he negotiated the arrangements.

Even with the thick tang of salt in the air, I could *still* almost taste her desperation. She repeatedly asked him if there was anything else she could do for him, constantly adding that she was *'happy to provide the best for such a high paying customer.'* Each time she asked, Kieran responded with a polite *'no'* and a flash of a smile that by the looks of it, made her ovaries scream. After the third time I heard her giggle, actually *giggle,* while helping him, I had to look away. *Of course,* the pretty blonde girl gets smiles and *'no thank yous'*, while anytime I asked him for something I got golden-eyed glares and the reminder that I was nothing but a *'thief'. Prick.*

After she finally let Kieran slip away, the two of us headed down the main road towards the steep path that led down to the sea caves. I did my best to ignore the hum of anticipation that vibrated through my muscles as we made our way in the direction Kieran was pulled toward the stars, choosing to focus carefully on my steps so that I didn't lose my footing on the loose rocks. We walked for about half an hour before the top of a rocky archway caught my eye.

The curve of the formation perfectly framed another rock, and the four circles arranged in a diamond that were lightly etched into it. My eyes followed the rock to the point where it emerged from the ground. There laid a dark opening, guarded by what looked like the most rotund man I had ever seen in my life. My heart pounded.

"There!" I shrieked with excitement.

If Kieran had said anything back to me, I didn't hear him. No longer taking care in my steps, my feet were charging towards the caves, my braid flowing in the wind behind me.

As I approached the beefy man who was standing guard at the entrance to the cave, I slowed to try and catch my breath. Instantly my lungs were filled with a foul stench that made me want to bend over and heave. I spotted the small fishbones and fins cluttering the man's feet first, then the cracked liquor bottle half buried in the sand behind him.

As I looked up at him, my nose burning from his stench, I tried not to stare at the bits of scales suspended in his black beard. He was entirely gross, and yet he had the audacity to look down his nose at me as I stood there, as if *I* was the unpleasant surprise.

I noted the iron gate that stood in the shadows of the cave behind him before choking out a 'hello'. His glance shifted from me to Kieran as I heard his familiar footsteps pad in from behind me.

"I'm assuming you are here to enter the Cave Match." The fish-man's words travelled over me, his voice loud but scratchy.

"Yes, we are." I responded, letting every bit of my annoyance through my lips.

His beady eyes shifted to me quickly. He lifted his lip in disgust before his eyes shifted back to Kieran.

"Do you have a passkey?"

I shifted my weight in my boots, crossing my arms. He was completely ignoring me.

"Yes, I do." I said through gritted teeth. I stood as tall as I could, palming the dagger that Kieran had just returned to me in my hand. The blade got his attention. "I was told that since this event is apparently run by distasteful barbarians, as a woman, to gain entrance I needed to bring along a man."

I swung my arm out and motioned to Kieran with the tip of my blade, who was standing beside me now. He dodged my blade's path with ease before his feet settled again with mine.

"Here is said man. And I have a passkey for entrance."

The round man looked down at me before unsheathing his own blade—it was long and the edges were spikey. Instead of a weapon with the traditional sheen of silvery metal, the sawtooth blade was ivory and dull like bone. He used one of the spikes to scratch at his teeth, picking free a piece of scale before spitting it at my feet. The glob landed mere inches from my boots.

I crinkled my nose in disgust, flipping my blade out towards him. I growled at him, using all of the self-control I had to not stab this idiot in the groin with my blade.

"What delightful company you keep." Again, the man only addressed Kieran.

But as my fingers gripped tighter around my dagger's handle, I felt a familiar touch graze the small of my back.

"You don't know the half of it." Kieran's voice was light, and when I threw him a quick side glare, he winked.

My cheeks heated, but I rolled my eyes before quickly turning my attention back to the load that was blocking the entrance, never lowering my weapon. The man leaned against the outer cave wall with both hands on his blade.

"To enter the Caves, you must first declare your acceptance of the regulations," he motioned to Kieran with the tip of blade, "then, you both may enter, assuming your passkey is correct." His blade then moved in the air circling between us.

"What are the regulations?" Kieran asked.

His hand was still resting at my back, but I could see that his other arm, his starcuffed arm, was resting atop his own sword.

"I can share them with you, Sir, *once* you accept them." The man gave a wicked smile, exposing his teeth that housed bits of fish tucked in the grooves.

My stomach lurched. He was positively revolting... and *annoying.*

"That doesn't seem fair." I couldn't help myself but respond, despite none of the man's words being directed at me.

The man kicked off the wall and closed the distance between us, dropping his face so that it was mere inches from mine. I slowed my breaths, taking as little air as I could manage so I didn't breathe in any more of the man than I absolutely needed to as I met his gaze fearlessly.

"Which part, Princess? The part that he must accept the regulations before entering, or the part that *you* don't get to hear?"

"Both." I didn't blink as I gripped my dagger tighter. If I had my star, this man would have been on his knees and begging for mercy minutes ago. I was so close to getting it back. All that I needed to do was get past him and into the caves. I heard Kieran pull his sword next to me, but thankfully he didn't move to use it—I didn't need his help.

Except, of course, I did. I had been told that I would be denied entry into these matches without a warrior, but I hadn't expected that it also meant I would be treated only as a prop to Kieran. That sneaky white-haired Flare player... They hadn't given me all of the information about these matches. I guess I couldn't blame them—if I had been the person in charge of the passkeys, gambling the knowledge away, I might not have been fully forthright either. But the more I thought about it, the more it annoyed me that I didn't ask more questions.

"You're at the Cave Matches, girl. *Nothing* about this event is fair."

Kieran stepped forward, sword in his hand.

"How long until the cave matches will end, do you suspect?"

His face was generally calm, but his grip on his blade and the look in his eyes was anything but. His tall frame towered over the man guarding the entrance. Kieran's commanding presence was enough to make the round man take a step back, his boot knocking into his old liquor bottle as he did so. I jumped at the opportunity to take a deeper breath, welcoming the refreshing wave of fresh pine and salt that filled the air around me.

I found my eyes fixing on the curves of Kieran's back as he faced the man. During this entire trip, he had barely turned his back on me. Which meant that I hadn't gotten many chances to see just how tightly his tunic stretched across his broad shoulders… to examine just how perfectly his pants fit from his waist all the way down to his boots.

"Hard to say." The large man responded, breaking my concentration.

I hadn't considered it before, but if there was a chance that perhaps the matches would soon be over, we could… just wait outside for Riggs to leave. It would be a perfect ambush. And it might also mean that I could avoid subjecting myself to any more dealings with whatever other assholes were associated with the matches. I only cared about Riggs.

The round man searched the area behind us with his eyes as if he was looking for someone. I turned around and saw only the empty path we had walked in on. When his efforts proved fruitless, he spat again at the ground.

"They go on for as long as there are competitors who are willing to fight. Depending on their abilities and stomach for blood, it could be over in a few hours, or even another few weeks. I heard the last time one of these matches caught traction like this, we had competitors fighting for nearly two months. We still talk about those cave matches on the ships."

My jaw fell. *Two months?* Neither Kieran nor I were going to wait that long to get to Riggs and get his stars. So, it looked like we were going in.

"And what if we find a way to bypass you?" I flipped my dagger in my hand, the blade glinting on the sunlight before catching it back in my palm.

The large man motioned behind him towards the iron bars.

"I'm the only one letting you through those iron bars, Princess. Poke me all you want with your little toothpick there, you'll still be stuck on the outside here."

I squeezed the handle of my dagger harder—again with that fucking *princess*. I was tempted to stab him, just for fun. I might not have the accuracy help from my star, but with such a big target, I can't imagine I could possibly miss.

"I accept the regulations."

I quickly looked up at Kieran, my mouth open to protest, but his gold eyes flared. I huffed and shut my mouth.

"Excellent." The man turned his attention to me. "Passkey?"

I spoke the words out loud for the first time since I had heard them after winning the Flare game.

"Feast of the fire, song of the sea."

The large man nodded and grabbed Kieran by the arm, yanking him in close. He brought his crusty beard right up to Kieran's ear. As annoyed as I was that I wasn't allowed to hear what he was saying, I was grateful that his scaly lips and teeth were nowhere near my face. I tried to read Kieran's face as he listened, but I couldn't spot a single emotion. He just stood there, taking in the regulations for entering the matches.

When the man was done, he stepped away from Kieran. Kieran rolled his sleeve up on the arm that didn't sport his starcuff as the man reached into the torch that was lit before the iron bars. He pulled out a small rod with some sort of design on the end, the curled bits of the rod glowing orange. Before I could put together what was happening before me, the man pressed the rod into Kieran's flesh.

"What the—" I started, genuine surprise bursting out of me.

But Kieran shot me with another look, and I shut my mouth. He didn't even wince as the man removed the rod, the design left in flaming red skin. I lifted an eyebrow as I watched Kieran show no ounce of pain or suffering from being branded. *Impressive.*

The large man returned the rod to the flames before flipping a hidden switch on the other side of the torch, causing the iron bars to swing open.

"The Devils long to play with thee." The large man said, finishing the rhyme, using his blade to guide us through the gates. We crossed the threshold of the bars, and he slammed them quickly shut behind us.

"Death awaits you both. Enjoy." A sinister grin spread across the man's face, and my stomach dropped.

Before this moment, I had been perfectly content using Kieran for entry into the matches, suspecting that the warrior requirement was to supply competitors to fight. But while I had known the matches were deadly from how Riggs had described them, not until the entry guard's parting phrase had escaped his fishy mouth had I really considered that bringing a warrior with me on this hunt for revenge and my star also likely meant bringing them to their death.

I shot a glance at Kieran, noting how the torchlight of the cave danced in his gold eyes. I couldn't read it on his face, but I could feel it in the air between us—he was angry, and whether it was at me or at the situation was impossible to tell. Guilt threatened to climb up my throat from where it was now brewing in my stomach, but I chased it away with a deep open-mouthed breath. My lungs filled with air laced with damp earth and must, and I found myself leaning in towards Kieran as we walked side by side, craving the wisps of fresh forest that billowed off of him as he moved.

"Care to fill me in? What were the regulations you agreed to? And what in the Moon was that branding for?"

His jaw worked side to side as he was considering his reply. I didn't like how nervous I became as I watched him, waiting to hear what I had missed.

"The brand is to mark me as someone with a guest." Kieran looked at me, and I couldn't tell if that was worry or annoyance in his golden eyes. Maybe it was both. Either way, I was suddenly filled with the sense that I was about to learn something that I didn't want to know, something I didn't plan for. "*And* the regulations were those of the matches themselves. I'm *apparently* their newest contestant, and *both* our lives now rely on my ability to fight."

I swallowed hard, his words sending the now too familiar jolts of fear down my spine.

"Both?" My jaw fell slightly open.

"Yup," he said, still walking down the path.

Fuck.

CHAPTER 27 | KIERAN

At all costs.

That's what I kept reminding myself as Talla and I headed towards the low rumblings of a crowd cheering at the other end of the cave. The regulations the grotesque guard had outlined had been simple enough. Fight, win, fight again.

Weapons of all kinds were accepted, but only weapons that were currently on your person upon hearing the regulations would be allowed. It was up to each opponent if the match was to the death or just to a yield. If I lost and lived, we were free to leave. If I won, I was free to leave, but Talla, as my guest, had to stay. If I won it all, we would both walk out of here with riches beyond our wildest measures.

I wanted to be angry with Talla for not being clear about what exactly her passkey signed us up for in these caves. After a few glares from me, she did admit that she had expected that I would have to fight, but by the surprised look on her face when I was branded she hadn't realized that her own ability to escape relied on my success or failures.

Typical thieves. They are always focused on what's in their best interests. I don't know *why* I had expected anything different from her. It didn't matter that over the last few days, it felt like something changed between us. But, it was no use getting too riled up about it—I needed to focus on how I was going to get us both out with all of the stars.

While we passed torch after torch that lined the wet, earthen walls, she badgered me with tips on how to fight Riggs. She explained how each of his stars and their magics worked in detail, along with ways he might use them against me. She went on and on, her voice lightly echoing around us as we walked down the torchlit path. There were no guards posted along the way, and for most of the journey we had the narrow passageway to ourselves.

Talla spoke with her normal, know-it-all tone, but I could sense that something was different. By the amount of times that she repeated herself she either thought me incompetent, which she almost surely did, *or* she was anxious. I spent our entire descent trying to reason out why she might be nervous. Was she getting cold feet about being at the matches now that we were finally here? Was she second guessing her ability to face Riggs after what he did to both her and Jetto? Did she wonder what would happen after these matches like I did? Or could she be... worried about *me*?

Whenever she stopped talking long enough for me to get a word in, I reminded her that I had already bested Riggs once, without even using my blade, and that I was a uniquely trained guard. Apparently that didn't mean shit to her, because every time she continued on like I hadn't said anything at all.

Just before we entered what I assumed was the main hall of the cave, we were stopped by two large men that stood on opposite sides of a thick raised chain. Each of the men were equipped with a set of sawtooth blades strapped across the front of them. I kept my hand on my sword in case either of them made any indication that they were planning on using them.

"Arm?" The guard on the left grunted.

The brand *hurt,* the skin around the fresh wound throbbed and stung as I turned my wrist over so it was in his view. He nodded before giving Talla an up and down glance that made me curl my fingers into my palm.

"Guests that way," grumbled the one on the right, using a fat finger to point to his partner on the other side of the chain.

I bobbed my head reluctantly in reply, wondering if I should say anything to her. *Goodbye*? *See you soon?* What were you supposed to do when you left the thief that you had reluctantly been traveling with to fight to the death so either of you had even a chance of escaping out of a criminal-filled cave?

I decided that I wouldn't say anything. But when I started walking towards the path on the right, Talla grabbed my forearm, pulling me to stop. Her fingers were careful not to squeeze too hard and agitate the raw and reddened skin from the brand that indicated that I had not entered these matches alone.

I turned to look back at her, the sight of her dark green eyes sent a rush of heat across my skin.

"Try not to kill him, Kieran." She was trying to keep her face neutral, but she wasn't trained to control her emotions like I was. Her eyes said it all. *Leave him for me.*

"No promises." I replied back, mustering a carefree wink.

I shouldn't have been supportive of her killing anyone, but I knew that the night Riggs had tried to kill her, the night that he *had* killed their friend Jetto, haunted her. Even though she hadn't said as much, I knew it because it would have haunted me.

As per usual, she rolled her eyes. But unlike typical Talla, this time she promptly looked away from me as I held her gaze. I noted how her free hand was nervously tugging on the end of her sleeve. For some reason, I wanted to grab it, even for a second, to settle her working fingers.

I didn't get the chance, though. The guard had already tugged my shoulders, pulling me away from her. I found myself quickly trying to memorize her face as I rolled my sleeve down, protecting the skin from whatever was awaiting me around the corner of this path. The fabric was surprisingly light against the wound, and I realized that I could now barely feel the sting of pain as I headed towards the match.

The main cave hall was wide and open, with tall clay ceilings that reached down in varying lengths of stalactites. Small red fly lights had been secured to the ends of the formations. How anyone managed to secure the lights was beyond me, but the effect was marvelously unsettling. The glowing red dots scattered above portrayed a darker and inverted version of the night sky.

There were six rings set up on a raised section of dirt, each lined with an earth wall that was about waist high. Crowds were scattered in the gaps of stalactites in a circle around all of the rings, clapping and cheering as men slashed at each other with whatever weapons they had on them. I was directed to climb up into the ring where I had just seen the throat of a thick black-haired man slashed by an even thicker blonde one. I watched as two men that were also equipped with sawtooth weapons dragged the limp body a few paces before it was hoisted over the wall.

This entire event was *sickening*. They had just discarded that man like he was a sack of dirt and nobody in these redlit arenas seemed to care. I didn't want to think about how they eventually disposed of all of the bodies that must be accumulating down here. The caves smelled like dirt and salt and metal, but they didn't smell like death.

They must be moving the bodies from the sides of the rings eventually, but no matter where they were taken, I was sure that they were not given any proper burial rights. I didn't want to think about how many souls had already been lost just for the sake of coins and ego. Anyone participating in these matches for their own gains was a criminal that was engaging in activities that were explicitly outlawed by the King, but that didn't mean they deserved to have their transition into death be so inhumane. Surely, the knowledge of their resurrection had not made its way to the castle, and I couldn't help but wonder what His Grace would do when it did.

I hopped over the earth wall of my ring, sending my boots into the ground with a thud that went unheard due to the clattering of the crowd as they prepared to watch a new match. My eyes had started to adjust to the dark red glow of the caves, making it easier to visually make out the events around me. Power buzzed up and down my right arm, and the pulling sensation on my wrist nearly demanded that I look a few rings down. It didn't take me long to spot him—long black hair flowed in the shadows as he effortlessly dodged every strike that his current opponent was so desperately trying to land on him. *Riggs.*

Even though my wrist told me we were heading towards a horde of stars, knowing that he was actually *in* the caves, and that I hadn't just entered a fight to the death for nothing, was reassuring. He was here, and he had the stars. Had Talla seen him yet?

I searched for her, wondering where they were keeping the guests of the fighters. It occurred to me then that for all of the scenarios listed out in the initial regulations, the man at the front gate hadn't said *anything* about the fate of Talla should I die. I wouldn't die, of course. But how many warriors already had? How many guests were now trapped and at the mercy of the sawtooth-wielding gang that seemed to be running the show?

Considering how uncivilized this entire operation was, I couldn't imagine that the guests were simply allowed to walk out of here unharmed. I swallowed hard—unable to stop the hypothetical visions that flooded my mind. Talla being thrown on the ground in the red and wet caves. Talla's wrists being locked in chains and dragged along the ground. Talla pinned down with a sawtooth blade at her throat, someone above her demanding that she let them—

No. I reclaimed control of my thoughts, sending the waking nightmares away with a hard blink. It wouldn't happen. There was no one down in these caves, no one in Larendi, that was a match for my training. If I couldn't find my own way to get out of these matches, I would just win the whole damn thing.

I had all but three more seconds to scan the crowds, searching for a glimpse of chestnut hair before the blade of an axe came careening towards my head. My first match had begun.

CHAPTER 28 | Kieran

Yield or to the death, it was our choice. At least that's what the regulations that I agreed to said. I would do everything I could to get my opponents to yield while down here—and the faster they yielded, the faster I might be able to go head-to-head against Riggs.

As I dodged another swing from the blonde competitor's axe, I determined that getting in the ring with Riggs was probably my best chance at getting his stars. The sawtooth-bladed guards kept an annoyingly close eye on everyone's whereabouts, so I doubted they were going to let me walk up and confront Riggs otherwise. Even if I *could* do that, it's not like he was just going to hand them over to me. No, he would want to get me back for leaving him tied up to the cart in the Middle Forests. He would *want* to fight me.

Within minutes, my foot was on the blonde man's chest, the tip of my sword poking lightly at the crux of his neck. His eyes were shut tightly as his hands shook against the ground. He made no attempt to escape as he held his hands in surrender over his head. I heard a high pitched shriek from a woman behind me. I didn't recognize the voice. He must have heard it too, because with his eyes still shut I saw him mouth words that too many men say when face to face with death.

"I'm sorry."

I lifted my blade so that it no longer touched his skin, but barely. By the look on the man who guarded our ring's face, physically signaling the yield wasn't enough. He had to verbally admit his defeat.

"Yield, and you can go back to her," I said, my words running down the edge of my sword.

"Never." His eyes were still closed.

I could hear the woman shrieking even over the chants of the crowd. I honed in on her voice, forcing my ears to decipher her words against the roar of the crowd.

"Get up, Thermont. Get him."

I shook my head impatiently at my competitor.

"For Stars sake, *fucking* yield."

But Thermont just laid there, still shaking. I growled in frustration as my grip tightened around my blade.

"Ok, fine. What if I yield? Will you accept that?"

I didn't *want* to yield, especially not in my first fight. If I had come here just to fight, this entire series of matches would be mine to lose. But I had stars to get. I had Talla's freedom to secure.

If I yielded, Talla and I could escape, but our chances of getting the stars from Riggs before Starcast would be almost zero. Then entering the caves and bearing this brand on my arm forever would be for nothing. I lifted my sword a little higher now. Thermont's eyes flashed open with a jolt of frantic, murderous rage.

I knew that look. I had seen it too many times in the faces of criminals over the years. When people become so consumed with their emotions, they don't listen to reason. There is no arguing with them. They have one goal and will do anything, risk anyone, to make it happen. Thermont curled the corner of his mouth up into a sideways smile.

"You are weak, Golden Eyes. And you'll die for it."

He clearly thought that I hadn't noticed the hidden blade in his sleeve, and that with the way I was standing, I wouldn't be able to defend myself against his attempt to slice the back tendons in my legs. But he didn't know who he was fighting against. There was no way this average man was going to best me, not when the King's own star-powered guards couldn't.

I didn't want to do it, but sometimes, the Stars make choices for you. I let gravity do the work for me as I stepped aside, dropping my blade so it fell straight down into the man's throat, pinning him to the Earth. My chest tightened as I watched life quickly leave his eyes before his body slumped against the red clay floor. It had to be done.

I turned my attention to where I had heard the woman crying for him but the red lights flared, temporarily blurring all of the faces in the crowd. I didn't let myself think of her fate now that her warrior was dead. I *couldn't*—not if I was going to keep my focus on why I was here.

Not two seconds after Thermont's limp body was dragged to the side of the ring and tossed over the edge another opponent was ushered in. I readied myself, wiping the blood off of my blade against the leg of my pants and taking a deep and calming breath before the fighting started again.

The matches continued for what felt like hours. Thankfully, several of my opponents had yielded almost instantly. Whether they knew that they would die trying to beat me or just immediately regretted their decision to enter the cave matches as soon as their first match began, it didn't matter. I didn't care why they yielded.

I let them walk away and prayed to the Stars that the next man to be ushered into my ring would be Riggs. It never was. I ended up having to kill two more of my challengers, both of whom shared the same soulless look that Thermont gave me in the end. Thankfully those two didn't have guests with them. Or if they did, they had remained silent when the end came.

From the brief glances around that I could manage, I gathered that the other rings were taking periodic breaks. At times, some of the rings were completely empty. I wasn't getting tired, in fact so far the matches had been almost too easy, even the ones that didn't yield. But, I had to admit, a break, even just for a sip of water, *would* have been appreciated. I had already lost my tunic and shirt, shedding them early on so that I didn't drench them in sweat and blood. A moment to dry off would be welcome, too.

Furthermore, a break could be my other way to get to Riggs... *especially* if Riggs and I had a rest at the same time. The constant pull on my wrist let me know that he was still fighting, though. And in the same ring that he had started in. The sensation hadn't changed even the slightest since I started fighting.

That is, it hadn't changed until my next challenger entered the ring. If I hadn't already been testing the pull from Rigg's stars, I would have missed it. But as the new warrior hopped over the wall, I could sense the slightest additional pull. It wasn't to the side towards Riggs, but rather, in front of me.

I looked the new challenger up and down. His skin blended in with the darker red tones of the clay. He was almost as tall as I was, and he wore long leather arm cuffs that laced up to his elbows. As he adjusted one of them, loosening the laces and shifting the cuff so that it was now facing the opposite direction, his eyes caught mine. The darkness in them reflected the red lights of the ceiling, making them glow like hot embers.

I raised my eyebrows at him, twirling my sword in my own cuffed arm. Even without my seeker cuff, I would have spotted what the man was trying to hide. I caught the tiniest hint of blue glow from his arm for a brief second before he moved his cuff. The fighter in front of me was carrying a star.

I felt the wicked smile curl across my face as I raised my blade, no longer thinking that a moment of rest might be nice. *Finally*. There was someone real to fight, and I was ready to show everyone in the caves exactly who they were watching.

CHAPTER 29 | TALLA

My eyes didn't know where to look. It was pretty hard
to see anything from where I stood with the other guests,
tucked away in a gap between the shadows of the stalagmites.
Everything was tinted red from the suspended orbs of light
above the rings, and every few seconds I found myself switching
my attention between Riggs and Kieran.

Riggs spent most of his time toying with his
competitors, like a cat with a mouse. He would seemingly trip
or fumble with his weapon, allowing the other guy to get
dangerously close to him before slaughtering them in one swift
motion. If it wasn't for the grotesque guards and their
enormous sawtooth blades, I would have found a way to sneak
to the earthen benches perched right next to his ring.

I might not be able to fight him myself, but I'm sure
one look at me would distract him long enough for an
opponent to at least draw some blood. He deserved much more
than that for what he did though—he deserved for all of his
blood to stain these clay floors. But watching him move with

such accuracy and stealth, I knew that the odds of that happening at the hands of any of these men were low.

Kieran fought a few rings down from Riggs... I had to hand it to him, he was an impressive fighter. *More* than impressive, actually. It was amazing to watch him move his sword like it was a continuation of his arm.

The red light glinted off of the gold hilt as I saw him slash and then roll, just like he did in his morning practice sessions. Sweat was shining on his toned muscles as he fought against whoever stepped into his ring. Even when that black haired man wielded accuracy magic—at least that's what it looked like by the way his wrist glowed and his blades always targeted the spots where Kieran's vitals organs were—Kieran was prepared. No trick seemed to get past him. I don't even think a single weapon hit his gleaming skin. He was untouchable.

Back and forth my eyes went, scanning between the rings. I held my breath anytime Kieran made contact with the ground, even though it was always purposeful, just as I did whenever Riggs ripped through his next opponent. The way that the two of them fought couldn't be more different.

Every step of Kieran's was controlled and calculated, like he was trying to do the least amount of damage to his opponent as possible. Meanwhile, Riggs' moves were showy and rushed, always ending with a spectacular display of bloodshed. Would Kieran show the same composure if he was face to face with Riggs? It seemed impossible watching Kieran almost effortlessly evade attack after attack.

But Riggs held the magic of at least four stars. Would Kieran be able to dodge those starpowered attacks? Or, would Kieran's blood layer the surface of the ring like the rest of Riggs' opponents?

My stomach flipped at the thought. Kieran was clearly fighting for yields from his opponent, seemingly taking his time defending himself before making any move for a kill. There was no way that Riggs would ever yield, especially not to Kieran, the Royal Guard who bested him in the woods. Kieran had shown that he would kill, though, if he needed to.

I shook my head a little when I realized the situation that was unfolding in front of me. Kieran wasn't going to lose. Neither would Riggs. Eventually, they would end up in a ring together. And if I didn't find a way to intervene... *Fuck*. I had to find a way to get to Riggs before that happened.

Breaking my attention from the rings, I looked at the few people that were huddled around me in the shadows. I was one of maybe ten other guests. We were mostly women, but there were some males, too, that were trapped alongside me between the clay walls and the guards. Several of them were crying, likely realizing that their risk to gain fortune and power hadn't exactly paid off. As I watched one man's body shake endlessly with his sobs, I couldn't help but wonder what was going to happen to him now that his warrior was dead.

All around in the cave was a crowd of people that I could hear, but couldn't see. The red lights illuminated the shadows in a way that made my skin prickle with fear. *Darkness* I knew. *Moonlight* or *firelight* I knew. But these red lights... they were something completely foreign, and they were just another variable of these cave matches that I had not been prepared for.

By the loud cheers and booms from their feet, these hidden people around me that weren't being held captive were clearly enjoying every second of this antiquated display of barbarian activities. Who exactly were these people? I didn't know Larendi still hosted so many gore-lovers, not with how quickly the land adopted Armund's dream. I bit down on my lip, but the clang of swords that came from Kieran's ring jolted my body, causing me to draw blood with my tooth.

I envied the people up in the stands. Not because these fights were my idea of entertainment, but because they had figured out how to enter the matches as an observer and not as a guest. I hadn't thought to ask more questions of the passkey holder. I hadn't even considered trying to figure out what entry into the matches would mean. When they had told me I needed a warrior, I hadn't even understood that my ability to escape would be tied to the one I picked. The longer I stood watching the matches, the more jealous, and ashamed, I became.

My mood lightened as I watched Kieran slam his competitor to the earthen wall so hard that it made the man yield. When I had hatched my plan that night in Ilken, using Kieran for his seeking magic and his warrior status was just a means to an end—to get me to Riggs. But now that we were here, now that my freedom was linked to him and his ability to fight... I never thought I would actually need the Royal Guard, and yet here I was thanking the Moon that Kieran was the warrior I had chosen.

I gave my body a light shake, clearing the sudden swell of gratitude and pride from my chest. I did *not* have time for that shit. It didn't matter how remarkable of a fighter he was, or how *good* he looked while doing it. I needed a plan to get myself out of here, and to get the stars from Riggs before Kieran could.

As I watched fight after fight, I found myself cursing everything around me. Nothing about these cave matches seemed to follow any sort of logic. From what I could gather, the competitors would randomly be rotated between rings at the mercy of the guards, though neither Kieran nor Riggs had yet to be moved. I couldn't figure out the interval, but sporadically each ring would also take a break.

Contestants and spectators alike would retreat towards the back of the open room that we were in, their dark figures disappearing down what appeared to be torch lit halls. It was the same direction that I saw guards head off in when they were removing bodies of the fallen. Eventually, the contestant would return, seemingly refreshed, to begin their next match. Surely, there must be an exit over there, but what else? *Where* were those contestants going?

During one of the relatively quiet moments in between matches, I decided that, despite my desire to hatch the plan on my own, I desperately needed more information. I looked towards the other guests that were standing with me and turned towards the one who seemed the most composed. She was a tall woman with lighter features that were tinted blood red in the orb lights. I leaned in closer to her.

"Do you know how these matches work? Do you know what's beyond the rings?"

Though I knew that she could hear me, she didn't answer. Her attention never left the rings.

I sighed, realizing that perhaps I should take a different approach with her if I wanted to get her attention.

"Which warrior is yours?"

She gave me a sideways glance before pointing into the ring next to Kieran's.

"The one with the bow."

I took my eyes off of watching Kieran effortlessly dodge a swing of an axe to watch a man with the largest quiver I've ever seen fire arrow after arrow. His opponent carried a shield that blocked each one, but by the way his arm quivered, it was only a matter of time before that shield would fall.

"He's on day two of fighting."

Day two? I didn't want to be here another hour, let alone another night.

"Have you been able to see him since you entered? Have you been able to leave this spot? I haven't seen any of the other guests move all day."

She shook her head, never looking away from her man in the ring.

"I haven't been able to see him. But if you want to leave, you can talk to him."

She pointed at the large guard that was blocking the path out before an agonizing scream broke across the hall. The woman started clapping—her warrior's opponent's arm had finally given out, allowing her man to send a flaming arrow right into his heart.

I turned on my heel to address the sawtooth blade-holding guards who blocked my way out of the guests area.

"What's beyond the rings? In those hallways?"

The guard, large and rotund like many of the others, stared down at me.

"More caves," he replied in a mocking tone that made me wish I could slap him.

"No shit." I crossed my arms.

The guard twisted his sawtooth blade on the ground, grinding up dirt as he did so.

"There's an exit back there, should you be so lucky to use it."

I swallowed hard, and gave Kieran a glance. He was going toe to toe with someone who was also carrying a sword. It was a few moments before Kieran knocked the blade free of their hand.

"But where do the competitors go before they come back to fight after the breaks?"

"The caves have many secrets," said the guard, "we allow competitors who are doing well to explore them."

Now we were getting somewhere. Since the guard was surprisingly divulging information when I asked, I thought I'd press further. *Moon knows* that I couldn't just stand idly by anymore.

"So, is the plan to starve everyone down here, or is there any food available?"

Just as I hadn't seen any of the guests leave, I also hadn't seen anyone eat anything. The drama of the matches had distracted me at first, but the ache in my stomach was now becoming unavoidable.

"One of us can take you over there." He pointed across the rings, just next to where the torchlit hallways began.

I squinted my eyes, but I could barely make out anything besides a small crowd of people huddled together.

"There is water and meat for sale during the day. If you can wait until night, we distribute what hasn't sold out to the remaining competitors and guests before we break." He motioned to the guests behind me. "That's what they're all doing. Waiting."

"Why would they just be waiting?"

The guard let out a frustrated breath as he motioned with his eyes to the rings.

"The guests aren't safe out there. Whose to stop someone from snatching you up and using you to get your warrior to yield? Or better yet, doing something to you to serve as a distraction?" His thin lips curled into a cruel smile as my hands found their way to my face, rubbing at my temples and across my eyebrows to clear my thoughts.

Everything here was so bizarre. How was *any* of this legal? If Armund banned using starmagic, even if it was to *help* people, because it *'reduced the incentive for crime'*, then surely these aggressive, glorified cock fights were banned too. It just goes to show that while the King claims to rule the land, beyond the walls of Mellin the people are governed by their own power. And now that starmagic was all but removed, most people were at the mercy of the self-serving desires of whoever held the sharper blade.

I dropped my hands and gave the guard an up and down glance, focusing on the large sawtooth bone blade. Every guard that I had seen in these caves carried one, but before today I had never seen anything like them. They were nasty, and they could do significantly more damage than my small dagger could.

"Why do you all carry those particular blades?" I asked, curiosity getting the better of me.

The guard grabbed his weapon, pulling it tightly against his frame as if he could sense my instinct to steal it.

"The customs of D.Z. are none of your business." The guard looked down his wide nose at me.

"The what?" I asked. I racked my brain for anything that gave me a clue as to who the D.Z. were, but came up short.

"It's not for the likes of you, *Princess*. Now enough, don't bother me unless you decide to use the services. You're distracting me from the show."

I mulled the possibility of shoving my blade into his throat for calling me *'princess'*, but I resisted. I shuffled away from him, bringing my attention fully on the matches—I could work out what the D.Z. was later, but I needed my mind to work out a plan to get to Riggs before he and Kieran were set to fight each other. I would have to wait until Riggs' ring had a break, whenever that might be. If I could time a trip to where the food and water was just right, I might be able to slip away. I just hoped that with my dark cloak I could somehow sneak through these red-stained shadows unnoticed.

Moon, I really couldn't wait to get my magic back.

CHAPTER 30 | TALLA

Lucky for me, I didn't have to wait long before I could put my plan into action. *Thank the Moon,* Riggs' ring was finally out on break as four guards came in to mop up the slurry of blood and mud from the floor. I followed him with my eyes, making sure he didn't slip away to the back halls without me knowing. He ran around the interior wall of his ring, raising his arms up and down to elicit louder cheers from the spectators.

I rolled my eyes in disgust and checked a few rings over. Kieran was effortlessly hitting flaming arrows out of the air, the arrows snapping and splintering with the contact of his blade. It wasn't until I noticed that the woman next to me was wincing at the exact same time that Kieran cracked an arrow into pieces that I realized her warrior had switched rings. He was now going head-to-head with mine.

Distress laced her cry as her warrior dropped to his knees with his hands raised to beg Kieran to let him yield. All of his arrows had snapped, and he had no other weapons on him to continue to fight. Kieran was sweating, his entire torso dripping and glistening from fighting in the damp caves for almost the entire day without a break.

I held my breath as I watched Kieran lift his blade so that it pointed up towards the red lights. His chest was heaving, breathing heavy from his constant physical exertion. Maybe the pause was just him catching his breath. Maybe he had intended to let his competitor go the entire time. But for a split second, as his golden eyes glared down at the helpless man, I'm pretty sure that Kieran thought about doing it—about ending the man's life then and there just because he *could*.

No one would have blamed him. I mean, these were the cave matches. Death was expected. *Moon*, I bet a bunch of people here absolutely hated how little bloodshed Kieran had caused despite dominating his rounds.

But Kieran didn't bring the blade down on the man. Instead, Kieran dug his sword in the ground and nodded, accepting his yield and therefore releasing the man and his guest from the cave matches entirely. The woman gasped with disbelief before wincing again as a guard entered the ring and slashed her warrior's arm with his sawtooth blade. The man screamed a guttural yell as his branded skin was torn open. While clutching his wound, he ran over towards us.

She pushed past me towards our guard, who let her pass. I watched her warrior hop down from the raised center of the room and meet her, embracing her tightly with no regard for the blood that was now dripping down her backside. I carefully traced their steps with my eyes as the two of them made their way around the exterior of the rings before their dark figures disappeared into the back network of caves.

I noticed Kieran then, sweaty and catching his breath, looking right in my direction. I wasn't sure that he could see me at first, but I nodded at him in acknowledgment anyways. His gold eyes flared before he responded with a wink as he flipped his sword over his starcuffed hand a few times. My face heated as I watched the metal twist and reflect the red lights from above.

For a moment, I forgot why we were there, why we were both trapped underground in a sea of greedy and bloodthirsty fighters. I forgot that he was a member of the King's Guard who was after stars, and that I was a thief who had used him to get the stars myself. I imagined that maybe he wasn't fighting to recover fallen stars, but instead he was fighting for me, for us. I imagined him being as relieved as the man he had just set free to get back to me. I imagined what it might be like to run out of here hand in hand—away from the red-tinted shadows and into the dark night.

But as that moment passed, I shifted my attention back to Rigg's ring, only to see that it was empty.

My stomach dropped as I scanned quickly around, but there was no sight of him. *Fuck.* I turned quickly to the guard to insist that I was seconds away from fainting, and that I needed food, now. Anxiety filled my body as he slowly nodded, his face twisted in annoyance. He alerted a nearby guard to escort me across the room. My eyes were still scanning the dim red cave for any site of Riggs, praying to the Moon that I didn't miss this chance because I was distracted by the Royal Guard.

Even though I couldn't see Riggs, I knew he was close. I could somehow feel his traitorous presence as the guard weaved me through the crowd that had formed around the food stands. I breathed a sigh of relief when I finally caught a glimpse of his unmistakable hooked nose pass in front of a torch just a few paces ahead of me.

This was it. I was so close to him. To my stars. To revenge. Now, I just needed to get away.

I forced my feet to stumble, launching my body forward so that I crashed into a few people in front of me. The impact caused several to topple onto the cave floor. There was a flurry of arms and legs as the guard who had escorted me scrambled to help people back on to their feet. By the time he had pulled everyone up, I was already gone. I was already several paces away, willing with all of my heart to stay hidden in the shadows, and thanking the Moon that it worked as I stepped silently into the back network of caves.

I pulled my hood up, hoping that it might help me blend into the dark clay walls even more as I followed Riggs. He weaved through a network of narrow cave hallways that were lit on the sides with the same small torches as the entry cave had been. *Right, left, left, right.* I tried to remember each turn that he took so I could find my way back.

Each step forward sent stronger waves of energy through my body. I was closing the gap between us. He couldn't see me. He didn't know I was here. This was it. This was the exact advantage that I needed to make him pay for what he did to Jetto. What he did to me.

He finally turned into one of the smaller passages and paused in a room that sloped down a bit from the entrance. At the bottom, I could make out a small pool of greenish blue water at the back. Minus the steam, the water looked just like the pond that I had found in the Orun Mountains. If *this* pool was calling to me, too, I didn't notice. My attention was fixated on Riggs as he sighed with relief.

He bent down to the water's edge, sending his cupped hands into the water before splashing some against his skin. I silently sneaked closer behind him. I couldn't take the risk of throwing my only dagger at him without accuracy magic—I needed to get closer.

He reached down again into the pool to bring a handful of water to his lips. I pressed a few more steps forward, fear and anticipation climbing up the back of my neck. Riggs paused mid-drink, and I froze. He leaned in closer to the water, as if something was in the pool that he couldn't quite see from his previous view.

I realized that he didn't see some*thing*, he saw some*one*. Me.

With the angle of the floor, the pool of water mirrored back the entrance to the room, which included me standing alone in my cloak. I could see the reflection of my green eyes in the water before they were replaced with the image of two dark ones. My stomach dropped as he leaned in further so that I could see his whole face on the water's surface.

Moon, save me, what the actual fuck happened to him?

CHAPTER 31| Talla

"I shoulda figured you'd be a bitch that wouldn't die easily." Riggs turned away from the reflective pool to face me, pushing his damp and greasy black hair out of his face.

I wanted to move, to put more distance between me and whoever this twisted version of my old comrade was. But my feet didn't budge. I couldn't do anything but stare at him.

Though he had the same tallish frame, the same hooked nose, and the same raspy voice as the man who I thought had been an ally, he was now unrecognizable. Power rippled off of him in a way that confidence alone never could. His skin, though flush with blood, was so ghostly white it was almost glowing. His body was slick with sweat that shined across unnaturally bulging muscles.

But the scariest part about the Riggs that was standing before me was his eyes... His dark eyes were completely flat. No light. No sign of life. They were soulless. They were lost.

How long had he been here fighting in these cave matches? Hours? Days? How many lives had he taken to do so?

He shifted his weight as he wiped his hands clean along his pants. I stared at his chiseled body, not because of how tight the muscles were, but because they were bulging in places that they shouldn't be. Large round bumps seemed settled under his skin in his arms, his shoulders, and his chest. The bumps were fairly consistent in size, about the size of a...

No. My heart started to race as I thought back to the morning after we had tracked down Callum and stolen back Mara's star, the one that had incredible healing magic. There had been no hint to where Riggs had concealed it, no way he could have compressed it in such a short amount of time. I had forgotten about it, distracted by the run in with the other thieves and then later with Kieran. But as I stood before him in the caves, I not only remembered, I knew where it had gone. Riggs had embedded the star into his body. That glow in his skin... it was from starlight.

He must have been able to see the realization on my face, because he curled his lips into a wicked smile.

"For every bit annoying you are, you aren't dumb. *Naïve*... but not dumb." He all but licked his lips as he started walking towards me, clearly hungry for another chance to kill me.

Now that I was in front of him, and I remembered that I had come in here with just one dagger and no plan, I worried that I might have just given him exactly what he wanted. *No, I* could do this. Starpower or not, I had used my dagger perfectly a thousand times. It had to be in my muscles somewhere, the memory of how to throw and strike with perfect aim. I tried not to let his menacing grin shake me, but the sweat forming at the back of my neck let me know I was failing.

"My years of thieving have taught me many things, but probably the most useful is that while it's quite easy to lift something off a person, it's near impossible to steal something from within one." He flexed his muscles so they tightened around the stars.

The blue hue was so faint, most eyes would write it off as a trick of the light. I held back the bile that was rising up my throat. What he did wasn't natural—embedding the stars into his body like that so that every breath he took, every move he made, was laced with starpower.

"Starpower has become so rare, very few people recognize the glow anymore. They just assume I have some sort of deformity that causes these bumps. It's made my time here very rewarding. There is just *nothing* like the look of complete shock on their faces when they realize they never stood a chance."

Riggs' low laugh echoed around us as he took another step towards me.

"How *right* it feels knowing that the power coursing through my veins is enough to take a life," he snapped his fingers that were stained red from blood, "just like that."

I took my own step backward, checking over my shoulder to make sure my exit was still clear.

"You are a sick son of a—"

Taking my eyes off of him was a mistake. Before I could finish my insult, he was upon me. His steps had been silent and taken perfectly to close the gap between us without any indication of him doing so. His hand wrapped around my neck and he squeezed, lifting me off the ground.

"Now now, Talla. No need for that."

I wanted to kick my legs, to flail in protest, but I knew that it wouldn't get me anywhere. So, I willed my body to stay calm and focused. I needed to utilize every ounce of breath that I could manage despite his tight grip on my airways to *live*, not fight.

"Though it's annoying that I'll have to kill you twice, it is nice I guess that I finally get to ask you how you managed to fool us all of these years?" He loosened his grip enough so that I had enough air to speak.

"W... What?" I choked out.

I had no idea what he was talking about, but I didn't waste the opportunity to cherish the increase of oxygen that his question allowed for.

"Did the bald man know? You two were awfully close. *Annoyingly* close in fact."

His mention of Jetto sent a shock of anger down my body, but it was soon replaced with increased confusion. Did Jetto know *what*? I didn't know if my lack of comprehension was from the pre-suffocation delirium or what, but Riggs was making absolutely no sense.

"Did he know *what*, Riggs? That you were a greasy, sniveling, bloodthirsty *traitor*?" My words were choppy without much air.

Riggs threw down the arm that was holding me up, slamming my body against the floor in the process. I gasped a few times, filling my lungs with as much of the damp cave air as

I could. He growled at me like a ground bear right before it goes for the kill.

"The accuracy! Your stealth. Your speed. Your apparent *Moonsdamn* healing powers!" Each word that he shouted was accompanied with bits of spit as it escaped his mouth. "You never had a superstar! You fooled us all for years. How. Did. You. Do it?!" His last words boomed around me as I was catching my breath.

I lifted my head to meet his soulless gaze. He might look different, and he might be more powerful than I was used to him being, but it was clear that underneath the magic, underneath the cloak of blood and death that he wore like armor, Riggs still had the same weakness that he had suffered from the entire time that I had known him—rage. When Riggs got angry, he let his ego run his actions. It was *always* his downfall.

His extreme anger at me for whatever he thought I had kept from him would be enough of a distraction for me to make my move. He might have the help of a powerful healing star to save him from a hurried slash of a blade, but there are some wounds, like a dagger through the heart, that starpower can't heal. I had to keep him mad. I had to keep him talking.

"You are a madman, Riggs. Of course I had a superstar. *You* fucking stole it from me." I carefully and as stealthily as I could slipped my hand into my cloak pocket to rest it on my dagger. *Thank the Moon*, Riggs didn't notice.

"And a load of shit it did me." He threw his hands up in frustration.

"I went through all of that effort to distract you, to weaken you, to lure you away from any chance of aid, and for what? A silly silver necklace with a measly encased *elemental* star."

The description of my pendant caught me by surprise. He knew that my star didn't just hold elemental magic. He had spent years in Brakken, activating elemental stars with me as we kept watch over them. Of course, they can be tricky to work, but their power is distinct from the other types of stars. He would know the difference between an elemental star and one with more extraordinary powers.

"Oh I tried for an hour to activate your *'superstar'* and all that I could manage to do was take the chill out of the air for a few moments. The only thing that even remotely made up for it was the fact that I was free to gather all of the useful stars that I wanted now that you were out of the way. And gather I did."

His skin tightened once more around the round pockets of magic that he had hidden inside of his flesh. As I took a step forward, I wondered how many people had entered the cave matches with a single star, thinking that it was their key to glory, only to discover that they were wildly outmatched by Riggs' hidden hold on magic.

My hand perfectly grasped my dagger in my cloak pocket now. I either needed him closer or looking the other direction for me to have a chance at driving it through his heart.

"Don't blame me because you are unable to activate a superstar," I said, lacing each word with every ounce of condescension I could muster. "Maybe the star realized that all you wanted to use its powers for was finding new ways to betray and murder your friends. Maybe it deemed that you weren't worthy of its magic."

He sniggered at me before cracking the knuckles in both his hands, a telltale sign that he was gearing up to use them.

"What? And *you* are? You and Jetto both were fools. You both deserved what happened to you. Truly, it was an oversight of death herself for not coming to claim you both sooner.

Hunting all over the land for stars that become rarer and rarer by the day. And to what? Just *give* that power away? Give it to people to grow their gardens or heal their naturally caused illnesses? There is no use fighting the darkness for them, Talla. She sealed all of our fates the moment we entered this world. They're going to die. Just like *you* will."

His pits for eyes widened. He was implying that I would be dying soon, but I couldn't let that happen. I was running out of time. I was blowing this opportunity to get my revenge. Why the *fuck* won't he come any closer? I took another risky step forward out of necessity.

"Why fight the darkness when you could become it, right? That's the point of this. You have always enjoyed killing more than the average thief. You were always hungry for it."

He lifted his brows and smirked.

"Guilty. You know, before, I was great at ending lives. But now, with these, I'm the best there ever was. You might have had a superstar for all of those years, girl. But now, I *am* one. I'm the greatest weapon the darkness ever created."

With perfect form, he launched a small blade at me. It had been perfectly aimed for my throat, but by some miracle I dodged it, feeling the cool metal woosh by my skin.

His chest was exposed, so I went to throw my own dagger. Before the blade left my hand, his arm reached my throat. His fingertips grazed my skin as I dropped to the ground and kicked my leg out. A loud crack filled the cave as I made contact with his ankles, knocking his legs out from under him and sending him to the ground. Realizing that I wouldn't get lucky dodging any more blades he threw at me, I decided it was now or never. From on the ground, I threw my dagger, sending the knife spinning in the air with the controlled strength I had summoned more times than I could count. It stuck right between his ribs on his left side, angled slightly in. *A perfect hit.* Relief flooded over me. *Thank the Moon* for muscle memory.

I stood up and dusted the red clay dirt off of my cloak as my legs shook from the adrenaline. I watched the movement in his chest slow as he laid there. I watched his eyes fixate on the blade as if he knew what the contact meant.

For thirty long seconds, I thought I had him.

But any sense of relief that I had felt faded as he started pulling my blade slowly out of his flesh. As the puncture started to magically stitch itself shut, I knew that I had not only failed, but I was now *fucking* weaponless. The blade was apparently too short to pierce the organ, and from the feral growl that escaped Rigg's mouth, I knew that it was a mistake that I was about to pay for.

"You idiot *bitch*!"

To my surprise, instead of throwing my dagger back at me like I would have done, he flung it at the ground, causing it to skid across the floor. I tracked it with my eyes, trying to quickly think of a plan to get it back—

Slam.

My back hit the floor with a thud that sent shattering waves of pain down each of my limbs. An involuntary shriek escaped my lips as he climbed on top of me, using his knees to pin my arms to the ground. His hand shot back to my throat, this time squeezing harder than before. His fingers gripped my neck like it was the handle of a dagger.

Fuck. He wasn't waiting any longer. He was going to kill me. Even though I couldn't breathe, I fought with every ounce of strength that I had. If I didn't break free of him right *fucking* now, I was going to die.

He leaned in close to me, his lips so uncomfortably close to my face. I could smell the remnants of blood and sweat that had dried along his neck. My vision started fading around the edges as he pressed his lips down onto my ear.

"Tell me. Did you cry when the bald man died? Did it remind you of when they came in the night for you and your mother?"

I paused my desperate attempts to break free from his hold as my brain slowly processed the words. I hadn't made the connection between the two events before. But now that he had mentioned it....

Memories of the night that my mother was taken from me, stabbed and left to die in her bedroom, consumed me. As layers of suppressed ache and pain and sadness started to surface, I let my body go limp under his hand. All of my efforts were now going to reclaim my mind. I had to keep myself away from the memories, from reliving that horrible night.

If I didn't... well It wouldn't matter if Riggs killed me. If I allowed myself to fall down that hole of despair that I constantly kept covered, I was as good as dead.

"Oh yes," he continued, clearly enjoying watching life slowly drain from my eyes. "I remember the story that you shared with us a few years ago. The details of it really stuck with me. I was sort of hoping my surprise would mirror that special night for you. After all..."

I didn't get to hear the reasoning behind Rigg's twisted actions. The room started fading to black as consciousness threatened to leave my body. But I did see him drop his jaw as he stared at something overhead, his beady eyes no longer fixed on mine, but on what was now above me.

"You!" He yelled, anger fully returning to his voice.

The veins in Riggs' head popped along the side of his eyes. His grip loosened enough that the tiniest amount of air could find its way into my lungs. The black fog clouding my vision started to fade. A familiar and commanding voice soon filled the room, and I couldn't help but smile. Not at what had distracted him. But *who*.

"Unfortunately, my previous offer to negotiate has expired, you sick son of a bitch."

Kieran.

By some grace of the Moon, Kieran had found us... found me.

It was the exact distraction that I needed. I broke free of Riggs as he stared in awe at the Royal Guard that was standing before him. Kieran kicked my dagger across the room to me, and I snagged it. As the handle hit my hand, something dawned on me. While my dagger was my only formal weapon, I did have something else tucked away into my cloak pocket that if used correctly, could make up for the fact that my blade couldn't reach Rigg's heart.

There was no time to second guess if it would work or not. With lightning speed, I pulled the bundle of grayweed out from my cloak and quickly wrapped the vine around my bloodied dagger. Riggs spun around in circles, trying to determine which of us to kill first. Kieran pulled out his sword at the same time that I launched myself forward, stopping Riggs mid-turn and slamming the weed covered dagger into his back. I pushed the blade in as deep as it would go, leaving only the handle above the skin.

Riggs howled in pain, flailing his arms to yank me off of him. Before he could grab me, I quickly unsheathed my knife, pressing my fingers on either side of the blade to make sure the leaves and stems stayed neatly inside the flesh. No sooner than the dagger left Riggs' skin did his magic start to quickly seal the wound shut.

Riggs now turned on me, his eyes were balls of fury as he reached his hand out once more for my neck. I ducked, anticipating his reaction. Almost immediately, his steps started to falter. I merely sidestepped him as he tumbled forward, falling so that his outreached arm caught him. The herbs worked quickly, their essence already disorienting him as it dissolved into his bloodstream.

This was it. *This* was revenge for what he did to me.

"What the—" he started, but he curled over his stomach as he heaved himself through a wave of pain.

The amount of grayweed that was now trapped inside of him would kill a normal man in seconds if ingested. I knew that the healing powers of his star would keep him alive a little bit longer, but probably not much. As he pushed himself back up to standing his voice choked out a few breathy words.

"What did you do, you *bitch?!*"

I flipped my dagger in the air before catching it again by the handle.

"I think I got your dosage just right, but it can be tricky to determine, especially considering all of the stars you hold."

The echo of his own words back to him quickly changed his fury into fear. He fell to his knees.

"But, just to be safe...." I plunged my blade into his arm, right next to where a dim blue light bulged from the muscle.

"No..." he gasped, but it was too late.

I had carved out the star that was embedded in his right shoulder, kicking it to the side after I heard it thump on the floor. He screamed again, but the wound started to heal on its own, albeit much more slowly than his previous injuries.

"You're not going to find it..." he said almost laughing, "You won't find your star. I was so angry at you, I threw it in a creek. Far away from here. It's lost."

I grabbed a handful of his greasy hair, pulling his ear right up to my mouth.

"You. Lie."

"You won't find what you're looking for by killing me."

I looked him dead in the eyes, wanting to make sure that my own were the last thing this worthless piece of shit of a man ever saw. I didn't recognize the tone in my voice as the words escaped my mouth at a near whisper.

"But I already have found it. I found you."

I aimed for a second lump to cut out before I paused, looking back and forth between my blade and Riggs. I had already gotten revenge for me, but this... this would be for what he did to Jetto.

I brought the tip of my blade up the side of Riggs' neck as unhinged tears escaped from his eyes.

"And that means I get to be the bitch that sends you into the darkness to rest not in peace, but in *pieces*."

I stabbed and sliced. I cut out every single star in Riggs' body. Even after I had removed the healing star, and his frame laid limp on the ground after finally succumbing to the effects of the grayweed and wounds, I kept slicing.

Everything was red. Redder than it had been outside of the cave match rings. The floor, my hands, my blade, my cloak. Everything around me became covered in crimson. Only the soft glowing orbs that laid scattered by my feet stood out from the blanket of blood.

I don't know how long I sat there, kneeling in Riggs' blood, staring at what I had just done. I couldn't bring myself to gather the stars that I had claimed.

I had completely forgotten that Kieran was in the room until familiar arms were around mine. I felt a phantom sensation over my hands and face, like they were being wiped clean. I felt the tug of Kieran's arms under mine, trying to pull me up. I think I heard him mutter something to me, but my ears didn't register the words. My legs were growing limp as he tried to pull me up again.

Before I knew it, I could no longer see the floor. The world spun, and as I tried to distinguish the difference between up and down, my vision faded into black.

CHAPTER 32 | KIERAN

I always knew that Talla could be dangerous—the
entire time that we had been traveling together, I kept that
information tucked away in the back of my mind. She stole and
killed for a living. She was a thief... and a rebel against the King.
I *knew* all of that, but it still wasn't enough to prepare me to
watch her carve Riggs into pieces.

It was only by the grace of the Stars that I had seen Talla
follow Riggs into the back cave at all. I felt the pull of the stars
shift as my sword cracked through my opponent's last flaming
arrow. It wasn't until after I had cracked the nose of my newest
opponent with my sword hilt that I realized that Talla was
missing. The hit split his face enough to make him yield
immediately—and *thank the Stars* for it. I hadn't really wanted
to kill anyone else, but if I needed to end my match so that I
could keep tabs on Talla, well... I might have considered using
the sharper end of my sword to make it happen.

I couldn't let Talla get to Riggs before I did, and not just because she wanted the stars that I needed to bring back to the King. Even from a few rings over, I could tell that Riggs was *thriving* down here. He didn't entertain the idea of yielding. He was claiming lives left and right, or so I guessed from the way that the crowd constantly cheered around his ring.

Even though Talla only had one dagger, she wouldn't hesitate to go after him the second she got a chance to do so. *Stars*, that's what she made me take her all this way for, wasn't it? I could feel that the stars were on the move, which meant so was Talla.

Everything in me wanted to follow her, but I couldn't just walk away from my ring... not until the sawtooth guards decided to give me a break. Even if I could fight my way past the few guards standing nearby, I wouldn't be able to get far enough without being resigned to fight them all. And by the time that I was done doing *that*, Talla could be dead. And that would be...

A crackly voice drew my attention away from the area where I had spotted her green eyes minutes before. A guard approached me and gave a twisted congratulations for my continued victories. He added that I had a small window of opportunity to take a break and refuel while they cleaned up my ring.

The words had barely left his mouth before I was over the ring wall and sprinting towards the back hallways. I barreled through the crowd of people that had started to form, trusting that the cuff on my wrist would lead me right to Riggs and Talla.

The pull strengthened as I ran down the network of caves that were on the opposite side of the raised platform. My feet flew around the turns, causing me to nearly lose my footing as I followed the seeking magic. I wasn't worried about being careful or quiet with my steps. I was too busy praying that I wasn't too late—that I wasn't going to walk in on Riggs having successfully completed his second attempt on Talla's life.

At least I had given her that dagger. She might not have her starmagic, but she would be able to hold her own. *Right?* At least until I could get there. As my feet pounded against the clay floor, I kept silently praying to the Stars that she could.

I would never have found them had it not been for my seeker star. There was nothing that gave away their location— no distinguishable footprints, no echoes of their voices, *nothing*. The caves were like a labyrinth, filled with dim torchlight, a musty smell, and, most notably, an uncomfortable silence. I had lost the roar of the crowd that was spectating the matches a few turns ago. Besides my echoing footsteps, there were no other sounds to distract me from my racing thoughts. I hated it.

Once I turned down that final passage, I finally heard something other than my own steps. Voices. Two voices, loud and angry. I knew it was Riggs and Talla.

I heard him question her about her *'superstar'*, whatever that was. I heard them go hand to hand for a bit. When I heard her gasping for air, I called upon all of the strength that I had to push my feet to move faster and harder. My thunderous steps served as a metronome to his final words to her until I swirled through the entrance, catching Riggs' attention.

My mind and heart were racing as I entered the room. I kicked Talla's blade in her direction and shouted words before my mind could even think of them. And then before I knew it, everything went red. I was frozen in place, my feet glued to the clay as I watched Talla work.

She was... mystifying. Horrifying and... *remarkable*. She hadn't shown her lawless side since she lost her access to magic, but this... I had never seen anything like this.

Over the last week and a half I kept trying to convince myself that at the end of the day, Talla was just an average thief. I ignored how unnaturally silent she was, the way that her steps never made any sound no matter the surface she walked on. I ignored how her scars, especially the angry one up her chest, were... different than they should have been. I had never seen wounds that healed with that silvery blue sheen.

But I couldn't ignore the way she moved with defying speed to retrieve her dagger, or how her hands worked with such vicious accuracy as she removed the stars from Riggs' body. Even though I could feel the presence of their power, I hadn't been able to see the stars hiding under his skin. But Talla could—her knife moved as if her hand was drawn to their exact locations.

When she finally stopped carving, Talla sat still as stone on the cave floor with her bloodied dagger in hand. Blue orbs laid unsullied in the crimson blanket that surrounded her. She made no effort to retrieve the stars that she had so brutally collected. I stood in awe at what she was—what she had *done*—for too long, unable to take my eyes off of her. Sitting in her blood stained cloak, surrounded by the stars in the dim cave, she reminded me of the gaps between the constellations in the night sky. She was the mysterious unknown surrounded by skyward magic. She was *darkness*.

Whether or not she believed Riggs in the moment, she surely knew the truth of the situation now. He didn't have her star. He had harbored several others, but he hadn't carried the one she desperately wanted... But *I* did. I had found her discarded silver pendant in the creekside before I found her that icy day outside of Ilken. If she found out that I had it... *Stars*.

She had just carved Riggs like a hog searching for it. Riggs might have betrayed her, but he was still a rebel like she was. I was a member of the King's Guard. What would she try to do to me if she discovered that I had held her star this entire time?

The damp air of the cave became laced with metal as the pools of blood began to cool and dry into the earthen floor. Talla's hands began to tremble as her adrenaline wore off. When she turned her head to look at me, my instincts flared. My hand shot back to my sword, ready to attack. But my grip relaxed on my blade when I saw the line of silver rimming her green eyes.

I walked up to her slowly before I bent down and gathered the stars one by one, placing them with the others I had collected. With each star I moved, I expected Talla to react. I expected her hand to shoot out, blade first, to prevent me from taking them. But she didn't move. Her eyes were wide and glassy, her expression vacant.

After the last star was collected, I called to her. I watched as silver tears started to roll down her face, leaving tracks through the blood as they moved down her full cheeks. My heart squeezed.

It felt like someone had just taken my sword and plunged it into my chest, dragging the blade down to slice me in two. Half of me wanted to run from her. To take the stars and *thank them* that I hadn't had to fight against her for them in the end.

I looked down at the brand on my arm, the one that signified that I had entered the matches with a guest. The skin was raised, but it was more pink than red as the mark was nearly healed. Between the scar on my groin and now this brand, this thief had marked me. And just like I couldn't turn around when I discovered her half-dead on the forest floor, I couldn't leave her.

At least not here, not in these caves. Not alone on the blood soaked cave floor in the slushy remnants of her former ally. Not when at any moment, sawtooth guards would come looking for Riggs to continue the fighting.

With my shirt in hand, I walked over to the glittering water, submerging it before lightly wringing it out. I gently wiped Talla's hands and face clean, removing as much of the evidence of her actions as possible. I tried to tell her that we needed to leave, but I don't think that she heard me. I leaned down and wrapped my arms around her before I lifted her off of the ground. The second that her body lifted out of the mess, her muscles relaxed against me.

I shifted to carrying her with my arms tucked under her, her head leaning on my chest. It was just like I had carried her from the clearing in the woods, except this time, the blood that stained her cloak wasn't hers.

I made my way through the network of caves, carefully retracing my steps. I was surprised that I could remember the correct turns to take considering how desperately I had been racing to find them. But I quickly found my way back to the main torch-lit hall that held the rings on one end and our freedom on the other.

The booms from the crowd echoed around us once more. Several sawtooth-bladed guards were walking towards us, grabbing hold of every man that they came across, staring down at their faces until shoving them aside in disappointment. *Shit*.

They were looking for someone, and I had a hunch that it was either Riggs or me. Both of us had been granted a break, but we had both been expected to return to continue fighting. Unfortunately for them, neither of us were going to be doing that. Riggs was dead, and I was getting out of here.

I turned my back against the crowd, leaning one leg up on the clay wall to support Talla's weight as I quickly reached for her dagger that I had pocketed. With gritted teeth, I made my best attempt to replicate the jagged cut I had seen the guard dole out to the man I had let yield over the brand on my own wrist. The cut that signified that I had a guest bound to me, but now we were both free.

The blade ripped through my skin, and I did my best to wipe the blood before returning my arm to cradle Talla. It wasn't perfect, but it had to work. If it didn't... well. We were getting out of here one way or another.

With my head down, I made my way quickly up the path. I breezed past exiting spectators, ignoring their confused gazes and pointed fingers until there was no one around us. The wafts of fresh sea air told me that we were getting closer to the exit. When we finally made it to the iron bars that blocked us from the open circle of fading daylight, the man standing guard looked at Talla first, then at me.

"Your arm," he demanded.

I turned slightly, my muscles straining as I tried to display my marked wrist without jostling Talla's body too much.

The man nodded, believing my faked release, *thank the Stars.* He reached behind him to pull the lever that opened the gate, and I carried Talla out of the cave arenas.

I filled my lungs with fresh, salty air, clearing them of the damp and musty breaths that had sustained me in the caves. The sea was glittering orange and yellow as the waves bobbed up and down in the setting sun. Talla's brown face was smooth and peaceful as she slept. She stayed asleep the entire time that I carried her up the winding and steep path that led back to the main road of Havetta.

When she finally opened her eyes, it was near dusk. Her body started to stiffen as her sleep was lifting, so I leaned over to put her down. Her feet hit the road with silence as she rubbed at her eyes. She looked around a bit before turning to face me. Her face was solemn, and I couldn't tell if she was consumed with relief, gratitude, or grief. Perhaps it was a combination of all three.

"Are you okay?" I asked her with complete sincerity.

She had just brutally butchered her old ally. Even if he deserved it, something like that doesn't sit lightly on you. I remember that feeling *all* too well from the things I had done before I was recruited to the King's Guard. I remember seeking justice for how the starpowered gangs treated my mother—how they treated Lor. Finding revenge can be incredibly enticing, but getting it comes at a considerable cost. And one that you likely end up paying over the course of a lifetime.

"Did you get the stars?" She glanced at the bag that I kept strapped to my back behind my sword.

I nodded, clutching at the strap and pressing it close to my skin. Silence lingered in the air between us as we just looked at each other. I knew at some point, we would find ourselves here. That after she had gotten her revenge, after the stars had been collected, we would no longer be heading in the same direction.

My stomach sank as I continued to stare at her, watching the way she bit her lip, her gaze switching between me and the bag. I didn't want to fight her. But if she decided to try to take them from me....

"Good," she said.

I could see the wheels turning in her head. My instincts flared, urging me to grab at my sword. I ignored them, instead reaching my hand out in the gap of sea air between us. My fingers looped around a stray chestnut curl that was blowing in the breeze across her nose. My palm lightly grazed her cheek as I tucked the strand behind her ear, cupping her face once it was in place.

Besides carrying her and riding with her, I hadn't intentionally touched her since the night in the grasslands. I held my breath as her eyes closed at my touch. When she didn't back away, I let out a sigh.

"So, what are we going to do now?"

It was the question that I had been dreading for days now, but I did my best not to let my nerves manifest into anything too noticeable. Was there a *we* anymore? Was there even one to begin with? I kept my hand steady on her face as she opened her eyes.

She took a deep breath before reaching her hand up and placing it on mine. She glanced down at the bloodied brand on my wrist before turning away to look at Havetta in the distance.

"Drink. That's what *we* are going to do."

I raised my eyebrows. Of all of the responses she could have given me, that was one that I had not been expecting....

She read the confusion on my face and gave me a soft smile.

"What?" she asked, flipping her braid over her shoulder, "you're telling me that you couldn't use one after all of *that* shit?" She gestured vaguely to the cliffs behind us.

I nodded, albeit a little suspiciously. I couldn't deny that a drink sounded absolutely fantastic.

"I could indeed, but..." There were too many things that I wanted to say to her, but I was struggling to find the words that matched the series of thoughts coursing through my brain.

In the end it didn't matter—she quickly pulled away from me, turning on her heel and striding towards town before I got the chance to say anything else.

325

CHAPTER 33 | TALLA

There wasn't enough wine in the world to fill the gaping hole that ached in my chest. But the second a drink hit my lips, I tried pretty damn hard to fill it anyways.

I stared deeply into the last sip of wine at the bottom of my clay mug. Riggs was dead—I had done it. I had found justice for Jetto and for myself... at *least* there was that. But that hadn't been the only thing I had wanted to get from Riggs.

None of the stars that I pulled out of his body were my superstar. None gave me the same familiar warmth and buzz over my skin as I held them in my hands. That idiotic, traitorous, son of a bitch. What had he said? That he dropped it in a creek because he thought it was *just another* elemental star?

The deep burgundy liquid rippled in my mug as my hand shook with anger. Nausea crashed over me as a flash of red and flesh filled my mind. Even with my eyes shut I could still see the crimson pools splayed out on the clay floor around me. I could smell the damp cave air mingling with the metallic scent of fresh blood. I had killed before, but I had never done anything like *that*.

My elbows were perched upon the bar top as I downed the rest of the drink and signaled to the bartender for another. After leaving Kieran along the main road, I headed straight to the bar situated in the lower level of the inn we had visited this morning. I'm sure that there were other bars in the city, but I needed to get a drink as fast as possible, and I already knew the way here.

I had to hand it to Havetta—though the thatched roofs and clay-walled buildings in no way resembled the feel of Brakken, the raucous atmosphere of this particular establishment almost made me feel at home. Now that dusk had settled in, the bar room was filled with patrons. Dancers and servers alike wore woven outfits of shells and clay beads that lightly jingled together as they moved across the floor. The wine, though less spiced than I preferred, went down smooth and quick. I was on my fourth mug—I didn't even give a shit about how my tab would be paid, I just needed to drink. I would rather drown in wine than in the memories of what happened in the caves.

As I brought my freshly filled mug up to my face, my eyes searched for Kieran. He was seated at a table at the back of the bar, apparently giving me space as I drank. In all black, he almost blended in with the shadows, but his gold eyes led my gaze through the crowd like beacons when I dared to look for him.

His attention was mostly on the group of ladies that weaved their bodies up and down each other on a raised platform in the center of the room. I didn't know why, but it annoyed me that he seemed so comfortable here in the chaos of the bar, like he wasn't used to attending fancy capital city parties or drinking out of gold mugs stamped with the sigil of the King. If I didn't know who he was, I would never guess that he was a member of the King's Guard. I might mistake him for just an average Havettan out for a drink.

Ok, maybe not average. Kieran was much taller than the rest of the men in the bar. Taller, broader, and more...

His gold eyes locked on to mine for the first time since I left him along the main road. The phantom sensation of his hand on my cheek returned as I licked the rim of my mug, saving a few drops from rolling down the side of it. Before I could blink, he looked away again to follow the dancer's bodies as they moved.

His dark hair was curling more wildly from being exposed to the salty sea air. Even still, the brown waves laid perfectly against his head. How was not even *one* out of place? How did he not seem weary or drained or concerned in the slightest? Kieran looked like he was content and in complete control. Meanwhile, the only thing keeping me from spiraling was the warm rush of the alcohol, and I hadn't been the one in the ring for hours.

I took another large sip from my mug, draining half of it in one go. I guess why shouldn't he be happy? He had gotten what he wanted, right? He was in possession of all of those stars.

'*So what are we going to do?*'

His smooth and deep voice still echoed in my ear.

We. I scoffed to myself. There wasn't a '*we*' beyond the fact that *we* had been traveling together so that *he* could lead *me* to Riggs. I was supposed to get my star so that *I* could make sure that *he* didn't have a chance to take them back to the King. That's how this had all started... but now?

I had to believe that it didn't matter that he had saved me yet again. He was just doing his job collecting stars for the King. And now, I had no star. And he had multiple. Could I really take on Kieran to get the stars back to Brakken? I had beaten Riggs without any starmagic, but barely... maybe I could?

A flash of red filled my mind before it warped into Riggs, his beady eyes lit with glee as he squeezed at my throat. The image twisted again, and I was sitting in the warm sea of red. I bit my tongue to force the rising bile and wine back down my throat. It wasn't enough, so I shook my head and silently begged the Moon for new imagery, *any* imagery, to consume me.

With my eyes shut, my mind flashed again. This time, the red memory was of Kieran. I replayed his broad muscled form dodging opponents with ease under the red stone lights. Red shifted to gold as his soft eyes blinked at me against the backdrop of the setting sun.

I downed the rest of the wine before catching the attention of the bartender signaling for a refill, and the memories vanished. Sure, maybe I could try to fight Kieran for the stars... but *would* I?

The woman behind the bar set the fresh drink down in front of me before she collected my empty mug. All I knew for sure was that what I needed now was to let go. I needed to let go of the red memories haunting me from the caves and mourn my lack of reunion with my star.

Only with a clear mind would I be able to come up with *something* to do about Kieran and the stars. And to get a clear mind, I first needed to forget. I was from Brakken, and if there's one thing we do right when shit is heavy or hurting, it's drink the night away. So that's exactly what I planned to do.

By the middle of the night, the bar of the inn was packed tightly with locals and travelers alike. A bard had posted up in the corner, stringing lively tunes from a mandolin that danced rhythmically in my ears against the chatter of patrons and shelled bodies. I was on mug seven when I decided to leave my stool at the bar and join them, letting myself blend into the mass of people. I twirled and swayed until the swings of the melody felt as much a part of me as my own breath.

I soon found myself leaning against a man as I danced, cherishing the way his hands found their way to my hips as I pressed my back against him. My shoulders hit just below his, and since the sensation didn't feel quite right, I turned to throw my arms around his neck. He was young, maybe even a bit younger than I was, but still handsome. His black hair was cut short along the sides and his warm, chocolate brown eyes lit with delight as he gazed at me. I didn't give myself an opportunity to hesitate as I pressed my mouth to his.

His kiss was hard, his tongue rushed in its movements against mine. I tried not to care—it had been far too long since I kissed anyone. And even longer since I let anyone's hands slide up and down my body. His hands moved from my hips up to behind my shoulders before they grazed the back of my neck. At the touch of his hands moving to cup my cheeks, I pressed myself away, turning my body again so that my back leaned against him.

My eyes wandered, some mysterious force pulling my gaze through smoke and dancers towards the back of the room to find him—Kieran. My heart jolted when I saw that he was no longer alone. Next to him, I could just make out a long golden ponytail tied with a ribbon, and I knew exactly who it was.

The desperate girl from the front desk was leaning over him, her stupid doe eyes locked on his. But even as she pressed her breasts against his shoulder and traced the neckline of his tunic with her finger, he wasn't looking at her. *No.* His gold eyes were fixed on me.

My heart pounded against my ribs. Knowing that I had him as an audience sent a wave of adrenaline through my body. I cracked a devious smile towards Kieran from across the room before I kissed the man behind me again, this time leaning back over my shoulder, grabbing his face with my hand. When I broke away, I snapped my attention back, hoping to catch Kieran's reaction. I swore that I saw his jaw working side to side. But he didn't move—he just sat there, never breaking eye contact until the innkeeper's daughter moved her hand up to his dark curls.

I had to turn away as she pulled at his jaw, turning his face to meet hers. I wished I had my dagger so that I could launch it and send that shiny gold ponytail sailing to the ground. A woman with cropped curls eyed me as I continued dancing. As she closed the gap between us, I fixated on how her lips were painted the same shade as her hair. *Red*.

I swallowed hard as I pushed the flash of a blood-soaked clay floor from my mind and focused on her moving hands. She held a black pipe to her face for a moment before pulling it away. As she exhaled, a sweet and pink-tinted cloud plumed from her nose.

I took a step forward from the man I had been dancing with towards her, my outstretched hand gesturing to her pipe in silent question. She looked me up and down before flashing me a wink and flipping the mouthpiece around. I put my lips on the stem and breathed as deeply as I could. I had never tasted an herb like it before. It was sweet and crisp and the smoke was lighter than fresh snowy air in my lungs.

The smoke did what the seven mugs of wine didn't. For the first time in hours, I couldn't feel the ache that had settled in my chest in the caves. I dared to try to recall my confrontation with Riggs, but to my pleasant surprise, no wave of red memories came. I forgot about the blood, and the loss of my star, and the blonde whore that was sitting on Kieran's lap.

Instead, light and airy visions of smoke mixed with dancing and shells and dark hair blended together until faded waves of color were all that I could see. I think that I might have laughed out loud before I leaned forward and kissed the woman in gratitude. Her kiss was more tender than my previous one. The combination of herbs and spices on her tongue sent a shiver down my spine as she kissed me deeper.

She pressed her body in closer to me, and then it was the three of us dancing. Our bodies swayed together in the shadowed crowd as the bard played on. It wasn't long before my vision swirled completely and euphoria set in. I didn't let myself look for Kieran again as I lost myself in the chaos.

CHAPTER 34 | KIERAN

Seven. That's how many mugs of wine I saw Talla drink, and that's not even counting whatever she managed to down before I walked into the bar. I was on my fourth, myself. Though, if I had to watch her kiss *one* more person, I was going to be on my fifth faster than I had intended.

Watching her with them shouldn't have bothered me so much, especially considering that I had my own potential conquest all but sitting on my lap, but the gnawing feeling inside my stomach made it *very* clear that it did.

After Talla essentially fled from my touch earlier, I had decided that I would give her space. I would let all of my unspoken thoughts and questions remain hidden. It was probably for the best that things between us—whatever those things were—would end this way. Tomorrow morning, Boli and I would be off to Mellin.

I had seven of the eleven remaining stars tucked safely in my nightcloth sack. The original plan had been to collect all ten of the recoverable stars that were scattered across Larendi, but despite my several attempts to locate them, I could not detect any other significant pull of magic. There were only two possible explanations for why that was: either the seeking magic in my cuff was malfunctioning or the King had miscalculated.

I didn't *want* to return to the capital without all of the stars, but either answer to my newfound lack of direction made it clear that I needed to talk to the King. Hopefully now that we had gotten Talla where she needed to go, Boli would finally let us travel without her. I couldn't imagine that the starthief would want to head south after this. She probably would be heading west—maybe even back to Brakken to find a new crew to run with now that hers... well....

I shook my head, hoping to clear the vivid memory of her kneeling in pools of blood after delivering death with her dagger like she had been *born* to do it from my mind. But when I reached my arm out to grab another sip of my drink, the image of her silver-lined eyes glowing against her red-tinted skin still lingered.

I didn't know where Talla would go or how she would get there. But I did know that as of sunrise tomorrow, our journey together would be over.

Trying desperately to direct my attention away from the crowd, Celeste curled her dainty fingers in my hair as she pressed her breasts into me. I allowed myself to breathe her in as she did so. Her golden hair smelled clean, like sea breeze and citrus. It was a pleasant departure from the damp and metallic scent that had burned into my nostrils inside of the caves.

Celeste was pretty, *sure*, but in a softer way than I preferred. Even in the candlelight, I could see how pink lightly flushed her ivory cheeks when I looked at her. Her sensual gaze and constant touch made it clear that if I wanted her, I could have her. It had been a bit since I had last visited the ladies of the Mile Dark, which meant that I should have been more than tempted to seek my release from her.

And yet I couldn't keep my eyes off of Talla. Her toffee-colored skin and black cloak *should* have made her blend in with the mass of people that were drinking and dancing. *Stars*, just a few hours ago she had held a striking resemblance to—*no,* she had *been*—the voids in the night sky, blending in with darkness. She should have been invisible in this candlelit room. But inside this bar, somehow, whenever I looked into the shadows of the crowd, I kept finding my way back to her. Just how my eyes always find their way to my favorite star at the edge of Siren in the dark.

That meant that each time that *boy's* hands moved up her body, I saw it. My fingers clenched tighter and tighter around my mug as I studied *each* tantalizing swing of her hips against the front of him. I had to bite my teeth down onto my tongue as she kept kissing him to prevent my fingers from crushing the cup into dust.

But not being able to look away from her also meant that I saw how Talla watched me, too. Unlike me, Talla wore her emotions plainly on her face. And while there were several emotions that I would have expected to read on her after everything that had happened today, her steadfast stare across the bar silently screamed only one—*challenge.*

Meeting her gaze sent waves of adrenaline through me, no different than the ones I was used to bearing before every starpowered training session back at the castle. With a centering breath, I let my grip loosen on my mug. As Celeste finally reached to pull my face to hers, I let her. I forced my lips to relax as she pressed hers into mine.

Being with Celeste tonight would have been easy—*she* was attainable. I should have taken the perfectly fine, normal, and *eager* blonde upstairs to send off this *very* long day by standing behind her and thrusting forward while she screamed out my name.

As we kissed, Celeste climbed up fully onto my lap, using her legs to straddle mine. My body played the part, sending my hands down the curve of her back to rest on her hips as she ground into me to the beat of the music. And while physically I was with Celeste, I couldn't help that my mind was elsewhere.

Maybe I didn't want normal. And Talla, well she was anything but normal, wasn't she? I couldn't deny the fact that *something* drew me to her. That *something* made me sick with fury every time that I imagined some asshole bringing a knife to her chest and carving that large, jagged scar into her beautiful brown skin. That *something* made me want to save her even after watching what she did to Riggs.

I pulled Celeste closer to me, holding her down by her waist to sit tighter against my lap as I silently pleaded with the Stars. I begged them to release me from whatever strange pull that Talla held on me. I asked them to remind me that the King had been clear with me about people like her. Anyone who sought starmagic for their own personal uses was a threat to the dream of reuniting the night sky, and even more so, to the Kingdom.

Instead of answering my prayers, I think the Stars chose to mock me. As Celeste's tongue was gliding across my bottom lip, I felt a stern tap on the shoulder. I pulled my face away from the blonde just enough to see Talla staring down at me with fire in her eyes. Though the music was loud, her words were easy to read on her swollen lips.

"Your key, Kieran." Both of her dance floor conquests were in tow.

My words evaded me as I stared at her. Her braid was loose, and several of her frizzing curls framed her face. Looking into her wild green eyes trapped the air in my lungs, making it hard to breathe or think.

I didn't *want* to give her my key. I didn't want her taking whatever unspoken game we were playing to the next level, especially not with the people behind her.

When I didn't give it to her right away, Talla held her hand out expectantly. She shifted her weight to her side, sending her hip out beyond her cloak. My eyes traced the outline, and I tried not to remember the way her body curved perfectly under the steaming bluegreen pond in the mountains. The image only grew stronger in my head as I heard her mention that she intended to use the tub that my room came with. The idea of her stripping down and wading into water without *me* there to watch....

I raised a brow at her before lightly shaking my head in protest. Talla rolled her eyes before slinging a half-hearted threat my way about finishing the castration job that she had started before. I started to playfully remind her that it would be hard for her to do so since *I* still had her dagger from earlier today, when Celeste suddenly jumped out of my lap.

The contents of Talla's mug were now seeping into my clothes, the wine drenching my tunic from my shoulder down to my waist.

"What in the *Stars* is wrong with you?" Celeste shrieked, staring down at the deep stain that now colored the front of her satin gown.

A defiant smile danced across Talla's lips that rivaled the one she gave me in the woods the first time we met. The steadfast cap that I held on my emotions cracked, allowing a tidal wave of annoyance to flood me. With my heart pumping more wine than blood through my veins, I stood up, swiftly pushing the table out from in front of me with stiff arms. I stared down at Talla, using every inch of our height difference to display how *ready* I was to escalate this unspoken challenge to a physical one.

But as I glared down at her with my fingers clenched tightly at my side, her eyes shifted. For a split second, her face no longer read stubborn or resistant. *No.* Instead I caught a glimpse of the other expressions that I had been expecting to surface from her tonight—sadness. Fear. Guilt.

That momentary crack was enough to cool my temper. I knew that underneath the mask of alcohol and herbs, she was paying the price for her revenge on Riggs. I could see that she was hurting, even if she clearly wouldn't admit it to herself.

With a deep breath, I let my shoulders fall. I reached my hand into my soaking wet pocket and fished out the small key to my room. Talla hesitated as she stared at the key before taking it from my hand, turning on her heel, and heading up the stairs. A heavy sigh escaped my mouth as I watched Talla and her partners disappear onto the second level of the inn.

I told myself that Talla could do whatever she wanted, and if she wanted to erase the events of today by lying with the two that followed her upstairs, then so be it. I wouldn't need my room tonight. I would find a way to salvage the evening with Celeste and soon find myself perfectly comfortable in her bed. And then in just a few hours, it would be tomorrow.

Perhaps giving Talla that key was the easiest way to leave her here. At least if she was upstairs tonight, she wouldn't be sleeping with Boli in the stables. Boli and I could get our first fresh start in the morning without the interference of the starthief in almost two weeks. In a few hours the stars would fade and the sun would rise. We would be gone, and I would probably never see Talla again.

The seconds after I handed over my key ticked by slower than it took the blades of grass to grow in the Highlands. I fetched Celeste a clean rag from the bar, and with careful dabbing did my best to help lift the stain. The entire time that my fingers ran the rag over her chest, my heart pounded. I even managed to order another drink, downing the entire mug in three swift gulps. Nothing helped.

I made it all but fifteen *excruciating* minutes before I dismissed Celeste and ventured up the stairs towards my room. As I flew up the stairs without even a second glance at the blonde standing on the bottom landing in disbelief, the only thing managing my nerves was the fact that fifteen minutes wasn't very much time. Fifteen minutes wasn't enough for the three of them to get very far... not when they were that drunk.

At least, not if you're doing it right.

341

CHAPTER 35 | TALLA

When my vision cleared, I found myself in a bedroom, soaking wet and sitting on the floor. I was alone, *thank the Moon,* because I apparently had overflowed the tub. Water had flooded the stone catch basin and was now pooling around me. My clothes were soaked through to my skin, and though my body was still buzzing from the wine, it wasn't enough to fight the damp chill of the cool water.

I quickly stripped myself naked, hanging the wet clothes to dry by the lit fireplace. I grabbed a long cloth from the cupboard and wiped myself dry as I stood by the flames before tossing it over the water on the ground. With nothing dry of my own to wear, I scampered to the bed, pulling the sheets close to me. I didn't know when it started to rain, but sheets of it whipped sideways against the window as I laid beneath the covers.

The humid sea air made the chill settle deep against my bones. Even with the fire lit and the thick covers of the bed, my body shivered. I *desperately* missed my magic.

Even though I was starless, and I knew that it wouldn't work, I tried to warm the room. I might have been more drunk than I realized, because for a *second* I actually thought it worked. The chill felt the tiniest bit less offensive... until it didn't.

The pillow tucked beneath my cheek became wet with tears as I pressed my face down into it. Jetto was finally avenged, but I felt nowhere near the amount of joy and relief that I had expected. In truth, now that the light and airy haze of the herb had lifted, I felt the opposite. I felt lifeless. And cold. And empty.

Riggs deserved to die, dammit. He was a *monster*. He was a monster who killed Jetto and who knows how many others for the sake of collecting stars. He had wanted to torture me. He wanted to imitate the worst night of my life for the fun of it. He wanted me to nearly drown in the memories of when that King's Guard came in the night to kill me and my mother before he sent me to the darkness himself.

Riggs was a monster who didn't just end a life, he was thrilled with making a show of it. He had wanted to make a show out of me. Now he laid in pieces on the floor because of what *I* did with my hands. His life wasn't the first I had taken, but with Riggs... I had been ruthless. I had been hungry and unstoppable and—let's face it. I had been *grand* with how shredded him.

All evening I tried not to compare my dagger's spectacular display of bloodshed with what I had seen Riggs do with his hands over the years. But I couldn't help myself from seeing the similarities. I had been just like how he could be, how

I had seen him so many times over the years. So, if he was a monster that deserved to die, what did that now make me?

The sound of footsteps approaching the door pulled me back to the bedroom. It dawned on me then that I had absolutely no idea *whose* room I was in or whose bed I had climbed into naked. I prayed to the Moon that it was neither the man or woman that I had been dancing with. I wasn't sure *how* I was going to explain the mess to them without looking like a sloppy fool.

As the oncomer lightly knocked on the door, I wiped my tears dry. Somehow I already knew who it was before I even saw the two familiar boots through the gap above the floorboards.

"What, *Kieran*?"

Did he follow me up here? If I thought that I didn't want the strangers seeing me like this, I definitely *knew* that I didn't want Kieran to.

"I just wanted to make sure you didn't drown yourself in there. I would hate to have to deal with that before I found my way to bed."

A hushed chuckle escaped me as I wiped at my face again, ensuring the tears had dried. *So apparently*, I was in his room, then. I guess I hadn't locked the door after I had entered it because not three seconds later did I hear the hinges squeak. They squeaked again as he pushed the door back into place before a soft *click* from the door lock followed.

"Jeez, I can hear your teeth chattering from here."

I peeked up over the covers hoping that my glare might send Kieran away, but he didn't see me. He was too busy surveying the mess of water that I had made in the room—*his* room. I watched his eyes flip back and forth from the pool of water on the floor to my clothes hanging up by the fire.

"You know, when you threatened to cut my balls off for *real* if I didn't hand over the key to my room so you could 'rinse the wine' out of your cloak," he held his fingers up in the air for that last part. I couldn't decide if he was reminding me that he knew that the deep stains in my cloak weren't from wine or suggesting that he hadn't believed it had been my reason to use his room in the first place. "I didn't realize that you didn't know how to properly work a tub. The water is supposed to stay *in* the basin. That's how you prevent it from getting all over the floor and your clothes."

My narrowed eyes widened a bit in surprise before I closed them tightly. I tried to piece together the events after I had taken a puff off of the red-headed girl's pipe. Everything had been swirls of light and shadows.

I could vaguely remember storming up to him as that annoying blonde girl was straddling his lap, but I didn't remember threatening him. Anything that happened while that herb was in my system seemed permanently recorded as a blur. Though, spitting such a threat at him did *sound* like something I would do.

"Oh...sh...shut. U...up," I retorted, my speech broken with shivers.

I was unable to focus on anything wittier to say with the cold that was pressing in on me. Kieran looked again at my clothes hanging up by the fire before switching his attention to me.

"It looks like you're sleeping here then?" There was an odd tone to his voice that I couldn't quite place.

"I... well." I stopped short, unsure of how to answer him. I hadn't planned on it, *no*. But as the rain continued to pelt the small window in the room, the thought of having to put on wet clothes and walk across the street to the stables to sleep next to Boli as I had been doing seemed like unnecessary torture. "Yeah, I guess so."

The silence between us made the rain sound like it was bits of metal, not water, that were hitting the glass.

"And here I thought if you were opting for a bed tonight rather than a stall, you would have chosen to share one with one of the multiple people who had their hands all over you." His tone shifted again, but though it was subtle in his voice this time, this shift was more readable. Was he... *jealous?*

I knew that he had been watching me downstairs as I danced and mingled in the crowd, but I hadn't been sure if his moves with Celeste had been for real or a part of some game. I sat up a bit, testing him, keeping the covers pulled up to not expose my chest. I focused on his eyes.

To his credit, his golden gaze never left my face. Not even as I intentionally let the blanket slip, casually exposing the right side of my collarbone. *Nothing* in his body language showed any reaction. I slumped back against the headboard.

"No," I huffed. "In my experience, the idea of three is often much more exciting than the realities of it. I think I just didn't want to deal with the logistics."

I couldn't help but wonder how *awkward* it must have been to dismiss both of my prospects before entering Kieran's room. I was sort of relieved that I couldn't remember it.

"*Ah*." He said, leaning against the mantle and sliding his hands into his pant pockets. I wrapped myself tighter in the blankets as a new wave of chills spread over me.

The silence ticked on as we watched each other.

"So, you can be going now." I motioned to the door with my eyes. He took his hands out of his pockets and crossed his arms.

"No way, this is my room. Albeit a bit wetter than I would have liked." He took another glance at the floor before he bent down and picked up the cloth I had haphazardly thrown on top of the water. He twisted the cloth over the tub, wringing out the excess water before hanging it up next to my clothes. The sight of his strong hands gripping around the fabric sent a temporary warmth down my legs.

"Besides, the inn is completely booked. And, despite how much I enjoy Boli's company, I don't find the stables as *homey* as you do." I ignored the slight as I burrowed myself deeper into the bed.

"Well I'm not leaving. I'm fr...freezing." I saw him look to the side, noting the steady pattern of rain that was beating against the window. He then slipped off his boots and unhooked the sword and bag from across his chest. He grabbed at the bottom of his tunic before he slid it over his head. The motion revealed his perfectly toned torso, and my mouth fell open.

"Exactly *what* do you think you're doing?" I couldn't help but stare as he took a few steps towards the bed, tossing his items on the small table that rested along the edge of the room.

I had seen him shirtless in the caves, but he had been further away. This close, I could see each one of the hard, muscular lines.

"If I am going to have to sleep in that chair, you can't be having your teeth chattering all night. I'm going to help you warm up." I looked at the chair that accompanied the table. Even if your feet were resting up on the table surface, it would be extremely uncomfortable to sleep in it, especially for someone of his size.

"Ok..." I said hesitantly as I watched him set his items down on the table, "but *why* are you taking off your shirt?" But as the words were escaping my mouth, he had already reached the side of the bed, grabbing at the covers.

"You spilled wine on me... more like dumped actually, when I told you I wasn't handing over the key to this room." He raised his eyebrows at me waiting for my reaction, but I didn't give one.

I didn't remember doing *that*, either.

"Or," he continued, "did you want me to climb into bed damp as well?"

An unexpected and breathy sound escaped mouth as he stepped closer. I found myself making a clear boundary of the blanket between me and the spot he was climbing into. As soon as his body hit the sheets, I already felt warmer. But as he shifted his weight, there was a sharp sting of something cold against my side.

"Ah!" I yelped, instinctively scooting away from him, and away from my at least semi-warmed spot. The metal buckle of his belt had found a weak spot in the blanket barricade.

"What?" he asked with a tone of surprise.

"Your belt."

"Would you like me to remove it?"

His level of calm was nothing short of lethal, the question sending a different kind of shiver down my spine. *Dangerous.* We were approaching dangerous territory in this room right now.

As much as my instincts were nudging me to answer, *'no'*, I couldn't deny that I was already feeling so much warmer. With the way that his body heat was already traveling through the sheets, banishing the chill from deep below my skin, the thought of saying *anything* that might get him to leave was too risky.

"What I'd *like* is to not feel like I was buried in sheets made of ice." It wasn't a yes, but it was close enough.

He didn't say anything else before his hand moved across his waist slowly unhooking his belt. My pulse quickened with the soft clang of the metal as it loosened, and then even more as it hit the floor echoing in the room.

As heat flushed my cheeks, I flipped my body over so that my back faced him. With as much determination as I could muster, I concentrated on the sounds of the rain rather than the tightening sensation that was growing in my abdomen.

"Just close enough so that I can fall asleep, Kieran. Then move your ass to that chair. And *don't* get any ideas." I barked the last line at him, though it probably had been a warning more for me than it was for him.

The prick actually *chuckled* in response.

"Oh, *that* I can promise." His words danced along the blanket barrier that I had installed between us, the warmth of his breath rustling the strands of my hair that were resting on my ear.

I didn't like the way he emphasized the word *that,* like the idea of touching me was something he would never consider. I didn't like that it sent an unexpected wave of sadness over me. I wasn't... disappointed that he wasn't going to make a move on me. *Was I?*

Rain. I had to focus on the rain. I had told myself that I would come up with a plan on how to handle Kieran and the stars tomorrow, and tomorrow was now just a few hours away. My eyelids tugged against each of my blinks as my muscles and bones silently ached. I was going to need at least a *little* sleep if I had any chance of regaining those stars from him. If I let myself acknowledge this pull that I felt towards the man who was laying behind me... The incredibly tall, skillful, and perfectly tone—

I shook my head lightly against the pillow as I burrowed further into the bed. *Rain, Talla.* And then *sleep. Moon, save me,* get the *fuck* to sleep.

CHAPTER 36 | Talla

What felt like hours passed as darkness swirled beneath my eyelids. Thanks to Kieran, I was no longer shivering from the cold. But despite my constant efforts, my brain would still not surrender to sleep.

I cracked my eyes just enough to register any hint of morning light peering through the window. All that glowed inside the room were the dying embers in the fireplace. Despite the rain continuing to pour down from the sky, the only sounds that my ears could register were the quiet and slow breaths of the man lying next to me. I knew that Kieran's hands were inches away from my body—my *naked* body. My blanket barrier was still intact, but barely. Did he realize that if he so much as lifted a finger, he would be grazing my upper thigh?

The remnants of the *barrel* of wine I had drank this evening to drown the memories from inside the caves still pumped through my veins. The brew tried its best to pull me towards him, *urging* my limbs to shift my body back just a *little* towards his strong and callused hands. The wine reminded me how well those hands could wield a blade and tempted me with visions of other skills that they might possess.

The white covers of the bed rose and fell in a steady, slight rhythm. Despite following orders for a living, Kieran apparently chose *not* to listen to me when I demanded that he didn't linger in this bed. I guess I really couldn't blame him for staying, though. His alternative for sleeping was that tiny uncomfortable chair. I wouldn't have listened to me, either.

I carefully turned my body over, hoping that the shift would be enough to finally send me into sleep. But as my cheek landed on the pillow again, it became clear that I hadn't realized that Kieran had moved his pillow closer to mine... *more* than closer. His pillow was now practically on mine. This meant that as I settled myself into my new position, my face rested mere inches from his. His eyes were closed as he lay sprawled on his side, his torso completely exposed with only the lower half of his body under the covers.

Moon, save me. I couldn't stop myself from studying him. My eyes started where the blanket met his waist, memorizing the length of his body and the way his tight tan muscles cut into a v before they disappeared beneath the sheets. My gaze moved up to his stomach, tight and chiseled from his apparent years of combat training.

Further up I examined his chest, which was just as broad and strong as the arm that rested by his side. I worked my way along his shoulders before scanning the line of his chiseled jaw. From our time on the road, he now sported a coating of short, but full, dark hair. My eyes followed the curves of his lips and his nose, remarking how they both were so perfectly placed beneath his ever so enchanting gold—

Fuck.

A racing jolt of energy dropped into my stomach as Kieran blinked at me. How long had he been watching me? Had he seen me just shamelessly study every inch of him that was visible?

I could have looked away and tried to pretend that I hadn't been all but memorizing every bit of him that I could see, but as he raised a dark, knowing eyebrow, blood rushed to heat my cheeks. I had been caught indulging in the view, so there was no point in stopping now.

I bit my lip as I lost myself to the gold of his eyes. Not the bright, shining gold akin to coins like they usually were in daylight. *No,* his hue now was soft and warm, like melted honey mixed with afternoon sunlight. I didn't know anything could be more alluring than the color of coins, but as I stared into his eyes, I found myself never wanting to blink.

My legs, betraying me, tucked up a bit to close the gap between us. My bare knees pushed through the pile of blanket until they grazed his leg. I subtly shifted my weight, causing my legs to fall slightly open.

The movement did not go unnoticed by the Guard. His gaze darted down to where the blanket had been moving on top of me. His eyes locked on my hand that was now acting with a mind of its own and reaching up in the space between us. He meticulously followed my fingers as they landed on the hard muscle of his chest. I silently begged the Moon that he couldn't hear my heart racing—especially as I felt his own heartbeat quicken at my touch.

But even as my fingers settled on him, he didn't move away. His face remained perfectly calm and neutral, his body unnaturally still.

His keen ability to subdue his emotions and fight his own physical responses to them was something I had envied while traveling with him. Such a skill was only mastered with rigorous discipline and control. Neither of which I was cut out for—I always struggled to remember that my mind was stronger than my body. My face almost *always* gave me away in moments of fear. Or of adrenaline. Or of desire. But Kieran's....

"I thought you said not to get any ideas?" There was a twitch in his lips as he spoke to me, and I could see the truth then.

He might have perfected his mask of calm, but right now, my touch was cracking it. If I kept going, if I pushed a little harder....

The challenge before me lit my body on fire.

Forget sleep—it wasn't coming for me anyway. I was now committed to seeing how far I could take this. My finger slowly moved up and down his muscles as heat built under my skin. Just *how* much of his control could I chip away? A *little*? His eyes widened at my movements, turning from calm to hungry. I bit my lip harder. A *lot*?

"I thought you said you'd promise not to?"

I reached my face up, pressing my lips into his softly, with a tantalizingly slow pace. He parted his mouth, but only slightly, before annoyingly pulling away after a second.

"Talla...." My name was both a question and a warning on his lips that made my core ache.

I knew then that I didn't just want to chip away some of his control—I wanted to *demolish* it. By the way his breathing started to quicken, I knew that I was close to making that happen. It was now or never. Come sunrise, there was a good chance that I was never going to see him again. It would be a shame to waste such a convenient opportunity to end up with my cake after having eaten some, too.

My hand started moving up his body to palm the nape of his neck. My pulse throbbed through my body, my muscles tightening as it traveled down my legs and back up. The steady beating of my heart ultimately settled to hum between my thighs that were already slick from the thrill of the tease.

Kieran's pupils grew wider as he gazed down at my lips. I used my toes to pull down the blankets just a *bit* to uncover my shoulders and the top of my breasts. Each breath of his hesitation sent an electrifying wave of adrenaline through me.

After everything, after the last two weeks, after what had happened in the caves, I needed *this*. I needed to win at something, and I needed it to feel like a win. I was going to break that control of his. I needed this release.

I watched his jaw twitch as his mask of calm cracked further. His eyes grew hungrier, his breaths less steady. But he still hadn't answered me. He still hadn't moved so much as an inch closer to me, despite the way my hands traced lightly along his skin.

Just as a glimmer of doubt in my ability to break him flashed through my mind, he moved. He brought his face as close as he could to me, his nose now lightly brushing mine. My hand grabbed tighter around his neck—I was *not* losing any chance that I had to lock him in close to me. Not when I was so close to winning this fight.

"Well?" I said, my voice sultry.

For the first time since he entered the room, he allowed his eyes to look down the bed. I watched him linger on my chest before they moved lower to scan the parts of me that were still hidden by the sheets.

My heart pounded in my chest as I waited. *Close.* I was close. Just one more crack. I lightly pressed my nails into the skin where his neck met his shoulders.

Gold eyes shot to mine, his pupils wild and wide.

"Well," the side of his mouth lifted as he smirked. "I lied."

With a jolt of victorious energy, I pulled his mouth squarely onto mine.

Kieran's kiss was everything the others I had received that night were not. Hot, smooth, insatiable. His hand found my lower back under the covers and pulled me to him with vicious strength, causing my skin to slam into his. I could almost taste the hunger on his lips as they moved, making room for his tongue to slide into my mouth.

He held me tightly against him for a few breaths before shifting his weight, now leaning on his arm that had been tucked under his pillow. I went to hook my leg around him to draw my body even closer to him, but his arm held me away.

The strength in his forearm locked my hips square against the bed as he seamlessly shifted his weight over me.

My center ached with need as the sight of him hovering over me made me feel small against him. Small, but in the *best* possible way. His mouth still covered mine as I felt his fingers trace the points of my hip bones before finding their way between my legs. In one swift motion, I felt him slide two of them inside of me, the sudden change in pressure catching the breath in my throat.

Moon, save me. His touch was *incredible*. Every stroke of his hand sent a wave of pleasure through my body. Tension was building in my core as desire traveled down my legs, curling my toes into the sheets. I kept trying to kiss him, to keep a claim over the situation that was beginning to undo me. But I couldn't help the gasps and moans that were escaping with each breath that I took.

His fingers worked faster and harder in response, and alongside the pleasure that was building inside of me was a complete and utter sense of awe.

It had been a while since I had found release, but I could not believe how *quickly* I was about to come for this man. His hands were just as skillful curved inside of my body as I had seen them wielding his blade.

I could live off of this sensation... this building pressure and pull and feeling of familiarity. It was like my insides were being drawn to him, and... *no.* I focused harder on the way my muscles hummed, identifying exactly where my body felt like it was being summoned to. It was to him, but also, *Past* him? Past him and towards the... table?

I peeked my eyes open and looked down to see the faint blue glow moving back and forth in the orange light of the room. Another moan escaped me as I tried to delay the inevitable.

He had chosen to use his dominant hand that bore his starcuff. The familiar pull of the seeking magic from his star was flooding my body with each pump of his fingers. Why the *fuck* had I never thought of using starmagic during sex? This was beyond, this was....

My back arched as I came, my eyes slamming shut as his fingers worked each pulse of pleasure from me. As Kieran went to pull his hand away from me, I desperately clawed at it. My fingers grasped the smooth and cold metal wrapped around his wrist, stopping him before he could do so.

My eyes locked on to his as he looked down at me with confusion. Magic traveled up my arm, dancing along my skin as long as I kept hold of his starcuff.

"No." I panted, trying to make words come out of my mouth despite my body still reeling from the release. "Not yet."

I wasn't ready to let go of the feeling of starmagic again, not when it felt so natural to have it coursing inside of me.

A devious grin split Kieran's face that made me swallow hard. To my surprise, he worked his hand to add an additional finger to fit alongside the others. My eyes widened as he stretched me at my opening, my free hand clawing at the sheets by my side.

He chuckled against my lips as he gently worked his fingers into a slow and steady rhythm, picking up where he had just left off.

"For someone who claimed they didn't want me to get any ideas tonight, you sure do seem to like them."

I wanted to roll my eyes at him, but before I could, he lowered his face, moving his kiss to land on my neck. His hand pressed against me harder as his lips traveled down the scar between my breasts. They grazed slowly over my stomach before he finally settled on the epicenter of my ache for him. As he continued to kiss me, he plunged his hand deeper, pulling his fingers upwards against me.

His hand and mouth worked in tandem as pleasure and magic railed me. I could barely breathe as my body tensed around him. My fingers found their way to his hair, gripping his dark curls tightly until I couldn't hold on any longer. My body shuttered with release a second time, the pleasure sending my eyes backward as my orgasm consumed me.

It wasn't until my legs stopped quivering under him did Kieran pull himself up so that his lips were once again in line with mine. Even though he was slightly panting, his face was lit with the cocky satisfaction of someone who knew that they had just given an incredible performance.

And incredible it most definitely had been. The first orgasm had ignited me, but the second... it had *unraveled* me. All of my thoughts and questions that I had suppressed during this journey with him—about who he was, about why he did the things that he did—came bubbling to the surface.

He leaned down, brushing his lips against the line of my chin when a question escaped my mouth before I could stop it.

"Why did you save me?"

Kieran furrowed his brow. "Which time?" he asked, turning his head a bit to the side.

As I watched the hunger fade from his eyes, I so desperately wished I could take my outburst back. *Sure,* that particular question was the one I had buried deepest in my mind. But did I really have to ask it *now*?

"In the woods." I answered him, barely audible to myself.

He looked at me for a moment, clearly contemplating his response, before he twisted his body from on top of me to settle down at my side. One of his calloused hands grabbed at mine and pulled it lightly to his waist.

His voice was low, but earnest as he held me to him.

"When I first saw you, the day you gave me this," he moved my hand so that my fingers trailed over his tightened pants. He guided me right down to the spot where I knew my dagger had impaled him. My breath quickened as he had me trace the length of him pressing tightly up against the fabric. "I noticed that instead of the darkness that I am used to seeing in the eyes of criminals, yours carried a spark. I didn't know why, but you were so obviously different than any other thief I've encountered before."

His hand moved up from mine to land on my chest. He traced the large scar that laid between my breasts and sighed. I hadn't told him how I had gotten it, or that it had been a member of the King's Guard who had given it to me. But somehow, I felt like he knew it was a part of the reason that I did what I did.

"I might not agree with your methods, but that afternoon I took a chance on the idea that perhaps you were working for something bigger than yourself. Like I was." His hand now lay flat on my scar, but his touch was warm, and sensual.

A staggering, and unfamiliar, current of nervous energy consumed me. *This* wasn't what I was expecting when I had committed to tempting him earlier this evening. Sex was one thing—but this level of intimacy... this was something wildly unknown to me.

"There is a certain magic to you, Talla," he said as he moved his hand to lightly graze the several silvery nicks that covered my ribs. "I mean *look* at you. Your wounds look like they were stitched back together with pure starlight." He moved his hand slowly across my stomach and up my arms, as if he was studying the exact patterns of scars that marred my skin.

As if reading my thoughts, he leaned down to kiss the scar that ran up the length of my chest.

"Your scars are beautiful, Talla. They glow against your skin just like the stars do against the dark. It is almost as if you were covered with the night sky... like your skin is made of it. It's like you're *made* of stars."

His words danced in my ears before sending a new wave of unidentifiable emotion through my body. I didn't have anything to say to something like that. I had no practice in responding to words that... *lovely* being spoken to me.

So instead of saying anything, I lifted my chin up and kissed him. Now that I was no longer focused on breaking through his control, I noticed how Kieran tasted of wine and smoke and trees in the snow. He returned my kiss without hesitation, his efforts shallow and slow. Then guilt rushed over me.

I pulled my face away from him and pressed my hand into his warm and muscled chest.

"I'm sorry. About the cave matches."

The details of what I was sorry for—specifically the fact that I had carelessly risked his life to seek my revenge, revenge that ended up feeling worse than the betrayal had—were left unsaid.

Kieran shook his head.

"Don't be. We both got what we were looking for," he reached up to move a piece of my hair away from my face, tucking it behind my ear. "Didn't we?"

No. Not really. Even though I never found my star, I nodded in agreement anyway.

Kieran motioned to the small window in the room that no longer framed the darkness of the night sky, but instead the grayish purple clouds that surfaced just before first light.

"Jeez. It's almost dawn."

Any heat that had existed between us was now cooled at that unspoken reminder—once that sun was fully up, there would be no common thread tying us together.

He had the stars, and he would be bringing them back to the King. I was a thief who couldn't let that happen.

Fatigue finally washed over me. My eyes felt heavy as he pulled my head onto his chest. I didn't have the heart to fight him even though I knew that in a few hours, I may likely never see him again.

I don't know when I started caring about that, but now that the moment was approaching with rapid speed, I couldn't help but wish the sun would take its sweet time when rising today.

The last thing I remembered was the way Kieran's thumb lightly stroked my cheek as I finally drifted off into a very deep sleep.

CHAPTER 37 | TALLA

Warm.

I was so warm. But as my heavy sleep lifted, I became aware of the familiar weight of a hangover pressing itself down onto my head. I turned my face to look at the man whose arm was draped around me. Kieran's dark curls laid in a mess along his forehead as he remained lost in sleep.

Something in my chest tightened as I watched him rest. Hooking up with a member of the King's Guard was *not* something I had ever expected for myself, and yet here I was—warm and, honestly, perfectly content lying skin to skin with him.

I lightly brushed a strand of his hair out from in front of his eye, hoping the sensation of my touch wouldn't wake him. It didn't. And while I was pleased to watch him as he remained asleep, I couldn't help that I was also a bit jealous. Not because I needed more rest for myself, but because, for him, the day where everything would change between us hadn't yet started.

After carefully slipping out from under his arm, I propped myself up. The ache in my head sharpened around my temples as soon as I was vertical. I groaned as I rubbed them lightly. I had a blurred memory of Kieran setting a tonic vial on the nightstand, and I needed it, *now*.

Carefully peering over his sleeping body, my eyes locked onto the little glass container filled with a soft purple liquid. I stretched myself over him, trying to grasp the vial without having to get out of bed. It was no use. Even after I tried to push against Kieran to give me the extra distance, my fingertips were still inches away. His firm muscles didn't budge as I carefully leaned my entire body into him, grasping desperately at the air.

Ugh. Perhaps I could go without the tonic. I went to lean myself back onto my pillow when a flash of pain jumped from my head to my eyes. It was as if my body knew that I had been considering falling back to sleep and therefore sent the pain in protest. *Never mind,* then. Tonic it was.

I slid out of my side of the bed, carefully touching my feet to the floor. The water that I had flooded from the basin had dried thanks to the hours of warm firelight overnight, but the air inside the room still felt damp. As I walked around the wooden bed frame, I took a curious swipe at my clothes that were hanging on the mantle. *Shit*, they were still damp.

On the ground in front of me was Kieran's tunic, the wine-soaked one that he had effortlessly discarded to expose his chiseled frame before he climbed into bed. I couldn't help but smile as I picked it up. Aside from the part that was still damp with wine, it smelled like him. The fabric carried comforting notes of amber and woods all blended with a hint of salt from the sea air. I breathed it in, letting the scents mingle deep in my lungs, before I slid it over my head.

Doing so, however, sent me off balance. I tried to stay upright, but it was like the ground was pulling my body, still heavy with grog and hangover, down to it. As I stumbled to the side, I instinctively reached for something to prevent my fall.

My hands slammed into the small table pressed against the edge of the room. Kieran's sword that had been laid carefully on the surface shifted some with the impact, but didn't fall, instead catching on the strap of his canvas bag. My eyes widened as recognition flooded me. *That* was his star bag, the one he never left unguarded. *Fuck* a healing tonic. I was going to use the healing star.

My fingers quietly slid under his blade as I carefully moved it to rest along the arms of the chair. I gently opened the canvas bag, silently pulling out the black night cloth sack that was inside. Even with the layer of fabric between me and the stars, the comforting buzz of their magics felt like home.

Turning the bag upside down, I dumped the stars out on the table. A soft blue light filled the room as I surveyed the stars that Kieran had collected. My tongue grazed the front of my teeth from behind my lips—I could almost taste the magic rippling off of the orbs as they glowed in front of me.

All of the stars looked essentially identical, and there was no way to determine which star was which without picking them up and activating them. My eyes scanned each one, wondering if I could guess correctly on the first try. As I admired the shining orbs, I unexpectedly found myself counting seven. I had anticipated the bag to only contain *six* stars, the one from Kieran's opponent in the cave matches and the five that *I* had... *recovered* from Riggs.

I scanned the stars laid out in front of me three times to make sure that my headache wasn't interfering with my ability to count. Each time, I arrived at the same number. There were in fact seven stars, as well as one small and mysterious bundle that was wrapped in what looked like ripped fabric. My headache waned as I contemplated the non-star package. What could possibly be in these wrappings that Kieran had deemed worthy of his utmost protection?

Deciding that the now minor ache in my head could wait a few more minutes without being cured with healing magic, I let my curiosity lead me to reach for the ripped fabric first.

As I started working on undoing the folds, a silver chain slipped out. The links were thin and delicate, but still sturdy. It wasn't the type of chain that would be worn for special occasions or that was likely to hold a fine jewel, this was for daily wear.

I kept unwrapping until the entire piece, or rather, *pieces* were in view. Still forged to the chain was one small silver plate, bent and scratched. Next to it, there was another plate with a jagged edge, like it had been cracked free from its other half.

My heartbeat thudded alongside Kieran's sleepy breaths as I looked down at the broken necklace that laid flat on the fabric against my palm. Even broken, there was no mistaking it—I knew this silver. These were two halves of my own, now starless, pendant.

A series of competing emotions bloomed in my chest, taking up so much space in my lungs that it soon became hard to breathe. I had essentially given up hope that I would find the pendant again after Riggs claimed he didn't have it. How was this silver lying in my hand before me? Riggs had ripped it off of me that night in the woods outside of Ilken before Kieran found me. How the fuck was it that it was now in Kieran's possession?

The raspy voice that had haunted my nights since the night of his betrayal sounded in my head.

'You're not going to find it. I threw it in a creek.'

Riggs had said that right before he died. I had assumed he was messing with me—surely he didn't just throw away a star because he was frustrated by it? But Riggs had been known for his angry and impulsive outbursts. If he hadn't been lying like I thought he had been....

A stir in the bed behind me pulled my attention away from the table. Kieran had rolled from his side to his back, allowing me to see the entirety of his broad chest peeking from out of the covers. I did my best to block the orb's bluish glow from shining in his direction, praying to the Moon that it wouldn't wake him. Only when his breathing returned to the deep and slow rhythm of sound sleep did I allow my focus to return to the table.

My anger and relief competed for my attention as I clutched the silver tightly in my hand. My star was *here*. That's why there was one more than I had been expecting. The magic that I had so greatly missed, and my key to successfully leaving with the rest of the stars, was right in front of me. I just had to figure out which one it was.

Without any further hesitation, I picked up the star closest to me. I relished the familiar rush and warmth of starpower that danced under my skin as I searched for the way to activate it. Using my mind's eye, I parsed through the intricacies of the magic. A vision of shadow and silence overwhelmed me, suggesting that the orb held stealth magic. My heart sank as I set the star back down.

That star had been Jetto's, the one he wore encased in a ring on his finger until that dreaded night in Tuul. I drew a circle across my chest in prayer for my fallen friend before continuing to pick the stars up one by one.

The visions that I received changed with each unique type of magic. Wind and flames followed by pinholes and steel and then breath and light. Elemental. Accuracy. Health.

My original mission to seek out healing magic to rid myself of my headache was completely abandoned as adrenaline coursed through my veins. There were just two stars left to try. One of them was *my* star. I picked up the one that shined a bit brighter and was met with a vision of sunlight and snow. Elemental again.

My heart skipped as I stared down at the last remaining star. I had been without my superstar for only two weeks, but the constant waves of fear and uncertainty in my abilities that came with navigating the world without it made it feel like a lifetime.

My fingers rubbed along the silver pieces tucked tightly in my palm. I would have to find a way to make the star wearable again... perhaps once I found my way out of Havetta, I would be able to find a metalworker to craft me another condensed piece. The trade was complex, and becoming increasingly more rare due to the drop in demand after Armund announced his dream, but there was bound to be someone along my way back home.

My hand shook as I picked the star up, ready to embrace the familiar whoosh of warmth and power, but...

I frowned. Holding this star felt no different than holding the last one. The only thing that had changed was that once again, a vision of steel and pinholes faded in and out of my thoughts. I set the star down and picked it up again. *What* was going on?

My motions became frantic as I picked each star up again, desperately testing their magics to see if I had missed something. Star after star, I got the same results. A frustrated scream threatened to escape my lips, but I bit down hard on my tongue to keep it from doing so.

Riggs's voice once again filled my head, a series of his final words in the caves running on a loop.

'You never had a superstar!'

'You fooled us all for years.'

'A silly silver pendant with a measly encased elemental star.'

'How. Did. You. Do. It!'

Questions and potential explanations swirled together in an incoherent storm inside my head. None of this made sense. It couldn't be possible. My mother had given me a superstar. She had given her *life* to give it to me. This entire time, it couldn't have just been an elemental star... could it?

I had been able to wield seeking and accuracy and other magics while wearing my star. I wouldn't have been able to do those things if it hadn't been a superstar.

Rigg's had to have been wrong. Riggs was a monster and a liar who liked to play games. He was the one who orchestrated Jetto's death to resemble my mother's. He had just been upset with himself that he couldn't wield a star that carried all of the magics, so he created an elaborate lie to throw me off my guard.

Thoughts raced in my mind as I clawed at any scrap of knowledge tucked in my memory that would help me understand why my silver was here but my superstar wasn't. Had Kieran only picked up the silver and not the star? Was the extra star before me just one he happened to collect before he crossed paths with me?

My eyelids squeezed tightly shut as I continued to think. I knew in my gut that explanation was unlikely. I was clearly missing something. There was some vital piece of information that explained what had happened to my superstar that I didn't have.

A different voice filled my head, one that wasn't devious and raspy, but instead deep and calming. It was Kieran's from our conversation in the grasslands.

'Hundreds of them.'

Books about the stars. My realization snowballed as my eyes darted to the sleeping guard. Kieran said that he had only read a little on the stars, but I hadn't pressed further into what specifically he knew. He knew about the constellations, which was something that our oral histories about the night sky had left out. What other secrets about the stars did the Guard keep?

If he picked up my star not too long after Riggs had discarded it, that meant it had been in his possession for two weeks. He could have easily done something to it in that time. Maybe he deactivated the multiple magics. Maybe—

Fuck. I looked down at his tunic that was draped over my body and curled my nose in disgust before ripping it off. Even with the tunic gone, I could still smell the salt and forest on my skin. I had to lean against the table to support my weight as my legs felt like they might buckle underneath me. Heat rose to my cheeks as my stomach twisted and fell like I was toppling through the air.

This whole time, I thought I would be in control at the end. Once I got my superstar, I would be unstoppable again. I thought that I was using Kieran until I gained my magic back. But he always *knew* that I wouldn't find it. He had always had the upper hand.

I wanted to burn the memory of last night from my brain. I wanted to scrub my skin clean of his scent that so eagerly clung to me. I wanted to forget the way that his body felt as he leaned over me and the way he smiled triumphantly after bringing me over the edge for the second time. I wanted to shred my scars free from his gentle touch and kisses that he gave me afterwards.

'It's like you're made of stars.'

The second I opened my eyes, my thought spiral stopped. He had lingered on that word, *made*. The more that I repeated it in my head, the more powerful it felt, like it called to something woven inside of me. *Made.* Had that been a hint at something else that he knew?

Made. Made of stars.

It was all too much. I was losing my grip on reality and already feeling the tantalizing pull of despair begging me to concede to my darkening thoughts. As I stood in the room stark naked before the pile of stars, the damp and cool air bit at my skin. The added sensation on top of the cacophony of explanations and memories was more than I could handle. The overload made me wish that I could just set fire to my world so that everything—the dark thoughts, the memories—would burn into nothing.

As a desperate attempt to control *anything* around me, I threw all of my mental energy into willing the room to warm. If I wasn't so *damn* uncomfortable in my own skin right now, maybe—

No.

There was a sudden shift in the air. One moment the chill was oppressively nipping away at me and the next, it was gone. My skin no longer felt any sting of cold, but rested as if it were basking in the warmth of summer sunlight. As seconds ticked by, the warmth didn't fade. I recognized the use of elemental magic, but I hadn't even activated any of the stars that were sitting on the table.

Made.

Fueled by instinct, I hurriedly grabbed my dagger. I sliced a shallow cut along the inside of my arm before setting it back on the table. Red blood rose to the surface of my skin before dripping silently to the floor. I didn't reach for the healing star on the table to stop the bleeding, testing the theory that was rapidly forming in my head.

I slammed my eyes shut again, throwing myself into reaching for healing magic the same way that I used to when carrying my star pendant. Sure enough, warmth and light again washed over me. When my eyes opened, all that remained of my cut was a shallow silvery blue scar.

"No..."

The word audibly left my mouth this time as I stared, jaw open at my new scar that matched my others. I was somehow pulling magic from stars, even when I wasn't holding them. But, *how*?

Made.

Morning had fully descended on the day. The glass panes of the small window were now illuminated by shining white clouds and blue sky. Everything that happened in the caves, in the bar, in the bed was officially behind me, dead and gone with the passing of the night.

There wasn't time to make any more sense of my new found ability to access magic. Clearly, there was a lot that I didn't know. There were secrets to the stars, their magic, and even how to move them between the sky and the ground that I had never contemplated before. And while I had desperately wanted to return the stars on the table back to Brakken as soon as possible to help the city survive, I *needed* to find some answers. I prayed to the Moon that four elemental stars that I buried before the last anti-Starcast would be enough to keep the harsh winter winds at bay until I did.

I grabbed my damp pants and cloak, shimmying them on as quickly and as silently as I could before pocketing what was left of my pendant. My focus returned to the table. The only other items that had been in Kieran's canvas bag were a writing stick, a few pieces of yellowed paper, and my wooden handled dagger.

I grabbed my dagger again, tilting the blade so that I could see the reflection of Kieran's sleeping body in the cool silver metal. Like my star, he had held onto this weapon of mine for a while, too. Thankfully, whatever he had done to my star couldn't have been done to this knife. There was no magic to ruin in a blade beyond its sharp and lethal edges. And by how cleanly it had just opened my skin, my dagger cut as good as new.

If Kieran knew things, the King knew *more*. And if I didn't need physical stars to access magic, then *all* I would need is this dagger to find my answers. I flipped my knife in my fingers as the hilt of Kieran's sword caught my eye. The gold metal glowed in the sunlight while the three small onyx stones embedded across the front swallowed it.

My lips curled into a vicious smile as I shifted my gaze to Kieran's exposed chest. *No.* I began to move silently. This dagger wasn't *all* I would need.

CHAPTER 38 | KIERAN

My mind drifted in and out of thought as I laid in bed next to Talla. I was clinging to my sleepy state, forcing my eyes to remain closed as I prayed to the Stars, begging them to find a way to keep shining. I needed to delay the onset of the day just a bit longer. Just long enough so that I could memorize the way that Talla's tucked body felt against mine before I left her forever.

The soft mattress cradled my sore body like a mother with her babe. After several hours of fighting in the caves, on top of the past few nights that I had spent sleeping on the ground, the cushion beneath my sore body felt better than any tonic. With the addition of the deluge of wine that I had consumed the night before, getting out of this bed before first light to do my reps would have been difficult. Talla's added warmth, along with her soft aroma of campfire and spice, made it impossible. So for the first time in years, I skipped them.

It had taken everything in me not to rip my pants off and bury myself in her after she kissed me. Her lips against mine felt like taking a match to the fire. With only a small touch, she had created an explosion of heat that blazed through me.

I knew that she had been baiting me. Her hunger for a challenge was painted plainly across her face from the second that she let her blanket slip. But I didn't care. *Stars.* She didn't even need to work that hard to get me to crack. I had been ready to take her from the second my eyes landed on her naked in my bed.

My cock ached as I had laid there next to her, the wine in my blood pulsing with each beat of my heart. Between the rain and the fire and the lingering taste of spice and wine on my tongue, it felt like the stars had curated this moment specifically to unravel me.

And unravel me it did. The moment that I finally snapped free from the leash that I had fashioned to control my impetuous desires, I couldn't wait to claim her. I wanted to find a way to leave my mark on her memory just as her blade and the brand had marked my skin. I wanted her to remember the Guard who had not only saved her, but *devoured* her.

From underneath my eyelids, I sensed a stirring in our room. My instincts flared, begging me to open my eyes to investigate, but I ignored them. *Not yet.*

I couldn't let go of these last few moments of relaxation, of peace, of her. The urge to awaken lessened as the sensation faded. With a smooth shift of my body, I readjusted myself and drifted back into my shallow sleep, letting my mind continue to run with each memory of the night before.

Watching her squirm beneath me as I curled my fingers inside of her was more intoxicating than any brew or herb in Larendi. Her shallow squeaks and breathy moans rang like music in my ears. And while that particular song would be one that I would gladly keep tucked away inside my head, it wasn't the only reason that I had been satisfied with the evening ending without me locked between her legs.

I had played games before. I had *won* games before. But my victory in claiming Talla on our last night together was different. She might have been in control of the *when* this would happen, I had been in control of the *how*. Watching her lose her command of the situation and then delight in the consequences was a high that I would chase for the remainder of my days.

I might not have learned much about the details of Talla's life over the course of our journey together, but I had learned enough. I had seen her scheme and kill and laugh and break—I knew that moments like the one I was giving her were rare for her. It had only been a few weeks since our first encounter in the Middle Forests. And yet, as my fingers worked in and over her silver coated curves, I felt like I had somehow known her for a lifetime.

It was for the best that I didn't fully cross the line. It was hard enough to imagine riding away from Havetta knowing that the spot she had warmed in front of me in the saddle would remain cold. If I had fully had her, even once, I somehow knew I would need her again. And that wasn't an option.

She might be *Talla* to me now, the girl who embodied both darkness and starlight, but she was still a rebel. A starthief.

Even though she hadn't made any moves to do so, I wouldn't put it past her to make one final attempt to take the stars that were sitting in my canvas bag—

My bag.

My eyes flew open. The sudden influx of morning light that glazed the room chased the wisps of memory away in a flash. This had been the longest that I had left stars unguarded.

My eyes struggled to adjust to the light as I frantically scanned the room for my bag. Everything around me was tinted yellow from the bright sun rays. Everything except...

I saw stars sitting exposed on the table, the black night cloth bag lying open on the ground.

Shit. Shit. Shit!

My heart sank as I realized that the warmth I had been clinging to in the bed had not been from Talla, but from the sun. The bed was empty next to me, the covers and sheets crumpled where her body had rested the night before. Talla's clothes that had been hanging on the fireplace were also gone.

My feet flew towards the table, my hands grasping the wooden edge so tightly once I was upon it that I thought I might crack the surface. Adrenaline fueled my breaths as I desperately counted the glowing blue orbs. *Seven.*

I breathed out a sigh of relief. *Thank the Stars,* she hadn't taken them. I leaned back into the chair adjacent to the table before combing my fingers through my hair. As I settled my hands back on the surface, I couldn't shake the feeling that while none of the stars were missing, something was off.

I picked up the nightcloth bag from the ground, feeling the fabric for anything still left inside. There was nothing. My attention flew back to the table in hunt of the wrapped silver pieces that I had carried with me for weeks. *Her* silver pendant. And where was my sword? I had left it on the table, but now....

It was then that I noticed the folded piece of paper with *'Royal Prick'* scribbled on the outside. My hand slid through the glowing stars as I reached for the paper. My instincts shot up, making my grasp surprisingly shaky as I unfolded the note to read it.

I gotta hand it to you. Your 'soft eyes' and hero-complex almost had me fooled. But I now see you for the selfish ass that you really are. Thanks for the tip about the library of starmagic, I'll be sure to let everyone know it was you who helped me discover the secrets that have been hidden in that damn castle for the last thousand years. I left the stars so that you couldn't track me—I think we both know now that I don't actually need them to get what I want. Once I've discovered the secrets that you and the bastard King have been hiding...

I turned the paper over, looking for the continuation of her note. My heart and my head competed for who could pound the hardest as my eyes quickly scanned her hurried words.

I will bring <u>every</u> single star back down where they belong. Don't worry. I'll take great care of Boli along the way— your sword should fetch us enough gold and silver to keep us going. She always liked me better, anyways, don'tcha think?
For Starlight, for <u>Everyone</u>, you fucking Prick.

Fuck. My fist closed furiously around the paper before finding its way to the table edge, flipping it to the ground. The clatter of wood on the floor was enough to wake up everyone that shared our hall, but I didn't care. Talla was gone. She had taken my sword. And my horse. And...

I looked at the stars that were scattered on the floor around me. She didn't take the stars, at least. I could still return them to the King. I would still complete my orders and the sky would still be finished. But... did that even matter?

Talla was going to get there before me. The chances of her discovering how to bring the stars down again were low, but Talla was special—deep in my gut I knew that if there was *ever* a rebel with a chance to block the completion of the night sky, it was her. Without Boli, could I make it in time to stop her?

At all costs.

I would have to try.

I was willing to do whatever it took, to pay whatever price to see the King's vision through to the end. But, *what the fuck*. I never expected this, even if I should have.

I should have chosen to run from Talla when I had the chance. Because now there was no choice. Talla, somehow, had her own magic. Her stealth, accuracy... the way she could heal her body, they were beyond any other explanation. She didn't need to hold the stars to pull from their power, and while I didn't know how or why it could be true, I knew that it was. The fate of the stars, *fuck*, the fate of my life, depended on me finding a way to stop her before she succeeded.

So now, my only option was to run towards her. Towards the thief with green eyes who had stolen my sword. Towards the thief with her own magic who had stolen my horse. And, despite currently racing towards dismantling everything I had ever worked for, I couldn't deny what the heavy ache in my chest meant. I had to run towards the woman who had somehow stolen my heart, too.

◊

ACKNOWLEDGEMENTS

First and foremost, I need to thank my husband, James. From day one, you have been the biggest supporter of this story. Without your help and sacrifice, I can't imagine how I could have written this book. Thanks for pushing me to write. Thanks for encouraging me when it felt like too much. Thanks for throwing the punches against my imposter syndrome when I was too worn out to do so. Thanks for working through plot holes and timelines. Thanks for being the best in house editor I could have asked for. The list could go on... thank you forever for all of it.

Thank you to all of my early readers, especially beta team readers who *gutted* through my first draft: my mother Dawn, my sister-in-law Molly, and my fellow Tar Heels, Elizabeth, Nikki, and Bri. You all provided invaluable feedback that helped make this book a reality. I feel lucky to have a group of avid readers willing to read and discuss a story fresh out of my brain with such kindness and support. To everyone near and far who did an ARC read, I am also grateful for you! You took a chance on this book as a debut novel from an indie author—I hope that it brought you as much joy while reading it as it brought me to share it with you.

Thank you to all of my friends and family who shared love and support for me throughout my transition into motherhood and my writing journey. Every bit made a difference in me getting here.

A special thank you to Colleen Oakley, author of *The Mostly True Story of Tanner and Louise* among other titles, whose encouraging words during a Literature Lover's Night Out event helped me accomplish a lifelong dream of completing a novel. If you haven't read any of her books, hop to it. They're a delight and you'll be supporting a creative spirit who showed me kindness.

And finally, a thank you to... you, the reader. I am truly honored that you're here, and that you let me share part of my heart & soul with you.

Originally from Central Maryland, Alysa now lives in Minnesota with her husband, daughter, and rescue dog. While her diverse geographic experiences and mixed cultural heritage have shaped her as a woman and writer, nature has ultimately been her biggest influence. As a lifelong source of inspiration, her love for the natural world allows Alysa to find "home" in the outdoors no matter where she goes. When she's not writing, you can most likely find Alysa barefoot in the backyard or snacking on something delicious.